STAGED FOR DEATH

A LAUREN KAYE MYSTERY

DALE KESTERSON

D1065753

Jumpmaster Press
Birmingham, Alabama

STAGED FOR DEATH

A LAUREN KAYE MYSTERY

DALE KESTERSON

For Karen —
Never, EVER ask "What could go wrong?"
in a mystery!
Wonderful to meet you —
best wishes

Kesterson
15 June 2022

*This one is for my high school music teacher,
with long overdue thanks, and for Jim and Heather,
as always, for believing I could.*

Acknowledgements

This one was especially fun for me to write. I never had any formal training as a singer; my chorus instructor in high school gave me a good grounding in the art and science of music. His tutelage allowed me to perform in various venues, including opera. The basic plot idea came to me years ago during the rehearsals of Gounod's *Romeo et Juliette* while I was performing as a member of the chorus of an opera company, although it has taken me thirty-five years to get it on paper. Despite not pursuing music in my higher education, all the experience in junior high and high school music enriched my life in more ways than I can enumerate. Music lessons in any form are never wasted. Not only is music a language on its own, but music training also instills discipline and confidence. I owe Mr. Rosen a huge, overdue bushel of thanks.

I would like to publicly thank Ruthanne Reid, whose encouragement was critical to me and who constructed my website. You are wonderful and your confidence in me has been magical.

I am unable to express my appreciation to Gene Rowley, Kyle Hannah, and the Jumpmaster Press team for their encouragement, support, and belief in me and my main trio of characters. To have the first novel published was a dream fulfilled; that this is now a series is a concept almost beyond my comprehension. You gave me a chance, and I am humbled. Gene and Kyle, thank you!

No undertaking of this magnitude would be possible without the love and support of my family. My husband has been wonderfully patient with the crazy hours I spend at the computer. Jim is my first critic and reader, always honest and constructive. I could not manage without my daughter Heather's love and encouragement; she is my cheerleader and my friend. You both give me far more than I sometimes feel I deserve, and I thank you.

1

My acting debut (and subsequent arrest for murder) traced back to a meeting with my advisor the first day of classes at Hofstra College. Once I looked back, I realized I should have known nothing I planned that day would turn out as expected.

I dashed from my apartment to the parking lot—late as usual—and glanced up at the overcast sky, something the weatherman missed in his forecast the night before. He also predicted light breezes. Nope, the brisk, cold wind felt slightly damp, too, which clinched the weather's defiance of predictability.

"No sunny skies and pleasant temperatures," I mumbled to myself. "So much for accuracy in weather science." I pulled my suit jacket tighter and stepped off the curb to my parked car. I stopped suddenly and stared at my little Triumph. It listed toward the front right on an extremely flat tire.

"Blast and bother! This I do not need."

I unlocked the car door and yanked it open, dropped my large shoulder bag into the passenger seat, removed my jacket, and proceeded to get the jack and the spare out of the trunk. I carefully knelt on the rough, cold concrete—I was in my best suit for an interview—and went to work. I spent the next fifteen minutes in a wrestling match with several inanimate objects; they all seemed determined to thwart my efforts. The tire iron slipped off a wheel nut three times and I pinched my thumb in the jack once. I swore under my breath.

Thunder rumbled in the distance.

"Don't you dare!" I grumbled, glaring upward. Another rumble provided my answer.

I hastened to finish. In a parting gesture, the jack fell on my knee the moment I released it. I deposited it and the useless flat in the trunk, resisted the urge to slam it down, and ran back up to my apartment to call my office.

"Boss, I know I'm late. I had to change a flat tire," I quickly explained. "I'll be in shortly. I have to clean up a bit first."

"Lauren, you have a nine-thirty appointment with the new director of the Parks and Recreation Administration," my editor reminded me.

"I remember." I glanced at my watch. Nine o'clock. My morning schedule was evaporating before my eyes. "I'll go directly from here."

"Good." He hung up.

With a sigh, I reached to pull up my hem to examine my throbbing knee.

"Swell," I groused. My skirt now sported a streak of dirty grease, probably acquired when the jack landed on me. My stocking looked like an application cloth for a lube job. I hurriedly changed clothes as I harbored a faint hope the day would improve.

My interview with our new official was downtown, and I drove to the City Hall building in Northwoods Glen, adjacent to police headquarters. The sign posted at the gate of the miniscule parking lot read *Full*. Two blocks farther down the street, I found a space at the curb. I scrounged around in my bag for change and fed the parking meter. The clouds made good on their threat while I walked back to the hub of city government. The downpour matched my spirits. Wet and cross, I entered the building and approached the information desk.

"I'm Lauren Kaye from the *Daily Gleaner*. Mr. Loesser is expecting me." I showed the shop-worn, bottle-blonde receptionist my press card. Pre-occupied, she did not bother to glance at it or me.

8

"Mr. Loesser isn't in today," she informed me in lackluster tones. The odor of fresh nail polish pervaded the area as she inspected her bright red fingernails. "Mr. Fredrickson said he would do the interview and he's waiting for you. His office is in room 304."

I turned toward the lobby elevator, but she called to me.

"Oh, you'll have to take the stairs—the elevator is out of order. The stairs are down that hall." She pointed over her shoulder while she looked at me. "Gee, is it raining outside?"

I smiled politely with clenched teeth but refrained from speaking. I figured once I started, it would be hard to stop.

The hike to and up the stairs did nothing for my state of mind, but I found the cluttered office. Stacks of books rested on the floor. The smell of stale cigarette butts sitting in an overflowing ashtray melded with the scent of his strong aftershave.

The interview lasted a mere fifteen minutes instead of the scheduled thirty because the assistant to the new director answered all my questions with monosyllables. No charts, no diagrams, no recitation of plans, merely flat single words. I ran out of questions before he ran out of yeses and nos. His terse responses reminded me of the police captain who worked at headquarters. Loesser had been far more loquacious on the phone.

I politely thanked Fredrickson for his time and departed. The rain diminished to a drizzle as I proceeded to the newspaper office.

My bad luck continued to hound me with all the devotion of a lovesick puppy.

My typewriter decided the day after Labor Day would be the best opportunity it would ever have to malfunction. *Maybe it answered to the same source that controlled the jack and tire iron?* My keys constantly jammed, and the resulting copy of my story filled up with typos my fingers did not initiate. I squelched thoughts of its mechanical destruction. I yanked the page out, crumpled it, and deposited it in my wastebasket to join the three other discarded sheets. I pulled a fresh page out of my drawer and prepared to start over.

"This simply isn't my day," I mumbled to no one in particular, "and it's not even noon yet."

My desk phone chose that moment to ring.

I heaved a sigh and grabbed the receiver. "Lauren Kaye."

"Article ready?" My boss took it for granted we all knew his voice.

"Request permission to use a sledgehammer on my typewriter," I brusquely replied. "Or at least permission to toss it in the trash."

"Meaning no."

"Boss, I'll get the pages to you as soon as I can get it typed."

"I want it this morning." The connection ceased with a click. Short and sweet. I assumed part of his penchant for brevity stemmed from always being on the phone.

I glanced at the clock on the wall. *Already eleven o'clock.* The other reporters in the city room ignored me and clanked along on their respective machines. The daily haze of cigarette smoke started to fill the air, drifting up to the ceiling. I took a deep breath anyway and slowly let it out in a silent whistle.

"Okay, that's it. No more coddling," I threatened my Remington. "I'll give you one more chance before I trade you for a Royal."

I fed the paper into the rollers and started once again.

Twenty minutes later I approached the news nerve center of the *Daily Gleaner.* I looked through the large windows flanking the editor's glass door and discovered one of my fellow reporters in what we called the hot seat. Bernie Slater, all five-feet-eight inches of him, stood behind his overly crowded desk. Palms flat on it, he leaned forward. His mouth moved without pauses, and although I could not hear words, I knew Sandy Martinson's ears were burning. I wondered what he did or did not do, for both carried penalties, I dropped into the chair placed by the last desk in the city room, which occupied a small doorless office off the

10

main arena.

"Sandy is getting a real chewing out," I murmured to Jake Savonne, whose ringside seat to the editor's office gave him more insights than the rest of us got.

"I think he missed a major aspect of his assignment," Savonne replied. "Bernie isn't happy."

"An understatement, from what I can see," I acknowledged. "I hope it doesn't carry over. I have a favor to ask him."

Savonne grinned. Red-haired and approaching fifty, the *Gleaner's* circulation manager, fooled a lot of people. To me, he looked about eighteen. "I keep meaning to ask if I can turn my desk around. There are times the show in the office gets distracting."

I chuckled. "I'll bet."

The door opened. Martinson trudged with his head down to his desk at the end of reporter's row and threw himself into his chair. Slater glanced around and spotted me.

"Lauren." The irritated expression on his round face did not encourage me.

"Can I have a minute?" I hesitated before adding, "Sir?"

A look of surprise crossed his face. "Come in."

"Good luck," Savonne whispered.

I rose and walked the last few feet to the door. At the threshold, I put my free hand behind my back and crossed my fingers. Savonne chuckled as I shut the door behind me.

"Have a seat." My editor waved me toward the rickety wooden chair. "It may have even cooled off since Sandy vacated it."

The hot seat creaked when I sat. Bernie Slater, whose frame was surprisingly spare in contrast to his round face, regarded me with curiosity. Thinning brown hair surrounded the growing bald spot which threatened to take over his head. His blue eyes stared at me from behind his horn-rimmed glasses. "Well?"

"Here's my assignment on the new parks administration." I handed over the sheets. "I got more out of my phone conversation with Loesser than I did the interview with Fredrickson, so I combined the information. Nothing jumped out at me, and I don't see any need for a follow-up."

"You could have given me this at the door." He sighed and let the sheets drop onto his desk.

My two added to the scattered pages on the small open space between the ever-present stacks of file folders. Those folders broke several rules of physics by not sliding around or falling over. The desk dominated his office, and the precarious stacks dominated the desk. His blotter was visible, barely, and the phone seemed gargantuan in relation to the remaining free space.

"I know, but I need to ask you a favor."

I watched while he picked up a pencil and started to doodle on his notepad. How he handled the pencil provided major clues to his state of mind. The entire staff knew the signs. His doodling told me he was relatively calm but not overly interested.

"Go ahead." He glanced up. "Your piece on the scandal was good, Lauren. Solid research and reporting." The pencil became a twirling baton.

"Thank you," I murmured. The compliment was rare.

"So, what's the favor?" He went back to doodling.

I cleared my throat. "It's the first day of the semester at Hofstra, and I have an appointment later with my advisor to find out what my schedule is."

"Take as much of the afternoon as you need." He glanced up and chuckled when my mouth fell open "You look stunned." He stuck the pencil behind his ear.

"Not entirely, but I'll admit to being surprised."

"Your classes are important, Lauren," he replied, serious again. "Check with me when you get back."

"I will." I rose. "Thanks, Boss!"

"Don't call me Boss," he admonished, but he smiled. "Go."

I flashed a thumbs-up at Savonne on my way out the door.

I tried to dismiss the notion I had somehow become the living embodiment of Murphy's Law. I considered getting the time off the easy part of my next quest. Not bothering with lunch, I headed to the Hempstead campus, about twenty minutes from the Northwoods Glen paper on Long Island. I knew the congestion at the college would get worse later in the day; it was bad enough at the moment. Campus streets crawled with cars and pedestrians; all of them would lose a race with a snail. Most of those on foot tried to follow printed maps and paid little attention to traffic. Resigned, I sighed and resisted the urge to demonstrate basic traffic safety awareness. I located a free spot in the back forty acres of the student lot. The rain gave way to feeble rays of sunshine, and I hoped the trend of my morning mishaps broke with the exiting clouds. Locking my car, I joined the slow-moving throng and aimed for my major's building with the determination of a quarterback heading towards a goal line.

Inside, the crowd intensified. One of the oldest in the school, the language arts building had its own, unique atmosphere. Smells of wood polish and musty books merged with the sounds of students and ringing office phones. The echoing of doors as they opened and closed punctuated the babble of the uncertain voices up and down the halls. The familiar sights and sounds made me feel like I had come home after a trip.

I fought through the wall-to-wall crowd of mostly lost students and wormed my way down the hallway of the English Department to the chairman's office. I turned the knob and entered. The squeaking door told me maintenance never oiled anything, but it served to announce my arrival over the clatter of typing. My professor's secretary halted her efforts and acknowledged me.

"Miss Kaye, welcome back." A prim and dowdy widow, Mrs. Jacobsen functioned as the stalwart guardian of the professor's gate. Her voice never expressed anything but boredom. She dug through an index card file and handed me my class schedule without rising, forcing me to stretch over her desk to reach it.

"Have a seat." Her attention returned to her typewriter. I sighed, dropped my bag on the floor, and took a spot on the uncomfortable wooden bench outside the courtroom-like railing of her domain. One glance at the card in my hand brought me back to my feet.

"Excuse me," I said, loud enough to be heard over the machine-gun noise of her attack on the keys, "there must be some mistake. I'm a night-school student and this card is for a daytime class. Besides, music appreciation has nothing to do with English or journalism."

"I'm afraid you'll have to take that up with Professor McKechnie," she automatically replied. Her eyes remained glued to her propped up copy. "He'll call you in when he's ready for you. Another student is with him at the moment."

I sank back onto the bench and prepared for a long wait. I doubted my advisor, who could stretch a three-word thought into a paragraph, knew the practical application of the words *brevity* and *punctuality*.

Five days into September with classes not yet in session, I faced a major problem.

To complete my degree, I switched from being a full-time student with a part-time job to working a full-time job with evening classes. I lost credits from my two-year stint at a university in the process, but I consoled myself with knowing I could whittle away at the courses I needed when I had the time and resources. Following two years of mind-numbing drudgery in a succession of dreary, impersonal offices, I landed a position with the *Daily Gleaner*. The schedule in my hand indicated McKechnie registered me for Music Appreciation from ten-thirty to noon on Tuesdays and Thursdays. *A daytime class with a daytime job? Nope, this won't work.*

The inner office door opened. A boy too young to shave scurried out clutching a notebook and his card. My advisor shook his head sadly as he watched the kid depart before he beckoned to me. I entered his sanctum and closed the door. The musty books lining the cases caused more than one student to sneeze during interviews.

"Miss Kaye, do allow me to anticipate what you are going to say. However, I should warn you at the outset of this conference I am unable to envision any viable way to circumvent it." John McKechnie, Chairman of the English Department, regarded me with what passed for his version of sympathy.

He settled himself behind his desk, on which each item possessed its own meticulous place. I once suggested to another student McKechnie's middle name ought to be *punctilious.*

"Sir, there is a problem." I remained standing and waited for an invitation to sit. Proper and formal manners ruled his office.

He motioned me to sit in the chair opposite his. I took the indicated seat and reined in my frustration so I could place my case before him.

"The situation is untenable, Professor." I deliberately used one of his favorite words. "I work full-time at the *Daily Gleaner.* I'll lose my job if I walk into my editor's office and announce I will be gone from ten to twelve-thirty Tuesdays and Thursdays."

"Surely they can cover your absence. Your employment description is copy typist, is that not correct?" An absent-minded professor who gave credence to the stereotype, he did not remember what I had told him on more than one previous occasion.

I sighed as I dug into the bag my co-workers think I use for smuggling anything from bricks to small corpses and pulled out a copy of yesterday's edition. I folded it to a specific spot, rose, and tossed it on his desk.

"Check the bottom of the second page," I urged as I resumed my seat. "It's the tag to a major story I did two weeks ago."

My work as a reporter for *The Daily Gleaner* had gained substance and a degree of prestige over the last few months. Despite a few daring souls who took glee in referring to me as the *Gleaner's* 'girl reporter,' I never claimed to be Torchy Blane or Brenda Starr. Once I demonstrated my abilities, I landed a few features; I suspected I got those because I doubled as a photographer. In addition, recent events proved my capabilities to handle more intricate assignments than those given to the pool of want-to-be Pulitzer Prize winners. With a knack for in-depth investigations, I tackled a local politician's suspected embezzlement and proved he accomplished his gains through the aid of an accounting firm. The resulting story netted me my first front page piece, complete with banner headline. I refused to risk my newly-won status to take music appreciation, which I considered a frivolous waste of time.

I regarded McKechnie's furrowed brow while he scanned the story through his rimless spectacles. Almost bald with a gray fringe of hair, even if he stood totally straight instead of his normal stooped posture, I topped him by three inches, although he outweighed me by forty pounds. Occasionally, his lips moved while he read, something I never noticed before. He kept his long straight nose in the paper until he finished.

"Local Politician Indicted." He gazed over the top of his glasses at me. "I remember the original story. You wrote it?"

"Yes, sir. I investigated it and broke the story. I've been a reporter at the *Gleaner* for two years." I sat forward on the standard wooden chair, grateful it did not creak. "Sir, I can't take a day class." I paused to regroup my thoughts so my words would not appear too impertinent and gestured at the paper he held. "If you require confirmation, call Bernie Slater. He's the publisher and editor."

"Bernard Slater is your employer?" McKechnie paused. "He once taught in this department."

"He bought the paper several years ago."

"I understand your position, but collegiate protocol dictates the curriculum, and it necessitates a course in the fine arts, either art or music." He shook his head and consulted my file. "Miss Kaye, we have given sway on quite a few rules for you over the course of your time with us. I regret I must convey my inability to recommend an alternate. Would you prefer art appreciation or a class on basic drawing?"

"There's nothing at night?" I forced myself to stay calm. Experience taught me a show of anger would make things significantly worse.

McKechnie shook his head. "Not at the present time. It remains an oversight which hopefully shall be rectified in the near future. However, any future implementations have little bearing on your current situation."

"I know this is awkward, sir. I trust you can appreciate my position. It took me two years to break out of the reporters' pool. My first major story covered Northwoods Resort and Beach Club a while back. I did the whole spread, including the photos." I did not add that the story behind the printed version should have been locked in a vault at Fort Knox.

"I seem to recall it." His face remained expressionless. He would have given Keely Smith a run for her money.

"I don't see how I can fulfill the class requirement and keep my job. Without the job, I don't have the money for school and without the degree, I'll lose my job." *Well, that last might not be true now, even though it was originally a condition for my employment. The boss let me off this afternoon because he considers my schooling important.* "When Mr. Slater hired me, our agreement was contingent on using my earnings to continue schooling. Isn't there anything else I can do to fulfill this?" I pleaded.

"Unfortunately, and here I reiterate, a fine arts class is required by collegiate protocols."

"Yes, sir." I kept a scrupulous account of my credits. According to my calculations, I lacked eighteen credit-hours to accomplish the big goal. The course on my registration card was worth a measly two.

"I comprehend the position in which you find yourself, yet I would ask for similar consideration of ours." Professor McKechnie paused and stared out the dirty window. I waited as patiently as I could. His attention returned to me. "A thought occurs to me, nonetheless. A potential solution might conceivably be at hand. Of late, I have become aware of what may constitute a remote possibility for an alternative. However, I warn you: it will necessitate a concerted effort on my part. Additionally, I would be prepared to wager you will not find it to your liking. Thus, I am hesitant to attempt it without some assurance of your acquiescence. Are you certain you can't manage the day class?"

"I'm absolutely sure it would cost me my job." I swallowed and took a deep breath, grateful he appeared willing to consider anything else. "Can you give me an idea of what you have in mind?"

"The music department has engaged to produce an opera in conjunction with one of the local high schools. From what I've been able to discern, they need supernumeraries."

"They need *what*?" My wide vocabulary missed that one.

"Supernumeraries." He repeated the word as if he enjoyed articulating it as he bounced it off his tongue. "Those are people on the opera stage who act as crowds or soldiers and such who don't sing. It is my understanding these performers are generally referred to as walking scenery, or extras, if you wish to regard it in that light."

"Oh! I think I saw something like that in a Charlie Chan movie. Number One Son and his fraternity brothers were soldiers in *Carnivale* in the film *Charlie Chan at the Opera*."

"You are correct," my advisor acknowledged with a slight nod. "Boris Karloff portrayed an opera singer, although I would not have cited that film as my primary example." He surprised me with an honest-to-goodness chuckle, despite his solemn facial expression. "I would be amenable to undertake the role of advocate to persuade the dean to allow you to trade the class requirement for your participation in the opera as a supernumerary, if you would subscribe in advance to accept the arrangement."

"Would rehearsals be at night?" I asked once I translated his words into colloquial terms. *I would kiss my evenings goodbye but since I haven't had a date in months, it would not be a major loss.*

"According to what I have gleaned in conjunction with this matter while monitoring open discussions in the faculty cafeteria, you would be required to attend rehearsals three nights a week to start, in all likelihood Monday, Wednesday, and Friday. In addition, rehearsals will be increased to every night the last week prior to the performances, and of course, the two stage performances themselves." McKechnie regarded me with hopeful resignation. "This is the singular alternative I can conceive, Miss Kaye. My hesitation to offer it remains my inability to extend my absolute assurance I can persuade the dean to allow the exchange."

"Professor, although it's not something I'd ordinarily ask to do, it would be easier than trying to attend a class during the day."

"I feel impelled to reiterate my cautionary statement. I am not in a position to guarantee the dean will approve the notion."

"I understand." I stood. "If you can arrange it for me, I would really appreciate it."

"If it would be acceptable for you to leisurely take some light refreshment in the student union coffee shop, I shall endeavor to speak with Dean Cranmore to procure a positive response for you this afternoon." His suggestion made him sound almost human for a change, despite his archaic phrasing.

2

If a fire marshal on an inspection tour happened to glance into the campus coffee shop, he would have run out of citation notices before he wrote up all the violations. Always busy, this first day of classes exceeded all sorts of limits. The large crowd created a hubbub with students comparing schedules, buying books, and meeting friends. Searching the noisy, crammed room from where I stood, I saw no open seats. The over-worked waitresses navigated between the tables as if they were on an obstacle course, squeezing between chairs and stacks of books. Clinking dishes competed with loud voices while students tried to hear each other over the din. Smells of coffee brewing and frying oil filled the air. Smoke from cigarettes wafted to the ceiling forming a blue-tinted haze denser than the one in the *Gleaner's* city room.

"Lauren!" A voice hailed me with targeted projection.

I scanned the room and tried to locate the source. I spotted a girl on her toes waving her arm with the enthusiasm of a semaphore operator; she stood beside a table sized like something out of a toddler's playhouse.

"Carmella!" I fought my way to her. She dumped an armload of books from a chair to the floor so I could sit.

"What on earth are you doing here?" She hugged me. "You take night classes."

"My one class for the semester was scheduled during the day and it won't work. My advisor is trying to circumvent the requirement, so I don't lose my job."

"Geez, that's tough. What's the course?" Carmella Viscotti

was petite and pretty in a cute sense, with dark hair and large dark brown eyes. I knew she was a music major beginning her junior year.

"One of yours." I teased with a smile. "Music appreciation."

"Not mine, thank you. I don't like the way it's taught even though it was designed to give an overview of classical music," she lightly retorted with a grimace. "We majors generally refer to it as *Music Depreciation*. Too bad you can't join the opera as a super. We'd have a ball."

"Funny you should bring up the opera. Actually, that's precisely what McKechnie is trying to do. Dean Cranmore has to waive the class and agree to let me be a supernumerary in the production as a substitute to meet the fine arts requirement for graduation. Music appreciation is not worth losing my job." I grinned. "You mean, you're in the production?"

"I auditioned for the chorus last spring. I'll be singing soprano. My high school teacher, Mr. Peterman, is one of the organizers, and I took two vocal courses with Professor Brier last year. Oh, they *have* to let you do it! Can you join the chorus? That's where I'll be."

"Assuming my advisor can swing it with the dean I'll settle for being a super. It's not in stone yet," I cautioned. "Besides, you don't want me to sing. Believe me, I can't. I remember Mr. Peterman, although I never took any of his classes. I admit it's nice I know someone involved. I'm going to be lost. What are you doing sitting here alone in this chaos?"

"I stopped in here to pass the time until I can catch a bus to my apartment. How long do you have?"

"I took the afternoon off to pick up my schedule. I didn't know it was going to be this complicated. Tell you what. If you'll keep me company until I know for sure what's going on, I'll give you a ride home."

"It's a deal. Anything to avoid the bus!"

Carmella and I met when I did my first breakthrough story. We lost touch when I got tangled in the political scandal.

I glanced around the densely populated room. "Have you seen a waitress? I could use a cup of tea."

"Not yet, but I've only been here for fifteen minutes. Speaking of waitresses. Did you know I'm working at Susan's Place?"

"You are? I knew Mr. Mallory recommended Jim but I didn't know Susan hired you, too. That's terrific!"

Susan's Place, the best Italian *ristorante* in the greater New York area, belonged to Gianni and Susan Gianello, friends of mine.

"You and Mr. Mallory helped us both, and I want to thank you."

"Nonsense! You and Jim were hired on your own merits. Mr. Mallory knew the Gianellos wanted more help to open for lunch a couple of days a week, and he didn't want a good waiter to go to waste. He simply arranged the introductions. Honestly, he has a knack for it. In fact, I once suggested he open an employment agency." I smiled at the memory. "I had nothing to do with it."

"Well, we haven't seen you at the restaurant lately," she said with a sly smile. "Miss Susan commented on it over the weekend."

"I investigated the political scandal which broke two weeks ago, and I didn't have time for much of anything. I know Susan will blister my ears for it the next time I walk in, too. I'd rather wait until I can hide behind Mr. Mallory. He's out of town at the moment."

"We saw your story on the front page of the paper. Congratulations!"

"My boss even complimented me on it today." I smiled. "Are you and Jim still dating?"

"Oh, yes." She blushed and lowered her eyes.

"Good!" I glanced up to see McKechnie at the entrance. I waved and got his attention.

"Miss Kaye," he greeted as he waded his way through a clump of students blocking the aisle, "I am pleased to relate, with a considerable degree of personal gratification I should add, I successfully advocated your situation and the option we discussed." An unexpected tone of wonder crept into his voice as he continued. "Dean Cranmore genuinely commended me for envisioning the idea." A rare smile graced his plump, usually deadpan face. "You need only report to Norman Brier tomorrow evening. He is the music department faculty sponsor for this endeavor. As such, he has the herculean task of coordinating the cast. In an effort to fulfill my quest on your behalf, I further undertook to discover the precise assignation of the rehearsals. However, I must confess my attempt to secure the information fell significantly short of my expectations. I would therefore suggest—"

"Excuse me for interrupting, Professor, but that's not a problem," Carmella piped up. "I'm with the chorus, and I'll make sure she gets to the rehearsal."

McKechnie held out my new schedule card.

"Thank you, Professor. It's a relief to have this settled. I am truly grateful to you, and I want you to know I appreciate your endeavors on my behalf." I smiled. "Who knows? I may even enjoy it."

"I surmise I need not remind you to have Professor Brier report an official grade to my office following the conclusion of the production. Please relay my regards to Bernard." With a distasteful sniff and disdainful glance around the coffee shop, McKechnie left.

"Bernard?" Carmella asked, puzzled.

"My boss, Bernie Slater. McKechnie may be the one person on earth who calls him Bernard." I regarded Carmella. "Now, will you fill me in on the opera production I signed up for?"

"It's Gounod's *Romeo et Juliette*. Professor Brier and Mr. Peterman have told us we'll be singing it in French. Of course, when the idea of doing an opera first came up, I was hoping for something by Verdi, in Italian."

"Too bad. You could have coached everyone else on

pronunciation, which would have been handy." I knew her family all spoke fluent Italian. "Thankfully, I can keep my mouth shut. Who's playing the leads?"

"Romeo, Lord Capulet, the Duke, Tybalt, and Mercutio are all from the New York City Opera Company. Vocal majors are taking the rest of the featured singing parts, and the college and high school choruses are being combined for the chorus. The orchestra will also be combined students."

"You left out Juliette."

"Professor Brier has asked a friend of his from France to come in as Juliette, but NYCO has a woman who can play her if that falls through."

"Is this normal? I mean, it sounds like it's not really Hofstra's production."

"It's not unheard of, really. No small company can stage something like this on its own. Stars learn certain roles, both leads and featured parts, as part of their repertoire. They perform all over the country, even the world, as guest artists. We've already had to recast one part. It was supposed to go to a student, but he dropped out of school. Professor Brier talked Mr. Peterman into taking the role himself."

"Wow! This is totally new to me. I've never even been onstage." I snickered. "Wait until Mr. Mallory hears I'm going to be on an opera stage."

"You mean wait until your boss hears about it." She giggled. "Just don't get ideas about doing an exposé on the backstage activity!"

"Never even entered my mind," I truthfully replied. "It's purely a way to fulfill a graduation requirement. It isn't as if I'll be investigating anything. I promise I'm checking my reporter's credentials at the door."

The harried waitress assigned to our corner of the coffee shop appeared the moment we rose to leave.

I knocked on the glass-fronted door emblazoned *Bernard Slater, Editor and Publisher.*

Slater, sitting with a phone handset glued to his ear, raised his eyes from the papers in front of him. He waved me in as he told it, "Okay. I can have someone out there tomorrow." He replaced the phone on its cradle and turned his attention to me. "You're back early."

"Boss, you're not going to believe this." I commented as I crossed his threshold and shut the door. The clamor of the city room dropped off to a hum.

"What happened?"

"Among other things, I bring you tidings from Professor McKechnie. He told me to relay his greetings to Bernard."

"McKechnie?" He chuckled. "That old fossil never did call me Bernie."

"Haven't I mention he's my advisor? He had me down for a Tuesday-Thursday class in Music Appreciation, from ten-thirty to noon." I made a face. "We had a discussion about it."

"I'll bet that is an understatement. You're smiling, though. I presume you weaseled out of the class."

"That's the bit you're going to find hard to believe. He got the dean to okay a trade of Music Depreciation—that's what Carmella called it—for a stint in an upcoming opera production as a supernumerary."

"As a *what?*"

Laughing, I explained the term, secretly pleased he did not know it either. His vocabulary tended to be more esoteric than mine.

"Oh, you mean like Keye Luke in *Charlie Chan at the Opera.*"

3

I met Carmella on campus at the appointed time, and she steered me to the music building where we descended to the basement. After greeting Carmella by name, a department secretary took our class assignment cards, checked a list, and handed us back an index card with a single letter. Carmella clutched hers, which sported a C. My card displayed an S.

My introduction to the world of opera did not impress me. The huge basement, with its cinderblock walls, was a rehearsal hall furnished with sections of folding chairs and not a lot else. Masking tape marked out the stage at one end of the cavernous room. I quickly discerned a pecking order of sorts, delineating status. We supers filled the lowest rung on the ladder of importance. The combined choruses came slightly above us, the featured players above them, and the leads on top.

Norman Brier introduced the guest performers to us, giving their names and describing their career highlights. Each one stepped forward and sang a few phrases from one of their arias. Naturally, we all applauded.

"This is unusual," Carmella murmured to me as applause for Mercutio died down.

"What is?"

"The guest leads don't generally attend all the rehearsals. I wonder if it's because this has never been done before." She caught my puzzled expression. "Combining pros, college students, and high school students."

"Remember," Brier closed his welcome, "every single one of

you is important to the production. This is a first. To our knowledge, combining professional singers, student vocal majors, choruses, and the combined orchestra has never been done before. This is a massive undertaking and it's going to be a lot of work for everyone, from the supers all the way up."

"See what I mean?" Carmella whispered. I nodded.

David Peterman, the high school music director, stepped up. "Music will be rehearsed by the choruses during class time. Featured players will be scheduled individually at first. The orchestra will work with their respective music departments. I would now like to introduce our two staging directors, Bill Gardiner and Andrea Jamison."

"Andrea will be primarily working with staging the chorus and the supers," Gardiner announced, "while I work with the featured players. Now, we want you to split into your assigned groups. You'll find the letter corresponding to your group posted on a section of chairs."

I did not know if these speeches scared anyone else, but to me the logistics seemed intricate. I glanced around. The S section held about thirty seats. I joined a group of about fifteen students who seemed to be as lost as I felt. The students holding the letter C congregated in an area next to us.

"Good evening!" Andrea Jamison greeted both groups. A thin redhead of about my height, she exuded energy. "You are the backbone of the production, playing the household members, party guests, and crowds. Chorus members, David Peterman will be in charge of rehearsing you musically, and I will be directing your movements. Supers, relax and take heart in knowing you can keep your mouths shut. Singing and walking at the same time is not as easy as it looks!"

One of the things Andrea did with us struck me as brilliant, or bizarre, or (more likely) both.

"May I see the hands of those who have never worked on a stage before?" She paused and glanced around. I smiled and felt better. My hand joined a throng of others in the air, both chorus and supers. "That's about two-thirds of you. With that in mind, I'll describe what happens next in detail. I am going to create characters for you, complete with a backstory. You will become those characters and act accordingly. I may decide you and a partner are married and having problems, or two of you are best friends. I may assign someone to play a drunk. I promise this will make it easier for you to be part of a crowd or party guests."

I watched as students got their characters. Andrea gave one couple the chance to 'fight' onstage. She went down the line giving each student a brief history as she made notes on her clipboard.

"Lauren, I'm going to pair you off with Albert as your husband." A tall, stocky boy lumbered over to me. "You are his mousy wife, and he is domineering."

I cringed as instructed while Albert grimaced his intimidation. His menacing worked more readily than my cringing.

"Good, but not what I want. Let's try you as a shy wall flower," she suggested to me. "Stand over there and look lost."

I grinned. "That's easy!" I followed directions and got a few giggles. Our director scowled and the giggles abruptly stopped.

"No, that won't work either." Andrea paused. The scowl softened to a frown, and gradually became a sly smile. "Lauren, you are way too expressive for either of those. Ordinarily I wouldn't do this, but I hate to waste talent. Are you familiar with Verdi's *Il Trovatore*?"

My blank expression gave her my answer. She chuckled.

"*La zingarella!*" Carmella piped up. She burst out laughing when Andrea nodded.

"Okay, give over," I put my hand on my hip and shifted my gaze between the two of them. Their smug smiles reminded me of a couple of kids planning a prank on a teacher. "What are you two talking about?"

"There is a gypsy chorus scene at the top of the second act in *Il Trovatore* with a sassy flirt," Andrea explained. "It's very famous."

"It's the *Anvil Chorus*," Carmella added. She helpfully hummed a few bars. "The chorus of gypsies sings about the flirt."

"Oh, yes. I've heard it, but I never knew its name or seen it performed," I mumbled, completely in the dark. I wondered what this had to do with my character.

"I think you'll be outstanding as an outrageous flirt," Andrea said with hearty finality. "Done."

Carmella nudged me as she giggled. "Verdi meets Gounod."

Word of my part in the production spread through the ranks at the paper faster than an eyedropper of ink in a glass of water. It created chuckles since everyone knew me totally incapable of carrying a tune. My lack of musical prowess became well-established at the first office Christmas party I attended. A talented reporter sat down at an available piano, inviting all of us to join in to sing some Christmas carols. Halfway through *Jingle Bells*, my boss politely suggested I serve punch instead and pointed to the other end of the room where the punch bowl sat. After that, for weeks I heard every possible variation on tone-deaf jokes. Once my participation in the opera was open knowledge, the jokes got dusted off and re-worded. I took the good-natured ribbing in stride.

A week into the rehearsals I received a summons on my way out of the news building.

"Lauren!" Roland Beesley's cloying voice got my attention as I walked by his small office. "May I have a word in private?"

Beesley, our cultural editor, considered himself one of the key players at the paper, and his request left no room for argument, any more than a royal command would.

"Yes?" I paused at his door, curious to know why I had been honored with his attention. He rarely bestowed his time on minions, and he did not joke. He took life too seriously to indulge in something as base as humor.

"Are you doing the opera for a story?" Beesley demanded. His heavy frame almost quivered. He reminded me of Sydney Greenstreet, right down to his raspy breathing. "This is *my* area. I don't care how much Bernie thinks you can do!"

"Roland, Mr. Slater had nothing to do with this. I'm in the production to fulfill a graduation requirement for my degree. I need a music or art class and they're not given at night, so my advisor arranged this instead. Honestly, it was this or lose my job."

"Oh, in that case, I apologize for berating you," the portly critic assured me, although I could not detect the smallest amount of regret in his tone or his beady, slightly bloodshot eyes. "You did do a reasonable job this summer on your resort piece and your political story had bite to it. I simply don't want you poking around for scandal. The fine arts, especially opera, are my bailiwick."

"Believe me, you can keep it. So far, it's a total mire." I sighed. "Can you give me a leg up on what the plot is? I'm familiar with the play, of course, but I'm a super and we're taking things out of order in rehearsals."

"Let me get you a copy of the libretto," he offered, apparently touched by my confusion.

"Libretto?" I asked, my eyebrows knitting together. "What is it?" *One more new term to go with this.*

"That's the text of what's being sung," he pompously informed me, always eager to demonstrate his superior knowledge of his area. "It should help. I assume they're doing it in English?"

"Nope. They are singing in French."

"How many performances?"

"Two. Friday and Saturday evenings, the weekend before Thanksgiving."

"Hmm," he murmured. "This might turn out to be better than I'd hoped. I thought Norman Brier might be grandstanding. Perhaps he could be serious after all." The first smile I ever saw

31

broke on his face through his affected indignation. It changed his whole countenance. He looked benign, almost insipid, rather than sinister. "I'll get you that booklet."

"I'd be grateful," I said sincerely with a smile. "Really. All of this is new to me."

By our fourth Friday, which marked a month of rehearsals, I knew where to stand, when to move, when to flirt, and when to emote with the chorus. I muddled through our scenes with my fellow supers, and we helped each other find our marks. I reached the point where I felt comfortable being a member of the crowd and started to enjoy being a part of the production. Andrea and Gardiner finally lost their disconcerting tendency to call out conflicting directions, which relieved us all. My flirtation partners and I embellished a few of Andrea's suggestions, and she complimented us.

Unfortunately, what little confidence I painstakingly garnered slipped sideways during our mid-rehearsal break that evening and smashed to the floor like a priceless Ming vase hitting bricks.

"Lauren!" Andrea called to me. "Would you consider taking a part?" She studied her ever-present clipboard.

"Forgive me for being blunt, but has someone around here lost a grip on reality?" I shook my head in disbelief. "I can't carry a tune!"

She laughed. "David informed us you never took any music classes in high school, but he didn't know why."

"Now that you know, why ask me to take a role?"

"It would be strictly pantomime. There is no singing score for Juliet's mother. Professor Brier and Mr. Peterman have agreed we need a countess for Lord Capulet. It's an optional role usually assigned to a member of the chorus, but we've been watching you. We think you'd be great for it." She smiled at me like the Queen bestowing the title of Dame of the British Empire.

I glanced at Carmella, who stood a few feet away waiting for me to take a break. She overheard Andrea's offer. Her grin threatened to make her ears fall off and she bounced up and down on her toes with glee.

"What would I have to do?" Caution and suspicion merged in my question.

"You would be Juliette's mother. Do motherly things. Go up to her at the opening party. When your nephew Tybalt is killed, come out on stage, and mourn over his body. Later accost Romeo with Count Capulet. In the scene where Juliet dies, you will mourn again. Alan Brockton, who is playing Lord Cap, can give you pointers and ideas on it." Andrea beamed at me. "You have a wonderful face for acting and most importantly you don't look down at your feet when you move around the stage. Let yourself get caught up in the emotions and run with it."

"I'm not old enough," I pointed out. Desperation crept into my voice with panic on its heels.

"None of the students are. That's what wigs and makeup are for. Costume fittings will begin Monday. We'll outfit you with a fancier gown than originally planned and get you a more elaborate wig."

"Will this mean more rehearsals? I have a full-time job, and I can't get time off during the day." I mentally crossed my fingers and grasped my last lifeline with the fervor of a drowning victim as I sought a way out of this new predicament.

"You know most of the blocking. Minor alterations will come naturally, so no extra rehearsals would be necessary."

"Can we try it and see how it goes? You know I've never been onstage before, much less done anything like this."

"Of course," she agreed while she smiled at my nervousness. "Let me introduce you to Alan."

I tried to avoid meeting Carmella's eyes while Andrea guided me across the rehearsal room to the professional players. During the short walk I felt like Hannibal crossing the Alps. After performing the introduction to the gentleman playing Lord

Capulet, she abandoned me in their midst.

"I hope you will all forgive me," I addressed them, "but I feel terribly out of place."

"Nonsense!" Alan Brockton, heavy-set and a few inches taller than my sixty-seven, had sandy brown hair touched by a distinguished bit of grey at the temples. He dismissed my fears with a wave of his hand. His hazel eyes glinted with humor. "If anything, blame me."

"You'll be fine," chimed in the man next to him. In his mid-to-late thirties, he stood two inches under six feet tall. Blond, well-built, and attractive (and quite aware of it), he took my hand and kissed it, continental style. "I'm playing Tybalt. You get to cry over me, Auntie, after Wendell kills me in the duel. I'm Ashton Harper, and I'm your favorite nephew." His clear blue eyes shined, and his smile held charm. "Congratulations on making it out of the supers' pool, and welcome to the real acting side!"

"Don't start, Ash, she's not a pro," cautioned the boyish-looking man playing Romeo. "Lauren, I'm Wendell Thorne. Be careful around Ash—he's been charming girls since kindergarten when he discovered they swoon over his smile." His laughing brown eyes presented a contrast to his reddish-blond hair.

"That's not fair," Harper complained, "you'll scare her off."

"Maybe it's not fair," a man with a deep voice and rugged appearance offered, "but it's remarkably accurate." With dark hair and dark eyes, he smiled at me from six feet of height. "I'm Desmond Raphael, the Duke of Verona. Call me Des."

"Don't let us intimidate you, Lauren." A stocky younger man with auburn hair and blue eyes joined in with a chuckle. "Most of us have known each other for years. I'm Jeff Sebring, playing Mercutio. Ash kills me, and Wendell kills him."

"I'm not intimidated," I assured them. "I think I can admit to being overwhelmed, though."

"There's a difference?" Harper questioned.

"Intimidation implies fear. Overwhelmed implies there's

more than can be handled at once," I explained. "This is my first time on any stage."

"You're a student?" asked Raphael.

"Yes, I'm a part-time English major with a full-time job. I got into this because it was the one way to avoid a day class in music appreciation." I shook my head. "Roland isn't going to believe this."

"Roland?" queried Thorne.

"Roland Beesley, critic for the *Daily Gleaner*, where I work." I shrugged. "He was afraid I might be stepping on his toes trying to get a story about the production. Little does he realize I could *be* the story."

"Maybe he'll go gently on us with you in the part," Thorne suggested.

"I doubt it," I responded. "He's acerbic by nature, and his ulcers have emphasized it. He cultivates his eccentricities, too."

"Let's go over some blocking and business," Brockton offered. He guided me to the side when Peterman began working with the chorus.

"Okay but you lost me. First, though, why do I have you to blame for this?" I whispered.

"I requested a wife for the show and suggested you. Your face is remarkably expressive." He chuckled softly when I rolled my eyes. "You just made my point."

"What do you mean by *business*?" I sighed. "Please, as I said before, I've never been onstage before in my life, and I'm completely lost."

"Stop me whenever you have a question." He smiled. "Actions onstage may be referred to as *business*. Gestures, body language, movement in a scene, and even facial expressions all play into it. Now, your first scene will be at Juliette's ball, which is the opening of Act I. As you already know, the supers and chorus are party guests. From now on, you will be part of the main action, closer to me. I'll be singing to Juliette, and you can move to my side and fuss over her a bit. Straighten something on her gown, put a piece of hair in place, clasp her hand, any gesture along those lines."

"Don't we need to go over this with the staging director?"

"I'll let you in on an open professional secret. If we try something and don't hear anything negative from Bill Gardiner, it's good. If he yelps no, we drop it."

"Bother! This gets complicated. Isn't it too late for changes? We're only eight weeks away from opening night."

"I suspect there's one more coming," he confided. "The girl Norm Brier chose to play Romeo's page, Stéphano, isn't strong enough to carry it, and she's having trouble with the idea of a trouser role. Ash is pushing for a change, and he wants it to go to the girl you were standing with earlier."

"Carmella?"

Brockton nodded. "She's got a beautiful voice and it's well-modulated. She's also cute in the perky sense the role needs. She's already off-score and David has told Norm she's a fast study. I admit Ash can be a jerk, but he's got a great eye for talent."

"Wendell's warning was serious, then." When he nodded, I continued, "I'll make a point of warning Carmella. She has a boyfriend, but she's emotional." I paused to word another question. "Why is Stéphano called a *trouser role?*"

"It's a male role sung by a female in trousers. The classic example is the Prince Orlofsky in *Die Fledermaus* by Strauss." Brockton noticed the return of the blank look on my face. "That one is used as a guest star role, and traditionally it's sung by a woman celebrity in trousers."

"Thanks. I'm not exactly up on all this."

"No problem. Now, when Romeo kills Tybalt, I'll lead out from the wings. You need to come running onstage after me. The female chorus will be with you, probably with two of them trying to hold you back. Kneel by the body, crying. Bill won't expect real tears, but if you can manage that it will add to the role."

"Hold a minute? I've got a good memory, but I want to take

some notes. Let me grab a pencil and my notepad." I dashed around the periphery of the room to my bag for the two items and returned to my new stage partner.

"The real key to this is for you to become Juliette's mother and react the way she would," Brocton assured me. He guided me to a corner farther away from the rehearsing chorus where we could sit down in private. "Tybalt is your favorite nephew, as Ash said. Let the emotions show on your face and in your actions."

"Okay, people," Andrea called out later that evening, "that's it for tonight. My notes will be posted on the board in ten minutes, so please take a moment to check them. Try not to forget everything we went over tonight while you enjoy your weekend!" She paused as Brier and Peterman strode across the room. "Stand by everyone. The big guys want a word."

Physically, neither of them qualified as big. Both of average height and build, the two men stood side by side waiting for us to quiet down. Brier, fighting a receding hairline, presented a slightly calculating face to the world with mild features including watery blue eyes. Carmella informed me he peered vaguely at the world partly due to being near-sighted. I found him to be warm and slightly absent-minded, except when it came to music. Peterman, head of the high school music department, struck me as more distinguished with a full head of dark and wavy hair, a thin mustache, and brown eyes which smiled most of the time. Personable and outgoing, he took on the role of peace-keeper of the pair.

"We have two changes to make in the student cast," Brier announced. "Please take seats."

I settled into a chair surrounded by the choir and the supers. The professional cast members lined up along the wall.

"Myrna Branston has decided the role of Stéphano is too much for her and she's stepping back into the chorus," Peterman informed the gathering. "It wasn't an easy decision and I applaud her courage in doing so. I hope you chorus members welcome her into your ranks once more."

The chorus kids cheered, and Myrna blushed.

"David and I have discussed her replacement at length." Brier took over. "Based on her high school work with David and her vocal class work here at Hofstra with me, we would like to offer the role to Carmella."

Carmella, sitting next to me, started to cry with a huge grin on her face. I gave her a big hug while everyone applauded. She blushed red.

"You'll be great," I told her, speaking under the tumult. "Jim will be so proud!"

Brier held out his hand to her, and she got up. I pushed her toward him. Peterman beamed at her, and she babbled her thanks.

"Our new Stéphano," Brier said with a broad smile as he officially presented her to the company. "Miss Carmella Viscotti." Whoops and hollers, cheers and applause greeted the words. She sank into a graceful curtsy.

"Now for our other change. We have decided to create the role of the Lady Capulet, which you may know is optional," Peterman explained. "It is not a singing role. It requires pantomime acting. We have chosen one of our supers for this, and she has accepted." Peterman gestured for me to come forward. "I give you Miss Lauren Kaye, the Countess Lady Capulet and mother of Juliette."

I joined Carmella in front to applause and bobbed a curtsy. I felt *my* face blush. *Heaven help us! This is nuts! How in blazes did I get myself into this?*

"Thank you and have a great weekend," Brier called out.

The chorus and supers surrounded us, all talking at once and showering us with congratulations.

Harper broke through the crowd. "Some of us are going out for coffee." He turned the force of his smile on Carmella while he managed to include me. "Join us."

"Where around here is open this late?" she asked, glancing

down at her watch. Mine said ten o'clock.

"There's a coffee shop in Northwoods Glen near the newspaper office that's open all night," I supplied. "Wilfrid's. It's about twenty minutes from here."

"That's the one," Harper nodded. "Alan discovered it last night in a moment of sheer desperation. You know it?"

"We journalists would expire without it," I replied with a grin. "It's a nice place, family owned and operated. They know every single *Gleaner* staff member and supply about half of our coffee and lunches."

"I promised Jim I'd stop by the restaurant on my way home," Carmella told us. "He's working late."

"Anyone got a nickel for a phone call?" I panhandled. Digging into my shoulder bag would have required more effort. My car keys lived in my coat pocket to save time.

Brockton handed me a nickel and pointed me to the backstage pay phone. Five minutes later I returned to the group.

"Carmella, I spoke to Jim," I told her. "He'll see you tomorrow. You can ride with me."

"But I was going to offer—" Harper sputtered.

"I'll go with Lauren," she confirmed, to his disappointment.

Brockton gathered up a few of the professional cast while word spread among the students. I hoped that the coffee shop could handle it. *Maybe I should have called Wilfrid's to warn them.*

On the drive over to the coffee shop in my two-seater, I passed along the warning I had been given about Harper.

"Apparently he thinks he's irresistible," I finished, "so beware. Instead of shaking my hand, he took it and kissed it."

"I'll be careful," she promised. "Playing Stéphano, I'll be tossed in with him for a few rehearsals because my character is Romeo's page and annoys Tybalt. Anyway, rumor has it that he's married."

"Even if he is, I doubt that will stop him. If you need help with him, let me know. You're much too kind to be nasty," I commented as I pulled into Wilfrid's. "Here we are, and here he comes."

Sure enough, Harper headed over to open the passenger door and gallantly assisted her. She accepted his offered hand as she got out, but she immediately pulled her hand away once she stood. *Good girl.*

Brockton and Thorne waited for us by the entrance with Emilie St. Claude, the French professional cast as Juliette. Petite and gorgeous, with casually styled short brown hair and green eyes, she gave the impression of being a mouse. The illusion shattered the moment she walked onstage and opened her mouth to use what Carmella called her *full stage voice.* Emilie could knock out any back rafters with no trouble. Bright, brilliant, and talented, she seemed shy by nature. I discovered, once she felt at ease, she could be quite funny.

"Hi, *Maman!*" our dainty lead soprano greeted me in her charming accent, smiling. "Congratulations on getting the part. I thought it would be nice if we got acquainted."

Wilfrid's, located in the downtown area of Northwoods Glen, was a typical coffee shop. A counter with stools stood in front of the kitchen area, with the regulation pass-through window and aisle for service and orders. Across from that, a row of booths gave way to a few tables. A folding doorway led to a room which housed a dozen tables that could be closed off for privacy. According to rumors at the *Gleaner*, Slater held more than one editorial conference, his word for a scolding, there. The sign in the main picture window blinked *Wilfrid's Coffee Shop* in neat blue neon script.

The six of us got a table, and Brockton ordered coffee all around. I did not say a word; our waitress, Ellen, caught my eye and nodded. She brought my usual teapot when she served the others coffee, placing it in front of me with a wink.

"How did she know?" demanded Harper.

"I've been here many times, Ash. I work for the *Daily Gleaner,* a few doors down the block from here," I explained. "Alan, if you're buying, you might want to get a couple of orders of toast. Wilfrid's wife Greta bakes the bread herself."

At his nod, I flagged Ellen. "Toast."

"The bread came out of the oven twenty minutes ago," she informed us. "Most of you are new here. You're in for a real treat."

"This is one of the watering holes patronized by our staff," I continued. "The other one is a bar two blocks away."

"Lauren's a reporter for the paper," Carmella told Brockton.

"Pardon me for asking, but what are you doing as a super in a college opera production?" Thorne asked. "I know you said you worked for the paper, but if you're a reporter, shouldn't you be past this?"

"I work full-time and take night classes." I poured out my tea and prepped it. "Before she died, I promised my mother I wouldn't give up college. Two years ago, when I got the job at the paper, my boss made completing my degree a condition of hiring me."

"What does your father think of this?" Emilie asked.

"Dad was killed during the Normandy invasion. My mother passed away two years after that. I'm on my own. It was scary at first, but I've come to enjoy it. I have good friends and colleagues. Life is never dull."

"That's for sure," Carmella said with a giggle. She nudged me. "At least playing Emilie's mother won't get you into hot water. The only fights and deaths take place onstage, not in real life."

"Deaths in real life?" Harper questioned.

"My first big story involved a couple of deaths." I glanced at Carmella. "This is just a class assignment, right, so taking the part won't be dangerous." I sipped my tea. "What could go wrong?"

Ellen brought a basket of toast with a selection of jams and honey. She stayed near the table while we helped ourselves, smiling when she heard all the *ooohs* and *ahhhs* the fresh bread got. She nodded at me and gave Brockton the check.

"Are you sure you don't want to try some of the jam?" I asked Harper while he slowly ate a half slice plain. "It's homemade."

"This toast is sheer manna, Auntie. I don't want to spoil its glory." He grinned. "I'm a purist and I like to savor my pleasures."

"While we are here, may I ask a question of you professionals?" I addressed them as a whole.

"I told you, ask us anything," Brockton responded for them. "Is it something about your part?"

"Nope, a general theatrical question which has bewildered audiences for years."

Harper laughed. "Uh-oh. Let me guess. *Break a leg?*"

"Well, that, too, but why is a green room called a green room when it isn't?"

"No one is quite sure," Brockton replied once the chuckles subsided. "Both traditions have many theories but there is no set answer to either one."

Opera became the main topic of conversation as the professionals shared backstage tales of other shows.

"In another production of *R & J,* the dueling choreography between Romeo and Tybalt went awry during our first performance," Brockton told us.

"Not guilty!" Harper quipped when I glanced at him. "I wasn't in it."

"Our Tybalt didn't die in the right spot," Brockton continued. "When I charged out of the wings, there he was, right where I wanted to step." He shook his head. "In mid-stride I had to change my footing, and according to my wife, I looked like a frog jumping over a log. It was the most awkward thing I've ever done on stage."

"That's nothing," Thorne put in when our laughter died down. "I was in an opera chorus during college, and we did *Il Trovatore.* The staging director put me on top of a crate in the

Anvil Chorus. I got so carried away with arm movements, I fell off during a performance!"

"A few years ago, I was singing Juliette in Paris with a minor company," Emilie related, "and my costume didn't fit right. The costumer quickly basted the sleeve on right before curtain. During the party scene I went to hug my father, and the entire shoulder seam ripped. I gestured in my aria and the whole sleeve fell off!"

"Someone should collect all these stories and publish a book of them," I commented while we laughed. "Most people think opera is so deadly serious!"

"You can title it *The Glamor of Opera*," Harper agreed to more chuckles.

Six weeks later, my phone jangled while I unlocked my door. I crossed the threshold of my studio apartment, dropped my bag on the floor near my desk, and grabbed it.

"Whoever you are, it's Friday and it's late." Tired, I knew it showed in my voice, but I did not bother hiding it. I sank gratefully into the comfortable chair next to my desk. Positioned to be handy to my desk or the kitchen, the telephone table sat between them.

"My apologies, but you weren't there until now. Do I get to ask why you haven't been home all evening?" inquired one of the most welcome voices in my world.

"*You* can ask me anything you want, anytime," I assured my caller. I stood and dragged the long phone cord across the room so I could sit on my convertible sofa and put my feet up. "You've been away for a while, and you've missed a few things. It's been over two months."

"Something like that," agreed Robert Mallory. "What's going on in your life?"

"I'm playing the Countess Lady Capulet in Hofstra's production of Gounod's *Romeo et Juliette*." Silence on the other end of the wire greeted my statement. I let it grow for a full thirty seconds. "I finally did it!" I laughed. "You are speechless with shock."

"Lauren, are you serious?" His rich baritone sounded perplexed. "I don't want to insult you, but you can't sing. Even with a chorus."

"Oh, I know. Lately I have been forcibly reminded by the entire newsroom staff that I'm tone-deaf. I am absolutely serious about the part, though." I gave a brief explanation to catch him up. "A month into rehearsals I got pulled out of the supers to do the pantomime part," I finished. "Tonight's rehearsal went long because we had our final fittings for costumes. I got my wig, too. It itches."

He chuckled, a warm and friendly sound. "I leave town for a few weeks, and you end up on an opera stage. When does it go up?"

"In two weeks." I gave him the dates for the weekend before Thanksgiving, not surprised he used the proper term for a theatrical opening. "We move to the actual stage Monday, and I'll have to figure out how to move around in that outfit."

"It's a good show. Are you enjoying it?"

"Once I got used to the idea, yes. The guy playing Tybalt should be doing Romeo. I think he's hit on every female in the production, but he's targeting Carmella."

"Carmella Viscotti?"

"You know she's a music major."

"Yes, but I didn't know she's in vocal music."

"She is singing Stéphano, which is great, but Ash keeps trying to move on her." I hoped he could not see my frown over the phone line.

"You're talking about Ashton Harper, the tenor from New York City Opera?"

"The one and only, I hope. Believe me, I'd hate to have to deal with two of him. The college brought in the principals. Juliette is from France, but the rest are from NYCO. Do you know him?"

"I've seen him onstage. He's quite good."

"No argument. I keep wishing he'd behave off-stage as well as he performs."

"Carmella's not taking it seriously, is she?"

"Nope, not at all. I've spoken to David Peterman about it, and he's tried talking to Ash, but so far nothing has worked." I sighed.

"So, David's involved in this."

"He's the assistant music director in charge of the chorus, half of whom are his students." I paused. "I shouldn't be surprised that you know him."

"Julie took vocal lessons from him. He's a great teacher."

"He got roped into singing the cleric. Mr. Peterman is diplomatic, but Ash isn't paying attention. I'm considering trying to divert his attentions to me. I can handle him, and I'm not sure Carmella can. She doesn't want to offend him."

"You must be desperate. Anyone else I might know in the cast?"

"Uh-huh." I ran down the roster. "Everyone has been great otherwise. Ash personally recommended Carmella for the role when the other student stepped back to the chorus. Carmella is incredible. Wait until you see her!"

"I'll have my secretary get me tickets. I may see if Julie can come home for it."

"You're a big help," I groused. "I'm nervous enough as it is! I'm not sure I want my best friend in the audience. Knowing you'll be there will be bad enough—you don't have to bring your daughter."

"She'd never forgive me if I didn't at least ask her," he pointed out. "You'll be fine." He chuckled again, then grew serious. "On another subject, I want to thank you for your extra work on the accounting firm. I found the information helpful. Your story on the political scandal was excellent, and the follow-up pieces were solid. Bernie told me he regards it as a first-class piece of investigation."

"I now have a nickname around the office."

"Oh?"

"Sandy Martinson dubbed me *the ferret* after he saw me in the paper's morgue files. Naturally, it stuck."

"Good lord!" He unsuccessfully stifled a laugh. "Not exactly flattering, even if it is accurate. What are you digging into at the moment?"

"My boss hasn't given me anything major since I got embroiled in this opera gig. I'm grateful. I really don't have time."

"When was the last time you went to Susan's?"

"The last time you took me there. I told Carmella I wasn't going back unless I could hide behind you, because Susan is going to rake me over live coals. However, she knows what's going on with the opera. Carmella keeps her up to date."

"What are you doing for dinner tomorrow night? We can brave it together."

"It's a deal. How about five-thirty?" I suggested. "If we go early fewer people will hear the scolding."

"I'll come get you." His laughter echoed as he hung up.

Northwoods Glen mixed old money families and the GI influx which settled on Long Island following the war. The township sported a few cafés, luncheonette counters, and coffee shops, with Wilfrid's at the top of the list. A handful of family eateries provided housewives a reprieve from the drudgery of cooking without breaking the budget. However, none of these could touch where I dined with Mallory that Saturday evening.

A small Italian *ristorante* called Susan's Place—one of the best restaurants anywhere in the greater New York area—sat in a small shopping center on the main drag in Northwoods Glen. Gianni Gianello, an Italian immigrant who arrived in the US in 1939 in search for freedom, brought his love of cooking with him. After the end of the war, he left his position as first under-chef at the famous Manhattan restaurant, Trioni's, so he could be his own boss. He hired a widow to be his hostess, fell in love with her, and they married in a small ceremony in their new professional home. Susan ran the front while her husband happily created the dishes that made the place exclusive. I never saw a menu. Mallory and I always chose whatever special the chef offered.

"Mr. Mallory, it has been much too long! Gianni was wondering when you would come back from your trip!" Susan, classically dressed as always in a long black skirt and a white blouse with a colorful scarf for a sash, greeted us as we entered. "Lauren, why have you not been here? You don't have to wait for Mr. Mallory. You know we'll take good care of you, on the house." She held up her hand when I opened my mouth to protest. "You took care of my Arlene, and we remember. So why haven't I seen you?"

"Susan, I have been so busy—" I began, but she cut me off with a wave of her hand.

"Now Lauren, listen to a grandmother." The kindly juggernaut would not be diverted until she finished with me. She bustled us to the back corner table reserved for special guests. "Your mother, God rest her soul, cannot speak so I speak in her place. You'll never catch a husband if you don't eat! And now you're in an opera? This is maybe good, but *oy!* More running around and more meals skipped! *Feh!*" Susan's Yiddish tended to leak out whenever she got emotional.

"Susan," Mallory struggled to hold back laughter, "I got back into town yesterday. This is my first dinner at home, and we came here."

"So where else should you go? This is where you belong, the both of you," she fussed. "Your usual?" At our nods, she hurried off, returning with a tray of drinks and a basket of the fresh breadsticks made daily from scratch. "Gianni will be out in a moment. He tried something new with the veal and would like you to try it."

"Whatever he recommends," Mallory told her, obviously trying to stem his own scolding.

We were the sole diners in the place since the main rush would start at seven. With limited tables and the knowledge they would not accept payment following the summer's events involving their granddaughter, we tried not to abuse their hospitality.

"Susan, they're here now," Gianello chided gently as he came up to the table. Mallory rose and the men shook hands. "We have missed you."

"Gianni, while I was on my trip, my client took me to an Italian place he swore had the best food he'd ever tasted," Mallory related once comfortably seated. "It was good, but it made me realize how thoroughly you have spoiled me. I told him that the next time we meet, he's coming to New York, and I'll bring him here!"

Susan beamed at her husband. "Of course! For now, they should try the veal."

"Certainly," the chef agreed and disappeared to get it.

"Lauren, what's going on with our Carmella and that man in the opera?" Susan asked me. "She's a good girl, and she has her Jim. Why is Ashton Harper being such a *noodge*? He's married and should know better."

"Honestly, I don't know. I saw Jim two weeks ago and reminded him Carmella isn't interested in anyone else. She's caught in an odd position, though. She can't be rude to Ash. They are working together, and he did push to get her the featured role." I doubted my explanation would satisfy her, but I tried anyway.

"*Feh!* That I understand, but it's not to like. They're good kids, Jim and Carmella. Good workers and they are meant for each other. Mr. Ashton has been a wonderful friend to us, but I won't have him upsetting her." Her lips tightened and she continued, "Lauren, you think of something and take care of it." Her stalwart conviction indicated she thought I could fix the situation.

The door chimed and as she turned to check on it, I caught Mallory's eyes and rolled mine. He winked at me

"Enjoy your dinner!" she told us with her usual smile. She left us to greet the newcomers.

"If Susan is on the warpath, I guess the situation is getting out of hand," Mallory observed. "Can you distract him away from Carmella?"

"I'm going to try," I confirmed, "and not because I'm a *femme fatale*, either. He thinks he's irresistible, and apparently no female has ever successfully countered that. It's not something I'm going to enjoy doing, but he's really putting pressure on Carmella. Her folks moved back to Merrick, and she got an apartment near mine. I've been taking her home after rehearsals so he can't."

"Susan says he's married."

"According to Wendell Thorne, Jeff Sebring, and Alan Brockton, he most definitely is. His wife is Rebecca Chernak, one of the leading sopranos with NYCO. Alan Brockton is playing Lord Cap, and I'm working pretty closely with him. He confided to me this is Ash's normal behavior when he's not working with his wife. He singles out a chorus member and dallies."

Gianello emerged from the kitchen with steaming plates of veal medallions in a buttery lemon and tarragon sauce with sautéed vegetables, and pasta in a lightly seasoned red wine sauce.

"*Buon appetito!*" the chef said when he served us with a flourish. "Let me know what you think of it, *per favore.*"

"This is amazing," I murmured after my first couple of bites. "The veal is so tender!"

"It's new, not anything close to standard dishes," Mallory observed a while later, "but you're right! This is excellent."

"This should be on the specials menu," I agreed. "I wonder what he'll call it."

"Let's get back to the opera," Mallory said once we sated our initial hunger. "Carmella is bright and attractive, so in a way I can't blame Harper. How are you going to approach this?"

"I plan on having a talk with Carmella and get her opinion first. As I told Susan, Ash was the one to recommend her as the replacement for Stéphano. I know Carmella feels obligated to him, so she's being careful. However, I also know she's concerned because Jim is getting upset."

"With reason?"

"No, I don't think so. Ash is handsome, charming, and talented. If she wasn't so well grounded to begin with, her head would have been turned after two weeks. Since she hasn't succumbed, he's putting more effort into it." I sighed. "What's worse is some of the other girls in the chorus are getting jealous of his attentions to her."

"Great, that's precisely what we need," he said with irony. He put down his fork with a sigh. "She needs to be able to focus on her music, not get tangled in backstage drama."

"Thank you for taking my word for this," I told him with a sigh of relief as I realized he accepted my observations. Mallory tended to be protective of his friends, but I never took it for granted. I took one more bite and laid my knife and fork across my plate. "Not to mention backing my part in this."

"You rarely exaggerate, and Susan agrees with you. We know she's a great judge of human foibles." He smiled back at me. "Can I do anything?"

"Have a chat with Jim the next time you see him. Assure him all will come right. Carmella is level-headed and knows Ash is flirting." Reassured by the thought Mallory once more took my word for a complicated situation, I relaxed.

I reflected that his support for me never wavered. Our relationship started when Julie and I became friends. He never belittled either of us as 'just kids'. After my parents died, he urged me to rely on him through any troubles.

"If you do this, you'll be walking a fine line," he warned. "Will the other students turn on you?"

"Me? I doubt it. I'm not part of the department, remember? I'm English, not music. As for Ash, he's coming across like a Lothario with an ego which won't accept there's a female who won't fall for him. I think he takes it as a personal challenge when one doesn't." I laughed. "I was chosen for Lady Cap because I can act. I guess it's time to do it backstage as well."

"All the same, be careful." Mallory signaled Susan, who immediately came to the table. "Susan, whatever he calls this creation, he's got a major winner. We'd like our salads now, please, before dessert."

She nodded and collected our plates. "I'll bring them out shortly."

"I've been meaning to ask you something. How are they doing the costumes for this?" Mallory asked me once our salads arrived. "I've seen the opera before, and the clothing can be intricate or fairly simple."

"I've been told this is the plain and simple version for the show." I picked up my fork. "The guys are in tunics and tights, with belts for things like swords. No neck ruffs and no short pantaloons for them. No capes, especially for the dueling scenes, either. We gals are in high-waisted, long, loose dresses with puffy upper sleeves that taper to our wrists. Mine is a light green brocade-looking thing with gold trim. My biggest problem is avoiding tripping over it and not catching the hem when I kneel or run." I stabbed a piece of tomato.

He chuckled, probably because he knew my coordination tended to be limited. "Do you have a hat or scarf?"

"They added a pale green hat with a thin scarf to my wig. The scarf hangs down below my shoulders. It's probably got a name, but I have no idea what it's called." His expression bordered on a cross between amusement and disapproval, like the one I always got when I went shopping with Julie. I hated shopping and she lived for it. "Well, you know how I am about clothes. I think I told you my wig itches."

"You mentioned it." He grinned. "Any costume changes?"

"Nope. I talked my way out of that. I was supposed to have one dress for the ball and another for the rest of the show. I got lucky. The gown they wanted to put me in for the opening party was way too big in the wrong spots." I grinned. "The wardrobe people couldn't figure out how to alter it, so I get to stay in the one gown the whole show."

Mallory's chuckles were dying down when Susan came by the table to collect our salad plates and refill our water goblets.

"Lauren was describing her costume to me," he informed her.

"Carmella told me you look pretty in your gown," she said with a smile.

"I guess," I replied doubtfully, "but it laces up the back and I need help getting in and out of it. She has it easier. All she has to do is strip out of her tights and undo her front tunic lacings."

Mallory and Susan laughed aloud.

"I think we're ready for our dessert," he told our hostess. His gaze rested on me. "I'd like to suggest a small piece of cheesecake, if it's available." He waited for my agreement before nodding to Susan.

"Of course, right away!" Susan picked up the salad plates and headed for the kitchen.

I discovered Monday night our rehearsal schedule changed from three to five days a week sooner than expected. Andrea and Bill stationed themselves at the door and handed out sheets with call times for each remaining night of the production. The notice board outside the green room announced a Director's Chat before the evening's rehearsal.

"Mr. Peterman and I decided to add two rehearsals this week to the schedule. Many of you haven't been onstage before and we want to make sure you are comfortable with your parts." Brier nodded to Peterman.

"Tonight, we are adding the technical aspects, such as lighting, for the first three acts," Peterman spoke up. "Tomorrow we'll do the same for the last two acts. Wednesday we'll add costumes and run the entire opera. We will continue to run the whole program Thursday and Friday. Next week, the orchestra will join us, and we'll run the whole show each night until the opening. This will give you the chance to become your characters and get used to the complete staging."

"Any questions?" Brier asked. After a minute of silence, he continued. "Okay. For those of you new to the stage, adding the tech aspects may require you to stop in the middle of what you are doing. Bill will call, *hold*. Stop what you are doing and wait until you are told to continue. Get ready and take your places for Act I."

"Lighting for a show like this gets tricky," Brocton informed me as we worked our way to where we started the party scene. It can be a lot of starts and stops. If we are really lucky, they'll get it right the first time."

"Yet it all appears so easy once it's together."

"If we do our jobs right, that's what the audience thinks because we make it look that way," he agreed. "Now you have an idea of the amount of work that goes into that illusion."

On my way to the stairs leading to the communal dressing room, I bumped into Harper. Instead of his usual grin, he gave me a drained smile.

"Anything wrong?" I asked, concerned.

"Oh, no—I'm just tired. Jeff, Wendell, and I ran through the duels this afternoon." He tried to perk up. "Wilfrid's after rehearsal?"

"Sure!"

The first complete, non-stop run-through happened Wednesday with costumes and accompanied by our pianist.

Following the duel between Romeo and Tybalt, Harper collapsed after he got skewered.

"That's our cue," Brockton whispered in my ear. He left me with the chorus ladies and strode out onstage. I counted three beats and made my entrance, almost at a run. I knelt by Harper's side. The men sang their lines, and Tybalt died, with his head in my lap. After some more singing between Romeo and Lord Cap, the men of the household picked up Tybalt and placed him on the funeral bier. I followed the funeral procession around the stage, as directed, sobbing into Brockton's arm as I clutched it.

This is actually going to work! I am SO glad I don't have to sing!

I bent over the body, supposedly crying while I massaged his hands. Bill Gardiner and Andrea agreed on this staging as one of my major dramatic moments. I made up my mind to comply as professionally as I could. I closed my eyes tightly, which Andrea had suggested. I lightly rubbed his chest and stroked his cheek with my fingers.

"Oooh, yeah, baby," Harper murmured in low tones, without moving his lips. "Oooh, that's *so* good. Rub my chest. Oh yeah, keep it up."

I broke up laughing.

"HOLD!" Gardiner roared angrily from the audience.

I froze. The pianist stopped. The Duke stopped. Lord Cap stopped. The chorus stopped.

"Lauren, I'm surprised at you!" The staging director came forward to the edge of the orchestra pit. "I realize this is your first stage appearance, but we all felt you were mature enough to take the part seriously. We took the chance on casting you, and up until this moment, you have done remarkably well."

"However," a second disembodied voice, which I recognized as Brier's, sounded out of the darkened auditorium, "if you cannot perform properly and professionally, we will eliminate the role of Lady Capulet, you will be dismissed from the company, and receive a failing grade." He joined Gardiner at the edge of the pit.

"I apologize, sir. It won't happen again." I replied, contrite and humble with my head down. I meant it with all my heart.

"See that it doesn't." Brier cleared his throat. "Let's go back to the beginning of the procession with Romeo starting *O Jour de Deuil!*"

We shuffled to the appropriate places on the stage.

Harper, lying on the bier, opened one eye and took a breath.

"Later," I hissed.

By the time we got to the same point in the scene, which Gardiner blocked to place us at the edge of center stage, I decided breaking one of Harper's fingers would be too good for him. While I acted out the rest of the funeral, I formulated plans.

Once we finished the show, I approached Harper in the green room with a smile on my face. Mallory once called it my menacing shark smile and confided it made him nervous to see. Harper, however, did not know me well. If he had, he would have run for cover.

"Ash?" I put my hand on his face. He smiled.

"Auntie, I want to ap—"

I grabbed his earlobe and used pressure.

"You supercilious, solipsistic, narcissistic, egocentric Lothario!" I spat, cutting him off. "How *dare* you entangle me in your infantile imbroglio? You could have gotten me fired, and I need this class to graduate! Of all the puerile, churlish, callow pranks!" I paused long enough to increase the force of my pinch on his ear while I drew a fresh breath.

"*OW!* Auntie, I—Ow!"

"If nothing else, you know how nervous I am about this! I would have thought you had more maturity and sense!" I dropped my hand, folded my arms over my chest, and treated him to my sternest glower.

"Lauren, please?" He put one hand on my arm and used the other one to rub his ear. "I meant it as a joke. I apologize."

I glanced around at our fellow players, who watched us with rapt interest.

"Please, Lauren? I really am sorry," Harper pleaded, abashed.

Brockton stepped up behind me. "Lauren, I heard Ash's antics and I have spoken to Bill and Norman. They understand." He placed his hands on my shoulders and leaned in closer to direct his words to me and Harper. "Please don't kill him. We're too close to opening and Tybalt is a complex role."

Most of those watching us chuckled.

"Thank you, Alan." I turned and smiled at him to show Harper alone had roused my wrath. "I appreciate it."

"Um, Lauren?" Harper hesitated. "May I ask a question?"

"Sure." I refocused on Harper, who stood uncertainly, scuffing his shoe, and twisting his fingers. His face was sheepish and crestfallen, but he also appeared surprisingly tired.

"Would you please translate all those high-powered words you just used on me?"

Everyone in earshot laughed, including me.

"I'll be happy to if you can repeat them back to me," I returned. He preceded me out of the green room. Playfully, I poked him in the sides with my index fingers. To my surprise, he jumped about four feet.

"Don't do that!" he yelped.

"Ah-ha—you're ticklish! Oh, boy!" I chortled with glee. "You had better behave, my friend. Remember our blocking? Misbehave and you'll end up in the orchestra pit!"

5

"Auntie Lauren!" Harper's tenor rang out backstage. "Join me for coffee once we divest ourselves of our raiment!" He made his way to where I stood with Brockton and Thorne, following our first non-stop run-through in costume with the full orchestra.

"Let me get rid of my wig," I called back. He laughed.

I watched him carefully while the grin on his face faded. I did not like what I saw. He looked more drawn and tired than usual. Thinking back, I recalled he had gradually appeared more drained as the rehearsal process continued.

Opening night, five days away, loomed large over our final week of rehearsals. I discovered the nickname of *Hell Week* rang true. We were down to our last four rehearsals and there had only been a few minor hiccoughs in this run-through.

"Tonight went well, smoother than I expected it to," Brockton offered.

"Really?" I asked in surprise. "I have no experiences for comparison, remember."

"It is always different with the full orchestra, not just the piano," he reminded me, "but for a first go with tech, orchestra, makeup, and costumes, it was good."

"I haven't heard any complaints from Bill about our actions," I mused, "but I figured if he had any he'd tell you rather than me."

"I've had some compliments on it from the other principals," he assured me. "I haven't passed them along because you keep telling me you're still nervous about it. Wendell likes the way you seem to be backing me in my confrontation scene with him and Des. Are you getting more comfortable with the part?"

"It's becoming more natural," I admitted. "I'm even becoming more used to the itchy wig. I'm learning to ignore it."

He chuckled in his deep bass.

"Well? Wilfrid's?" Harper prompted when he joined us.

"Ash, if I do, we'll have to make it short. I have to be at my desk by seven-thirty in the morning for an assignment."

My relationship with Harper gradually shifted with full endorsement from Carmella. Although his attitude remained Lothario in Tybalt's costume, we struck an amiable compromise. If everything stayed, even all would be well, which I had reported to Mallory on the phone the evening before. The tenor seemed content to enjoy my company so far, without pushing too hard to advance to anything more serious.

"No problem." He grinned at me. "From what I could see from my bier, you did well in the procession."

"Just see to it that you stay dead once you are on that bier," I reminded him, with a cutting edge to my voice. "No more shenanigans. Agreed?"

He smiled in response.

"Agreed?" I persisted while Brockton and Thorne chuckled.

"I did apologize for that." He unsuccessfully tried to look contrite. "I promise I'll play dead."

"If you so much as wiggle a finger, I'll tickle you and you'll end up entangled in the tuba." My initial detection that Harper was ticklish got reinforced when I discovered how little it took to make him jump—my hole card ace. Our stage blocking put us right at the edge of downstage center, a few feet above the orchestra pit. "I'm nervous enough without having to worry about you acting up."

He put an arm around my shoulders. "You keep saying you're nervous, but you're doing fine." He squeezed me in a one-armed hug.

"Let me change so we can get out of here." I carefully

disentangled myself. "I think I have reached the point where I could do the funeral procession in my sleep. I want some tea and you're buying." I glanced at the other performers. "Wilfrid's in half an hour!" I announced, hoping for some moral support. Brockton and Thorne nodded; Harper frowned.

"Oh, I can't!" Carmella exclaimed. "I want to review material for a test tomorrow."

"I can drop you on my way to Wilfrid's," I told her, glancing at Harper in time to see his frown deepen.

"I think I'll pass tonight also," Emilie said. "I feel quite tired, and I want to get to bed early."

I headed to the women's communal dressing room where Carmella and I helped each other out of the intricate costumes.

"Lauren, I want to thank you for your help with Ash," she shyly said. "He's been a perfect gentleman to me this past week."

"He's not really bad," I told her while I scrubbed my makeup off. "I think he does a lot of the flirting because he can."

"Today is Monday and we open Friday," she murmured. "I still can't believe I'm singing solo out there."

"This is the first of many roles for you. Your voice is glorious. I hope some of your family comes to see you." I knew she came from a large Italian family. One of her uncles—as charming as he was powerful—made me nervous. I wondered if he liked opera enough to attend one of the performances.

"My mother has tickets for both nights." She giggled. "Jim will be sitting with her. Papa hasn't decided yet, and I'm not sure anyone else would be interested."

"Mr. Mallory is talking about having a cast party after the performance on Saturday at Susan's. He also told me that his daughter will be home for an early start to her Thanksgiving break." I rinsed off the soap and sighed at my reddened reflection in the mirror. "My skin may never recover from this stage makeup."

"Here." She offered me a jar. "Put some of this cream on. It'll help. How old is his daughter?"

"Thanks!" I rubbed some on; it soothed my irritated skin. "Julie's twenty-one."

"Are you sure about giving me a ride home? Won't Ash want to ride with you?"

"Probably. If Wendell and Alan are going, they'll take him." I smiled. "There are advantages to having a two-seater."

Wednesday, two days before we opened, I got a message at the *Gleaner* to be at the auditorium an hour early. On my way to the door, Beesley cornered me to ask why.

"I haven't got any idea," I truthfully replied. "Last night's rehearsal went beautifully."

I arrived at the auditorium to find the entire company in varying degrees of panic.

"Oh, Lauren!" Carmella greeted me in anguish. "It's terrible! Emilie is sick and can't sing! And Ash just told me he isn't feeling good. He looks exhausted."

"Bother! What's going to happen?"

"Mr. Brier and Mr. Peterman are discussing that now." Her big brown eyes welled with tears. "I don't see how we can manage to open."

"I thought you said that City Opera had a soprano who could step into the part," I recalled, frowning.

"You know by now there's more to an opera than singing. All the timing, blocking, costumes, wigs. It takes days to get it right." Carmella sighed, forlorn. "We need a miracle."

"What's Emilie's problem?"

"Some sort of throat infection. She's not supposed to even talk. The doctor has treated her, and she'll be okay, but it may not be in time."

The entire company assembled in the auditorium's downstairs rehearsal hall. I thought we stayed strangely quiet for a group of performers. Carmella and I slipped into seats next to Thorne and Brockton.

"Any word?" I whispered, taking a glance around. I did not see Harper. "Where's Ash?"

"He is in the office with Norm and David," Brockton told us, keeping his voice low. "They're talking with Ash's wife, Rebecca Chernak. Juliette is one of her signature roles. Becca is a wonderful singer but she's bigger than Emilie."

"Alan, most females over the age of thirteen are bigger than Emilie," I pointed out. He chuckled.

"Besides, she'd have to deal with all the blocking and timing of movements," Thorne added, also low-voiced. "I've worked with Becca and she's terrific, but even if they could get the costuming right, there's not enough time for her to learn what she'd need to know."

"Here they come," I whispered.

"That's Becca," Brockton confirmed.

Norman Brier, David Peterman, and Ash Harper walked to the front of the room accompanied by Emilie St. Claude and a woman I had never seen before. Emilie trudged alongside Brier, almost dragging her feet, totally dejected. Brier pulled a chair over for her. Peterman did the same for Rebecca Chernak, who gazed around uncomfortably as she sat. Brier stood between them. Harper came over to us and took a seat next to me. Carmella's observation was accurate. He appeared exhausted, even while he gave me a half-smile.

"Ladies, gentlemen, I want to thank you for all the hard work you have put into this production so far," Brier stated. "I'm sure you are all aware that we currently have a problem to overcome if we are to open the day after tomorrow." He put a hand on Emilie's shoulder. "As of now, Miss St. Claude is unable to sing. A specialist has taken charge of her treatment, and we have hopes she will recover in time to grace these halls with her voice, but we cannot count on it. Therefore," he continued, putting his other hand on Becca's shoulder, "I have asked Rebecca Chernak to join us." He took her hand and brought her to her feet. "It is my pleasure to present Miss Rebecca Chernak, one of the leading sopranos with the New York City Opera Company. We are extremely lucky to have her!" He bowed to her, and she dipped her head to us as we applauded.

"Obviously," Peterman said as he stepped forward, "Miss Chernak cannot take over the part *en toto*. What we are going to attempt this evening is use a television camera pointing at the stage to show action on a monitor backstage. Miss St. Claude will perform onstage, and Miss Chernak will sing the part into a microphone, matching Miss St. Claude's lip movements."

Murmurs and mutterings greeted his words.

"This has never been done to our knowledge," Brier picked up the explanation, "but in theory it should work. We are relying on your help, support, and patience while we try this out." He glanced at his watch. "Report to the green room in costume at your usual cue times. This will be full dress with orchestra."

Harper beat a hasty exit when we stood and started to disperse.

"Come with me," Thorne murmured to Carmella and me. "I want you to meet Becca."

I tried to hang back; Brockton overruled me by taking my arm. I glanced at Carmella, who shrugged.

"Becca!" Thorne called to her. Her face lit up when she saw him.

"Wendell! Alan!" she replied with the barest of smiles. "Familiar, friendly faces."

An inch shorter than me, Rebecca Chernak, although slender, possessed a noticeably fuller figure than the petite Emilie St. Claude. Attractive, with dark brown hair and grey-green eyes, she appeared pre-occupied and worried.

Brockton introduced Carmella as Stéphano.

"Ash tells me you are going to be one of the top voices in the country if you keep up your training," she told the nervous girl. "I'm looking forward to hearing you."

"All I've ever wanted to do was sing," Carmella shyly managed to say. "Miss Chernak, I saw you perform last year, and

I want to thank you for helping us. This is my first featured role, and I would be heartbroken if I couldn't do it."

Thorne presented me as Brockton's wife, which got a short laugh.

"I've heard that you don't sing at all," she told me.

"Believe me, it's much better this way." I shrugged.

Becca smiled. "I was also told your face is expressive and you're doing well with the pantomime part."

"My mother tried to curb my tendency to make faces, but finally gave it up as a lost cause." I smiled. "I'd like to add my thanks for all here. From the way it's described, you are stepping into a real challenge."

"I've never done anything like this before." She shook her head. "I don't think anyone has."

"Lauren, we should get ready." Carmella tugged at my sleeve. "You're on in the first scene, remember?"

Brockton gave us each a quick hug, and we scampered.

Amazingly, the story unfolded the way we rehearsed it. To my ears, Becca's excellent voice sounded like it lacked the expressiveness of Emilie's, but what I knew about opera would not fill one of my small notebook pages. Once the final curtain descended and the last notes of the orchestra faded, everyone heaved sighs of relief. David Peterman stepped to down center of the stage and called for us all to report to the rehearsal hall before changing.

Norman Brier joined us with Becca Chernak while we found seats. Emilie sat next to Becca, and David Peterman stood with Brier.

"I can't tell you how proud I am of each and every one of you," Brier said, wiping his brow. "Most of you are students and you came through like professionals. The sound synchronization worked." We applauded while he bowed first to Emilie and then to Becca. "Thank you both!"

"I asked a couple of friends to sit out in the audience to make sure the sound came across cleanly," Peterman added. "Now we'll see what they thought."

Our heads turned as one toward the door, which opened to admit a tall, attractive man in his early forties with incredibly blue eyes and a lovely girl about twenty-one. I stifled a chuckle, while Carmella giggled. Mallory caught my eye and gave me the tiniest negative shake of his head. *Okay, if that's the way you want to play it, no problem.*

"Robert Mallory has been an opera buff since he was in college, and his daughter, Julie, was one of my vocal students," Peterman explained. "I have asked for their honest opinions. I did confide to Robert that our Juliette was being doubled." He turned to Mallory. "We're all nervous about this. How did we do?"

"David, the whole production is impressive. I know you were all on edge because of the extreme difficulty with your leading lady, but it didn't show. The dubbing was effective. I only saw one instance where it was even noticeable." He bowed his head toward the two sopranos, one in full regalia and one in street clothes. "As David knows, I've seen most of your leads in other roles, and they didn't disappoint us. Excellent performances all around." He smiled at the rest of us.

"The big surprise is the caliber of the chorus," Mallory continued. "You were extraordinary! You made it hard for me to believe that you are high school and college students. However, just because I said you're good, don't think you can slack off. I have tickets, so I'll know!"

We laughed.

"Mr. Peterman told my father about the dubbing," Julie added. "I didn't know and only one tiny thing gave it away. My father is correct about the chorus, though. We never did anything like this when I was in high school. I envy you all."

"Notes are on the board. Check it, please, before you leave!" Andrea called out over the babble. "There are a few remaining rough spots, no matter what Mr. Mallory said!" She greeted

Mallory with a big smile, and he gave her a hug. I smiled to myself. Andrea typified his usual dates: tall, attractive, vibrant, sophisticated, and intelligent.

I caught Julie's eye and echoed her father's negative when I approached Bill Gardiner who stood next to her.

"Any complaints?" I asked.

"Not about you. You'd have heard before now if I had." He winked. "All sins forgiven. You and Alan have concocted some creative business between you. Lady Cap is real, and that's exactly what we wanted. I love the touch of you cradling Ash while he sings his last line to Alan."

"Thank you," I told him sincerely, "I think I needed to hear you say it." I happened to glance over at Harper and saw him wobble, then stagger, to avoid falling. "Excuse me," I said to Gardiner. I moved to face Tybalt, whose face almost sagged with fatigue. "Everything all right?"

"Just tired," he replied, hedging. "You were terrific." He seemed wan even with his makeup on. "I guess it's time to change back to being Ash. Auntie, have you met Becca?"

"We met earlier," Rebecca Chernak said with an edge of asperity when he placed a hand on my arm. "Alan said you and he had worked on your part. I hope I get to see it," she continued in a slightly warmer tone after Harper left us. "Hopefully, Emilie will recover enough to sing."

"I'm not an expert on voices, but I loved your performance," I honestly told her. "The camera worked?"

"Well enough for me to match most of her mouth movements," she replied with a shrug. "This is going to be tricky."

"I admire you for even attempting to tackle it."

"I didn't want to see the production fold if there was something I could do to help out," she responded. "Frankly, I was doubtful it would work."

"Apparently it did. Mr. Mallory seemed impressed."

"If you'll pardon me for changing the subject, I would like a personal word with you. I see you are one of the students listed in the program. Forgive me, but you don't strike me as a typical college co-ed."

"Probably because I'm not," I conceded. "I'm taking night classes because I have a full-time job during the day. This," I waved my hand down at my costume, "is to fulfill a fine arts requirement for my degree."

"I see. You're not a music student?"

"Heaven help us, no! I'm afraid that would be a complete waste all the way around." I winced and gave a tiny shudder. "I'm tone-deaf and terribly misplaced in music. I work full-time for the *Daily Gleaner*. My advisor worked out a deal with the dean because I can't take a day class without risking my job." I rolled my eyes. "The pantomime role was not my idea—I never dreamed I'd end up with an acting part."

"Life can be strange," she admitted with another shrug. "I didn't mean to pry, but I—I'm concerned."

"Concerned?" My echo of her words slipped out.

"Ash usually flirts with a chorus member during rehearsals. You don't fit his usual profile, so I was wondering."

"He's a friend," I asserted, "and he's been quite helpful. This is my first time on a stage, and I've been extremely nervous, even before tonight. Bill and Andrea have been patient with me, and most of what I do onstage was Alan's idea. All the pros, including Ash, have been terrific. I'm only mildly nervous now, rather than totally petrified." I did my best to be disarming. She gave me a brief smile.

"Excuse me, Lauren?" Carmella interrupted. "Most of the girls are leaving the building. Are you ready to get changed?"

"Absolutely." I smiled at Becca. "I found that if I wait a few minutes, the crowd around the sinks in the dressing room thins out a bit. With about two dozen females and four sinks, it can get interesting up there."

Becca laughed. "That's an understatement!" Her laughter died and she grew serious. "Before you run off, Carmella, I want you to know I fully agree with Ash, You have a beautiful and expressive voice. I'm sure Norman and David can recommend teachers. I hope you keep working on it."

"Thank you," Carmella blushed. "I'm a vocal music major, and I hope to continue after I graduate." She tugged at my arm. "Let's go, or we'll never get out of here."

In the now-empty dressing room, she slumped against the wall. "Wow! Somehow, I can't quite see her together with Ash. She's so contained and he's so open."

"That's a good way to put it," I told her.

"Why didn't you say hello to Mr. Mallory?"

"Simple—he signaled me not to." I tried to get the laced fastenings behind me undone. "Blast these things!" I sighed in exasperation.

"Here," a girl's voice said, "let me help. You're hopeless, as usual." Fingers brushed mine to one side and easily accomplished the task. "There."

"Being able to see what you're doing helps," I groused. I turned around and gave Julie a big hug. "It's great to see you! When did you get home?"

"This afternoon. I couldn't believe it when Daddy told me that you are in an opera." She giggled. "Of course, I had to come see for myself. You were good!"

"Carmella, I want you to notice how surprised she sounds," I teased. "Julie, this talented girl is Carmella Viscotti. Carmella, this is Julie, Mr. Mallory's daughter."

They nodded to each other. Julie, about the same height as Carmella, had auburn hair and deep blue eyes which were replicas of her father's. Always impeccably dressed, she regarded my utilitarian office clothes with a sigh of resignation.

"Lauren," Julie began, in admonishing tones I knew well, while she held up my plain blouse.

"Don't start," I warned her. "I came straight from the paper." I turned to Carmella. "Remember those lovely clothes I had at the resort this summer? Julie picked them out. If I wore anything she'd approve of to work, all the guys would faint."

Carmella burst out laughing. "You two remind me of me and my brother."

"I've wanted to meet you since Daddy told me about you," Julie told her. "I didn't know you were one of Mr. Peterman's star students. Your voice is amazing."

"Thank you," Carmella murmured, blushing once more.

"You're going to have to get used to this sort of compliments," I offered. "There will be a lot of them."

Carmella asked Julie about the dubbing. "Your father said he thought it sounded all right."

"Mr. Peterman told Daddy about it, but I honestly didn't know. The one time it sounded funny was when the singer held a note a tiny bit longer than the actress did." Julie smiled. "It's astounding that it worked that well."

"Everyone's twitchy about it," I commented while we descended the stairway to the stage door. "It's never been done before, but it beats canceling the performances."

"Amen," Carmella fervently added. "My mother is so excited about seeing me onstage she's even accepted that I'm not going to be wearing a pretty dress like the rest of the girls."

"Oh, but remember the rest of the girls don't get to sing a solo in a featured part," Julie pointed out, "and you do. You need to remind her about that!"

"Exactly," I agreed.

Mallory waited with the custodian, who obviously wanted to close up.

"Carmella! It's great to see you again," Mallory greeted her. "You were terrific onstage!" He gave her shoulders a squeeze and laughed when she blushed beet-red. "Most impressive."

"Told you," I whispered, which made her blush even deeper. "I'm going to take Carmella home, and then find my bed."

"Oh," Julie said, disappointed. "Lauren, I was hoping you'd stay at the house."

"If I stay with you, we'll talk all night. As odd as it may

sound, I have to be at my desk first thing in the morning."

"Julie, you're on vacation," her father pointed out. "Some of us have to work."

"Or have classes in the morning," Carmella put in with a smile.

"Okay, but I will not accept any excuses after the final performance Saturday night," Julie warned. "Carmella, I'd love to have you spend the night at our house. I feel as if I already know you."

"I'll have to see if my mother has plans, but thank you," Carmella shyly replied. "I've heard about you, too."

"Daddy, that reminds me," Julie said and turned to her father. "Uncle James has been trying to reach you. He and Aunt Lydia are opening the house up at the lake for Thanksgiving. He wants to know if we want to join them. Mrs. Fiddler asked me to relay the message."

"We'll talk about that after this weekend."

"Do you have tickets for Friday or Saturday?" I asked out of curiosity.

"Both," father and daughter stated together.

Carmella laughed. "So does my mother! My boyfriend will be sitting with her."

I groaned. "Swell. I guess it's nice to know if we mess this up, we'll have friends out front!"

Staged for Death

The final dress rehearsal, traditionally scheduled to take place the evening before opening, fell on Thursday night. I checked my call sheet at my desk and discovered I needed to be at the auditorium at six o'clock.

I checked the time as I typed up some notes I made on a light assignment one of my co-workers asked me to complete for him. I promised to have it done by two-thirty, but my watch said three o'clock. My phone buzzed. I picked it up, ready to explain the delay.

"Lauren Kaye."

"Office. Now." The connection ceased with a click.

I wondered what current transgression of mine bothered Slater this time. I admitted to myself my track record at the paper included more dressing-downs than kudos. I mentally shrugged. I knew I would soon be well informed in excruciating detail, and dutifully reported to the editor's office.

I knocked on the glass door, which shielded him from the clattering and chattering of the city room, and poked my head in. "Here, Boss."

"Come in," Slater instructed without looking up from behind his desk. The large desk, with its unsteady stacks of files, never seemed quite big enough for what it was holding up.

I entered and closed the door. If I was in for a berating, I wanted to keep it private.

"I wanted a word with you about the opera. Take a seat." He closed the folder he held in his hands and carefully added it to one of the precarious piles.

I sat on the edge of the creaky wooden chair. I disliked it, not simply for the thought of a reprimand but also because it was rickety. It always felt on the verge of collapse.

"How is the production going?"

"Honestly, I'm no judge. I do what I'm told. Tonight is the final rehearsal."

"So, Roland explained to me. He'd love to see it. Any chance you can arrange it?"

"Nope, only by invitation. From what I understand, normally there wouldn't be a problem, but we have a slight situation and it's making everyone antsy."

Slater sat back in his chair, playing with a pencil. After getting tired of trying to cram grammar and spelling into the thick skulls of his college students, he purchased the *Gleaner* and transformed it from a weekly yellow sheet to a respectable daily while doubling the circulation. He took a chance on me two years ago when I tired of office clerical work.

"What is going on?" He rolled the pencil between his fingers. "I suspect Roland would give up at least one meal to find out."

"Wow! He must really want to know." Our fine arts critic took his meals seriously, which his size evidenced. "I'm sorry. I wish I could tell you, Boss. I can't. We've been asked to keep it quiet, and I can't break that trust."

"How did Robert Mallory get in last night?" He sat forward in his chair, twirling the pencil like a cheerleader's baton.

"Why am I not surprised you know he was there?" The expression on his face stopped me—he was obviously not in the mood for banter—so I desisted. "David Peterman, one of the music directors, personally invited the Mallorys. Mr. Brier and Mr. Peterman wanted an honest, unbiased opinion of the production. Knowing Mr. Mallory as well as you do, you can assume he got it." I grinned. "Did you ask him what he thought?"

"He offered me a ticket so I could see for myself. He said it would be good for me. He did add that the chorus is surprisingly good for students."

"Well, apparently I'm doing okay, at least according to the staging directors." I sighed. "It has been a novel experience. I'm really glad I don't have to open my mouth. What I do is tricky enough without having to sing."

A knock sounded on the door, and Slater waved an invitation to enter. I carefully swiveled in the creaky chair to face the newcomer.

Roland Beesley stuck his head into the doorway. "May I join this little conference?" he asked in his oily voice.

"Sure, Roland, come on in."

After settling his bulk into the remaining chair, Beesley gazed steadily at me. "Something is up with the production. Don't bother to deny it. All the signs are there. Tonight is the final dress rehearsal, and I demand to see it."

"Roland, I don't know what your sources are, but it's not my call," I explained. "I honestly haven't got that kind of authority."

"Can you contact someone and request I be allowed to attend?"

"Why don't you wait until we open tomorrow?" I countered. "This is our final rehearsal."

"The press, which in this case means me, is usually invited to attend the final dress." He leaned far enough forward to teeter, and his chair squeaked in protest. "Try."

I frowned. "I'm a super with a pantomime part," I pointed out. "I'll check on it for you, but don't hold your breath."

"There is something amiss or Brier wouldn't be hiding, and I want to know what it is." He rose with some difficulty and a lot of wheezing. "You obviously won't open up about it, therefore I shall have to see for myself." He turned and came as close to stalking out as his physiognomy would allow.

"With that attitude, I'm not going to plead for his admission," I muttered.

"Lauren, please, ask," Slater advised. "If it's a firm no-go, call me here and I'll tell him."

"Thanks, Boss. I'd hate to have to give him the bad news myself."

"You're sure it will be a negative."

"Roland correctly implied I know what is going on and why the press hasn't been invited." I shrugged. "I seriously doubt they'll lift the ban simply because I ask them to make an exception."

"It will open tomorrow night, right?"

"That's the plan. However, we genuinely need tonight with no prying eyes." I sighed. "I'm not holding out so I can scoop a story. I'm a member of the cast doing what's best for the production. Take the ticket Mr. Mallory offered you and see for yourself."

"I think I will. Robert told me he has four tickets for each performance."

"Then he can spare one for you." I grinned.

"Now, go." Bernie Slater waved me to the door.

"Yes, sir." I rose.

"I mean, leave for the day."

"What gives, Boss?" Poised to leave, I turned to face him. With my hand on the doorknob, I asked quizzically, "Are you sacking me?" *That would tear it after all I've gone through to make sure I could keep the job!*

"No, no, I promise, nothing like that," he quickly assured me. "I've been pleased with what you've done for us. Also, if you need tomorrow off, let me know."

"You're offering me a day off?" My mouth dropped open, so I closed it.

"You've been honest with me today, and I appreciate it. You've done a great job with every feature I've handed you, and you're really working hard on this opera," he explained. His round face crinkled into a smile. "I can't give you a raise, so I've decided to give you some slack with your hours. Let's say you are doing research for a story."

"Rollie won't like this," I cautioned him, using the nickname we dared not use to the critic's face. "He's spreading the word I'm your pet and he'll take this as a sign you are favoring me again."

"Little does he know." Slater chuckled. "Have you figured out I work you harder than most?"

"It has crossed my mind more than once," I admitted. "I know you push me to keep doing better, if that's what you mean. Doesn't matter, though. Rollie is probably not the only one to think that way."

He nodded. "If it doesn't bother you, it doesn't bother me. In this case, however, we simply won't tell him."

I got to the auditorium and found some changes in the technical arrangements had been made.

Television camera number one gained a twin positioned at another angle along with a director and a second technician. I assumed the additions comprised an attempt to give Becca a better chance of doubling Emilie.

"Mr. Peterman!" I hailed him when he passed me backstage. "Will the rehearsal be recorded?"

Totally preoccupied, he gazed at me like he had never seen me before.

"Never mind. I apologize for bothering you. You undoubtedly have more important things on your mind."

He gave me a weak smile. "I'm sorry, Lauren. It's nothing personal. To answer your question, I don't have the foggiest idea."

"I really hate to ask this, and normally I'd let it pass, but my boss at the paper insisted I try. Is there any chance you would let the *Gleaner's* critic in to see the final rehearsal tonight?"

Peterman's absent-minded gaze changed to a stare, and he regarded me like I suddenly grew a second head and turned purple before his eyes.

"I'll take that as a negative. Again, never mind, I'm sorry to bother you."

"Wait a minute." He put a hand on my shoulder. "I have an idea. Come with me."

He led the way through the backstage maze of wardrobe, makeup, and storage rooms to an office marked, *Director of Music*, and knocked. At hearing, "come in," he held the door for me to enter.

Norman Brier, seated behind a desk, greeted us. From the way he looked, he could probably use at least three nights of sleep in one stretch.

"Yes, David?"

"Lauren asked me if we would grant admission to the paper's critic for tonight's rehearsal."

"Have a seat. I know you work for the *Daily Gleaner*." Brier gazed at me through tired eyes. "In what capacity?"

"I'm a reporter. I get special assignments, usually involving in-depth research."

"You're not the critic."

"Heaven help us, no." I shuddered and they both snickered. "I'm asking because my boss Bernie Slater, our publisher and editor-in-chief, requested me to. Roland Beesley, our cultural editor, has heard a few rumors that something is up around here, and he's desperate to see the rehearsal."

Brier closely regarded me. "You're not doing a story on the production?"

"Absolutely not! Mr. Brier, I'm here by special arrangement because I can't graduate without some kind of fine arts class." I grimaced. "I give you my word, I haven't told anyone outside the production anything about it other than I have a pantomime part," I assured them. "Anyone who knows me finds the whole situation hilarious."

"Why?" Peterman asked. "I know you didn't sing in high school, but I also know you were busy."

"I'm basically tone-deaf." I grinned. "The idea that I have a part in an opera is laughable. I've never set foot on a stage before and I admit I've been more than a bit leery of the entire process."

"You're doing a great job," Peterman told me. "We're pleased with your work, and Alan is praising your acting abilities."

"Thank you. I'll take all the compliments I can get. My knees finally stopped knocking together about the time we moved to the stage."

Both men chuckled again.

"About the rehearsal tonight?" I prompted. "I need an answer one way or the other."

"If we let him in, it would be a good test for our doubling," Peterman commented to Brier. "Maybe we should consider it."

"Risky. Absolutely risky, although you're correct," Brier admitted. He glanced at the clock and then me. "All right. It's almost four o'clock now. What is his name and how do I reach him?"

"My editor is Bernie Slater. Our critic is Roland Beesley. They're both at the office. If you want to give me credit for it, it could help me out. Our critic is a real snob and thinks women should stay home." I refrained from adding anything more. Beesley needed to be experienced to be believed.

"The number?"

"Northwoods seven, five-eight-zero-eight."

I sat back in my chair and listened while he spoke first to Slater, and then with Beesley.

"Mr. Beesley, assuming you attend the rehearsal—" He paused for a moment before he continued. "I would like to speak with you afterwards before you leave the building." He paused again. "Yes, Miss Kaye did make the request on your behalf." Another pause. "I certainly shall. Ask for Mr. Gardiner, our staging director, when you arrive. He'll show you to your seat." Short pause. "You're welcome. See you this evening." He hung up and regarded me with something approaching a sly smile. "You're right. He would have promised almost anything, possibly up to his first-born, to see the show tonight."

"Thank you for the credit. I presume you are going to use him as the final acid test."

"If we can get it by him, we know we knocked it out of the park," Brier stated with a sigh issuing from his toes. "Thank you for bringing this to me." He leaned back and closed his eyes, dismissing us.

"Lauren, how is Ash?" Peterman asked once we were back in the hallway.

"I know he doesn't look good. He claims he's just tired." I shrugged. "He's not keeping late hours, unless there's someone involved whom I haven't seen."

"Carmella?"

"Mr. Peterman, Carmella has a wonderful boyfriend and hasn't given Ash Harper anything but polite refusals. You'll meet Jim Pomeroy tomorrow night. He's a great guy and they're meant for each other." I held up my hand when he started to speak again. "For my part, I've been friendly but firm. We've gone out several times after rehearsals, but there have always been others around."

"His performance is up to his normal standards, but he looks ill." He glanced each way down the hall; one of the stagehands came toward us carrying a bucket and mop. "Let's go to my office." He took me through the maze to a small closet masquerading as his office. Barely room for a desk and two chairs, the desk was more cluttered than the one in front of Slater. "Have a seat. And stop calling me *Mr. Peterman*. I'm David. We're in this together."

Nodding, I moved some papers off the second chair, sat, and waited.

"Lauren, Robert Mallory confided to me that you are an investigator," he began and hesitated. He stared at the floor for a moment. "He also vouched for you being totally trustworthy."

"I like to think so," I responded, wary of where he wanted to take this. "I've done some work for him."

"If Robert trusts you, I guess I can. This is delicate," he told me. His usually smiling brown eyes appeared worried. "And confidential."

"I carry a few secrets," I candidly admitted. "Is there something I can do for you?"

"Ash Harper can be a bit of an ass, but I've known him for years and I'm worried. I was in his dressing room two days ago and saw a syringe." Peterman rubbed his face with both hands. "He can be a wild party guy. I hope he's not doing something stupid, like drugs."

I frowned while I mentally reviewed all the time Harper and I spent together. I saw the beginnings of a pattern but nothing concrete. Yet. However, there was something going on even if it did not make total sense to me at the moment.

"I understand your concern, and I share it. I doubt it involves drugs. His behavior isn't erratic enough."

"You'd know?"

"I've had some dealings observing the effects." I left my statement there. "Mr. Peterman, I mean, David, may I ask you something?" At his nod, I continued. "How well do you know Rebecca Chernak?"

"I was in their wedding four years ago, but Becca's a hard person to get to know. Ash seemed to settle down after they got married, but in the past two years he's gotten his old reputation back for outrageous flirting." He gazed at me. "Has he made a pass at you?"

"Honestly? Nothing serious, or at least nothing I have taken to heart. As I said, we've gone out for coffee, and we've talked, but that's been it. I let him know that I'm not a giggly chorine panting to score with an opera star, and he accepted it. I will admit I steered him away from Carmella. However, he doesn't seem to be chaffing for a conquest."

"Even that is curious." He lightly massaged his temples with his fingers. "See what you can find out. I may be concerned about nothing, but that syringe was real."

"Is he in the building?"

"Let's find out. He usually comes in early. I know Becca is

here, going over the technical aspects with the television people."

We made our way down to Harper's dressing room in the basement. His door stood slightly ajar. I waved Peterman off and knocked.

"Come in."

I pushed the door open. The tenor, with his eyes closed, rested in his recliner.

"Ash?"

"Lauren. What a nice surprise," he greeted me without moving. "I'm resting my eyes. Pull up a chair and sit down." His voice lacked any sign of his earlier spirits.

His dressing room befitted one of the principal players: divan, lounge chair, lighted mirror on a vanity makeup table, a sink, a small refrigerator, and a screened area for changing. I took advantage of his closed eyes to study his appearance. Tired and pallid were two adjectives I would have used in a description. Dark circles, clearly visible without his stage makeup, underlined his eyes. I got an overall impression of listlessness, with none of the vivaciousness he had when we met.

"Wow. This dressing room makes the community room for the chorus seem positively slummy," I quipped to break the silence.

"Slummy?" He opened his eyes and smiled. His face was etched by fatigue. "Is that a word?"

"Probably not." I smiled back. "But it's descriptive, so maybe it should be. We have four sinks to serve almost two dozen women." I sat on the small couch. "I've been worried about you. Forgive me for saying this, but you don't look well."

"I've been really tired," he conceded openly with no frivolity or teasing. "I'm not sure why."

"That's your only symptom?"

"That really seems to be it. I'm having some trouble concentrating, but that goes with being tired." He started to sit up and I pushed him back. "Okay, I'll be good."

"A marked change in attitude, if I may say so." I chuckled.

"Are you sleeping well?"

"I think so. At least I was before Becca showed up." He sighed deeply and it sounded like it came from his toes.

I thought about my conversation with Becca and her concern about me. *Maybe she accosted him about it because I'm not an eager chorine.* "Ash, are you two fighting?" I gave my voice a smidgen of scorn.

"No, nothing like that. Becca mumbles in her sleep and I'm a light sleeper." He closed his eyes again. "Can I get you to come back for me at five? I think I'll try to nap."

"No problem. See you later."

I eased back into the hallway and pulled the door shut. Three steps down the corridor, I met Becca Chernak coming down the stairs.

"Is Ash here?" she asked with a frown.

"David asked me to check on him. I knocked and stuck my head in to ask him a question, but he seems to be asleep. At least, he didn't say anything. He's in the reclining easy chair, and his eyes are closed."

"He didn't sleep well last night," she confided. "I was surprised to see how tired he looks."

"Shall we move to the green room?" I suggested. I let her lead because my sense of direction—what there was of it—did not mix well with rabbit warrens and mazes. I easily got lost. "Is the extra camera going to help? I saw it when I came in."

"I hope so. There's a director now, too. Bill and I went over Emilie's blocking with him so he can keep up with her. The better the close-up, the happier I'll be."

"According to Julie Mallory, the one time the doubling showed was the time you held one ending note a tiny bit longer than Emilie did. That's a remarkable accomplishment." I wanted to keep her off the subject of her husband if I could.

"Frankly, I hope Emilie recovers enough to sing, at least Saturday's performance. I'd like to see the production."

"Were you planning on it before this happened?"

"Ash and I always try to see each other's shows. We're in so many together that it's a nice change to sit in the audience once in a while." She remained silent while we navigated a hallway. We entered the large green room and found seats. "You're here early. I hope you didn't get fired."

"Funny, when my boss told me to take the rest of the day off, I asked him that same question." I chuckled. "No, I haven't. In fact, this is sort of a gift from my boss. He's pleased with the way I've handled two major stories. Apparently, I'm not eligible for a raise, so he gave me some extra time off with pay. He also asked me to do him a favor, which is highly unusual for him."

"I heard Norm telling the camera people that the *Daily Gleaner's* critic is going to be out front this evening." She scowled. "I thought they were keeping the press away from us."

"Well, I confess that was the favor. David and Mr. Brier decided if Roland doesn't trip to the doubling, it will mean we knocked it out of the park, to use Professor Brier's phrase." I sighed. "Our critic has gotten wind of something going on, and he put pressure on our boss."

"Who, in turn, put pressure on you," offered Des Raphael, strolling up to join us. "Norm is correct, though. If we can get it past Beesley, we're home free."

"Hello, Des," Becca greeted him with marked warmth, her voice sultry. "It's good to see you."

The way they gazed at each other made me feel like a fifth wheel on a tricycle.

"Becca, I thought you did a remarkable job last night," the bass informed her. "It was beautifully sung, as always. I must admit, as much as I admire Emilie's voice, this production didn't seem right without you."

"Thank you, Des. That means a lot coming from you." She gave him such a brilliant smile that her eyes echoed it.

Raphael turned to me. "Lauren, I've been meaning to compliment you on your work. For someone who has no stage experience, you're doing a remarkable job. You and Alan make a believable couple, which is exactly what we need for this."

"Thank you. I'll take all the moral support I can get," I murmured. "I feel terribly out of place."

"Have you ever considered acting?" he asked.

"Ugh, thanks but no thanks." I grimaced. "This is close enough. Once I'm done here, it's back to the typewriter for me. Frankly, I'd rather write than speak."

Raphael laughed. Becca barely reacted; apparently, she reserved her beaming smiles strictly for Desmond Raphael. Backstage life, I reflected, could be interesting.

Staged for Death

7

A few minutes before five, once I made certain Becca Chernak and Des Raphael went off somewhere to get a bite to eat, I wound my way back to the basement hallway. I knocked on the door to Tybalt's dressing room and entered.

"Ash?"

He was up and he held a thin syringe in his hand. He jumped at the sound of my voice and almost dropped it.

"Lauren," he snapped in a loud stage whisper, "come in or stay out, but close the door!"

"You asked me to wake you at five. I'm about two minutes early." I stated while I complied. Two steps into the room, I spotted a small bottle on the table next to the lounge chair. The pattern I had noticed completed itself and fell neatly into place. "Do I get to ask what you are doing, or shall I guess?"

"I'm not shooting drugs," he retorted.

"Begging your pardon, but insulin is a drug."

"You're sharp." He pulled up his shirt and gave himself the shot. "Join me for a quick bite? I have to eat something now."

"Sure. There's a café around the corner. We can walk."

While we walked, he asked me to keep his diabetes confidential.

"I will, of course. You should know me well enough by now to realize that. But Ash," I protested mildly, "it's nothing to be ashamed of. If it's under control—and I've watched you when we've been out—you should be fine."

"Up until recently, I have been."

"What's been happening? I've noticed you've become increasingly tired." His reluctance to admit more was palpable. "Please, Ash, trust me?"

"Two weeks ago, I started feeling odd. Last week was strange and the past few days have been more than peculiar. I've never been so tired. I seem to feel worse every week." He gave a sigh of resignation. "Right now, I have reached the point where all I'm hoping for is to get through the two performances."

"Who does know about this?"

"This?"

"The diabetes."

"You and Becca."

"You need to tell David," I urged.

"Why?"

"He saw a syringe in your dressing room, and he's afraid you're doing something stupid, like hard drugs."

"God above! That's rich!" Harper threw back his head and laughed. "I can believe it of David, though. He's a worrywart. Honestly, he should know me better than that."

"Please, Ash, let him know? He's got enough, with everything else going on, to genuinely concern him and he doesn't need more, especially since he's wrong." I paused while he opened the door. "If you don't, I will."

"Okay, Auntie, I will, when we get back. I promise."

We got lucky. We saw no one else from the company in the café. The hostess seated us and after a quick perusal of the menu, we ordered sandwiches.

"Oh, I don't think you've heard the latest. The *Daily Gleaner's* cultural editor will be attending tonight's rehearsal."

"I thought Brier was keeping the press out."

"That changed this afternoon. Our illustrious critic decided something sinister must be going on around the production when he didn't receive an invitation to the final dress. I wouldn't spill it, so he demanded to be present, and I do mean demanded. He put pressure on my boss, who dumped it on me. I admit I was the one who asked, but Brier issued the invitation."

"Why?"

"He and David seem to think if they can get the dubbing by Roland, we'll be okay tomorrow night."

"Becca must be fit to be tied. She keeps hoping Emilie will recover."

"Des was with her when I saw her last. I get the impression Becca is a cool customer. I doubt much throws her for long." I paused for a moment, sorting out my thoughts. I wanted to be tactful, which never came easily to me. "Ash, may I ask a personal question?"

"Of course. Ask me anything, Auntie."

"Why do you come on to every female who walks across your path when you really don't have any intentions of following through?"

"Who says I don't intend to follow through?" He gave me a lewd grin.

"Down, boy! You made a pass at Carmella, and then at me. Nothing happened." I cocked my head to one side; his grin stayed. "I'm serious, Ash."

"Lauren, all joking aside for a moment, please bear in mind, I'm a gentleman at heart." The mocking grin faded. "I don't force my way. I never have. I enjoy the company of women, and they seem to reciprocate." He smiled at me, plain charm without hype. "Carmella has her Jim. I'm not sure who commands your interest, but it's definitely not me."

"So, the Mack truck routine is window dressing?"

"And fun." The grin returned, brimmed with mischief. "However, if I thought for one moment I could entice you into a deeper relationship, I would."

"I won't ask why you would consider it." I watered down my response with a smile. "Becca told me I don't fit your usual profile."

"You don't. You're more, well, I don't know how to put this without sounding like a complete cad," he complained. "You're real, not symbolic. The flirting is a reflex. I do it simply because I don't like to be alone. Becca can't understand that."

Our sandwiches arrived and we ate in silence for a few moments.

"I may be talking way out of turn here, but what is going on between her and Des Raphael?" I regarded my BLT and took another bite. The bacon could have been crisper, but I decided not to fuss. "I'm not trying to pry but I am curious. I saw them together for a few moments this afternoon."

"Des has always put her on a pedestal, and she likes that kind of adoration. I'm not sure how deep it goes." He shot a shrewd glance at me. "Not much gets by you."

"A friendly foe once told me he's not sure he will ever be able to take in everything I do when I look at a scene."

"A friendly foe?" He chuckled. "That sounds intriguing."

"It's a long story, but his comment is valid." I smiled at Harper. "Take you, for instance. I was beginning to see a pattern before I walked into your dressing room today. We've been out for coffee several times. The picture puzzle didn't fall together, at least not completely, until I saw the medication, but even before that I had suspicions."

"Pattern?"

"Certain basic things were consistent. No sugar or milk in coffee, half a piece of toast with no jam or honey, no sweets, no snacks, and such. I was trying to combine all of it with your fatigue and make it all add up. I know, from a friend who has the disease, that dealing with diabetes depends on keeping things even. You're probably out of balance at the moment."

"Could be." He reached across the table for my hand. "Keep it confidential?"

"Absolutely." I squeezed his hand.

"Ah, Lauren, you're one in at least a thousand, if not a million. You're worth much more than a short dalliance."

"Thank you, I think. However, please understand I will not consider dallying with you while you're married." I grinned, took my hand back, and glanced at my watch. "Time to finish and get out of here."

We approached the auditorium stage door and watched a cab pull up to the curb. Roland Beesley stepped out in full regalia.

"Oh, *bother!*" I pitched my voice low and gave the word plenty of venom.

"Who's the whale in the fancy suit?"

"Roland!" I called out. He stopped and waited for us to approach him.

"Lauren, I understand I have you to thank for my invitation to the dress rehearsal." Impeccably dressed, Beesley enclosed his bulk in a dark suit complete with vest and watch chain; his trousers and the handkerchief in his breast pocket had creases sharp enough to cut cheese. A homburg and ebony walking stick provided the final touches to his outfit.

"I was able to talk to Mr. Brier and Mr. Peterman, as you and Mr. Slater requested. They issued the invitation."

"I thought you'd be inside by now."

"I do eat once in a while, in spite of what you guys think. My call is for six." I smiled at him and turned to my companion. "Ash, I'd like you to meet Roland Beesley, cultural editor and fine arts critic for the *Daily Gleaner*. Roland, this is Ashton Harper, with the New York City Opera. He's our Tybalt."

They nodded. I noticed Ash didn't reciprocate when Beesley extended his hand, and I wondered why. The critic's pudgy, gloved hand fell limply to his side.

"Mr. Harper, I have heard you perform other roles, and I'm eagerly anticipating seeing you this evening." Beesley regarded me with some interest. "I'm supposed to meet William Gardiner."

"Bill should be right inside," I told him. "Ash, you need more time in makeup than I do. I'll see Roland gets to Bill."

Ash gave me a quick hug. "I hate pompous jerks," he whispered in my ear, and vanished down the stairs. I stifled a snicker.

"Mr. Harper appears fatigued," the critic commented as we entered.

"We've been at it pretty hard, and he takes his part seriously. He's a professional and Tybalt is a demanding role," I offered what I hoped he would accept as a logical observation. We did not need any rumors started. I spotted Gardiner and waved to him. "Ah, here's Bill."

The staging director joined us and I introduced the men.

"Norm told me to expect you." Gardiner greeted the newspaper man. "We have chosen a prime seat for you."

They turned to go down the side stairs to the auditorium floor. Right before they disappeared, Gardiner glanced back at me and rolled his eyes. I managed to curb my laughter until I got to the stairs which led up to the communal dressing room.

"What's so funny?" Carmella asked when I entered, chuckling. "I was afraid you were going to be late."

The six other girls in the room giggled among themselves, not paying us any attention.

"Bill just met the *Gleaner's* critic. You'd have to know Rollie to fully understand. He's almost a relic from the Edwardian era." I got started on my makeup.

"I heard the critic had been invited," Carmella murmured with a shudder.

"You, my dear, have absolutely nothing to worry about. In fact, I'd be willing to bet right now he will undoubtedly try to take credit for discovering you. As for being late, I wasn't. I've actually been here since about three forty-five. My boss let me go early, and he's offered to give me tomorrow off."

"Wow!"

"I know what you mean. I'm impressed, too." I made a face in the mirror. "I even asked if he was firing me."

Carmella giggled. She pulled her tunic over her head.

"I wish I was better at this," I said while I tried to get my eyeliner on straight. "Julie keeps telling me it's easy, but she also thinks shopping is fun. That, by the way, is something you two have in common. How come you're changing up here? I thought they gave you a dressing room."

"They did, but when Becca joined the cast, she was going to share with me. I offered to move back up here so she could have it," Carmella said in tones so low I almost missed it. "The paint and brush squad applied my finishing touches. They want to make sure my makeup is right, and I can't get the hang of putting my wig on straight."

"Becca will probably freeze me out completely the next time I run into her if she finds out I had a light supper with Ash."

"I saw her coming in with Des when I arrived." She wiggled into her tights. "If there's anything going on there, I don't want to know."

I kept my mouth shut. Secrets were secrets and these were not mine to share. Instead, I asked her to do up my back fastenings, which were more along the lines of lacings.

"Have they told the critic about the voice doubling?"

"Absolutely not! I think they want to see if he catches it on his own. Sort of a final test. I know Mr. Brier has asked to talk to Roland after the performance before he runs off to do his story." I adjusted my gown and slipped into my shoes. "On to wigs!"

With our heads properly wigged, we reported to the green room.

"This is what I have dreamed of all my life," Carmella whispered to me, her eyes reflecting her excitement.

"You deserve it," I whispered back. "If I can help, I will."

She grinned at me before she hurried off to join the students gathering in the main rehearsal area.

Alan Brockton came up to me. "She's really talented."

"I've known her since this past summer," I volunteered. "She's sweet, and much too polite and nice to be nasty. If someone or something gets in her way, I will do my best to remove the obstacle, and I'll have help!" *Would I ever have help! And high-powered! Bother!*

I found a seat and kept my mouth closed. The accompanist

worked with the chorus in the main room while the soloists worked with Peterman in another area. Carmella warmed up with the soloists after Peterman caught her amid the chorus and ordered her to where she belonged. Once they finished, the soloists joined us peons.

Norman Brier stood on a chair and beckoned for us to gather around. Peterman, looking anachronistic in wig, makeup, and street clothes, stayed on the ground at his side.

"Since nothing works better around here than the grapevine," Brier began, smiling as we laughed, "I assume you all know that the *Daily Gleaner's* critic is out front. He has *not* been told about the vocal doubling. We want to see if he catches it."

"Who is he?" asked Raphael.

"Roland Beesley," I supplied from my position in the back. "He's the one out front who looks as if he belongs in Edwardian London."

More laughter. *Heaven help us, we need it.*

"You've worked hard on this, and I know it's going to pay off," Brier said. "Tonight's the last test run. Everyone break a leg."

"But please, not literally," Peterman quipped. "I don't think we could deal with another crisis."

I heard a few amens murmured among the chuckles.

"Overture in ten minutes!" Gardiner called out. "Those up in the party scene take your places in eight. Opening choir, be ready to step out when the overture ends."

Instead of having the curtain rise to open the production with a full chorus prologue before the party scene, David Peterman and Bill Gardiner carefully selected a small ensemble from the chorus to file out in front of the curtain when the overture finished. The eight choir members explained the feud between the two families of Verona in the same manner as the prologue of Shakespeare's play. Once done, they retreated to the wings and joined the rest of the chorus and the Capulets on-stage during the musical introduction of Juliette's birthday ball. Following that, the curtain rose on the party, which opened the first scene of Act I.

When I asked Brockton about it, he told me this approach kept the flavor of the play while it gave more students better stage experience. Again, what I know about opera would not fill a small notebook page. I wondered what Roland Beesley would think of it while I stood in my place with Emilie and Brockton, waiting for the curtain to go up.

That proved to be my last moment for wondering about anything for the rest of the performance.

During the ball, Emilie clung to my hand as much as she did to Alan's arm. I hoped it appeared natural. Her acting during Juliette's first aria seemed marvelous, and from what I could tell, Becca's dubbing hit all the marks.

Unable to stand in the wings while Carmella did her solo part because of the television equipment, I managed to sneak around and enter the auditorium. I grabbed a seat off to the side. From our rehearsals I knew which would give me the best view of her antics. I watched her cavorting around. She almost dropped her sword when she drew it, yet even the mistake worked since she played a brash young boy.

When Sebring entered as Mercutio, I ran backstage again so I'd be in the right place for my next entrance.

After Tybalt did in Mercutio, Tybalt and Romeo danced the second duel. Once Thorne finished slicing and stabbing Harper, they ended a bit farther upstage than usual. Brockton, standing next to me in the wings with the women of the chorus, chuckled while we waited for our entrance cue.

"See what I mean?" Brockton whispered in my ear. "You have to watch where he lands."

I nodded. At the appropriate moment, he stepped out. Right behind him, with two of the ladies trying to hold me back as directed, I acted out my struggle to get free in view of the audience. Crossing to Tybalt, I dropped to my knees to cradle Ash's head and shoulders in my lap for their final exchange. I felt more confident performing it now that I knew Gardiner thought it a good dramatic piece of business. *Geez, even the slang works for me now.*

Tybalt died in my arms while Capulet strode forward to confront the Duke. I rose and when the men loaded Harper onto the bier, I stayed behind Brockton. He and I joined the funeral procession while everyone onstage sang, "*O Jour de Deuil!*" which, in French, means, "Oh Day of Woe!" Once we arrived at down-center stage, the location where Ash Harper earned me the stern reprimand, I acted out my weeping bit. Raphael, the Duke, called for peace. Brockton, as Lord Capulet, vowed there would be no peace and voiced his sorrow at Tybalt's death. Raphael banished Romeo. The curtain came down on Act III.

My next entrance occurred during Juliette's death scene at the end of Act IV. Brockton and I watched Emilie 'die' from the wings waiting for our cue. More weeping to do.

We made our final exit and found seats in the green room. Fortunately, the fifth and final act did not involve us. Strictly for Romeo and Juliette, it showcased the two leads. Harper joined us while we tried to relax a bit. Last up were the curtain calls. The entire ensemble took the first one; it whittled down slowly to Wendell Thorne and Emilie St. Claude.

"You really should consider acting," Brockton told me. "You're a natural for it."

"Ash, would you happen to have a bar of soap on you? I'd like Alan to wash his mouth out," I mischievously said. "He can then pass it to Des, who made the same comment earlier."

Both men laughed.

"Sorry, Auntie, but I don't have any pockets in this rig. I guess I should confess I was going to agree with him." Harper favored me with a wry smile, "but I'll back off. I hate soap in my mouth." Even his smile lacked his usual energy.

"I ran out front to see Carmella's big solo scene," I admitted.

"She is incredible, although you guys know me well enough to realize I don't have the background to properly judge anything here."

They both nodded.

"You're right, though," my stage husband told me. "She is exceptional."

"I have recommended her for a NYCO scholarship, once she graduates with her music degree," Harper volunteered. "Alan, can you imagine her as Adele in *Die Fledermaus*?"

"Easily! I could see it as a signature role for her. Ash, I'll be happy to second her for the scholarship. Maybe it would be possible to have her start some lessons before she graduates."

"That's worth checking," Harper agreed.

Brockton nodded. "We certainly can't let her amazing talent languish."

"I know she's concerned about having money for her studies," I confided. "She has a part-time job on weekends at the best Italian restaurant in the New York metropolitan area to help with her expenses, but I know it's not going to be enough on its own." I also knew she had one wealthy relative who would probably assist her, although I doubted she would ever approach him for help.

"Wait a minute. She works at Susan's Place?" Harper asked, astounded.

"Carmella works the weekend lunch hours there, sometimes spilling over to the evening," I said. "You know about Susan's?" I gave him a surprised smile.

"Oh, yes, although Becca and I don't get there as often as I would like to. I helped Gianni get started when he left Manhattan five years ago." Harper sat back. "It's a small world."

"Gianni and Susan are friends. I met Carmella earlier this year when I did my first big story," I put in quickly, "the one with the dead bodies. Carmella's steady boyfriend also works at Susan's. They got the jobs when Robert Mallory made introductions."

"You can leave this in our hands, Lauren," Brockton said. He leaned back with a satisfied smile. "I'm sure Des and Jeff would also be willing to help."

"Help with what?" Sebring asked, joining us.

"Getting Carmella set up with a scholarship to study with NYCO," Harper explained. "I've made the initial recommendation."

"I will gladly help. I was going to suggest it. Has anyone made sure Laszlo will be here tomorrow night?"

"He will be," Harper confirmed. "If nothing else, he wants to see how this dubbing rig works. Becca and I spoke to him last night. He's bringing Joseph Rosenstock."

"When he sees her perform, he may offer it on the spot." Sebring noticed my confusion and turned to me. "Laszlo is NYCO's director and Joseph is one of our conductors. This will be better than an audition because she'll be in a known role."

"The real bonus is she won't know it's an audition, so she won't be any more nervous than usual," I offered.

Des Raphael strolled into the area. "You people look like cats contemplating a trapped mouse. What's going on?"

"We're discussing getting Carmella a scholarship with NYCO," Sebring said.

"Great minds working alike. I just spoke to Joseph about her," Raphael told the group. "He's planning to come with Laszlo tomorrow."

"Okay, guys!" I seriously interposed. "Listen up and trust me. I know Carmella fairly well, and I can assure you she would panic if she knew anything about this. Not syllable to her about this until after Saturday's performance. I want your promises." I got nods and agreement from all four of them. "Good. Thank you."

"Are you always this protective of your friends?" Raphael asked.

"Des, I'm an only child, and since my parents died, I've been on my own. My friends are now my family. If I see some way to help a friend, I do what I can."

His eyes, steady on mine, reflected a strange emotion I could not name as he digested my response.

"That's how it should be," Harper said with a weary smile.

Gradually, the cast gathered, and at the appropriate moment, we took our places onstage for the curtain calls.

Moments later I headed back into the green room, this time with Carmella. Becca came in and joined us.

"You look as tired as I feel," I told her.

"This is work," she admitted. "I got caught up in the part, and during one of the arias, I almost knocked the microphone with my arm when I absent-mindedly did a gesture."

"I wonder what our critic thought," I murmured. "My main concern is his ear for voices. If he knows your voice well enough to identify it *as* yours, he'd realize it wasn't Emilie singing." I sighed and gave a slight shrug. "If you understand what I'm trying to say. I'm usually more coherent than this."

"I understand perfectly, I'm afraid," she agreed, "but unfortunately we can't do anything about it."

I got up when we were called back on stage to practice the curtain calls which Bill and Andrea decided to change for the third time. I had visions of us getting all three sets of directions confused with everyone tripping over everyone else.

Once more back in the green room, I commandeered a couch and put my feet up. I finally started to relax when I heard a voice asking directions to wherever the cast gathered.

"Uh-oh, here he comes," I muttered, trying not to cringe.

"Lauren," came the oily voice, "I wish to congratulate you on your acting abilities."

"Thank you, Roland," I replied as sincerely as I could to the man. "I've never done anything like this before, and I appreciate the compliment."

"Norman Brier asked me to meet him here." Beesley glanced around, his face uncertain. I guessed he needed a seat large enough to safely support him. I jumped up and moved to a chair so he could use the divan.

"He should be here shortly," I said. "Meanwhile, let me introduce you to Carmella Viscotti. She's a music major in her junior year. Carmella, this is Roland Beesley, fine arts editor and critic for the *Daily Gleaner*."

Carmella gave him a big smile. I never thought I'd see the *Gleaner's* Sydney Greenstreet simper at anything, but that is what he did. I glanced at Becca, and she rolled her eyes.

"Miss Viscotti, I cannot tell you how much I enjoyed your performance as Stéphano. I've rarely seen it done as well."

"Thank you," she murmured almost inaudibly, dropping her eyes and blushing. "This is the first featured role I've had."

"Young lady," intoned the pompous critic, "it will not be your last. I am prepared to give you my personal guarantee on that."

I resisted the urge to groan at his toadying while I made a note to tease Carmella about her blushing. "Roland, I'm sure you recognize one of the leading sopranos of the New York City Opera, Rebecca Chernak."

"Miss Chernak," he gushed. He pronounced it *Kernak* instead of *Shernak*, and she winced. "I have listened to you sing many times. It is a pleasure and an honor to meet you at long last."

"Excuse me, Roland." I rose. "I'll see if I can find Mr. Brier—"

"Let me," Carmella cut me off. "I want to get out of this wig." She dashed out, and I sat down again.

"Overall, Mr. Beesley, what did you think of the production?" Becca, always cool, dropped her demeanor to outright frosty, probably the result of his fracture of her name. I thought he should have known better, with all the posturing and bragging he did about his superior intellect. Inwardly I smiled at his mistake.

"It is difficult to believe the chorus is comprised of high school and college students," he pontificated. "Of course, the principals are all seasoned veterans. Miss St. Claude's voice vaguely reminds me of yours, which is, of course, all to the good." His obsequious attitude, coupled with his unctuous voice, caused more than one to wince.

Score one for our side – he didn't catch it! I caught Becca's eye and winked. She almost smiled.

"Oh, here's Norm," Becca said, rising. "If you will excuse me?"

"Of course, dear lady." He tried to bow while seated, which did not work. He struggled to his feet and leaned forward a bit. Undoubtedly, this constituted his version of a bow, but I hoped he stayed upright. He looked like he could topple over.

"Mr. Brier, let me introduce Roland Beesley, critic for the *Daily Gleaner*," I said formally, also getting to my feet. "Roland, this is our musical director, Norman Brier." I stayed long enough to hear Beesley start gushing again before I excused myself. I hastened out of the room before I broke up laughing.

I stopped at the wig room, and bareheaded once again, made a beeline for the dressing room.

"He really enjoyed your performance," I told Carmella. "Rollie is gushing all over again to Mr. Brier."

"He's an odd one," she giggled. "Did he suspect about Emilie's voice?"

"He told Becca, and I quote, Miss St. Claude's voice vaguely reminds me of yours, which is, of course, all to the good. End of quote." I grinned. "It worked!"

We finished changing and returned to the green room. Most of the cast stood or sat around, listening to Brier recount Beesley's raves. "Becca, Emilie! Congratulations again, it seems to have worked!"

I joined in the applause.

"Is he coming back for the opening?" I asked.

"I doubt we could keep him away at this point," Peterman replied with a wide grin.

"I hope you realize Roland will probably try to take all the credit for discovering Carmella." I snickered. "There won't be a lot you can do about it. I'll try to pull a string or two and get our boss to make sure it doesn't come out that way in print."

"She's our discovery," Ash put in. His grin matched Peterman's. "Norm's, David's, and NYCO's!" He put his arm around her shoulder while everyone in the room applauded.

Carmella's face turned beet red.

Friday morning, I woke to my alarm at seven and stayed conscious long enough to call my boss and accept his offer of the day off. Never a morning person, I luxuriated in going back to sleep. I knew when someone in the world wanted to find me, they could use my phone number if they knew it. I figured sooner or later, the phone—in easy reach on the floor—would ring. Of course, it did.

I opened one eye and checked my clock. *Ten o'clock.* I picked up the receiver.

"Hello." I doubt I sounded articulate even with the one word.

"Lauren! I tried calling you at the paper, and they told me you had the day off," Julie's voice bubbled over the line. "Since that's true, let's go out to lunch!"

"I might be awake by then," I replied, entirely non-committal. "What time shall I pick you up?" Julie possessed a license but those of us who knew and loved her conspired to ensure she never had to use it on the grounds of safety for all concerned.

"How about eleven? That gives you an hour, if you don't go back to sleep."

I sat up and stretched. "Okay. I'm moving. See you in a bit."

Julie knew me almost as well as her father did. I got up, folded my convertible bed back into its daytime configuration of a sofa—mostly to avoid the temptation of climbing back into it—and trudged to the bathroom. While I brushed my teeth, the phone rang again. I picked up the receiver.

"I'm up, I promise," I told it through toothpaste and brush.

"You sound like you're strangling," Mallory laughed.

I took the toothbrush out of my mouth. "I thought you were Julie making sure I hadn't gone back to sleep."

"Are you two going to lunch?"

"That's her plan."

"Where are you going?"

"No clue. I'm the wrong person to ask. I haven't had a cup of tea yet. Check with her. You can also tell her I'm up."

"That's fine." He chuckled. "I'll see you later."

I got dressed and made my first cup of tea. Years of trial and error convinced me two cups formed the absolute minimum of caffeine before I made coherent compound sentences. I never drank coffee. I sat on my sofa and sipped my tea.

Opening night! Heaven help us, what a thought!

The phone went off again.

"Hello?"

"Kaye, what's this I hear about you cavorting around on an opera stage?" a gruff, almost gravelly voice asked point-blank with no attempt at social graces.

"Good morning to you, too, Captain," I replied, smiling to myself. "It's all true, which I'm sure you know."

"Robert Mallory was here for a moment to drop a ticket for tomorrow night's performance on my desk," he grumbled, "and told me if I wanted a real treat, I should plan to use it. How in blue blazes did you get involved in an opera?"

"Class requirement," I informed Police Captain, Daniel O'Brien, and related the circumstances. He was the one person I knew who called me by my last name, and somehow, it always amused me. Shortly after we met, O'Brien declared he considered my first name phony and asked my permission to use my last name. Since he addressed his officers in the same manner, I assented.

"So, it's Romeo and Juliet."

"Technically, it's *Romeo et Juliette*, being sung in French." I snickered when he groaned. "I'm sure he also said it would be good for you."

"He did."

"Last time I spoke to Mr. Mallory at any length, he mentioned throwing a cast party at Susan's after the second performance."

"He mentioned that, too. He also said he saw the show Wednesday night at a rehearsal. Apparently, you were impressive."

"He and Julie were both there. Thanks for not sounding surprised," I sincerely told him. "I have a copy of the libretto in English if you'd like to borrow it."

"What's a libretto?"

"Basically, it's a script of what's being sung. The opera follows the Shakespeare play closely, with two exceptions. There's an extra character named Stéphano, who is Romeo's page. It's always sung by a young girl, in this case Carmella Viscotti."

"Carmella? You mean our Carmella?" O'Brien, part of the chaos during my first major story, had escorted her to a dance in order to fit in with club members at an exclusive resort.

"The one and only." I smiled again. "She truly is incredible. She even impressed the *Gleaner's* critic last night."

"What's the other change?"

"Romeo doesn't die immediately after taking the poison, which gives the star-crossed lovers another chance to sing one more duet."

"Figures." He sighed. "If you want to drop that libretto by my office, I'll return it Saturday."

"Will do. I'm going to lunch with Julie, and I'll stop by after I take her home."

"You know where my desk is." He hung up.

I reflected that while my boss liked to keep things short and sweet, O'Brien whittled brevity down to the point of being brusque.

Well, well. O'Brien is going to brave the terrors of an opera performance. I'll have to tease Mr. Mallory about this. I checked my watch. *Oh, bother! Not enough time for a second cup.*

I arrived at the Mallory home at two minutes after eleven.

"Miss Lauren," Mrs. Fiddler greeted me warmly, "Miss Julie is upstairs in her room."

"Mrs. Fiddler, I'm here on time because I skipped my second cup of tea. Can we correct this tragedy so I can finish waking up?"

"Certainly." She smiled. "I always have the tea kettle on when I know you're going to stop by. You go on up, and I'll bring it to you."

Mrs. Fiddler, whose duties included everything from cooking and cleaning to guarding the residents from annoyances, functioned as a governess and surrogate mother figure to Julie, and by extension, to me. Her appearance generally fooled newcomers. Although not a tall woman, she held herself ramrod straight with posture I envied. She parted her dark hair, now showing streaks of grey, in the center and wore two long braids as a crown across the top of her head. The immaculately pressed housedresses she wore as her uniform were always topped with a starched apron, and her feet were shod in sensible shoes. None of this gave a hint of the iron will behind her high forehead and blue eyes. Although a naturalized citizen of the U.S., her speech gave her English origins away.

I climbed the familiar stairs. Every kid needs a refuge when the going gets tough at the parental homestead, and this had been mine. Following my mother's death, the Mallory home became the one place I knew I would always be welcomed when the world got too complicated to cope with on my own.

The beautifully decorated mansion held none of the usual pretensions of a palace. The comfortable atmosphere, set and maintained by the incomparable Mrs. Fiddler, thrived even though the foyer out-sized my entire studio apartment. Rooms on the ground floor included Mallory's office, the living room, formal dining room, kitchen, bathroom, what he called the den, and in a small wing of its own, Mrs. Fiddler's quarters. Stairs from the foyer led to the second story hallway which branched out in two directions. Six bedrooms, three bathrooms, a master suite with its own bath, and Mallory's study comprised the upper floor. At that moment, the door to his study was closed; I guessed he had received a phone call. The open door to Julie's room, at the front of the house, welcomed me.

"I made it!" I called out as I approached.

"Good! How did the final rehearsal go last night?" Julie, standing in front of her mirror, checked her outfit. The coppery material of her shirtwaist dress accentuated her auburn hair and clear blue eyes.

"It went surprisingly well. There was a second television camera and a director to help with the monitoring, and it worked even better than when you were there. The *Gleaner's* critic saw it and didn't catch on to the voice double."

"That's great! They are really going to use it?" She turned away from the mirror and gave me a hug.

"As far as I know. I haven't heard that Emilie is ready to sing tonight." I sighed. "As good as Becca is, I wish you could hear Emilie. To me, her voice is more expressive, and there's a lovely clear quality to it. We're hoping she can sing the role tomorrow. Even Becca said she wants to see the production rather than sing it."

"I hope so. We have tickets for both nights."

"Miss Lauren? Here's your tea." Mrs. Fiddler appeared in the doorway holding a mug.

"Oooh, thank you so much," I said, gratefully accepting it. She went back down the hall and I told Julie I skipped my second cup. "I knew I could get one here."

"Where are you two off to for lunch?" Mallory leaned casually against the door frame.

"Daddy, are you still planning a party at Susan's after the performance tomorrow?"

"Yes. I was on the phone with Susan making all the arrangements. Starting at eleven, the restaurant is ours. Gianni will have a variety of dishes for an *après-theatre* supper. He's delighted because he hasn't done one since he left the city. I spoke to David Peterman, and the primary cast is to be invited. The chorus kids will have their own party at the college, which I told David I would sponsor." He quizzically regarded his daughter. "Why did you ask?"

"If we're going to be there tomorrow night, we don't need to lunch there today."

"I can agree with that," I said. "When was the last time you had a sandwich at Wilfrid's?"

"Wilfrid's and that marvelous bread! Yes, that would be terrific." Julie beamed. "Daddy, would you like to come with us?"

"No, I think I can manage without the girl talk." He grinned. "You two have catching up to do. Besides, I have some work I want to get done."

"We'll be back before two o'clock," Julie told him. She gave him a hug and kiss on the cheek.

We got into my car, and I drove around the circular driveway.

"I'm glad Daddy sold this car to someone we know." Julie patted the dashboard of my Triumph. "I've always liked it."

"He told me he wanted to make sure it had a good home. I needed a car, and I think he likes the idea that he occasionally gets to drive it. I know he didn't charge me what he could have gotten otherwise."

We got to Wilfrid's ahead of the noon rush, although the crowded parking lot indicated the coffee shop's usual brisk weekday lunch business. Handy to a large section of offices in the area, it catered to most of them.

"Uh-oh," Julie murmured. "Are we going to be able to get a table?"

"We'll see."

Inside the entryway, I managed to catch the eye of Wilfrid's daughter, Jenny, who acted as hostess. She grabbed a couple of menus and beckoned to us.

"Lauren! And Julie, right?" She smiled and led us to a small table toward the back of the coffee shop. "This is the best I can do right now."

"It's fine, don't worry about it," I assured her. "Judging by the parking lot, I was afraid we'd have to wait for a table."

"Grace will be with you shortly," she said with a nod. She took off to take care of a customer at the cash register.

"Well, we're not exactly in a hurry," Julie acknowledged and studied the menu. "What are you going to have?"

"The chicken salad sandwich." I left my unnecessary menu unopened.

"Sounds terrific. Oh—they have that wonderful creamy cole slaw, don't they?"

"Yes."

Grace showed up at the table. "What will it be?"

"Chicken salad sandwiches," I answered, "and instead of potato chips, we'd like sides of cole slaw."

"Drinks?" Grace moved to the side while Jenny put down a mug, a pot of water with a teabag hanging out, and a small pitcher of milk. "And for you?" Grace asked Julie.

"Coffee."

Our waitress finished scribbling on her order pad and left us.

"What's the latest on your love-life?" I queried. "Last I heard you were dating an engineering major."

"Not anymore. He showed up drunk at my dorm to pick me up for a date." She made a face. "I refused to get in the car. He got mad, and I went back inside."

I laughed. "Happy to hear it. Anything else going on?"

"No, although I brought a term paper home with me to work on, in case I manage to have extra time."

Julie and I spent the next hour and a half catching up, laughing, and commiserating with each other. Both only children and closer than most sisters, we went back eleven years. We did everything together when we were kids, even though I was exactly three-and-a-half years older. It never mattered. Mallory watched over me as carefully as he did her.

When Jenny brought the check to me, Julie grabbed it.

"Daddy's orders," she told me.

"I'm not arguing." I raised my hands in surrender, then looked at my watch. "Oh, blast and bother! It's almost one-thirty. I'll drop you at the house. I have an errand to run, after which I'm going to try to take a short nap. Can you call me around four? I told Carmella I'd pick her up to take her to the auditorium."

"No problem. I'll also tell Daddy and Mrs. Fiddler. One of us will remember." She laughed when I groaned. "Silly, you know I'll remember."

I drove to the police station after dropping Julie at the mansion. O'Brien correctly surmised I knew where to find his desk. The surprise, if I wanted to call it one, came when I saw him seated behind it going over paperwork.

"Good afternoon, Captain." I dropped a large envelope on his desk. "I even put it in a plain wrapper for you."

"Gee, thanks," he grumbled. He raised his head and aimed his grey eyes at me. His dark hair held a sprinkling of grey and its unkempt state showed the usual signs he had been running his fingers through it. He had abandoned his usual grey suit, for once. He tended to wear it like a uniform. Today he wore a dark blue suit with his normal white shirt. His grey tie may have been the single one he possessed. If I ever decided to shock him with a Christmas present, I planned to get a garish one and dare him to wear it. The only hat I ever saw on his head graced his coat rack, a fedora. Grey. Of course.

"I didn't want your men to get confused by seeing you with an opera libretto," I explained.

"Can you sing?"

"Nope. Not a note, and I admit I am eminently grateful for

that. I'd hate to have to sing and walk and act all at the same time. I'm having enough trouble with walking and acting. It's a pantomime part. They decided I would make a good Lady Capulet because I can make faces."

He laughed out loud. Apparently someone on his staff thought it a rare sound, because a head popped in the doorway.

"Captain?" Sergeant Walt Evans leaned into the room. "Oh, pardon me. I didn't realize you had someone with you."

"Hello, Walt. It's been a while." I greeted the officer.

"Hi, Lauren. We've heard you're in the opera at Hofstra."

"I don't sing. I'm a supernumerary."

"I beg your pardon?" Evans scratched his head, puzzled.

"In the movies, it would be called an extra. Walking scenery."

"My folks have tickets for tonight," he told me.

"I think they'll enjoy it. It's a good production."

"Evans, I assume you have something to do?" snapped O'Brien.

"Yes, sir." Evans smiled at me. "Have a great performance."

"Thank you, Walt." After he withdrew, I turned to O'Brien. "He was just being nice. He poked his head in to see if you were all right. I suppose no one around here is used to hearing you laugh."

"Kaye, Evans has things to do, and so do I." O'Brien did not quite growl it.

"I'm going." At the door, I stopped. "Please, Captain, come to the performance. I'd like you to be there. I can use the moral support. I've never done anything like this before, and it's scary."

"I'm sure you'll be terrific. If you botch it, I'll let you know." He almost smiled but caught himself in time. "Now get out of here."

I went back to my apartment and stretched out, not expecting to fall asleep. I did, however. My phone rang, which prompted thoughts of traveling back in time to slit Alexander Bell's throat.

I hated waking up to a ringing phone.

"Hello?"

"Did you get a nap?" Mallory asked.

"Surprisingly, yes." I yawned. "I thought Julie was going to call me."

"I told her I would. I wanted to wish you a broken leg."

"Ah, yes, in the true theatrical tradition. Thank you." An idea struck me. "Mr. Mallory? There's another theatrical tradition which comes to mind. Would you get some flowers for Carmella? I think she'd love that."

"Already planned. I thought I'd bring them backstage and have one of the ushers take them out to her at the curtain call."

"If they're red roses, her face will match them."

"She does blush beautifully," he acknowledged with a chuckle. "Lauren, I want you to know I'm proud of you."

"Thank you. You know how much that means to me."

"I'll see you after the performance in the green room. David gave me a backstage pass for the two nights."

The Music Departments of Hofstra College and
Northwoods Glen High School Present
Charles Gounod's *Romeo et Juliette*
Friday the 17ᵗʰ & Saturday the 18ᵗʰ of November
Director of Music and Conductor: Norman Brier, Professor
of Music and Vocal Studies Hofstra College
Assistant Director of Music: David Peterman, Music
Department Chairman, Northwoods Glen High School
Stage Manager: Jerome Levine
Staging Director: William Gardiner
Assistant Staging Director: Andrea Jamison

Principal Cast:

Juliette, *daughter of Capulet*	(soprano)	Emilie St. Claude
Roméo, *son of Montague*	(tenor)	Wendell Thorne
Frère Laurent, *a cleric*	(bass)	David Peterman
Mercutio, *Romeo's friend*	(baritone)	Jeffrey Sebring
Stéphano, *Romeo's page*	(soprano;trouser role)	Carmella Viscotti*
Count, Lord Capulet	(bass)	Alan Brockton
Tybalt, *Lady Capulet's nephew*	(tenor)	Ashton Harper
Gertrude, *Juliet's nurse*	(mezzo-soprano)	Stephanie Jewell*
The Duke of Verona	(bass)	Desmond Raphael
Pâris, *a young count*	(baritone)	Alexander Mercer*
Grégorio, *Capulet's servant*	(baritone)	Richard Lakeland*
Benvolio, *Montague's nephew*	(tenor)	Andrew Stiers*

| Countess, Lady Capulet | (pantomime) | Lauren Kaye * |

Male and female retainers and kinsmen of the Houses of Capulet and Montague, maskers and the ensemble, played by the Hofstra College and Northwoods Glen High School Chorus Members*

*denotes student role

The Combined Orchestra of Hofstra College and Northwoods Glen High School Conducted by Norman Brier

Setting: Verona, Italy in the 14th Century

Curtain is at Eight O'clock in the Evening

I realized all the books and films about theatrical opening nights described them as thrilling, yet I always assumed the effusive hyperbole to be apocryphal and exaggerated. I discovered those observations were much closer to reality than I ever imagined.

Prior to opening night, I did not appreciate the marked difference between a rehearsal and a performance before a live audience. I felt a special electricity in the air which set up a flow between those of us on the stage and the audience in the seats in front of it. Veteran cast members told me the audience was a multi-eyed monster hidden in the dark. I did not understand it until I stood on my first mark with the houselights down. From our rehearsals, I knew performers could not see the people in front of them with the stage lights on, yet a real audience made it totally new.

Their reactions reached us out of the darkened auditorium, like sounds from disembodied ghosts. Applause greeted the solos; gasps met the tragic moments. I heard some laughter at the antics of Stéphano. We created magic and dispensed it to our audience. The energy enveloped me like a tingling blanket. Emilie, perfect in her pantomime with Becca as her voice, brought the character of Juliette to life. No hitches, no glitches, no bumps. The whole thing proceeded smoothly as if each one of us existed exclusively to perform these specific parts.

Three ushers stayed busy at the curtain calls delivering flowers while the audience stayed on its feet.

Emilie, smiling broadly, received several bouquets. She took one to the wings to Becca, whom she brought out on stage, although no one knew why but us. Carmella burst into tears when she received not one, but three, bouquets. Jerome Levine, our stage manager, brought a large bouquet of red roses to me along with a single white carnation with greens and tied with a red ribbon. I almost dropped them out of sheer surprise.

Finally, the curtain came down for the last time, and the applause out front ebbed to a stop. We filed off to the green room, reluctant to let go of the triumphant moment.

Carmella almost knocked me over with her enthusiasm when she hugged me. Tears of joy flowed down her face as she grinned through her ruined makeup.

"Three! Three bouquets! Three! I can't believe it!" Her beautiful smile lit her eyes.

"You earned them," Harper said from behind her. "Any cards?"

She fumbled the flowers, and a bouquet of pink roses hit the floor. Harper picked it up and wobbled a bit when he got up. He withdrew a card from the cellophane wrapper.

"This says, *You were wonderful! Jim.*"

Carmella squealed and bit her lip. "Oh, how sweet of him!"

I found a card in her mixed bouquet and read out, "*The first of many roles for you! Robert Mallory.*"

"He's so thoughtful," she murmured while she handed Harper the third one, another bouquet of roses, this time red. Her hands shook as she took the first two from him. She wiped her eyes with the back of one hand, completing the damage to her makeup.

"*You have made the family proud. Uncle.*" Harper read aloud. "Uncle?" He regarded the two of us in turn.

Carmella and I gasped.

"Oh, my goodness," she murmured. She stared at me with her brown eyes bigger than usual. "I didn't think he would know about it, much less come. My mother must have called him. I'm glad I didn't know."

"He's proud of you," I told her. I turned to Harper and added, "Carmella's uncle is a wealthy businessman." *Okay, I pulled the punch. It sounded much less frightening than the truth of admitting he wielded significant underworld power.* "I doubt he'll come backstage, since he sent the flowers."

"Who sent yours?" she asked.

"No card," I concluded after a brief search of my fragrant red roses. "Maybe it was a mistake." I kept digging. "Oh, there's a card with the carnation." I opened the small envelope and gasped again. I turned to Carmella. "This is also from your uncle." My card read, *Brava! Always with my sincere regards, V.* I shivered slightly and handed her the card.

She took in the sentiment, looked up, and stared back at me. "I guess he was here. I know you impressed him," she said, her tone low.

"As long as he's on my side," I murmured back. "That was thoughtful of him. I wonder how he knew I was in the show."

"If I had to guess, it was my mother," she whispered and handed back the small missive.

"No card with the roses?" Harper asked, grinning. "Can't you guess?" He took a step toward me and staggered. I reached out to steady him, and he slipped his arm tightly around my waist for support. He loosened his grasp once he regained his balance.

Carmella smiled. "Ash, was it you?"

"I cannot tell a lie," he said with a broad grin. He studied the expression on my face and hastily added, "well, at least not to you two. Alan and I got them for you."

"You deserve them," Brockton told me, giving me a hug. "We thought we'd surprise you, but there should have been a card." He glanced questioningly at Harper, who shrugged.

"I promise, I ordered one." Harper dropped his arm completely to his side when Levine approached.

"Lauren! This one just arrived for you." The stage manager smiled and handed me a bouquet of yellow and white roses.

I thanked him and drew out the card. "Ah, these are from you. *For my Auntie, our Lady Cap. Ash and Alan.* Thank you both!" I gave them hugs. "That leaves the mystery bouquet."

"A mystery bouquet?" Mallory made his way through the throng. He could have passed as a model for a debonair advertisement for Brooks Brothers in his elegantly tailored tuxedo. His deep blue eyes glinted with an emotion I did not recognize. "No card?"

"Mr. Mallory, you are the one who sent them to Lauren!" Carmella exclaimed. "Of course! Thank you so much for mine. They are lovely."

"There should have been a card, Lauren," Mallory whispered to me. He slipped an arm around my waist and gently kissed my cheek. "It probably fell out in the car. Maybe someday I'll tell you what it said." He glanced around at the rest of those around us and raised his voice. "Ladies and gentlemen, I'd like to congratulate you all. You gave a magnificent performance!"

Under the cover of all the congratulations flowing throughout the room, I showed Mallory the card and the white carnation.

"He also sent a bouquet to Carmella," I whispered.

"He was here, but not with his sister. I spoke with him briefly at intermission. Although he knew Carmella was studying music, her performance made him realize how talented she is. He asked me to make sure she has what she needs to continue her vocal studies. I am to let him know if he needs to assist her. I agreed to be a conduit if we need one, since she would never ask." Mallory kept his voice low. "He mentioned you could have a career in theater, but nothing else." I moaned, and he chuckled. "He considers you a friend." When I shivered slightly, he added, "Relax and take it as a sincere compliment. I believe that's the way he means it."

"May I have your attention please?" Peterman called to us. He hopped up to stand on a chair.

The babble subsided.

"We are hearing glowing reports from audience members," he said. He beamed like a lighthouse in a storm. "I also had a word with Roland Beesley, the *Gleaner* critic, and Andy Johnson from the *Times*. Both men were praising you all to the skies."

We whooped and hollered.

Norman Brier, looking dapper in his tuxedo, slipped into the room and stepped up on the chair next to Peterman. "It gets better!" I suspected if his grin got any wider, his ears would fall off. "The two critics have each requested tickets for tomorrow night's performance, which I am truly pleased to say is now *SOLD OUT!*"

Pandemonium burst out into the room.

"Wilfrid's in a half hour," Mallory spoke softly in my ear. "Bring Carmella." He fought his way out of the room. Brockton turned to say something to Carmella, who stood next to me.

I turned to hug Harper and grabbed him when he sank to the floor. He pulled me down, and I struggled to avoid falling on top of him.

"Alan," I stage-whispered from my kneeling position. Brockton glanced around, and I reached up to tug at his sleeve. "Ash passed out."

"Let's get him out of here. He needs air if nothing else."

We propped the tenor up between us and managed to get him downstairs to his dressing room. Harper was semi-conscious by the time we put him in his lounge chair.

"Where's Becca?" I asked Brockton. "We need to know if he ate anything for supper."

"I saw her with Des a few minutes ago. I'll find her and let her know he collapsed." He pulled the door closed after him.

"Ash?" My voice trembled and my hands shook while I loosened the neck of his costume. "Can you hear me?"

"Lauren, I feel awful." He swallowed. "Water?"

I got some from his refrigerator and held the glass steady so he could sip it. "Ash, did you eat supper?"

"Yes, I had a light one."

"Do you need food or a shot?"

"Not sure. Let me try orange juice. Some in the fridge."

"Okay, and if this doesn't work, how much insulin do I inject?"

"The case is on the dressing table and the syringe is marked."

I poured a small glass of orange juice and propped him up, leaning in behind him to make it easier for him to swallow. I waited to see if he guessed right.

When he got more disoriented, I drew a shot and gave it to him the way I had seen him do it. The speed of his recovery amazed me. Within ten minutes, he formed sentences and he no longer resembled a corpse although his makeup could not hide how drawn he looked.

"What do you need now?"

"Probably some food, like cheese. I don't want the shot to send me the other way. There should be some in the fridge."

"There is." I crouched in front of the small appliance. "Ash, that shot was the last dose out of that vial." I held up the small glass drug vial which was now almost empty.

"You can toss it. I have at least one more in there, don't I?" His speech slowly improved.

"Two." I dropped the vial into his trash basket.

"That will get me through the weekend." He rubbed his forehead. "I need to change into real clothes," he mumbled as he got to his feet.

He staggered. I took two steps toward him and got my arm around his waist to steady him. Becca chose that moment to open the dressing room door.

"I sincerely hope I'm interrupting this cozy scene," Becca tartly observed from her stance in the doorway.

"Becca, he collapsed," I explained. Once he rested safely back in his recliner, I went to the fridge.

"Dearheart, I folded up in the green room. Lauren and Alan brought me in here," Harper related while I dug around for cheese. "I was in no condition for games, Becca."

"Lauren, I'm sorry, I didn't know. I assumed he was up to his usual tricks," Becca's tone reflected the chill of her gaze, which contradicted her apology.

"Cheddar or Swiss?" I inquired, ignoring her as I knelt in front of the small appliance.

"How about a bit of each?" Harper answered. "Not much."

I found a knife and a plate, carved off small pieces, and handed them to him on a napkin. "I'll put the rest away."

"You're terrific," he gratefully replied. "Thanks." He stared up at Becca. "I ate supper."

"Is Ash all right?" Brockton stuck his head in the door. "Lauren, Carmella's out here waiting for you."

"I'll be right there." I regarded Ash. "Robert Mallory is hosting a gathering at Wilfrid's, if you feel up to it. You're both welcome to come."

Raphael stopped by next. "Apparently most of the gang is heading for the coffee shop. I'll be happy to drive you all over."

"Des, I'll be taking Carmella, if you can bring Ash, Becca, and Alan." I smiled at Becca. "You really should come. It's a great little place."

"You'll find it comfortable and a bit quaint," Harper told his wife with an almost-normal grin. "I think we should."

"All right," she agreed with a notable lack of enthusiasm.

"I'm going to get changed. I hope Carmella's willing to tackle my laces. I'm hopeless *and* helpless trying to get them undone!"

Brockton waited outside in the hallway with Carmella; both exhibited concern.

"What happened?" Carmella asked. "Is he okay?"

"He's fine. I think Ash simply overran his energy with the performance. Alan, Des will bring you, Ash, and Becca. I'll drive Carmella but on the sole condition she helps me get out of this!"

Carmella and I headed toward the stairs leading to the women's communal dressing room.

"Lauren! Your wig!" Emma, one of our company dressers, hailed me in the hallway.

We stopped.

"If you will stay still for thirty seconds," Emma commanded, "I can get this off of you. You're my last victim, and I want to get back to the hotel."

"Gladly," I fervently agreed. "It itches." Once freed from it, I cheerfully scratched while Carmella and I climbed the stairs.

I set a record as a quick-change artist getting back to civilian clothes once Carmella untangled the laces on my gown. Harper and friends greeted us in the parking lot when we got out there.

"On to Wilfrid's!" Carmella and I yelled together.

"On to Wilfrid's!" the men chorused in reply. I did not hear Becca's voice, but I figured she would feel above such nonsense.

"Heaven help us! They sound operatic even when they're speaking," I commented to Carmella while I started the Triumph and put it into gear.

She dissolved in laughter.

Staged for Death

10

"Good morning, sleepyhead," Julie greeted me the next morning. "Sit up and I'll put the tray on your lap. Mrs. Fiddler decided our very own opera personality needed her tea in bed and sent it up for you."

"You'll spoil me." I sat up, stretched, and glanced at the bedside clock. *Ten-thirty.* "It was glorious sleeping in!"

"It should happen more often," Mallory commented from where he graced the doorway. "I mean both spoiling you and the luxury of sleeping in. I'm glad you decided to stay here last night."

"After the performance and the late-night snack at the coffee shop, it seemed to be the thing to do." I gratefully sipped my tea.

"The *Times* has a glowing review of the production," he informed me. "Also, Bernie called to congratulate you. After getting no answer at your place, he called here."

"He's learning. It only took him two years," I observed. "Heaven help us, what a night!"

"Just think, you get to do the whole thing over again tonight," Julie reminded me.

"Not quite," Mallory said. "David also called. You are to report to the auditorium this afternoon at three for a quick pick-up rehearsal."

Since I was half asleep, it took me a minute to make sense of the message. My mental gears finally meshed, and it clicked. I grinned. "Becca told me she wants to see the whole performance from the audience. I'm glad she'll get the chance."

"I missed something," Julie complained with a giggle. "What are you talking about?"

"Logic," I said promptly and laughed at the face she made. "Following the great opening we had, the one possible reason to have a pick-up rehearsal would be to let Emilie warm up in the part. She's feeling better and ready to sing. Simple reasoning."

"It's always so simple after you explain it," she said with a sigh.

I chuckled. "You'll get there."

Julie played cards like a duck swam, and I loved her like a sister, but aside from the bridge table, logical thinking eluded her.

For our pick-up rehearsal—a term meaning a short, refresher rehearsal—we ran through the party scene, the balcony scene, and the final act with piano and no costumes. Brier called, "That's it!" and we took it as a signal. The whole company gave Emilie a rousing ovation. Becca went up the stage stairs, applauding.

"How do you feel?" she asked the French star.

"Much better. Becca, you've been wonderful, and I thank you." Emilie's accent added charm to her words. "I must confess, singing felt incredible." She turned to those gathered onstage. "Thank you all! If you will excuse me, I'm going to rest for a few hours."

"Emilie, hold a moment!" I called out while I climbed the stage steps. I extended a white paper take-out bag. "I stopped on my way over and got something for you."

She unfolded the top and peered inside. A big smile formed on her lovely face as she gazed at me. "Wilfrid's?"

"Of course. He sent his chicken salad sandwich with his best wishes. He heard you were ill and apologized because he never makes chicken soup."

The entire company broke out laughing.

Harper tapped me on the shoulder. "Auntie? May we take you

for an early supper?" He nodded to Becca, Brockton, Thorne, and Raphael.

"Oh, thank you! I wanted to talk with all of you anyway. I have an invitation to extend."

The two music directors joined us, along with Carmella. We descended on the local café where Harper and I dined the night of the final dress rehearsal. The manager got a head count and grabbed two waiters to put some tables together. Once we placed our orders and had our drinks, I stood.

"On behalf of all tone-deaf people everywhere, I salute the singers and musicians of the world." I raised my water glass.

"Hear, hear!" they chorused.

"There we go again!" Carmella grinned. "Lauren commented yesterday that even off-stage and speaking, we sound like we're an opera company."

We all laughed. I invited them all to Susan's Place after the performance. "Robert Mallory is hosting it. Primary cast members are in for a real treat."

"What about the students?" Carmella asked.

"Robert provided funds for a separate party on campus for them," Brier told her. "They won't be left out."

"As a student singing a featured role," I added mischievously, "you have your choice of the two parties to attend."

Carmella giggled. "I do?"

"Yes. However, I feel obligated to advise you, Mr. Mallory was emphatically informed by Susan that you have a much simpler decision to make. You have the choice of going to Susan's or facing her wrath the next time you show up for work."

"Hmmm," she murmured, pretending to mull it over while we chuckled. She giggled again. "I think I'll go to Susan's."

"That's quite prudent of you." I grinned and sat down.

"What is Susan's Place?" Raphael asked. "I keep hearing about it, but is it a restaurant?"

"Des, it's the best Italian restaurant in the whole of New York," Becca informed him. "It's small, family-owned, and you'll love it. It's owned by Gianni Gianello, who used to work at Trioni's in Manhattan. He moved out here about five years ago."

"Trioni's? That's the top Italian place in the city," Raphael commented. "How do you know about Susan's Place?" he asked Harper.

"Gianni wanted his own *ristorante*, and I helped him get set up," the tenor replied. "He said he was tired of being told what to cook. Susan is his wife. The food is exquisite."

Becca turned to me with a questioning glance. "They don't usually cater. How on earth did Robert talk the Gianellos into this?"

"He's known them since they opened," I explained, keeping it vague. I nodded to the young soprano. "Carmella works there part-time."

"So does my boyfriend," she chimed in. "The Gianellos have almost adopted us. Seriously, I wouldn't dream of not going there tonight."

"Susan hired Carmella and Jim, among others, so she could open for the lunch trade," I told Becca. "Des, you're in for a real treat. According to Mr. Mallory, Gianni is cooking up some special dishes for this."

While we ate, I kept an eye on Ash Harper. His demeanor worried me; his wan appearance emphasized the lack of his usual high spirits. Even though I knew what was going on, and he admitted to being tired, it went beyond that. He appeared almost completely drained of energy. I hoped he would make it through the performance.

When we got ready to leave, Brockton picked up my check and Raphael picked up Carmella's.

"Thank you, gentlemen, for supporting poor students," I quipped. Carmella giggled and blushed.

On the walk back to the auditorium, I strolled with Harper, who hung back slightly from the rest of the group.

"Ash, will you be all right tonight? Forgive me for being

blunt, but you genuinely seem ill."

"I don't feel quite right," he admitted, "but I think I'll be okay."

He deliberately slowed our pace. We watched while Becca and Raphael passed us; she took Raphael's offered arm. They walked slightly faster ahead of us.

"I don't mind admitting I'm concerned," I commented. I tried to avoid staring at the two singers, arm in arm, walking with evenly matched steps.

"I'm not sure what happened last night. I did a shot before dinner tonight, and I'm planning to grab a piece of cheese before Act III to make sure I'm okay. The balance gets tricky when I'm performing, and the dueling is more tiring than simply singing. Tybalt is one of the more active roles I do."

"I want to make a phone call," I told him. "Have you got a nickel?"

"You don't carry a purse, do you?" He pulled out a handful of change. "Here, have three."

"I don't carry a small handbag, because I tend to walk off and forget it." I sighed. "Over the years, I have driven my friend Julie to despair. She's dainty and thinks I should be more like her."

"Mallory's daughter? The one who was with him the other evening?"

I nodded. "We met eleven years ago and grew up together as best friends. She positively hates my satchel, as she refers to my shoulder bag." I grinned at him. "One of my coworkers swears I could move a body in it."

Harper laughed aloud and made no attempt to choke it. "I am so glad we met. You go make your call. I'll see you later," he told me once we entered the building.

I fed the phone a nickel and dialed one of the first two numbers I ever memorized. I sat on a convenient stool while the connection went through.

"Mallory Residence," Mrs. Fiddler answered.

"Mrs. Fiddler, is Mr. Mallory around?"

"Hold the line, Miss Lauren, he's right here. I want to wish you the best of breaking a leg tonight."

"Thank you, Mrs. Fiddler." I heard her hand over the receiver.

"Lauren? Is everything all right?" Concern shaded his voice.

"So far," I replied. "I'm basically checking in with you. The rehearsal went beautifully, and Emilie sounds magnificent. You're going to be astounded because she's inspiring everyone else to up their performances. I'm wondering if Rollie will notice the difference in voices and ask about it. I may bring that up to Mr. Brier."

"Probably wise. Did you invite the principals for tonight?"

"I had a light supper with most of them, and yes. They're looking forward to it. By the way, did you know Ash helped Gianni get set up when he left Trioni's?"

"Gianni told me that yesterday."

"Carmella asked about the chorus kids, and Mr. Brier made the other announcement. She'll be with us, of course. She got a giggle out of the choice Susan gave her. I told her that the decision to join us was prudent."

He chuckled. "Anything else?"

"You gave O'Brien a ticket."

"Yes, and I also gave one to Bernie."

"Where are your seats?"

"First row mezzanine, center, seats M14 through M17." He paused for a moment. "Lauren, what's wrong?"

"I want to be sure I can find you if I need to." I hesitated. "Nothing's wrong, at least nothing I can pinpoint."

"Lizzie," he began, using the nickname he created from my middle name. Combined with his tone of voice, I knew he wanted to be serious. "Something *is* bothering you. What's going on?"

"Nothing. At least I hope it's nothing. I have an odd feeling. I honestly can't put a name to it. It's almost as if I am waiting for something else to come crashing down on us." I paused. "Thank you for not laughing at me."

"I never do," he said, his voice somber. "Be careful. I'll see you after the performance. If you need me before then, send someone to get me."

"I promise."

We hung up and I reflected on his response. He never did laugh at me; with me yes, many times. Never at me. He never brushed me off and always found time for me when I needed to talk. Our relationship, based on mutual trust, evolved from parent-child to close friends in recent years. My nickname began as a way to let me know a decision was final and gradually evolved into reminder of our friendship and mutual trust, although lately he also used it to tease me.

I snapped out of my reverie to see Norman Brier walking past me, his nose buried in the *New York Times*.

"Mr. Brier?" I called softly, not wanting to startle him.

"Yes?" he responded absent-mindedly until he looked up. "Oh, Lauren. What can I do for you?" His attention remained focused on the paper. "The box office is turning away people who want to see the production! Andy Johnson gave us a great review in the *Times,* and he specifically mentions Carmella."

"You need to make arrangements for copies of the paper so the cast can have them. I'll take care of that for the *Gleaner*. Meanwhile, I was wondering what, if anything, you are going to tell the two critics if they notice a difference in Juliette's voice tonight."

"Good Lord! I hadn't thought of that," he exclaimed. "How sharp is Beesley?"

"Beats me. However, after he repeatedly stated to us Emilie's voice was vaguely reminiscent of Rebecca Chernak's, he is bound to notice the change. Becca winced every time he massacred her name when they met backstage, so he'll never be her favorite person, even with his groveling." I grinned. "The man from the *Times* may regret printing his review today."

Brier's face broke into a wide smile. "You could be right about Beesley." His expression became serious again. "Come with me. I want to talk to David."

The three of us met in Brier's office.

"David, Lauren has brought up a point about the change in Juliette's voice. Do we want to alert the critics before the curtain and explain what we had to do?"

"Oh!" Peterman replied, startled. "Good heavens, I never thought about it."

"Neither did I," Brier admitted. "Lauren pointed out there is a noticeable difference between Emilie's true voice and Becca's. These guys are pros."

"I figure if I can notice it, they will," I chimed in.

"This could be a problem. We certainly don't want to antagonize either of them," Brier mused.

"Roland Beesley raved about the show to our editor, who will be here tonight by the way," I tossed out. "His review will be published tomorrow in the Sunday section, and he could incorporate the second voice saga as part of his. Andy Johnson doesn't have that option unless he wants to do a human-interest story."

"What's the *Gleaner's* number?" Brier asked me.

"Northwoods seven, five-eight-zero-eight."

"Do you have any contacts at the *Times*?" he asked hopefully as he jotted down the number.

"Sorry, no."

"Any ideas on how we should handle this?" Peterman asked me.

"For Beesley, I'd start with the angle he originally brought up, when he suspected something was going on behind the scenes. You might want to admit now that he was right. Tackling it from that direction might ease it a bit." I rose and bowed. "Please leave me out of it this time, though. I'm going to find a spot, dig a hole, and hide."

"What?" Brier said, stricken. "Why?"

"Roland Beesley will figure out a way to blame me."

"I was going to ask for your help with this," Brier stated with a frown.

"If you want help with the *Gleaner*, you don't want me. You want Robert Mallory."

Peterman rubbed his chin and gazed at Brier before switching a thoughtful glance at me "I don't suppose you have his number."

"Northwoods six, four-two-one-seven." I flashed a grin and escaped.

Carmella and I decided we did not have enough time to do anything outside the auditorium. Peterman found the two of us relaxing in the green room when he searched me out.

"Thank you for your assistance," he told me, collapsing into a chair. "Norm spoke to Andy Johnson at the *Times*. He was definitely not pleased. Roland Beesley, on the other hand, gushed his sentiments, telling us he has the utmost admiration for us as a professional production, since we went to great lengths to uphold the tradition —"

"—the show must go on," I finished for him. I crossed my eyes. "Heaven help us, did he really use that hackneyed phrase?" At his nod, I groaned. "Well, you won him over. He was highly skeptical about the whole endeavor when he first spoke to me. The *Times* critic was probably irked because he can't go back and redo his story. My boss will be pleased, though. It gives us a leg up over the big guys."

Carmella told us she wanted to get something from the dressing room and took off.

Peterman leaned closer. "I want to thank you for getting Ash to finally tell me what his problem is. I can't believe he's ashamed of it."

"I can. We're halfway through the twentieth century, yet some ideas about health problems remain solidly rooted in the sixteenth." I sighed. "I'm very worried about him. He doesn't look good."

"No, he doesn't. I made him promise to have a thorough

checkup with his doctor after we close."

"I'm glad to hear it."

Carmella rejoined us, holding something behind her back.

"Mr. Peterman? Would you please sign my score?" Smiling shyly, she extended her music with a pen.

"I'd be happy to." He beamed as he fulfilled her request. "Make sure you get everyone to sign it. This is your first role, but it won't be your last."

She blushed and skipped off to find others.

"She's a lovely girl with a brilliant talent," he observed. "I'm pleased she's getting recognition."

"I met her this past summer while I did my first feature story. She's gracious inside and out, with nothing pretentious in her makeup." I checked my watch. "It's after five-thirty. I think I'll grab a program and get some signatures."

"You?" Eyebrows raised; he gave me a quizzical stare. "I wouldn't have guessed you'd want it."

"I have a few streaks of sentimentality, which surface every now and then in spite of my efforts to hide them. It may be Carmella's first of what promises to be many roles, but it's probably my one and only stage venture. I think I should be able to prove I did this." I smiled. "Frankly, I may not be able to believe it myself. Where do I find a program book?"

"I have a few in my office."

"Into the rabbit warren again," I mumbled. I caught the puzzlement on his face. "I have a lousy sense of direction."

A few minutes later, with Peterman's autograph in my booklet, I started knocking on dressing room doors.

"Alan?" When he called for me to enter, I poked my head in. "Can I get you to sign my program book?"

"Lauren! It would be my pleasure." He bestowed a broad smile on me. "Oh, I'd like you to meet my wife, Lisa."

I shook hands with her. Lisa Brockton, a lovely, petite, blonde with dark brown eyes, gave me a mischievous smile. "I never thought I'd be meeting another wife of Alan's."

"Oh, dear, I hate to break up a happy home." I grinned back at her. "You should know most of what I do onstage has been on his instructions. I've been grateful for all his help because I have never been onstage before."

"He has told me you are a very talented actress. Have you considered taking lessons?"

"Uh-oh," broke in Brockton, "here we go again. Don't repeat the question—she'll go searching for a bar of soap!"

I laughed. "He's right. I have a full-time job with the *Daily Gleaner*. I'm doing this to fulfill a graduation requirement." I reached for my booklet. "Seriously, Alan, thank you for being patient with me. See you later!"

Back in the hallway, I resisted the urge to see what he had written. I decided to try for Des Raphael's autograph next.

I knocked on the Duke's door and entered once I heard, "come in." I found Becca with the bass, sitting more or less on his lap.

"Hello!" To give them a moment to untwine, I glanced around the room. His dressing room was about the same size as Brockton's but not as nice as Harper's. Papers and folded newsprint sheets were strewn on the makeup table. One had a photo of a horse. I smiled and handed him my program.

"I'm collecting autographs. I know once this is all over, I'll never be able to convince myself I actually did this, so I want proof."

Raphael chuckled. "I keep telling you that you have done remarkably well for someone with little or no training."

"I agree," Becca chimed in, to my surprise. "I would suggest acting lessons, but I have been told it's not a good idea to bring up."

I grinned. "I honestly prefer writing. Becca, would you also sign my program?"

"Of course." The diva added her signature under his. Their scribbles—no other way to describe them—were illegible.

"Thank you. I want to thank you again, Becca, for helping us out with your singing. It would have broken more than a few hearts around here to have to cancel after all this work."

I made Emilie my next stop.

"*Maman,*" she said with a laugh. "You have been so kind to me, and I will always remember that wonderful bread from Wilfrid's." She took my program, wrote something in French, and handed it back to me.

"Um, Emilie? Would you mind putting the translation down as well? I speak and write one."

She laughed as she reached for it. "*Bien sûr!*" She glanced up at me. "That means, *of course.*" She signed it, and as I left, she called out, "See you at the party scene!"

I ran into Jeff Sebring coming down the hall to his dressing room.

"Lauren! You're here early," he greeted me. "What's up?"

"I decided to get some autographs in a program book. This is such a departure from my normal activities I need to be able to prove I was here." I offered the booklet to him, and we stepped into his modified cubbyhole.

"You just missed Carmella," he said. "She was doing the same thing," he said as he scribbled something and his name. "There! Thank you for asking. I'm not quite used to signing autographs."

"I suspect you'll get lots of practice." I chuckled and regarded his scrawl. "You certainly sign with a real flourish."

Jeff walked off, smiling, and I continued down the hallway. Thorne's dressing room door was open. I knocked and handed him the program. He grinned.

"I know better than to suggest acting lessons," he commented as he scrawled on his page, "but it is theater's loss if you won't."

"If I ever get tossed off the paper, I'll bear it in mind," I replied as he chuckled.

I saved Ash Harper for last.

I knocked. No reply. I knocked louder. "Ash? It's Lauren."

The door opened. Carmella, her face unnaturally pale, shot

past me without seeing me. Her teeth caught her lower lip and her hand clenched her rolled up score. She ran to the stairs. The echo of her steps quickly diminished as she raced up.

"Ashton Harper, have you done something to upset that girl?" I demanded with some venom.

"I gave her a hug and a kiss." He attempted to appear contrite. "Nothing more. I also signed her score."

"She's on the brink of a wonderful career, and if you do anything to interfere with that you will have to answer to me." I scowled. "She doesn't need any of your games."

"Lauren, I promise I want nothing but good for her. She's a great kid, and I want to help her career."

"Then lay off the personal stuff! You've been wonderful this past couple of weeks. Don't ruin it now!" I folded my arms across my chest.

"I may have overdone it a bit. Chalk it up to pre-performance nerves."

"Carmella's a sweet girl and doesn't need you playing around or distracting her. She's too nice to be rude to you, but I won't let you get in the way. Period."

"Problem?" Brockton, going by the opened door, stopped and leaned into the room to ask.

"Nope, simply a matter of an attitude adjustment," I reassured him with a smile. "Sorry if I got too loud."

Brockton went on his way down the hall.

I turned back to Harper. "Okay, I'll let it pass for now," I relented and held out my program. "Friends?"

"Friends," he returned with a grin. He wrote for a moment and flamboyantly signed it. "I don't want to see you angry ever again, Auntie, especially at me. Once was enough."

"All you have to do is make sure you don't try anything stupid." I noticed the door to his fridge opened a crack and crossed the room to close it. Something stuck out a bit too far and I re-arranged the two blocks of cheese before shutting it. I took a deep breath and let it out. "Ash, please don't forget to have a snack before your fight scene."

"I won't. Scoot and let me rest a bit."

"Sure." I left him and went in search of Brier. I finally cornered him in the auditorium as he came out of the orchestra pit.

"Mr. Brier, would you sign my program book?"

"With pleasure. I want to thank you for your help with the newshounds," he said. He added his scribble. "Oh, and please drop the *mister*. My name is Norm. Use it."

Next, I found Bill Gardiner and Andrea, the two staging directors, together in the green room with our stage manager, Levine. All three signed, and I thanked them for their time and patience.

"You should take a couple of acting classes," Gardiner added when he handed back the booklet. "You have a genuine, natural talent for this."

Andrea nodded. "I agree."

Levine opened his mouth, but I cut him off.

"I think you all should know when Alan Brockton suggested it the other day, I asked if anyone had a bar of soap handy so he could wash his mouth out," I stated. "I appreciate the thought and encouragement, but I'll stick to my typewriter." I shuddered.

I left them chuckling.

Back upstairs, I found Carmella.

She was sitting in front of the mirror, shoulders slumped, staring at her reflection. I stood behind her.

"I have a request," I said gently so I did not startle her. "But first, what's wrong? I saw you dash out of Ash's dressing room a bit ago. What happened?"

"He made another pass at me, I think, but this one felt different. It's as if there was something serious about it." She scuffed her slipper on the floor, obviously uncomfortable.

"Did you say anything?"

"I told him I'd be very angry if he did it again, and he wouldn't want to get me or my family angry."

"Especially your uncle, but he doesn't know that," I murmured. "I wouldn't worry about it. I laid into him a bit after you went tearing past me and he realized he overdid it. I think he genuinely wants to help you advance professionally. I told him if he upset you again, he'd have to answer to me. That's the way we worked it out for rehearsals. Deal?"

She smiled, at ease again. "Deal." She heaved a sigh of relief. "Now, what's your request?"

I held out my program book. "I'm collecting autographs, and it's your turn to sign." I handed her my pen.

"It's my first autograph." She shyly smiled. "I'm glad it's for you. Will you sign my score?"

"Of course. Probably the only autograph I'll ever do." I did my scribble and looked at hers in my book. "You're going to have to learn how to scribble your signature. This is too neat and legible," I teased.

"I'll put it on my list right below learning how not to blush." She giggled.

"Do that." I silently gave thanks that she was herself again.

She flipped through her score. "This is going to be one of my treasures."

"Rightfully so," I agreed. "Did you get Becca's autograph?"

"Yes. She's been nice to me. Oh, when I saw Emilie, she told me she's going to watch for me to appear on a major stage in a few years." She sighed and smiled.

As we entered the green room, the NYCO cast members greeted Carmella like one of their own.

"Lauren, this is what I've dreamed of all my life," she whispered to me. "I can't believe it."

I made a note to bring it up with Mallory. I knew he would agree that her way should be smoothed to continue her studies.

Although the afternoon seemed to drag on, once the chorus kids arrived back at the auditorium, time telescoped. One minute it was six, and the next time I checked my watch, it jumped to seven. I made sure the students with singing roles—all of them good, but no one else close to the incredible talent Carmella possessed—knew they had the option of coming to Susan's after the performance or staying on campus for the other party. I found out the professionals intimidated them. They each told me they planned to stay on campus and attend the party in the music department.

The chorus kids told me something similar. The high school students found the college students a little clannish, but I figured the party would help. I considered the notion some of the high school kids would eventually move to the college music department.

"I'm not surprised," Peterman said when I mentioned it to him. "However, Norm and I have discussed doing this next year, and we're sure it will all work out."

"You're going to do this again?"

"The response has been overwhelming." He grinned. "We're sold out and turning people away. It's been a lot of work for everyone, but it's worth it. Plus, it provides valuable stage and technical experience for the students."

"Do me a favor."

"Certainly. I can pencil you in for another pantomime part, if you're interested."

"Absolutely *not*! I was going to tell you to forget I exist."

I took off while he enjoyed his laugh.

Once in costume and wig, I moved to the green room. I found a spot where I could take some time out. I felt like I sat in the eye of a hurricane, with another storm front yet to engulf us.

I never believed in the premonitions of others and never experienced any myself, yet some part of me felt decidedly uneasy. I knew it had nothing to do with nerves or stage fright. Opening night showed me capable of performing my part, although the thought of going back out onstage caused a few butterflies in my stomach. My concern for Ash Harper, following his collapse, formed part of it, along with lingering worry about Emilie.

I acted on instinct, if I wanted to acknowledge that much, to find out the specific location of Mallory's seats. I felt better knowing he and O'Brien would be in the house.

I hope I'm seeing nothing but shadows of my own imagination, but at least I know where to find help if I need it.

I snapped out of my reverie when the warm-up exercises began.

Staged for Death

11

The house lights went down.

The overture played and the hand-selected ensemble sang the prologue. The curtain rose on the party scene.

Alan Brockton and I knew Emilie embodied perfection after she sang two phrases. The fixed, artificial smiles on our faces became genuine. We caught each other's eyes and in unison turned glowing gazes at her. After she sang her solo piece, she grasped our hands and squeezed them with a smile that matched ours. I straightened one of the ribbons in her hair and happily sighed.

That's a relief! Now if nothing else goes wrong we'll have this in the bag. The vague feeling of unease persisted. It hung over me and haunted me like heavy thunderclouds before a deluge.

Emilie's recovery and her flawless performance inspired everyone from the chorus to the leads to boost their own. The audience sensed it. The intensity of their reactions increased, further spurring each member of the cast to reach beyond themselves. I found the interplay between performers as fascinating as the rapport they built with their audience. The special, almost electric, energy increased and flowed, distinctly real in a way I appreciated but which I could not begin to describe in words.

I planned to check on Harper during the brief break between acts but got waylaid. Gardiner cornered me with Brockton when we came off-stage.

"You two were marvelous," he told us, almost babbling with excitement. "The emotions were there, and you both were every inch the proud parents! I've never seen it done better!"

"Honestly, Bill," Brockton responded, "most of our reaction was sheer relief at hearing Emilie's voice as clear and strong as always. It was easy to smile for real."

"Whatever it was, it was magic." He clapped us on the back. "We're using the cameras to record this. I'll arrange a screening for the entire cast." He hurried to an exit to go back into the auditorium.

I watched Act II on Becca's monitor backstage. Thorne and Emilie worked extremely well together, which we all knew. I thought her voice blended with his better than Becca's. I saw Harper headed downstairs, hopefully to his dressing room to eat a piece of cheese before his duel. I worked my way over to go down but stopped when Carmella stepped in front of me.

"Emile sounds incredible, even better than Becca did," she gushed. "Oh, this will be even more wonderful than last night!"

I chuckled. "Take it easy. We have the rest of the show to do."

She giggled, nodded, and ran off to talk to another student.

I did not see Harper again until he made his entrance for the big fight scene which consisted of his two duels. Tybalt first fought Mercutio, and after Romeo picked up Mercutio's sword, his bout with Romeo took place.

I left my post by the monitor when the ladies of the chorus began to congregate for our entrance. Brockton wormed his way through them to get to me. As Capulet, he always led me out onstage after Tybalt fell. I stayed behind him at the line which divided the wings from the area which could be seen by the audience. He blocked most of my view.

"Uh-oh," he muttered softly while he watched the action on the stage. I moved to his side and peered out. "They moved around again." His hand squeezed my shoulder. "Careful. Here we go."

He strode out. I counted to three and then made my entrance, hampered by the two chorus ladies, exactly the way Gardiner planned it. I saw Harper lying on the stage in an odd position and hurried to him. I dropped to my knees and cradled him. His eyes opened and he tried to speak to me.

"Can't sing," he whispered.

Fear clutched at my throat and chest. I felt the color drain from my face. I bent farther over him to catch his words and held my breath so I could hear him.

"Keep the show going. Must go on—" His normally strong voice faded off to nothing.

I barely caught it with all the music.

"Becca—did—" Harper gasped. "Becca—did—my—sorry—so weak—" His faint voice shook as he struggled to talk. He gripped my hand.

Stunned, I sat back on my heels. Terror painfully gripped me; my voice caught in my throat, which suddenly closed.

A passage of music brought my attention back to the stage. Brockton sang his first line of their final exchange and turned toward us. I looked up at Brockton, panic-stricken. He saw my expression and, without missing any words, came to us and knelt.

"Alan," I whispered, "he's not acting!" A sinking feeling of horror engulfed me, and a terrible chill settled over me despite the hot stage lights. I shivered and tears filled my eyes.

Brockton's face, inches from mine, creased in a frown. He stood and turned, singing on his cue without waiting for Tybalt's final lines.

Harper sagged in my arms. "Lau—ren—help—"

He passed out. His hand slipped away from mine.

I struggled to hold his limp, dead weight on my lap.

Brockton swore Capulet's revenge. I untangled myself from the genuinely unconscious tenor and stood trembling, wringing my hands. My vision blurred with unspilled tears.

My instinct to screech out that Harper needed help became unbearable. *I cannot do it—I promised Ash we would finish!* I clenched my fists and beat my hands against each other to control the impulse. Brockton and I confronted Romeo. *Ash needs help. NOW!* The Duke made his entrance. *Ash, please—don't die.* We got Tybalt onto the bier. *This is what he wanted—the show must go on. He was serious about that.* The company proceeded to do the funeral march. *Why is the stage suddenly bigger than it was in rehearsals?* I automatically followed. *Stay calm—do it like we rehearsed it.* Brockton slipped his arm around my shoulders. *Heaven help us, will this* never *end?* I leaned into him while we walked. I bit my lip without realizing it.

"*Ah, jour de deuil et d'horreur et d'alarmes...oh jour de deuil.*"

The company sang and we made our procession all the way around the stage to downstage center. *If I scream everyone will panic.* I wanted to scream despite Harper's wish for the show to continue. *I can't scream! I can't scream!* I did not notice when I started to cry.

The scene played out. Unheeded, genuine tears streamed down my face. I felt mired in a nightmare, yet I knew it to be real. *Please, heaven help us! Day of mourning, of horror and alarm—it's too appropriate!* Shaking and scared, I kept murmuring to Harper, holding his hand, rubbing his cheek.

"We'll take care of you, my friend. I won't let you die," I whispered under the music and singing. I hoped, prayed, he could hear me.

The Duke issued his decree of banishment to Romeo. Finally, the curtain descended, closing the act. At last—intermission.

House lights came up. The lights behind the curtain came up.

We moved off the stage. Levine and the cast stood around us waiting for Harper to jump off the bier. He did that every time we played the scene, springing back to life with a grin. This time he stayed unmoving on the wooden platform.

"He *really* passed out! Please!" I pleaded with those around me. "Jerome, please! He's unconscious! We need to get him to his dressing room. Get a doctor!" I thought I yelled it, but it came out as a whisper. They all stayed put, like I had spoken to them in another language.

"Move!" Brockton snapped.

I marveled at how sharp he made the word with so little volume. I took a deep breath of relief when the stagehands picked up the bier.

"I'll get the house doctor. He's in the audience," Levine tossed at me over his shoulder as he dashed to the auditorium.

I ran down the stairs to the dressing rooms. The stagehands got Ash onto his divan and left.

I tried to revive him by talking to him while I loosened the neck of his tunic. I put a folded towel under his head. I knelt on the floor beside him, wiped his face with a wet washcloth, and massaged his hand. I felt a pulse, and I saw slow respirations, yet I could not get him to respond. I heard Brockton outside as he gave more orders, trying to keep the corridor clear. Finally, the doctor arrived.

"I'm Dr. Rossiter. Does he have any medical conditions I should know about?" he asked Brockton in the hallway.

"Doctor? Please, come in!" I called over my shoulder. Once the man entered and closed the door, I added, "He has diabetes. From what I can tell he has trouble balancing it when he performs."

"I'm Steven Rossiter," he told me as he pulled a stethoscope out his bag. "I'm the doctor on-call for the auditorium when there's a show. I don't usually attend, but I love opera, so I was in the audience tonight. The stage manager came for me. If Mr. Harper has trouble, he's probably what we call brittle, meaning little or no leeway. Has he eaten lately, Miss—?"

"Lauren Kaye. He gave himself a shot before going out to dinner. He ate well but it wasn't a heavy meal. I know he was planning on coming down here to grab a piece of cheese before the third act. He collapsed briefly last night and required insulin after orange juice didn't work."

"It's probably not insulin shock then," he said thoughtfully, "so I'll try insulin. Do you know where it is?"

"There are two vials in the refrigerator."

He got the vial from the shelf. I opened the dressing room door. The crowd in the hallway thinned out a bit because the stage manager called Act IV places. One of the stagehands saw me and asked if he could do anything for me.

"Can you get one of the ushers to go to the center front row of the mezzanine, seats M14 through M17, and ask Robert Mallory and Daniel O'Brien to come down here?"

He repeated the seats and names. I nodded and he took off.

"Alan," I spotted him in the hallway on his way to the stage. "Becca should be here."

"I'm due back onstage. I'll get Des for you. He'll know where she is."

I turned back into the room. "Doctor? I'm trying to locate his wife."

"Miss Kaye, I don't want to alarm you, but he's not responding to the insulin. Have someone call an ambulance."

The stagehand returned with Mallory and O'Brien.

"Ash Harper collapsed," I told O'Brien. "We need an ambulance five minutes ago."

O'Brien asked the stagehand a question and they left at a run.

"Are you all right?" Mallory's face showed his concern for me as well as for Harper.

"I'm trying not to scream," I replied while I tried to stop shaking. My fingernails dug into my palms. "I feel like I am trapped in a nightmare where I'm in a quagmire being sucked down and I can't wake up."

Mallory moved to a position near the door.

"Make way," a familiar gruff voice commanded the gathering crowd. He plowed past Mallory into the room. "Doctor, an ambulance will be here within five minutes."

The doctor nodded his acknowledgement, then knelt beside the couch. His fingers rested on Ash's wrist. He regarded me. "Do you know how to draw a shot?"

I nodded. "I learned when my mother was ill, and I did it last night for Ash."

"I need another dose of insulin."

I opened the refrigerator, took the front bottle, drew off fluid to the mark on the barrel of a fresh syringe, and handed it to the physician. "Here, Doctor." I put the vial back in the refrigerator in front of the second one.

"Hold his arm steady."

I did as he directed.

"Ash, hang on," I murmured, kneeling again. "Please, hang on."

"Where's Ash?" Becca demanded from the doorway. "Robert, what's going on?"

"Becca, your husband collapsed on stage," Mallory briefly explained. "A doctor is with him now." He guided her into the hallway and pulled the door closed.

"Doctor," I said quietly while I stood, "Ash's wife is outside." I went to the door and opened it, nodding at Mallory.

"Miss Chernak, please come in. Quickly!" the doctor called.

Becca, regal and beautifully dressed in a pale blue formal ensemble, entered, and gasped. Her hand flew to her throat, and she moved to stand near her husband's head. She reached out to touch his face but did not complete the move. Her gloved hand dropped to her side.

"What's wrong?" She dropped to her knees beside him but maintained a slight distance.

"I believe he's slipping into a diabetic coma," the doctor told her. "He's not responding to the insulin, and I've called for an ambulance. I'll take him to Northwoods Memorial."

Her face fearful, she rose and backed away from the divan, stopping when she bumped into the refrigerator. "I'll come with you, Doctor, if that's all right." Becca turned and realized for the first time I was next to her. "Des is outside, and I want to let him know. Will you stay here?"

"Certainly." I bit my lip again to quell my trembling and my comment; she left the room. I knelt beside the physician. "Doctor, I don't understand. None of this is new to him. What went wrong?"

"If he gave himself a shot before dinner and ate something, his actions were correct, so I can't say for sure," he replied. "I've given him two shots of insulin and he's not reacting to it. I'll know more at the hospital."

"The ambulance is here," Mallory announced from the doorway. "They're bringing a stretcher down now."

I brushed Ash's face with my hand as I rose. "Ash, please, hold on," I whispered. I moved to stand back out of the way. Becca joined me, as cool as ever, with no sign of her earlier anxiety.

They got Harper onto the stretcher and out the door. Becca followed. Mallory came into the room, took one look at me, and pulled me into a reassuring hug. I clung to him like a drowning victim grasped a life preserver, once more realizing the strength he represented in my life.

"You have a scene coming up." He lightly brushed my cheek with his fingertips as he released me.

"What?" I forgot I needed to go back onstage. "I can't. I mean, I don't know if I can do this."

"You're on in about five minutes. Juliette's fake death scene," he gently reminded me. He handed me his handkerchief and I blew my nose. "Come on. I'll take you upstairs."

"Wait, I want to check something." I noticed the refrigerator door slightly ajar again. I freed my arm and crossed the small room back to the refrigerator. I opened the door. I saw one bottle of insulin on the shelf, along with Harper's cheese, orange juice, and a pitcher of water. I searched the floor around the couch. Nothing. I checked the wastebasket, which stood under the table at the end of the couch near where we placed Harper's head. Again, nothing.

"What are you searching for?"

"There were two bottles of insulin in there a few minutes ago.

There's only one now." I frowned. "I was trying to find it."

"Maybe the doctor took it."

Raphael appeared in the doorway. "Lauren, Alan is waiting for you." He nodded to Mallory. "I'll take good care of her." He took my arm and marched me out of the dressing room.

"Des, tell me how in the world I am supposed to do this after what has happened," I pleaded with him while we climbed the stairs. "Please?" Tears welled up in my eyes again. I was sure my eyes and nose were red and blotchy. I did not care, even if I matched Rudolf the reindeer.

"Lauren, Ash would want us to carry on."

"I know. He said so onstage when he collapsed." I sighed. My tears threatened to spill down my cheeks again. I clenched my hand; my fingernails stung my palm as they cut into it.

"Put your fears and sorrow into what you're doing on the stage," he advised. "As far as Lady Capulet knows, Juliette is dead. Use what you are feeling to enhance the part." He smiled sadly down at me and gave me a brief hug. "It's not much, but it might help."

Brockton waited for me in the wings. "Let the shock show," he murmured, slipping his arm around my shoulders. "It's an emotional scene, so let it all show in your performance."

I nodded. "I'll try."

We did the last scene of Act IV. I took the advice of the professionals and once again, real tears streamed down my face. The curtain came down, and Peterman met us when we came off.

"Lauren, what's wrong? You were really crying earlier, and you're doing it now. Alan is stunned and shocked. Acting is one thing, but that's not what I'm seeing. What happened?"

We steered him to one side of the hallway immediately outside the wing for privacy.

"David, Ash collapsed. He's on his way to Northwoods Memorial with your on-call physician and Becca." Brockton kept his arm around my shoulders. "Lauren?"

"Right before he passed out onstage, Ash whispered to me

that he wanted the production to keep going," I told the music teacher, my voice shaking. I took a deep breath and slowly let it out. "Please, it's all we can do for him. He's in good hands."

"The rest of the company will find out soon enough," Brockton added. "Wendell and Emilie don't need this right now. Neither does Norm. It would serve to distract them and add more pressure."

"Good heavens," said Peterman, his face pale under his makeup, nodded his agreement.

I leaned against Brockton. "Heaven help us."

"Amen." He gazed down at me with sympathy. "What do you want to do now?"

"I left Robert Mallory with another friend in Ash's dressing room. I'd like to go back there, if that's okay with you?" I asked Peterman.

"Fine." He shook his head sharply, attempting to come to terms with the circumstances. "This is a real jolt. Any ideas about how we should handle telling the company?"

"After the curtain comes down, you might want to get everyone in the green room and make an announcement," Brockton suggested.

"Ash won't be at the curtain calls, and there will be a lot of speculation. I'd also suggest catching Norm before doing it and telling him in private." I sighed. "If I can, I'll start circulating the word about the green room assembly among the chorus people."

"Good idea."

"I have one once in a while," I admitted. "On top of everything else, we don't need rumors flying around. I'll be back up in a couple of minutes."

I found Mallory and O'Brien sitting in Harper's dressing room. They rose when I entered.

"Whatever you do, don't ask if I'm alright," I cautioned them. "I'm not and I have to be back onstage in a few minutes for the curtain calls. I wanted to let you know that David is going to have everyone meet in the green room so he can make an announcement." I clenched my fists to stop myself from shaking. Stinging pain in my palms reminded me to ease up.

"Lauren, what can I do?" Mallory asked. His deep blue eyes gazed into my reddened ones. His strength flowed to me.

"Don't hug me again, I'll collapse into tears," I truthfully replied. "Once I let go, I may not be able to stop."

"I think we should go back to our seats. I'll leave during the curtain calls and wait in the green room for you," he told me. "Danny, make sure Bernie and Julie get to Susan's." The police captain agreed.

"Oh, that brings up the parties," I said while the three of us went up the steps. "I'm going to suggest we go ahead with them. I know it sounds hokey, but I think Ash would want that. He was insistent that we keep the show going."

I got to the wings in time to watch Romeo and Juliette begin their last exchanges. Carmella worked her way toward me, a huge smile on her face.

"Where have you been?" she whispered.

"Shhh! I'll tell you later," I whispered back. "Keep it down. Wendell and Emilie are still dying." We moved out of the wings to the hallway. I tried to re-focus my thoughts on the production.

"I'm so wound up!" She bounced on her toes. "You were amazing tonight," she added, giving me a hug. "It was *so* real!"

"David Peterman wants us all in the green room immediately after the curtain calls," I murmured to her. "If you want to, start spreading the word. *Quietly*, please."

She nodded and began to circulate. *At least that's a constructive step.*

Although I realized my preoccupation with the backstage events increased my impatience, I found myself wondering why it took so long for our two kids out front to die. They did. At last.

The curtain calls followed. First, the entire company, minus one, took a bow. Second, the leads, again minus one, took theirs. The third seemed a bit trickier. Bill Gardiner staged us so the featured students moved forward, and I joined them. The fourth one, reserved for Emilie and Thorne, was supposed to be our last. They received tumultuous applause on opening night, but tonight, the audience's ovation threatened to shake the building's foundations when they took their bows. The crowd rose to their feet. Levine delivered more bouquets for Emilie; she gave her Romeo a rose. The audience stayed on its feet, not letting up. Thunderous applause continued after the curtain went down. Peterman motioned everyone back on stage for a final company bow. Even preoccupied with concern for Harper, I recognized it as thrilling, heady stuff.

After the final curtain, Levine stepped to downstage center and held up a sign: *Green Room Before Changing*.

12

Mallory grabbed my arm and pulled me to one side when I passed through the doorway of the green room. "Any word?"

"I was going to ask you that." I nodded to the front of the room. "Here's David. Where's Norm?"

Peterman motioned to us. "I haven't told Norm yet. Would you do that before he comes in? I'll keep the cast here."

"Since I'm the one who saw it happen, I suppose I should be the one to tell him," I wearily agreed. "Come with me?" I asked Mallory.

"Of course." He slipped his arm around my shoulders. His support, steady and strong as always, coursed through me. "David, I think the parties should go forward. The cast did a terrific job, even better than last night, and they should celebrate. Ash collapsed, but that shouldn't stop everything."

Peterman nodded. "You're right, of course. I think Ash would approve."

Brier approached the green room, exhausted and elated at the same time. Mallory and I moved out to the hall.

"I'll leave you alone," Peterman said softly as he pulled the door shut from within.

"Something wrong?" Bewildered, Brier shifted his gaze between us.

"Norm," Mallory reported, "Ash Harper was taken to Northwoods Memorial."

"Dear lord! Why?"

"He collapsed on-stage at the end of his duel." I related the events and what steps we took. "Alan, David, and I take responsibility for not closing everything down immediately or letting you know before now," I finished. "The last thing Ash told me onstage before he passed out completely was, he wanted the production to continue."

"Oh, no!" Brier exclaimed, dumbfounded. "Why did he collapse? He fainted last night, too. Is he sick?"

"It's not general knowledge," I chose my words carefully, "but Ash has diabetes. From what the doctor said, I gathered control can be difficult under stress."

"Why does he hide it?" Brier asked, perplexed.

"He probably feels no company would have him if it became known," Mallory replied.

"He could be right about that," Brier sadly acknowledged. "Who does know?"

"Becca, David, me, and now you two. Let's keep it that way. He collapsed. No need to say why. Agreed?" I asked. They nodded.

"Lauren, you and Alan did a great job holding things together," Peterman said when he rejoined us. "Norm, I hope you forgive us for not telling you when it happened."

"You took on a heavy burden, but I agree it was for the best. This is awful." Brier shook his head as if to clear it and sighed. "Has there been any word from the hospital?"

"None," Peterman replied. "Of course, calling the office would not exactly be helpful with no one in it to answer the phone."

"The cast needs to know," I pointed out. "I'm sure his absence has been noticed by now. Norm, that's one burden I'll happily shove on to your shoulders."

"Okay, I'll call it a collapse without going into details. What about the two parties?"

"If Ash wanted the show to go on, he'd probably feel the same way about the parties," Peterman observed.

Brier nodded. "You know him better than I do. Is Becca at

the hospital?"

"As far as we know," I said. "She left with the ambulance."

"Right. I'll make the announcement and send everyone to change and party," Brier said.

We entered the large room. Mallory guided me to stand with Brockton and Raphael. Carmella popped up out of her seat to join us. I suspected her excitement proved too strong for her to remain seated, and even standing, she bounced up and down. The room quieted when Brier and Peterman stepped up onto their accustomed perches.

"To stand here and say, '*Well done, everyone!*' doesn't begin to express how proud I feel of all of you," Brier stated. "The audience gave you a stunning ovation. Now give yourselves a hand!" He wiped his forehead with a handkerchief.

They did, complete with whoops and hollers. It lasted for about a minute.

"I'm arranging for extra copies of today's *New York Times* and tomorrow's *Daily Gleaner* to be delivered to my office. Anyone who wants a copy, please stop by my office on Monday."

More applause greeted the announcement.

"I'm sure you all know by now, with our grapevine's efficiency, there are two parties tonight. The one on campus is in the basement rehearsal hall of the music department and is open to all students, high school and college, including anyone with a featured role. Refreshments are in place, you lucky kids, courtesy of Mr. Mallory." Brier paused while Mallory waved and drew applause. "The other party is for the leads and featured players and will be at Susan's Place."

"Wait a minute, Mr. Brier! Did you say that the students who had featured roles can take their choice of parties?" Alex Mercer, the college senior who performed Paris, yelled out.

"That's right," Brier replied with a smile. "You guys are lucky!"

"Alex, *you* are coming with *us* to the student party," stated Stephanie Jewell, who sang Gertrude, Juliette's nurse. She put her arm through his.

"Umm, I guess I'm going to the student party," Mercer said, smiling at her while everyone laughed. According to our vaunted and sometimes accurate grapevine, they became a dating couple during rehearsals.

"Where's Tybalt?" called out Richard Lakeland, who performed Grégorio. "I mean, Ash Harper? I didn't see him after the duel, not even at the curtain bows."

"Dick, thanks for asking," Brier acknowledged. "I'm afraid this isn't good news. Ash Harper collapsed following his duel with Wendell Thorne and has been taken to Northwoods Memorial. His wife Rebecca Chernak, who so beautifully doubled Juliette's voice last evening, is with him. We haven't received word from the doctor attending him, but I know you will add your thoughts and prayers that he makes a speedy recovery."

Murmurs of agreement and sympathy rippled through the cast.

"I've known Ash for a long time, and his first thought was for the production," Peterman took over from Brier. "I know it sounds corny, but as he collapsed, he insisted the show continue. I know he would want you to celebrate a magnificent performance done well beyond anyone's expectations. This was somewhat of an experiment to see if it could be done and whether it would be well-received. The answer to both questions is a resounding *yes* thanks to your hard work. We are considering making this an annual event."

The chorus kids cheered.

"Before you scatter, I have some final notes from the wardrobe department," Brier called out when the noise leveled off to a low babble again. "Please make sure your wigs are returned properly to the makeup room, put your costumes on their hangers, and bring them down to wardrobe. Once that is done, you're free to leave and enjoy the parties! Thank you one and all!" Brier finished to loud applause.

In the dressing room, I fidgeted and squirmed while Carmella attempted to untangle my laces so we could turn in our costumes and go. My movements made it more difficult. Antsy and anxious, my thoughts focused on Harper.

"Lauren, please quit wiggling! Can you take me to Susan's?"

"Sorry. I'm wound up and worried." I did my best to stand motionless.

"I understand, but if you don't hold still, I'll have to cut the dress off you and wardrobe won't like that." She tugged on something. "About my ride? Am I going with you?"

"That was the original plan. If I don't, Mr. Mallory is here, and he can take you. He sent Julie to Susan's with Captain O'Brien, and she'll be the hostess until he gets there."

"Mr. Mallory always seems to be around when he's needed."

"I know, and I've always been grateful for it. I remember when my dad was killed on D-Day, he helped my mother with the paperwork. After Mom died, Mr. Mallory made it clear that if I needed anything, I was to call him first. Julie is the center of his world, but he always makes time for friends. Speaking of parent-type people, I wanted to meet your mother. Was she here again tonight?"

"I couldn't have kept her away." She giggled. "Jim took her home, and he's going straight to Susan's after that. Mama isn't much on late nights. She's giving a party for me tomorrow to celebrate my stage debut. She told me to be sure to invite you, too. I'd like to ask Mr. Mallory and Julie, but I don't know how."

"Sure you do. Walk up to them and say, 'would you please come to the celebration party my mother is giving for me tomorrow?' I'm sure you can handle that," I teased.

"You make it sound so simple."

"It is. There's nothing tricky about it, especially with the Mallorys. You want them to come, all you need to do is ask. Logical cause and effect."

"That's hard for me."

"How strange. Julie says that a lot."

"There," Carmella said as the final lacing knot yielded to her fingers. "You're free."

"Another major advantage of a trouser role," I moaned. "Easier to take off. Let's get out of here." I grabbed my cavernous shoulder bag.

Costumes dutifully delivered, we headed for the green room, or as I put it, our home away from home. Mallory waited there with Raphael. Both men rose.

"Any word from Becca about Ash?" I asked the bass.

"I just spoke to Becca at the hospital," he solemnly related. "Ash is not responding to treatment."

"Oh, no!" Carmella murmured and put her hand to her mouth with her eyes wide. "He's *got* to get better."

"I've offered to go over to the hospital to stay with her, but she won't hear of it."

"Mr. Mallory, you need to get over to Susan's," I urged. "It's your party and Julie is probably close to panicking. I'll bring Carmella."

Mallory turned to Raphael. "We can call the hospital again from there, and any news can be relayed to the rest of the company." The tall man nodded, and he continued, "Is there anyone else left here that needs a ride?"

"I could use one," Thorne announced. He strolled up to us. "Somehow or other, I seem to be last."

We were bundling up to brave the chilling November wind outside when Emma popped out of a doorway and called to me with a wave.

"Lauren, I'm glad I caught you. We found this in your costume pocket." She handed me a small brown paper bag and hurried back to her domain. I regarded the bag, which looked like a child's school lunch sack.

"I didn't know my skirt *had* a pocket," I confided to Mallory while I opened it. "Uh-oh. This is a bottle of insulin." I held the bag so he could see for himself. "Heaven help us, I'm totally in the dark here. I have no idea how it got stuck in my pocket."

"Is that the one you were searching for earlier?" He peered into the opening.

"That would be my guess." I scowled. "I swear I put it back in the refrigerator." I folded the top closed and dropped it into my bottomless shoulder bag. "Someone is playing serious games."

"We can discuss this later. For now, let's go," Mallory suggested, "before Susan gives us up for lost."

We saw Norman Brier and David Peterman in the parking lot, debating about which car to use. I realized we witnessed part of a long, amiable debate.

"This is funny," I called over to them. "I think this is the first time I've ever seen you two disagree on something. I would like to point out, though, if you keep it up much longer, all the food will be gone. How about picking one or taking both?" I unlocked my car.

They both laughed and piled into the larger car.

Staged for Death

13

Susan met us at the door of the restaurant. One look at her face told me to brace for one of her good-natured scolding's.

"Lauren, you are teaching Carmella bad habits," she stated purposefully as her opening gambit. "Already Mr. Mallory is here."

"Susan, the sole reason he got here before us is he went through a yellow light, and I stopped when it turned red."

She waved off my excuse. "So how did the opera go? Our Carmella was a hit?" The proprietress gave the young singer a big hug. Carmella blushed. I grinned and nodded, and Susan continued. "I told my Gianni the next time she sings we will close so we can hear her!"

She showed us to the u-shaped arrangement made of three of their four long tables. One stretched across the width of the restaurant with the others forming the sides; the unused round ones were folded and stacked in the back alcove. The settings took away my breath. Susan had laid out her good crystal glassware, bone china, and sterling flatware on beautiful snow-white linens. In addition, centerpieces of flowers and lighted candles graced the tables. Gianello chose to place individual covered serving dishes on each table rather than serve buffet-style. The overall impression was of an intimate family gathering rather than a standard late-night after-theater supper. The smells arising from them were tantalizing.

Julie jumped up from her chair and ran to us, giving Carmella a big hug.

"You were marvelous!" she told the young singer. "Everyone was. I got goose bumps several times." She turned to me. "Lauren, you were perfect." She hugged me.

Julie took Carmella by the hand and led the way to an empty chair next to Jim Pomeroy, who stood and gave his girl a hug and kiss on the cheek. They both blushed.

I glanced around. Des Raphael was absent at the moment. I guessed he would probably be calling the hospital from the pay phone outside, although I wondered why he had not used the phone at the hostess stand. Mallory gestured for me to join him in the middle of the head table, which put me between him and David Peterman. Alan and Lisa Brockton were there; Emilie sat between Wendell Thorne and Jeff Sebring. Julie found a seat between Pomeroy and Danny O'Brien. Norman Brier took one end of the table, and I assumed they saved the other empty one for Raphael.

"All the other featured singers went to the campus party," Mallory informed me. "Bernie left to put the finishing touches on the Sunday edition, and Des is calling the hospital."

"I surmised as much." I waved at O'Brien, who nodded.

I sank into my seat gratefully and downed most of the water in my goblet.

Susan brought my usual pot of tea, and I smiled my thanks while she refilled my water goblet.

"Tea?" Peterman observed, startled. "You know that Robert has ordered champagne and wine. Why are you drinking tea?"

"Mr. Mallory is a marvelous host," I acknowledged. "David, I've been parched for over an hour. The water cooler supplied enough during the show, and that glass I downed helped, but now I need the tea."

"If you are around her for any length of time you'll realize tea—and she'll put milk and sugar in it—is Lauren's lifeblood," Mallory informed him. "Trust me. You don't want to be around if she hasn't had her normal quota. She can't create compound sentences in the morning before she's had two cups."

The high school teacher chuckled. "I'm like that with my coffee."

Raphael entered the restaurant. "I'd like to run to the hospital. The doctor told Becca that Ash has stabilized and is resting quietly enough for her to take a few hours away from the place. I thought it might be good for her to join us." He focused on Mallory. "I came over with you."

Mallory strode around the table, and I followed.

"Robert, I'll be happy to chauffeur," O'Brien volunteered, standing up to join us. "I'll make sure they have this number to call in case anything changes."

"Thank you, Danny," Raphael agreed. "I appreciate it."

Mallory nodded and the men left.

"They'll be back, Susan," Mallory explained while she slightly frowned as she watched two of her guests leave. "They'll be bringing Rebecca Chernak with them. I believe you know her."

"Yes. Her husband helped Gianni strike out on his own. She was against it. I heard them arguing one night at Trioni's. I went to meet Gianni about the hostess position, and I was waiting for him." The frown on her lovely face deepened and her brows drew together. "Mr. Ashton told her he was going to help us, and she said he'd regret it."

"I know that last isn't true," Mallory replied. "He's proud of this place."

"I heard Becca describe your restaurant as the best Italian restaurant in the New York Metropolitan area not more than five hours ago," I added.

"*Feh!* Now she says things like that." Susan bit her lip and earnestly addressed Mallory. "We paid back every bit of what he gave us long ago. Mr. Ashton didn't want to take it, but my Gianni insisted. He has come out here once in a while to eat, but his wife is rarely with him."

"Susan, it's her loss," I steadfastly stated.

"I pray that he recovers. He's a good man with a big heart."

She hesitated a moment before she continued, "Mr. Ashton has had trouble like this before."

"I know," I confirmed. "Apparently you know why."

"He told you, which surprises me not in the least." She gazed at me with a knowing half-smile.

"His meal choices gave him away?"

She nodded. "I'll tell Gianni that Miss Becca is coming. He'll want to fix her something special." Off she went to the kitchen.

"She's a grandmother above all things," Mallory said, chuckling.

"Definitely," I agreed. "If she didn't have anyone to fuss over, she'd have to adopt someone new. However, that's an interesting insight into Becca."

"While we have a moment to ourselves, I'd like to bring something up." Mallory glanced at the tables to make sure no one paid us much attention. "What about that vial of insulin?"

"I *know* I put it back in the refrigerator after I drew the second shot for the doctor." I scowled. "I didn't realize the dress had a pocket, and I don't have any little paper bags. I have no idea why it was put in my pocket or how. I don't like this."

"Neither do I."

"Daddy! Are you two coming back to the table?" Julie called out from her seat.

"Of course, we are. We're plotting a few surprises."

"We are?" I whispered.

"We can always come up with something," he whispered in return with a wink. I rolled my eyes as he led me back to our seats.

Gianello came out of the kitchen carrying a tray with four bottles of champagne. His clean apron and stiff chef's hat, which looked tall enough for a magazine advertisement, gave him an even more professional appearance. Susan and Pomeroy placed wine stands and cooler buckets around the tables, and she produced a tray of champagne glasses from the wait-stand by the kitchen entrance.

"Mr. Mallory, my dear friend, you honor my *ristorante* with your presence, and tonight you host these talented people. You ordered champagne for the party, and I have your bottles ready for you to take home. These are from my personal cellar." He bowed while we applauded. "I have two regrets about this evening. The first, my good friend Ashton Harper cannot be here to celebrate with us. We pray he will recover. The second, my Susie and I did not get to hear our Carmella make her operatic stage debut." He gestured to his wife, who moved to stand next to Carmella.

Susan pulled a small, wrapped gift box from her skirt pocket and gave it to Carmella.

"You have become like family to us, and we wanted to give you something to remind you of your special night."

Half-laughing, half-crying, Carmella got the little box unwrapped. She opened it and gasped. Her hands trembled as she held up a dainty, gold chain necklace with a golden note pendant on it. She stood and threw her arms around Susan first, then the chef. Words failed her totally, but her feelings showed on her face.

"A golden note for your golden voice," Gianello told her. "It's engraved on the back."

"I can't read it," she said through her tears of joy. "My eyes are blurry."

"Let me see it." Julie squinted. "*R&J*, and the date."

"It's all they could fit," Susan told Carmella. "It's to mark the day."

"Thank you! It's beautiful." Carmella sat down to applause and buried her head against Pomeroy's chest, which made him blush.

I caught Susan's eye. "That gift was inspired."

"It was my Gianni's idea." Susan gave Carmella a hug and fastened the necklace around her neck.

"I may never take it off," she said happily with more tears flooding her eyes.

The door chimed and Becca, Raphael, and O'Brien entered.

"That was fast," Brier commented.

"Robert, the next time I need a ride somewhere, warn me you are sending me with a policeman," Becca told our host. "The reason it didn't take long is he used the lights and siren," she added to Brier.

"I thought you wanted to get here while the party was still going on," O'Brien said, totally unruffled. Mallory and I laughed.

"Policeman!" Sebring exclaimed.

"Danny was in the audience tonight strictly as a friend of mine," Mallory explained. "He is, however, captain of the Northwoods Glen police department."

"You haven't opened the champagne yet?" Nonchalant, O'Brien questioned his friend while he sat down.

"I was waiting for you," Mallory replied.

"I got here as fast as I could." O'Brien shrugged.

"Oh lord, yes," groaned Becca, leaning against Raphael.

During the laughter, Mallory stood and tapped his glass with a fork.

"Susan, Gianni! Please join us!"

Pomeroy pulled up chairs for them and Becca.

"After years of watching you perform, it has been a privilege getting to know all of you this past week and my pleasure to host this celebration. I've attended Gounod's opera several times, and this was by far the best production I've had the pleasure of seeing." Mallory picked up a bottle of champagne and whistled at the label. "Gianni, this is most generous of you."

"You never let us properly thank you for what you and Lauren did for us this summer," Gianello replied. He shrugged and waved his hand to encompass the gathering. "It's to enjoy with friends."

"You also brought Carmella and Jim to us, too," added Susan.

"My friends, you are in for a special treat," Mallory announced to the rest of us. He started to wrestle with the bottle. "Assuming I can get it to cooperate." The cork suddenly flew out and hit Carmella on the forehead. She squealed and laughed. "The baptism of a new star of the opera stage—by cork!" Mallory quipped while he poured.

Once he saw we all had glasses, Mallory raised his. "To a magnificent performance all around!"

"Hear, hear!" we chorused and sipped the champagne. He sat. Emilie stood and raised her glass.

"I would like to thank all of you for your efforts, support, and assistance when I was ill. I especially would like to thank Becca for her wonderful work as my other voice."

"Hear, hear!" we called out and sipped again. She sat.

Jeff Sebring rose and raised his glass. "With my respect and undying devotion to the two lovely leading ladies present, I would like to be the first to salute one of the up-coming stars of the opera stage, Miss Carmella Viscotti!"

"Hear, hear!" we cried in unison, and all took another sip as he sat.

Julie got to her feet. I moaned, which got me an elbow in the ribs from her father.

"I would like to congratulate my best and dearest friend, Lauren Kaye, for taking a simple school assignment and turning it into an acting debut."

"Hear, hear!" the group yelled, and everyone took another sip. Julie sat.

"Have you people rehearsed this? You sound like an opera chorus," O'Brien mockingly complained.

Everyone in the room broke into laughter.

"We've heard the comment before," Carmella told O'Brien. "Twice that I know of."

The toasts and accolades ceased abruptly when the telephone rang. The entire company froze while Susan went to her podium to answer it.

"Susan's Place, this is Susan speaking. We are—" She stopped, and her face contorted like she experienced a sudden, stabbing pain. "Please, hold the line. She's right here." Susan covered the mouthpiece with her hand. "Miss Becca, it's the hospital."

Becca took the handset. "This is Rebecca Chernak." She listened for a few moments; her face paled. Susan pulled out her stool and guided the diva to sit. "I understand. I'll be there as soon as possible." She placed the phone back on its cradle and faced us.

"Ash has taken a turn for the worse. They've asked me to come back," she announced in a trembling voice. "Danny, can we use the lights and siren?"

O'Brien, already on his feet, held the door open for her. "We're half-way there," he assured her. "Robert, I'll be in touch."

"Go. If you need anyone, ask."

Less than five minutes later, the phone rang again. We sat in silence while Susan answered it. I held my breath and prayed we would not get more bad news.

"Susan's Place, Susan speaking. We are closed for a private party." She paused to listen. "I'm sorry, Mr. Harper isn't here." Another pause. "Mr. Thorne? Certainly! He's right here." She covered the mouthpiece. "Mr. Thorne? This is for you, a gentleman named Laszlo Halasz."

Thorne rose. Brockton, Sebring, and Raphael held up crossed fingers.

"Laszlo? It's Wendell. Ash isn't here, but Alan, Jeff, and Des are with me." He listened for more than a minute. His smile grew broader and broader until he resembled Lewis Carroll's Cheshire Cat. "I certainly will, with pleasure. Thank you!" He hung up the phone and nodded to the other three NYCO members. "Yes."

"Outstanding," Raphael said with a grin. Jeff Sebring nodded with a brilliant smile on his face.

"It would have been unthinkable otherwise," Brockton cryptically added. He winked at me.

"Now it is my turn to offer a toast. I only wish Ash was here to do it in my stead, since it was he who suggested this first."

Thorne picked up his glass and turned to Carmella. "Jeff saluted you as an up-coming star of the opera stage. That is now a certainty. On behalf of Laszlo Halasz, the artistic director of the New York City Opera organization, it is my honor and great pleasure to inform you that you are being awarded a full vocal music scholarship by the New York City Opera Company."

"Congratulations!" called out David Peterman, standing and clapping.

"Brava!" yelled Norman Brier as he stood.

"Wait!" Carmella protested, stunned. Crestfallen, she stared at her two teachers. "You don't understand—I can't! It requires an audition to qualify for it, and you know I'm not good at that. I'd never be able to do it!" Carmella's outburst verged on tears, and she clenched her hands into fists which shook as much as her voice did. "I'd be too nervous. I'd make mistakes." Her voice faded and she bit her lip, visibly shaken.

"Carmella, I don't think *you* understand. You don't have to audition. It's been awarded to you. All you have to do is accept," Brockton gently explained. "Laszlo was in the audience both nights, together with one of our conductors, Joseph Rosenstock. They saw and heard you as Stéphano. That was your audition. Your performance in a known role was more than enough to convince them you deserve the scholarship."

"Wendell told me about it," Emilie spoke up, "and I knew it would happen the first time I heard you."

"One of the things I have always liked about New York City Opera is their willingness to nurture new talent, be it singers, musicians, or composers," Sebring told us. "Ash knew once she was heard, Carmella would find her first professional home with us. We made certain Laszlo would attend at least one of the performances."

"*Dio Mio*," Carmella murmured. She fingered her new necklace. "Oh my! I can't believe this!"

"To Carmella! May her talent grace the stage for years to come!" Brockton stood and raised his glass.

We all stood. "To Carmella!"

Carmella blushed and smiled through more tears. "I can't wait to tell my mother. She's not going to believe me!"

Laughter followed her statement.

"There's an easy answer to that," I told her. "How about tomorrow afternoon?"

"Oh!" Her big brown eyes widened. "Lauren, that's a wonderful idea!" She stood. "My mother is having a celebration for me tomorrow afternoon. I know this is short notice, but if you would all come and be there when Mr. Thorne tells her about the scholarship, maybe she'll believe it. I know she won't believe me if I tell her."

Pomeroy laughed. "She could be right. Her family is proud of Carmella and her mother loved the performance, but she may need convincing. It will strike her as being too good to be true."

"Give us the time and place, and we'll be there," Sebring stated while the Brocktons nodded.

"I'm not leaving for another three days," Emilie told her, "if Wendell will give me a ride, I'd love to meet your family."

"You're all so good to me," Carmella said, her eyes bright with emotion and a few happy tears. "Mr. Gianni? Miss Susan wasn't sure if you both were coming."

"With this news, I won't stay away," Susan said decisively and raised her eyebrow at her husband.

"We didn't close for the opera, so we will be there for your party," Gianello agreed. "Do I need to bring anything? I'm a pretty good cook," he added. His comment elicited chuckles.

"Mama has it all planned," she replied with a smile. "You and Miss Susan will be my special guests. No working allowed." She rose, got a pad of paper from the hostess podium, and wrote simple directions to her mother's home. She passed them out to Brocton, Thorne, Susan, Sebring, and me.

"I know you took me there once, but I don't want you to get lost."

"I think I can manage," I said, "but thank you." I pocketed

the notepad sheet and pulled a chair next to Norman Brier. "If I may?"

"Of course—and congratulations! Your work and your performance were impressive."

"That's what I wanted to talk to you about. Remember I got into this to fulfill a class requirement."

"Oh. Yes, yes, of course. I'll have a word with John McKechnie and Dean Cranmore on Monday. I believe the dean was in the audience tonight, and I'll be sure you get full course credit for an A."

"Thank you. It was an interesting way to get one."

"You earned the grade and more. I promise I will let him know."

I returned to my seat at the table. We chatted while we devoured the wonderful dishes Gianello placed before us. I tried to avoid staring at the telephone although everyone knew it would ring again.

At one-thirty in the morning, it did. A heavy silence fell over the room.

"Susan's Place, this is Susan." She listened for a moment or two. "Yes, Mr. O'Brien. A moment, please?" She turned to summon Mallory, but he was at her elbow. "For you."

"Danny, what's the word?" Mallory asked.

I saw the news fell at least marginally to the good side because I knew him so well. Long years of acquaintance taught me to read the slightest shift in the tension of his neck and shoulders. Lisa Brockton gripped her husband's arm. Peterman asked me if I could tell.

"I don't want to guess," I dodged. "Let's wait for him to announce it."

Mallory put the phone on its hook and turned to us.

"This crisis has passed, and Ash is currently holding his own again. Danny will be taking Becca back to the hotel. He promised her he would drive like a normal person rather than a crazed maniac." The quip drew a few snickers. "After he sees her to her room, he's coming by here, so I'm afraid you'll have to put up with us a bit longer," he told the Gianellos.

"Not to worry," Susan assured us. "Because we aren't opening for lunch we can sleep late."

"Is Ash going to recover?" Thorne asked the question foremost on every mind.

"Apparently, it is touch and go. Danny may have more when he gets here. I think he wanted to keep the call short in order to get Becca to the hotel. She's had a rough time."

"Once we hear from Captain O'Brien, I'll take Carmella home," Pomeroy offered. "I will have room in my car for anyone who needs a ride back to the hotel."

"Oh. Carmella, I was hoping you and Lauren would spend the night at our house." Julie pouted, something out of character for her. "Mrs. Fiddler is eager to see you both."

"I'd love to!" The young singer shyly smiled. Abruptly, her facial expression changed, falling into dismay. Her hand flew to her cheek. "Oh, no—I can't!" Carmella moaned, chagrined. "Oh, dear. I had a small bag packed, but in my rush this afternoon I must have left it on my kitchen table. I don't have my things for overnight."

"Believe me, that is the least of your worries," I assured her with a snicker. "Julie has enough clothes to open a store, and something will fit. We won't get much sleep, but it'll be fun." *Mrs. Fiddler will love her.*

Carmella turned to Pomeroy. "What do you think?"

"You're wound up, and you won't sleep anyway." He gave her a hug. "You should enjoy yourself. You've earned it."

"Jim, if you'll take people back to the hotel, I'll take the two girls with me," Mallory said.

"I'll have room for one," I piped up.

"We have our car, too," Lisa Brockton pointed out.

The discussion kept going until O'Brien returned.

"Sorry I couldn't go into details on the phone," he stated when we clamored for news of Harper. "The doctors didn't want to unduly worry his wife. Ashton Harper has not responded well to treatment, and they are trying to find the reason why. He is holding his own for the moment."

"Has he regained consciousness?" I asked.

"Not entirely. He has moments of partial lucidity, but that's about it."

"We were discussing how to get these people back to the hotel when you came in," Mallory told the policeman.

"Becca's in her room. I offered to take her for something to eat or a cup of coffee, but she insisted on going straight back."

"That's Becca," Raphael commented. "When I get back, I'll check on her to see if she needs anything."

Thorne and Sebring exchanged meaningful nods, which implied a long story behind the unspoken words. I suspected a translation of the manuscript would be required to understand it.

We sorted ourselves out. Brier and Peterman left first, after congratulating Carmella once again and thanking the men who arranged for her to be heard by the NYCO's company director. O'Brien offered to take Des Raphael back to the hotel. I surmised he wanted a word with the bass about Becca's relationship with Harper. Pomeroy volunteered to transport Emilie and Thorne, while the Brocktons offered to give Jeff Sebring a lift.

O'Brien pulled me to one side. His eyes swept the room to make sure we would not be overheard before he spoke. "You'll be at Mallory's in case I need you?"

I nodded. "So, you're suspicious, too. I have something I think you should have checked." I dug in my bag for the small paper sack.

"What am I holding?"

"Captain," I addressed him by his title since I presumed the whole thing would become official, "the costume people found this in a pocket of my stage dress. I am ready to give a deposition under oath that I put this bottle back into the refrigerator in Ash's dressing room after I drew a shot for the doctor. Since it turned up in a paper bag I never had, in a pocket I didn't know existed,

I'm curious."

"Especially since the medical people are baffled by Harper's condition," he agreed. "Here and now, did you tamper with this in any way?"

"If you dust it, you'll find my prints. I drew a dose from it at the doctor's request. There will be prints on it belonging to Dr. Rossiter, and of course, Ash. Other than that, I haven't done anything to it." I stared into his grey eyes while they probed my brown ones. "I've never lied to you and don't intend to start now."

"I don't like the way this is playing out. I've heard that you threatened him for coming on to Carmella."

"I said if he did anything to hurt her, he'd answer to me. If you consider that a major threat, I wish you luck."

"It could be construed as one."

"Yes, I suppose it could if you're fishing for a motive."

"I've also heard that you've been playing up to each other."

"More motive?" I sighed and shook my head. "Captain O'Brien, I give you my word. I have done nothing to harm Ash Harper. You can take that to the bank."

His piercing gaze found my steady one coming back at him. Wordlessly, we held that pose for a slow count of ten

He frowned. "I want you to know that if I find anything unusual about this bottle, you're my first stop."

"Understood." I broke eye contact to gaze over his shoulder. "Des is standing next to the car. You'd better go."

He nodded, said his goodbyes to the Gianellos and the Mallorys, and left.

"What was that all about?" Julie asked.

"Nothing much," I evaded the question and nodded to our hosts. "I think we should leave these two wonderful people to clean up and close."

The four of us said our goodbyes to the Gianellos.

"I offered to help clean up, but I got scolded," Carmella told us as she got into Mallory's car.

Julie laughed. "That sounds about right. Lauren, don't get lost."

"Julia Elaine Mallory, I may have a lousy sense of direction, but I can find your house from here!"

Staged for Death

14

"I will *not* allow you to go up there! She's asleep. They all are."

Mrs. Fiddler? What poor soul earned the receiving end of Mrs. Fiddler's wrath?

A man answered the housekeeper. Through a sleepy haze, I identified O'Brien's gruff voice, but I could not understand the words.

Alice Fiddler rarely raised her voice. Somehow, she developed the knack of putting power into her words without raising her volume. I envied the talent and wished more than once I could learn it. I heard the exchange because I slept lightly, and my ears worked. From the sounds floating up, I figured she planted herself at the bottom of the stairs, physically barring the way. The door to my room stood open.

"Please wait in the master's office." She stated it as an order. Mrs. Fiddler, when roused to anger, left no room for quibbling, and he knew it.

"Yes, ma'am."

I listened to her muffled footsteps as she climbed the stairs and passed my door. She stopped at Mallory's study, the room next to mine. Julie and Carmella spent the night in Julie's room down and across the hall.

"Mr. Mallory, I'm sorry to disturb you, but Captain O'Brien is here and wants to see Miss Lauren. He was insisting on charging up here, but I managed to stop him." Alice Fiddler's voice, back to normal, reflected a hint of pride. No one, not even

O'Brien, got to storm her castle without her permission. "He's waiting in your office."

"Thank you, Mrs. Fiddler. You can leave this to me."

Footsteps approached my room, followed by a knock on my door frame. "Lauren?"

"Here, I think," I mumbled through a yawn. "What time is it?"

"Eight. Danny O'Brien is downstairs demanding to see you."

"I thought I heard that. I wish I could learn Mrs. Fiddler's trick of yelling without adding volume to her voice." I stretched and rubbed my eyes. "If you'll stall him with a cup of coffee, I'll throw some clothes on and come down."

"I'll have Mrs. Fiddler bring you a mug of tea." He paused in the doorway. "Any idea what's so urgent?"

"I'm not awake enough to have ideas." I murmured. It was not an entirely truthful statement.

I grabbed my robe and padded to the bathroom. O'Brien's attempt to breach the battlements, even when he knew better, gave me a solid idea of what I faced. Mallory would have imploded if I explained it to him.

Eight o'clock. Ungodly. Way too soon to be conscious.

I recalled the early hours of the night. Upon arriving at the house and as expected, Julie, Carmella, and I had talked for an hour before I left them to get some sleep. Mrs. Fiddler fussed over Carmella, as I suspected she would. Unknown to us, she attended last night's performance. The news of the scholarship elicited a sniff and the comment, "of course they gave it to her." Julie and I told Carmella once the Fiddler Decree issued forth, any doubts vanished.

I crawled into my bed ten seconds before I fell asleep, about four hours ago. I knew O'Brien's patience would be tested by any delay, but I did have to get dressed. I suspected neither of us would enjoy whatever happened next. I hoped Mallory would attend the grilling.

Back in my room I contemplated my closet, where I kept a

few changes of clothes. The room was mine to use anytime. Over the years, I discovered keeping some of my things here in the mansion made logistics easier. Occasionally, I noticed something new would appear in the closet which I did not remember buying, but Julie loved to shop. I did not share her views on it, and she delighted in surprising me with full encouragement from her father. It took me a while, but I learned to accept it on the grounds I could not fight them both.

Mrs. Fiddler knocked on the door and entered with a mug. "Perhaps you would like some help?" She smiled as she handed me the tea.

I nodded. "You really do spoil me."

"Orders from the master. He knows you're not up to making decisions yet." While I sipped, she laid out one of my skirts, a blouse, and a jacket; she dug into the chest of drawers for appropriate underwear. "Finish your tea and take your time dressing." She gave me a big smile. "You were terrific onstage."

"Thank you. It was fun, for the most part. I never realized how much work went in to making a show look effortless. I got an A for it."

"As you should have," she intoned with a typical sniff. She pulled the door closed as she added, "I'll tell Mr. Mallory you will be down soon."

I finished my tea, dressed, and brushed my hair into a semblance of its normal style. It is brown, straight, and long enough to put up. Once done and out of my way, I forgot about it. My eyes did not appear as bleary in the mirror as they felt from my side of them. The sand I felt in them did not show.

I made my way downstairs to the kitchen and handed over my mug. "Refill? I have a feeling I'm going to need the reinforcement."

Mrs. Fiddler nodded while she set up a serving cart. "I'll see to it and bring it with the rest. They are in the office."

I knocked on one of the carved oak double doors off the foyer and entered as instructed.

Mallory called the room his office. I referred to it as the library. Floor to ceiling bookcases lined two walls, with additional ones flanking a fireplace on a third wall. The mantelpiece held a clock and his prized photos. A table with two chairs sat under the picture window overlooking the back lawn; a door next to the window opened onto the landscaped terrace. A Persian carpet muffled most of the sounds from outside.

I advanced to the main feature of the room. Mallory sat behind his mahogany desk, which dwarfed everything else. O'Brien had taken his usual place in one of the two comfortable chairs in front of it. I stood behind the other one and faced the desk.

"Good morning, Lauren." Mallory rose and greeted me with a smile. "I'm sorry your night was so short."

"I had a feeling this would happen." I regarded O'Brien. "I take it something dicey showed up." I sat down.

He nodded. "I said you'd be my first stop."

"Danny, what's going on?" Mallory resumed his place in the leather chair behind his desk.

"When we were leaving Susan's," I explained, "I gave the captain the small paper sack with the insulin bottle in it. I suggested he have it checked. He said if anything funny turned up, I'd be his first stop. Since he's here, I assume something did."

"This needs to be completely confidential," the veteran police officer stated. His steady gaze met Mallory's. "I know it's your office in your home, but I'd rather do this here than down at the station." He paused and waited for a response. I got the impression his emotions were barely under control.

Mallory nodded. "Go ahead."

"By confidential, I mean alone." O'Brien's forehead wrinkled like a sideways accordion.

"I'd rather stay, if it's acceptable," Mallory replied. He used a tone of voice I never heard before. It sounded like it had steel reinforcement rods in it.

"You are not a lawyer." O'Brien's shoulders stiffened as he

distinctly enunciated each word. His cold and harsh voice rivaled a Siberian winter.

"No, I'm not. However, as you mentioned, it's my house." Mallory's unyielding tone left no doubt about his position. "You know I'm capable of confidentiality. The other two girls are upstairs asleep. Mrs. Fiddler will bring in coffee service with Lauren's second cup of tea, and hopefully some juice and toast. We'll be left alone and undisturbed."

O'Brien silently glared at his host who unremittingly stared back. Skirmish lines for a battle had been drawn.

"Danny, it's either here with me, or you'll have to take her to the station." Mallory regarded his friend, and I wondered, not for the first time, what their relationship was. It puzzled me the first time the three of us were thrown together. I asked about it more than once, but neither of them saw fit to offer any kind of explanation other than the vague promise of, 'someday we'll tell you.'

"I don't want to make it official."

"Then don't." Mallory's matter-of-fact response underlined the determination visible in his face.

A knock sounded on the door. Mallory rose, crossed the room, and opened it. Mrs. Fiddler rolled in a small serving cart with a tray containing three glasses of orange juice, a coffee pot, two cups, a sugar bowl, a milk pitcher, a rack of toast, a small pot of jelly, a mug of tea, and a teapot with more hot water. The three of us watched in silence while she took small plates, silverware, and napkins out of the drawer on the cart, placed them on top, and maneuvered it next to the desk.

"Thank you, Mrs. Fiddler. We are not to be disturbed unless someone calls for Captain O'Brien."

She nodded and withdrew, closing the door.

"Well, Danny?"

"Blast it! I don't want to have to do this at all and I definitely don't want to take her down to the station." O'Brien sighed, and it came from his toes. "Cheese and rice! I almost wish she hadn't given me the bag." He ran his fingers through his graying hair.

"May I say something?" I rose and reached for one of the juice glasses. "I don't know what was in the vial I gave the captain, but I'm almost certain I know what wasn't in it." I drank the juice and replaced the glass. "Is Ash Harper alive?"

"Yes." Blunt speech was built into his nature and underlined his professionalism. I discovered that quirk the first time I worked with him.

"Good." I usually tried to match his brevity. "The vial wasn't filled with insulin." I resumed my seat.

"Yes and no."

"Great. Are we playing twenty questions now?" Mallory asked. He glowered at the officer.

"Hold." I regarded O'Brien. "There was insulin in the vial?"

"Yes, there was."

Mallory sat back in his chair and sipped his coffee, watching the two of us the way a hungry owl regarded a couple of field mice.

"That's surprising. He didn't respond to the first shot from that bottle in the dressing room. The doctor asked if I could draw a med, and when I said yes, he asked me to draw the second shot. If there was insulin in the vial when you had your lab check it—" I frowned. Thinking came hard because most of my mind hid behind a foggy curtain of sleep. "That doesn't make sense unless—" I looked up. "Diluted?"

He nodded. "That's it. I went back to his dressing room early this morning. I got the remaining bottle from the refrigerator and had two men go through the backstage garbage. They found one other bottle, with a just a few drops left." His grey eyes bored into me as if he attempted to see into my soul. "I assume you used logic to get to that conclusion."

"I did. I'll bet the bottle from the garbage was stronger than the bottle I found in my pocket and the one in my pocket was stronger than the one you got from the refrigerator." I reached for my refilled tea mug which had my requisite milk and sugar in it.

I gratefully took a sip.

"That's what I expect them to find."

"Poor Ash. No wonder he continually felt tired." At his sharp inhale, I glanced up. "Captain, I've been working with Ash Harper since the beginning of September. Of course, I noticed something was going on, but I couldn't pin it down."

Mallory helped himself to another cup of coffee and poured one for O'Brien.

"So, what's the problem?" he asked the police captain, handing him the steaming drink.

O'Brien took a piece of toast. "The only tangible thing we have is two bottles of insulin with Lauren's fingerprints. The way she summarized it, plus her prints, would be enough to take her in for attempted murder."

"You found her prints on two bottles?" Mallory queried, his voice edgy enough to saw wood.

O'Brien nodded. "The one in the bag and the one found in the garbage."

"Uh-oh." I stared down at the mug in my hands. I glanced at O'Brien and shrugged. "Sorry, it slipped out." I took another swig of my tea. "I drew the last shot from the discarded one on opening night. The vial in the bag was the one we used last night."

"I have another problem," he told Mallory. "Rebecca Chernak is pressing me to make an arrest." He hesitated, like he hated to finish his statement.

I knew why, so I said it for him. "Me."

Unhappily, O'Brien nodded again. "She doesn't know about the fingerprints, either. If and when she does find out, I may not have any choice."

"Danny, you can't arrest Lauren." The calm, factual words of the statement belied the force Mallory put behind them. He sat straight up, and a muscle in his jaw twitched.

"You honestly think I *want* to?" O'Brien's broad, craggy face turned red and not from blushing. "For the record, I don't."

"Mr. Mallory, he may be forced to. If Ash does die and the vials are brought up, it's murder. My fingerprints are on them both. It's circumstantial, but it could back him into a corner, especially if there's a lot of pressure. Becca probably has powerful friends." I glanced at O'Brien, who glumly stared into his coffee.

"This is absurd!" In a low, harsh whisper Mallory made his feelings clear. He leaned forward in his chair. "Utterly ridiculous!"

The two men tried to out-glare each other.

"Hold." I broke the silence. "Let's take it from the basics we have." I found, to my surprise, my hands were steady when I reached to put my mug on the cart. "Ash is the victim of tampered insulin."

"You didn't tamper with the insulin." Mallory stated it as fact.

"I don't think she did." O'Brien decided his statement needed to be stronger. "I don't believe she did."

"You don't?" Mallory observed. "A moment ago, you didn't sound sure." His voice remained chilly enough to modify freshly brewed hot tea into an iced beverage. He got to his feet and loomed over his desk, leaning on his fists. Deep blue eyes met dark grey ones.

"She wouldn't be stupid enough to dilute it, use it, hide it, and forget to take it out of her pocket!" O'Brien snapped at his friend. "Much less give it to me unasked." He turned to me. "Even though the bag was handed to you in front of witnesses, no one else saw what was in the bag."

"I beg to differ," Mallory informed the veteran police officer. "The woman from wardrobe handed that bag to Lauren in my presence. Lauren then showed it to me." He slowly lowered himself into his chair and leaned forward. "Lauren also swore she put the bottle she used last night back in the refrigerator after drawing the shot on the doctor's orders."

"Did you see her draw the shot last night?" O'Brien fired at

Mallory.

"I did. I was in the dressing room. It happened while you were going after the ambulance."

"The doctor can confirm he asked me to do it," I mused aloud.

O'Brien turned back to me. "You didn't have to hand it over."

"I know, but I was suspicious of his collapse. He promised to be careful and take precautions after he collapsed the first time. You said Ash is alive."

"For the moment, yes."

"What kind of chances are his doctors giving him?" Mallory asked.

"No one is sure." O'Brien admitted. He rubbed his face with his hands. "Like I said, the doctor is baffled about his condition. Rebecca Chernak is convinced she's going to be a widow any time now."

"Captain O'Brien, officially and for the record, I did not tamper with the insulin. I will dictate a sworn statement to that. Let's assume, at least for the moment, you believe me." I poured and prepped another mug of tea, picked up a piece of toast, and spread some of Mrs. Fiddler's home-made apple-cinnamon jelly on it. "You have questions." I waved my toast in the air as a gesture. "Go ahead."

Mallory settled himself in his chair behind his massive and beautiful desk with its carved legs. The first time I took the seat behind it, I asked him to leave the desk and chair to me in his will. Despite the circumstances, I gazed at it longingly and sighed. He ignored me. He pulled a notepad out of a drawer and uncapped his favorite fountain pen. O'Brien poured another cup of coffee and took out his notebook and a pencil.

"Why—" His voice cracked and wavered. He cleared his throat and started again. "Why did you make a play for Harper?"

"Ash was flirting with most of the females in the chorus in turn, but I noticed he kept circling back to Carmella. She was getting tense, and Jim Pomeroy was becoming upset. I decided to see if I could divert him."

"By having him focus on you?"

"It seemed the safest way to defuse the situation. David Peterman tried talking to him about it, and Carmella tried to ease away from him. Nothing worked. I did what I could to redirect his attention to see if that would help.

"Did he come on to you?"

"Not precisely. We simply spent more time together. I figured I was more capable than Carmella to walk the line between flirting and getting serious."

"So, it wasn't serious?"

"Not at all. We became friends." I returned his hard stare with one of my own. "Nothing more."

"His wife seems to think it was more than that and others have agreed with her."

"I can't help that," I returned, keeping my tone even. "He recommended Carmella for the part of Stéphano. She felt she had to be nice, and I tried to make sure it didn't get out of hand. What I did kept Carmella off his radar. That's all there is to it. Friends."

"Saturday evening before the performance she was seen running out of his dressing room, visibly upset. You were seen going in immediately after that and heard threatening him if he didn't leave her alone."

"That's not quite accurate." I recounted the scene in the dressing room. "I guess my side of it was loud because Alan Brockton was passing by the door and asked if there was a problem. I told him no, it was a matter of an attitude adjustment."

"Okay, I learned in our first go-round that I could check you with a tape recorder. What happened in his dressing room the night before?"

"You mean after he collapsed in the green room on opening night?"

"You were alone with him in his dressing room, weren't you?"

"Ash crumpled during the gathering after the performance, and I literally caught him. Alan Brockton and I got him to his dressing room, and I sent Alan to find Becca. At Ash's request, I helped him drink some orange juice, and when that made things worse, I gave him a shot of insulin according to his instructions. He started to recover but tried to get up too soon to change his clothes, and he lost his balance. Becca walked into his dressing room at about the same moment I had my arm around his waist to steady him. She said, *I sincerely hope I'm interrupting this cozy scene.* Ash explained what had happened, and she apologized to me. She wasn't warm about it, but she did apologize."

"You used the vial in the refrigerator?"

"There were three of them at that time. I used the one in front, so it has my prints on it, and I drew the last full dose. He told me to toss the empty vial. That was the one your man found in the garbage. The syringe was marked, and I had seen him give himself a shot Thursday, the night of final dress."

"When?"

"The night of final dress?" I waited for his nod. "About five. Earlier, he asked me to make sure he was awake in time to have a light supper. I got there a couple of minutes early and found him giving himself a shot of insulin. That's when he admitted to me he has diabetes. Ash and I went out to supper, by ourselves, immediately afterward and were back before the rehearsal."

"Who else knew he used insulin?"

"At that time, Becca, of course, and then me. I told him he needed to tell David Peterman, who's a friend of theirs in addition to being a part of the production."

"Why Peterman?"

"David had asked me to find out what Ash's problem was after he spotted a syringe in Ash's dressing room. They're good friends and he was hoping Ash wasn't doing anything stupid, like hard drugs." I paused. "When I relayed that to Ash, he laughed and said he thought David knew him better than that."

"Did Harper ever discuss his relationship with his wife?"

"Obliquely, yes. He told me he flirted because he didn't like being alone, and it was something his wife never quite understood."

"Becca thinks there was more to it than friends because you weren't the type of girl he usually went after."

"They both told me that, give or take a few words. Apparently, I'm not."

"Did Harper mention his wife's relationship with Des Raphael?"

"Again, obliquely. I asked him what, if anything, was going on between Des and Becca because I noticed her attitude toward our duke was warmer than it was with anyone else. He explained Des has always put her on a pedestal, and she likes that kind of adoration." I shook my head. "I won't even attempt to analyze that, but those were his words."

"Okay, say I buy all that as being on the level," he muttered, scribbling in his notebook. "Now I have a big one for you." He glanced at Mallory, probably to give his eyes a break from me, and brought his gaze back to me. "Why didn't you raise the alarm on stage when he was passing out? You could have screamed, cried out, or called out. Anything besides continuing to play the scene." O'Brien drained his coffee cup and put it back on the cart.

"Ash knew he was sinking. He struggled to tell me he wanted the show to continue." I gazed straight into the probing dark grey eyes. "I considered, briefly, overriding his request. At the same time, I realized it would have created chaos and probably taken just as much time to get him off-stage and into his dressing room. Possibly even more in the resulting panic it would have caused." I paused to gather my thoughts. "I know you saw the scene, but you have to understand what happened. Tybalt was supposed to make a dying request of Capulet. That's the cue for Capulet's response. Ash didn't sing his last lines. I was kneeling with him, and I looked up at Alan. He saw something was wrong and he knelt beside us, something not in our staging. Alan picked up his cue from the music and sang without Ash's plea, which kept the pace of the act. Alan didn't even blink when I said Ash wanted us to carry on."

"No one questioned that?" he asked, incredulous.

"No one." I carefully considered the question. "I'm including Becca in that, too."

"Isn't that callous?"

"These people are totally immersed in what they're doing. The duel was Ash's last scene. To give you a better idea of the dedication they have, when I asked Des Raphael how I was supposed to go out onstage and play my last scene, knowing Ash was on his way to the hospital, his first words were, *Lauren, Ash would want us to carry on.* Des and Alan both suggested I put what I was feeling into my part."

O'Brien's skepticism etched his face. "Right."

"Fine." I bristled. "Let me add this. Other than the people in the wings when we exited, most of the company didn't notice anything unusual until Ash failed to show up for the curtain calls."

"Danny, what are you trying for?" Mallory, who followed the questions closely without comment, spoke up.

"I'm grasping for a reason to look at anyone besides Kaye for motive and opportunity." O'Brien flatly stated. His eyes were hard, his face glum, and he looked exceedingly uncomfortable. "She had the opportunity. She has been in and out of that dressing room for days and she knows her way around syringes."

"You can't be serious about her motive," Mallory countered. "She wanted to kill him because he made a pass at Carmella?"

"Okay, so it's not the strongest one I've ever seen," O'Brien retorted. He ran his fingers through his hair. "She was also heard saying she wouldn't let anything get in Carmella's way, or words to that effect. Blast it, at the moment it's all I have. *She's* all I have."

"Have you heard any other ideas from the people you have questioned?" Mallory probed.

"Raphael's theory is that Harper may have been stringing Lauren here along toward a full-blown affair, and when he pulled back, she went off the deep end."

"Hold!" I protested. "That's even worse! You are saying I either committed murder to help Carmella get to the opera stage, or I did it because I fell for him and he brushed me off? No thanks!" I glowered at him.

"I admit I'm snatching at will-o-wisps. Remember I'm being pushed to find answers."

"I hope you don't settle for Lauren because you can't find anyone else." Mallory's caustic comment startled O'Brien and he grimaced.

I studied Mallory. His blue eyes were darker than I had ever seen them. *Heaven help us, he is ready to explode at O'Brien, and in my defense!* I shivered.

O'Brien returned his attention to me. "Have you got any better candidates?"

"I'll work on it." I sipped tea. "You drove Des Raphael back to the hotel after the party last night. Did you talk with him at all, other than getting his lame idea about my relationship with Ash?"

"Apparently, the New York City Opera people have known each other for years. It's no big secret that Harper likes to flirt. It's also common knowledge Chernak had both Raphael and Harper on the string before she married Harper. Brockton's marriage is happy, which is nice to know, and Thorne and Sebring are single. None of that is new."

"In other words, I remain your prime suspect." I scowled.

"I admit other than your fingerprints it's all circumstantial. But yes, you are."

"Wonderful. Swell, even." I knew my scowl deepened when I saw Mallory wince. "This has gotten us precisely nowhere."

"I noticed." O'Brien face was as gloomy as he sounded. "I was hoping we'd find some other stone to turn over."

We sat in silence long enough to hear the clock on the fireplace mantle strike nine-fifteen.

"I'd like to see Ash," I murmured.

O'Brien missed it. "Huh?"

"I'd like to see Ash," I repeated, using slightly more volume.

"I'm not sure that's a good idea," Mallory gravely said. "If anything should go wrong, you might be worse off."

"If he can talk or respond in any way, I want to ask him a couple of questions. Nothing in lurid detail, just simple and basic yes or no questions," I elaborated. "O'Brien can even stay in the room."

"I can see one or two advantages to it," O'Brien acknowledged. "Let me give it some thought and check with his doctor before we decide."

"Fair enough." I tried to formulate an intelligent version of a question I wanted to pose, but the phone rang. Mallory ignored it, knowing his housekeeper would get it. It stopped after the second ring.

Mrs. Fiddler knocked on the office door.

"Mr. Mallory, the call is for Captain O'Brien," she announced when told to enter. She withdrew.

O'Brien stood and took the call on the desk phone. "O'Brien."

His side of the exchange consisted of occasional grunts before he finished with, "Stay with him. We'll be right over." He hung up and dubiously regarded me. "Ash Harper is fully conscious and asking for you. He wants to see you and only you and won't answer any questions until he does see you. Come on."

"I need my bag," I managed to blurt out while he hustled me toward the front door. "It's upstairs."

"Make it fast."

He waited at the bottom of the stairs with his arms folded. Mallory, standing next to him, looked like his face had been carved in the granite of Mt. Rushmore.

"Don't tell Carmella what's going on, at least not yet. She'd never forgive herself if she even catches a glimmer that I might be suspected of harming Ash because I tried to protect her." I regarded them both. "I want your word, gentlemen." They both knew I meant it, although O'Brien did not know me as well as

Mallory did.

"Agreed," Mallory murmured.

"I'll go along with it unless, and until, it becomes necessary to drop it," O'Brien told me, characteristically leaving himself an out. He firmly grasped my arm and propelled me out the door.

15

At the hospital, O'Brien pulled into a *reserved for official use* parking spot.

"Before we go in, I want you to know I don't believe you had anything to do with the attempt. None of what I may have to do officially is personal," he advised, "and I will do my utmost to give you a fair break."

"I appreciate that. Honestly, I know you consider me a meddling pest, but you at least listen to me."

"I learned the hard way I can't ignore you. If you get any ideas, I want to hear them."

"I'll have to finish waking up first. Did Ash say why he wanted to see me?"

"My man told me Harper wanted to see you, adding the request was forceful."

"Is Becca with him?"

"Not as of that call, which is one reason I wanted to get you here." He got out of the car and circled around to open my door. "I'm not going to leave any loopholes. I'll stay in the room with you."

"If it gets to where you shouldn't listen, will you put your fingers in your ears?" I knew the crack pushed my luck, but I always counted on humor to help tense situations. I reminded myself a curtain of sleep reigned over my mind. I hoped O'Brien realized it.

"Cute." A typical response. He surprised me when he opened the door of the building and allowed me to precede him.

"Your manners are improving," I wryly commented. "You must be taking lessons from Walt Evans." I snickered a little while I passed him. He snorted.

We went up the elevator, passed by a nurses' station, and stopped outside a room with a uniformed policeman outside.

"A guard?" I whispered.

"Yes, and it's a private room."

"No chances and no loopholes?"

He nodded.

"There's a doctor with him," the officer informed us, "but it's not Dr. Rossiter."

Curious, I entered without knocking. A tall man in a white lab coat bent over Harper. One hand behind his back held a large syringe.

Something struck me as wrong. More than one something and all extremely wrong.

"Doctor!" I yelled as I dashed across the room. *"What are you doing?"*

The man turned away from the bed and backhanded me. I crashed into the bedside table and stuck my foot out to trip him. I lost my balance and tumbled to the floor, landing on all fours. My hand closed on a slipper, and I picked it up.

The phony medic stumbled over my foot but did not fall. Something flew out of his hand, and I used the slipper as a makeshift baseball mitt and caught the glass syringe before it hit the floor and shattered.

O'Brien charged into the room. The man swung at him. O'Brien ducked and retaliated. O'Brien's punch landed on the assailant's chin. Down he went, sprawled on his back.

The guard followed behind O'Brien and stood with his gun pointed at the man on the floor.

"Glass jaw," O'Brien muttered, massaging his hand.

I inspected my prize without touching it. I gasped and shuddered. The plunger of the syringe was pulled out, ready to inject its contents. The large barrel of the glass syringe contained nothing—plain air.

"Lauren?" Harper rolled on his side to peer over the edge of the bed at me. "What was that all about? What is going on?"

"Give us a moment, Ash." I straightened myself out a bit before standing. "Do you know that man?"

Harper shook his head. O'Brien's target slowly got to his feet with an assist from the officer. The man's sullen face showed a slight swelling around his jaw, courtesy of O'Brien's fist.

"Why?" O'Brien barked at me.

"Phony." I hotly returned, concise and similarly blunt.

"I got that when he slugged you. How?"

"Hold a moment." I turned to the tenor. "Ash, did he do anything to you? Did he give you any shots or medication?"

"No."

"Thank God," I murmured. I slumped into a handy chair next to the bed, clutching my makeshift mitt.

"What's going on here?" demanded Dr. Rossiter from the doorway.

"Please, Doctor, come in and close the door." O'Brien pointed to the intruder and gestured his officer to come forward. "Briggs, cuff him and hold him," he ordered. He turned back to the doctor. "Dr. Rossiter, can you identify this man?"

"His name is Ken Stone, one of our night orderlies. Is everything all right?"

"You tell us," O'Brien requested, although it sounded like another order. "How's Harper?"

"Coming along nicely," the physician replied, studying the chart.

"Daniel O'Brien, police." O'Brien flashed his badge to the orderly. "Stone, I have some questions for you. What were you doing in here?"

"Nothing. I was just talking to the guy." Stone's surly voice matched the beady brown eyes which peered out from a broad, fleshy face. His mouth formed a thin line.

"You told me you were a doctor," Harper insisted.

"Not true." Stone's face now matched his name. A huge muscular man, he towered over O'Brien. He glared at the five of us in turn.

The singer started to protest. I put a hand on his arm and shook my head; he leaned back on his pillows. O'Brien asked the orderly a few more questions to no avail. Our phony physician turned into an extremely large clam.

"Take him to the station and hold him. He talks to no one from the outside, and I mean *no one,* until I order it. No calls," O'Brien decreed.

"I want a lawyer," Stone glowered at O'Brien.

"We'll take care of all that at the station."

"What is—" Dr. Rossiter sputtered.

"Be patient for one more moment, Doctor." O'Brien cut him off. He was not harsh yet made his point. Once the pair vacated the room, O'Brien turned to me.

"*How?*" he barked, repeating his query with more emphasis.

"Sloppy shoes. Lab coat didn't fit. Dirty fingernails. Syringe pointed the wrong way. Shall I go on?"

"Cheese and rice, Kaye! Why didn't you say something?"

"No time. By the way, he dropped this." I offered the slipper with its prized catch. I knew better than to tell him not to touch the syringe. "Note the barrel is ready for injection. It's empty."

"I suppose you saw that, too?"

"Not clearly. The whole picture was wrong."

"Dr. Rossiter, without touching it, what do you make of this?" O'Brien took the slipper and let the genuine doctor take a close look at the syringe.

The practitioner paled. "I think Mr. Harper owes this young lady his life." He perched on the corner of the bed. "An injection of that much air into the intravenous line would probably have killed him."

"Would someone please tell me what in heaven's name is going on?" Harper sharply demanded. "We could start with why I'm in the hospital with this." He sat up and waved the arm with the IV line. The two bottles on the pole next to his bed rattled.

"Ash, I know you have a bunch of questions," I said. "Hold on for another moment or two, please? I promise we'll explain everything. First, though, we have to decide how to handle this." I stared at the floor.

Harper reclined against his pillows.

"Miss Kaye, what do you mean?" Rossiter asked.

"Captain, correct me if I'm wrong. What we have here are two attempts on the life of our Tybalt."

O'Brien nodded, his face set in a scowl.

"*WHAT?*" Harper popped back up like a jack in the box. "Lauren, you're kidding, right?" He reached for my hand and gripped it.

Rossiter gasped. "I didn't think of it that way, but you could be right."

"Ash, I wish I was kidding. You asked what you are doing here. The answer is simple. The shots you have been giving yourself haven't been the right strength of insulin. Someone, call him the butler, diluted your insulin supply. It's why you've been dragging."

"God above," he murmured. "No wonder I felt like warmed over horse manure."

"It's also why you collapsed onstage and didn't respond to the shots we gave you last night in your dressing room," Dr. Rossiter confirmed. "You started to recover when I got you here because what I gave you was genuine."

"So, you're saying someone—you called him the butler?" Harper asked me.

"That's Kaye's pet name for a bad guy we can't identify yet," O'Brien explained. "Like—"

"The butler did it," Harper acknowledged with a wry smile. "Got it. You're saying the butler deliberately tampered with my insulin, figuring I'd eventually collapse and die." He sighed and lay back. "This is just plain nuts."

"Nuts or not, it came uncomfortably close to working," I

pointed out. "Ash, who knows you are a diabetic?"

"You, Becca, David, and anyone else who found out in the last forty-eight hours. I'm losing track," he dryly observed.

"Understandable," I commented absently with my thoughts elsewhere.

"Kaye, I know you well enough to realize you have an idea cooking. Care to let the rest of us in on it?" O'Brien studied my face. "We might even help." Sarcasm dripped from his words.

"I'm working on it." I squeezed the tenor's hand. "Ash, I realize this is tough for you to accept, but we need to know. Can you think of anyone who would want you out of the way?"

"I'm having trouble believing that the butler is someone I know." Dismayed, Harper shook his head. "It's going to take time to get used to."

"Time is something we don't have," I told him. "For now, though, we have to decide if you're going to get better or take another turn for the worse."

"*WHAT?*" A unison chorus of the single word exploded from all three men.

"Explain," O'Brien growled.

"We have three pieces of evidence, right? And two of them point straight to me."

"*You?*" Harper's expressive face added incredulity to the word. "Captain, you can't seriously think Lauren is behind this!"

"No, I don't, but she's right about the evidence. Her fingerprints are on two of the vials of diluted insulin. One was found in her costume pocket, and we dug the other one out of the auditorium's garbage."

"She's been helping me!" Harper vehemently exclaimed. "She drew a shot for me after opening night!"

"She also drew a shot for me last night in the dressing room before we decided to bring Mr. Harper to emergency," Rossiter confirmed.

"Calm down," I said. "The vial was planted on me. Captain O'Brien agrees I didn't do it."

"What's the other evidence?" Rossiter asked.

"This syringe Stone dropped."

"Hired?" O'Brien switched to monosyllables.

"Coerced?" I proved I could do it, too.

"Good heavens," Rossiter murmured.

"The butler diluted the insulin, doing it by making each vial progressively weaker," O'Brien explained. "The effect was gradual."

"When he did collapse," I added, "we got Ash here in time and he began to recover. Our unknown adversary upped the ante by getting the giant to inject air into Ash's intravenous line. The way I see it, the butler is someone who not only knows Ash well but is close enough to him to have access to his medication. Couple that with enough skills to partially empty the insulin vials and top them off with sterile water, find a motive to drive it, and you have a case. Simple."

"Oh, sure. It's simplicity itself." Once more O'Brien's sarcasm dripped all over the floor or would have if given physical form. He glared at me.

Harper groaned. "God above."

"Dr. Rossiter, did Becca mention what time she would be back up here today?" I asked.

"No specific time. I gave her a sleeping pill to take after she got back to the hotel, so it's entirely possible she's still in bed."

"She will be," Harper offered. "She usually sleeps late, and if she took a pill, it could be noon before she gets up."

I glanced at the clock over the door, which indicated a few minutes after ten. "Hopefully, that will give us some time." I started to sigh. A yawn interrupted it. "Pardon me. I got about four hours of sleep."

"Let me see if I have this straight. You are suggesting we do a set-up." O'Brien's normal scowl deepened, a sight not for anyone faint-hearted.

"It's a thought." I stretched and yawned. "Before we get to that, though, I have a question for the doctor, if you don't mind."

"Oh, please, be my guest." O'Brien's facetious acquiescence startled me.

"Dr. Rossiter, last night we first heard that Ash wasn't responding, then he was holding his own, and finally that he had a turn for the worse. Would you fill in a few details?"

"When we arrived here, I got the IV line started, ran some blood tests, and immediately started titrating insulin into his system. I had to go slowly, of course. At first, we got no response, but after an hour, he began to come around. At that point, I had him moved to this room." He regarded his patient. "You were touch and go for a while."

"I don't remember anything after asking Lauren for help onstage," Harper said. "Even now, I'm not sure I actually said it."

"You did," I assured him. "It was faint, but I caught it."

"Doctor, were you with him continuously?" O'Brien cut off the sentimentality.

"In the emergency room, yes. Once we got him up here, no."

"I apologize for going over this again, Doctor." I stifled another yawn, "Please feel free to correct me. Des Raphael called Becca from the party. She told him that you, Dr. Rossiter, had informed her that Ash was stable enough for her to leave. O'Brien drove Des over here to pick her up and brought them back to the party. Later, she got a call saying he had taken a turn for the worse. O'Brien raced back here with Becca, waited with her, and eventually took her to her hotel. Right?" I looked at the doctor and the policeman in turn.

"Accurate," O'Brien nodded. "You're frowning. Why?"

"We're missing something."

It took him a moment to catch up. "Blast it! You're right."

"I'm lost," Harper complained. "What's missing?"

"Ash, you went from *stable and holding his own* to *turn for the worse* in about an hour." I turned to Rossiter. "The reversal must have had a cause. Can you suggest any reason or cause for that reversal?"

"Truthfully, no. I was here when Miss Chernak was joined by Mr. Raphael. Mr. Harper was stable, showing signs of regaining consciousness. I had to leave while they were here, but they were getting ready to depart for the party. About an hour later I was notified by one of the nurses that Mr. Harper had stopped reacting to stimulus. I examined him, found he was definitely losing ground, and called Miss Chernak to come back. We basically had to start over." Rossiter shrugged. "Sorry I can't be of more help."

"That's fine, Doctor," O'Brien said.

"Thank you," I added. It never hurt to be polite, and O'Brien usually skipped it. "Doctor, could Ash have been given something to set back his recovery?"

"Such as?"

"What would throw him back into a major imbalance?" I eyed the two bottles on the IV pole, one of which was labeled D5W.

"You don't pull punches, do you?" Rossiter followed my gaze. "Yes, enough of a dextrose solution added into the IV would have done it. Easily, if your butler was adept at handling solutions and needles."

"Would you have suspected anything out of the ordinary?" O'Brien's question showed he had boarded my train of thought.

"No, I wouldn't have," Rossiter thoughtfully replied. "In fact, given that he didn't respond to the insulin shots in his dressing room, it would have been accepted as metabolic failure." His facial expression turned sheepish. "I'm ashamed to say this, but the air in the intravenous line would have also been accepted as heart failure."

Harper moaned. "Would someone please wake me up from this nightmare?"

"Ash, I know you're reeling from all this. Bear with us a bit longer? It's scary but I think you're going to be all right," I reassured the tenor.

Harper clung to my hand and squeezed harder.

"Um, Ash? I don't mind you holding my hand but please

watch the circulation."

"Oh, sorry." He eased up on it. "I'm trying to get used to the idea that the butler—and I like that by the way, somehow it makes it less personal—is trying to kill me." He looked at me and I nodded. "Now what?"

"Yes, now what?" O'Brien skeptically echoed. He emphasized his words by folding his arms across his chest.

"We know the butler is behind this, unless we want to explore the possibility that Ash has two people after him."

"God above! Please, no," groaned Harper. "One's bad enough."

"Didn't think so." I gave him what I hoped passed as an understanding and sympathetic smile. "I'm piqued. No, it's much stronger than that. I'm fuming, indignant, and resentful. I've been set up to take the fall for this. However, if Becca starts pushing, O'Brien will have to arrest me."

"What? Wait a minute. Becca is pushing for your arrest?" Harper stared steadily at O'Brien. "Is this true?"

"Unfortunately, yes," O'Brien said. "She knows about one vial although she doesn't know we found Kaye's fingerprints on it."

"Well, I'll stop her," Harper forcibly stated.

"No, you won't." I stood up and lightly kissed him on the forehead. "You won't even be able to talk to her. My dear friend, I regret to inform you that you are going to slip into a coma."

"I am?" Harper's eyes grew wide enough to meet over his nose and his mouth fell open. He turned to regard his doctor. "Am I?"

"It could happen, I suppose," Rossiter slowly said. "Assuming, of course, Captain O'Brien agrees."

O'Brien stared at me, astonished. "You're serious."

"We need time to figure out what's going on. I'm the patsy, so the butler is safe for the moment. Remember that Ash is, first and foremost, an actor and he's coming off a performance where he had to play dead. What more could we ask?"

"We could start by asking him if he can do this, and we could ask his doctor if he's medically up to this. We could also ask them both if they want to go along with this," O'Brien dryly suggested.

"I admit I'm scared," Harper immediately broke in, "but I'm more afraid of letting this hang over me. Patience is not one of my traits and I don't think I could bear the uncertainty. Whatever you want me to do, sir, I'll give it all I can."

"Captain, if I can assist you, I shall certainly do so," Rossiter assured O'Brien, "but please be aware that my first concern is for my patient's well-being." He shook his head apprehensively and added, "I think you should also know that I'm a terrible liar."

"Doc, if you want to sell a lie, hide it inside a truth and hesitate a lot," Harper advised. "In your profession, you might also want to sound sympathetic and sorry."

"Tips from a master," O'Brien grumbled. "Assuming you have a plan, Kaye, how do we proceed?"

"More of a suggestion than a plan. First, keep the giant on ice. That's essential."

"I can hold him for twenty-four hours without charging him, no problem."

"The butler will be wondering why Ash is still alive. In addition, he will probably wonder what happened to Stone. However, he can't start deep inquiries without tipping his hand. While he mulls that over, you can catch me doing something dastardly to enhance the frame around me."

"Another attempt?"

"Uh-huh. I can be caught with one of Ash's syringes and the bottle of insulin you took from his dressing room this morning. You, of course, arrest me."

"I don't like that," O'Brien flatly stated.

"Mr. Mallory won't either, but his actions will be convincing," I replied.

"Hold! You are saying I don't get to tell him about this in advance? *Cheese and rice!* Do you have any idea how vehement his response will be?" O'Brien's broad face turned red.

"His reactions have got to be real," I pointed out. "The butler is cunning and calculating. If he—or she—wasn't, we wouldn't be in this mess. One false step, and we lose him."

"What good does it do to have you under arrest?" Once more, O'Brien combed his hair with his fingers.

"We need time. This will buy it for us, enough time to arrange a few things."

"I'm confused," Rossiter interrupted. "How does your arrest buy us time?"

"The key is my supposed complicity. The butler has set me up as the stooge. If I'm under arrest, he should realize he can't make any major moves because it will put me in the clear."

"You have a very strange way of thinking, Auntie," Harper commented.

"You're just noticing that?" O'Brien sardonically queried. "Pay close attention. It's probably going to get a lot worse."

"What have you got in mind for me?" Rossiter asked with the barest hint of a smile.

"Doctor, I would suggest you stage a valiant battle for his life. Keep him on the knife-edge of dying." I grinned at Harper. "You're going to love doing this, but don't ham it."

"Kaye, this is not a game," O'Brien warned.

"Believe me, I am all too aware it's not a game. It's much more than a game—it's a war, declared by the butler. *We* are going to turn it into a war of nerves." I addressed the doctor. "Call Becca, encourage her to visit. Tell her it may help Ash if she's here. Be concerned about preparing her for the worst, should it happen. Imply there's little, if any, hope. Make her believe it may stretch out into days. This will put everything back to where it was last night." I shrugged. "You get the idea. Draw it out. Build suspense. Then leave him alone at some point."

"Wait a minute! I'll be a sitting, no, make that a comatose duck," Harper pointed out, "all by myself."

"No, you won't be alone," O'Brien said. "I'll assign a babysitter to hide in your closet. Or your bathroom, whichever affords the better view through a crack." He regarded me with a degree of acceptance which surprised me. "Nominations?"

"Walt Evans?"

He nodded.

I smiled at Harper. "Please don't fall asleep and start to snore. It would spoil the effect."

"I'll try not to."

"Pardon me for asking this, but I'm curious. Could this be construed as entrapment?" Rossiter asked.

"If I understand the concept of entrapment, it means a crime occurs after police intervention, which would not have happened otherwise. Correct?" I waited for O'Brien's nod of confirmation. He instructed me on the definition himself as part of my lessons on how to avoid lousing up his investigations. "We are trying to prevent the completion of a crime which has already been attempted. If we wear him down, the butler will jump when we play our final card."

"What's that?" Harper asked.

"We present an opportunity for the butler to finish off a comatose patient and catch him in the act," I said. "Ash, you're the bait. It's a trap, not entrapment."

"Failing that, if the butler thinks you are dying, and we play on his nerves enough, when you are presented as alive and well, he should crack," O'Brien stated.

"Yet you say I have a strange way of thinking," I commented while I checked the clock. "Captain, I need to get out of here. I'll wait an hour or so and come back on my own. If you can take me back to the house, I may be able to avoid explanations to the girls by simply being up before them."

"I'll send for Evans and Morse. Morse can take you back to the house while I brief Evans." O'Brien left the room.

"I'd like to run to the cafeteria and grab some breakfast," Rossiter told me. "You'll stay?"

"Doctor, you're catching on." I smiled. "Secrecy is essential to protect Ash. You and I are the only ones besides the police who know what's going on, and it needs to stay that way."

"Confidentiality is part of my job," he acknowledged with a nod. "It's crass to say this, but it's exciting to be a part of this—this—this—" He groped for a word.

"Sting operation?" Harper supplied.

"Close enough." I chuckled.

"Miss Kaye, are you part of the opera company or a member of the police department?"

"Heaven help us, neither. I joined the opera as a super for a class requirement. In real life, I'm a reporter for the *Daily Gleaner*. O'Brien puts up with me because he can't ignore me." I sighed. "By the way, my name is Lauren."

"You should consider acting," Rossiter told me. "You were wonderful as Lady Capulet."

"We've all said that," Harper agreed, grinning widely while I grimaced.

"Please, I have enough problems. I don't need more." I glanced at Harper. "You're not helping."

"Speaking of breakfast," Harper ignored me, "do I get any?"

"I'll bring something with me, but if you're on the verge of a coma, I can't send in a tray." Rossiter chuckled.

A thought struck me. "You can't send in nurses either. Do you have a nurse you can trust?"

"As a matter of fact, I do. I can hire her for special duty. I'll arrange it."

"Doctor, thank you for taking care of me," Harper sincerely told the physician. "Go get your breakfast. I'll take your leftovers." After Rossiter left, Harper turned to me and slyly smiled. "Alone, at last! Tell me about the party. How are Gianni and Susan? Was Laszlo in the audience? Did he like Carmella?"

"We missed you at the party." I described the champagne toasts and O'Brien's reactions. "Oh, and the Gianellos gave her a lovely gold note pendant engraved with *R&J* and the date for her debut."

"Gianni and Susan are terrific."

"Susan rakes me over live coals every time I set foot in the place. She seems to think I never eat." He opened his mouth to comment, but I glared, and he shut it again. Instead, he raised his eyebrows with another question. I did not need telepathy to guess what it was.

"Carmella got the scholarship."

"I was certain if Laszlo heard her, she'd get it."

"I was right about her being too nervous to audition. It was the first thing she said after Wendell announced it. Alan carefully explained it to her. She's convinced her mother won't believe it's true, so everyone was invited to a party this afternoon."

Harper reclined with a smile, which faded as a knock sounded on the door.

O'Brien entered with Evans. "We're all set. Morse is waiting in the lobby to take you back to Mallory. Where's Rossiter?"

"Breakfast. Also, he's going to arrange for a private nurse whom he trusts to take special care of Ash so we can keep traffic in and out of here limited to those we want." I nodded to Evans, who winked at me.

"Get out of here," O'Brien growled.

"Where will you be?"

"Around."

"Swell. You can be so helpful."

16

Morse, whose first name turned out to be Charlie, patiently waited by an unmarked car at the hospital entrance.

"Miss Kaye?" he asked politely. He held the door for me.

"I hope you don't mind if I fall asleep on the drive," I told him once I settled into the seat.

"It's a ten-minute trip." He smiled and started the engine.

"It's been that kind of a day."

I dozed but jerked to awareness when Mallory opened the car door. He studied me while he extended his hand to assist me getting out of the vehicle.

"I'm exhausted, and I look it," I said to cut off what he probably wanted to say. "Let's not discuss it."

"I wasn't going to say a word. How's Ash?"

"Holding on. He did recognize me." Barely in time, I remembered to hedge. *I hate lying to him, but Ash is right—you couch a false implication inside a truth, and it is believable.* "Is anyone else up?"

"Both girls are asleep. You could use a nap," he shrewdly observed

"What I could use is a day in a room with a guard at the door." I took his offered arm, thanked Morse, and we went inside.

Mrs. Fiddler's face reminded me of Susan's when I skipped eating in the restaurant for a month. "Can I get you something, Miss Lauren? Tea, perhaps?"

"Lovely, Mrs. Fiddler."

"Coffee for me. Would it be possible to get a light brunch for the two of us?"

"Certainly."

"Bring it to my office," Mallory told her, "and thank you."

Once inside the library, he guided me to one of the chairs at the table under the picture window.

I gratefully sank into the easy chair, and he sat in the other one.

"You were waiting for me out there."

"Danny called to say you were on your way back. Do I get to know what's going on? He told me to ask you."

I wanted to open up and dump the entire situation into his lap. His demeanor made the temptation, already strong, overwhelming. I found it difficult to resist the concern on his face. His electric blue eyes bored into me, like he could see clear through to my soul. He gazed at me expectantly, not pushing. He rarely demanded or shoved, one of the things I liked about him. *Nope, better to keep it covered.*

"I'm sorry, Mr. Mallory. At this point you're better off not knowing." I yawned and stretched.

"At least tell me that you and Danny are working together."

"We are. It's strange, in a way, too. I got the feeling once or twice he actually values my opinions and ideas." I rubbed my eyes with the heels of my palms.

Mallory chuckled. "I knew there would be periods of peace between clashes. You two are good for each other. I saw that the first time."

Mrs. Fiddler brought in the serving cart. A warmer with scrambled eggs, a rack of rye toast, the small pot of apple-cinnamon jelly, the coffee pot, and my tea pot graced it, along with the plates, mugs, and flatware.

"This looks terrific, Mrs. Fiddler. Thank you," I said with a weary smile.

"Let us know when the girls wake up," Mallory instructed her. "You can close the door."

"I'll be going back to the hospital later," I told him while we served ourselves. "O'Brien wants me there if and when Ash wakes up."

"What about Carmella's party this afternoon?"

"I won't be spending the day at the hospital, just part of it." I spread the jelly the housekeeper made from scratch on a piece of toast. "I wish we could find a motive behind all this. I'm not thrilled with the one Des is touting." I dug into my serving of eggs.

"I haven't been idle while you were gone," Mallory assured me. "I have some friends in high places in opera, as you know."

"You have friends in a lot of the high places, including one I never expected," I muttered, recalling my meeting with Carmella's uncle.

"I called a few and asked them to do some digging for me. I'm waiting on the results."

The phone rang twice. Mrs. Fiddler knocked on the door.

"Yes, Mrs. Fiddler?"

"The girls are awake, and Miss Lauren has a telephone call."

"Thank you. You can leave the door open, please." He motioned to me. "Take the call at my desk and try not to drool," he teased.

"Hello?" I settled myself in his chair and leaned back with a satisfied sigh. Mallory rolled his eyes.

"Lauren! It's Alan. Is there any word on Ash? I called the hospital and was told his condition is stable for the moment." Worry colored his expressive voice.

"Alan, I was up there this morning after he asked to see me. He knew who I was, but that was about it. Dr. Rossiter is watching him closely, and he promised he'd let me know if anything changed."

"Was Becca there?"

"Dr. Rossiter told me that he gave her a sedative to take last night when Danny O'Brien got her back to her hotel. She may not be up yet."

"Is Carmella's party still on for this afternoon?"

"As far as we know. Last night she mentioned her mother has planned it for between two and four this afternoon, so we should plan to get there around two o'clock."

"Can we see Ash?"

"I wouldn't push it right now. Dr. Rossiter said he's going to encourage Becca to visit, but I suspect he wouldn't recommend a crowd."

"Thanks for the update and call if you find out anything else. I'll see if I can track down Jeff and let him know. Des will probably find out from Becca. We'll see you at the party later."

"I wouldn't miss it. Tell Lisa I said hello." We hung up.

Mallory cocked his head to the side, listening. We heard the two girls come down the stairs, giggling.

"I think they're getting along," I observed. "They went to sleep giggling, and it sounds as if they woke up that way."

I perfectly timed my comment. My remark prompted a choking laugh, and most of the large swig of coffee Mallory took ended up in his napkin.

"Are you all right?" I asked, returning to my chair.

"Oh yes." His blue eyes twinkled with laughter. "Your timing makes Milton Berle seem like an amateur."

"Don't you start!" I warned.

"Start what?" His voice sounded totally innocent, although the mischievous glint in his eyes contradicted it.

"In the past few weeks, at least four people have seriously suggested I take up acting," I confessed. "It's ridiculous."

"Not entirely," he observed. "Here they come."

"Good morning, Daddy," Julie sang out and crossed the room to give him a hug. "Good grief, Lauren! When did you get up?" Her robe matched her pajamas, but then she had a talent for coordinating outfits.

"Trust me, you don't want to know. It was way too early."

"I haven't slept this late in a long time," Carmella commented. "It was wonderful! Mr. Mallory, thank you for having me." She wore a robe and nightgown set I recognized as one I helped Mallory pick out for Julie's birthday.

"Our pleasure," her host told her.

"Mr. Mallory," Mrs. Fiddler said from the doorway, "if you and Miss Lauren are finished in here, may I suggest the breakfast nook would be more appropriate for the girls' breakfast?"

"I think we've been politely told to move," Mallory observed while he watched as his housekeeper gathered up our plates and placed them back on the cart. "Shall we?"

"Mr. Mallory, may I use your telephone?" Carmella shyly asked. "I would like to call my mother."

"Go right ahead. When you're ready to leave, let me know and I'll take you over there." Mallory rose and motioned Julie and me out. "Come on, you two. Let's give her some privacy."

We settled in the breakfast room, a comfortable, sunny alcove off the kitchen. Carmella joined us, smiling.

"Mama is excited that the opera people are coming to my party," she told us. "I didn't tell her about the scholarship yet. She's cooking, and I didn't want to distract her. She'd be furious if she let something burn."

"What time does the party start?" Julie asked.

Mrs. Fiddler put filled plates in front of them.

"She told me she'd like people to start arriving around two." Carmella glanced at the kitchen clock. It lacked a few minutes to eleven-thirty. "Mr. Mallory, I should go to my apartment before I go home."

"I'll be happy to run you to your place and then on to your mother's." Mallory checked his watch. "I'm familiar with Merrick, but I need specifics. Taking you beforehand will help. We can leave shortly after you finish your breakfast." He turned to me. "Shall we drop you at the hospital?"

I did some fast calculations. "I can drive."

"I'd rather take you," he replied, and I bristled. "You're tired and it's going to be a long day," he quickly added.

I considered it. The telephone interrupted. Mrs. Fiddler picked it up.

"Mallory Res—" Her greeting halted. "Yes, sir. Hold the line, please." She extended the phone to me. "Captain O'Brien."

"Kaye." *Why not? He used it.*

"You're on, kid. Becca is awake. Raphael is taking her out to eat before they come up here."

"I'll be there before noon. Mr. Mallory seems to think I should be driven rather than drive."

"He's probably right," O'Brien conceded. "It would also remove the complication of what to do with your car later."

"True. I hadn't thought of that."

"Better yet, let me come get you. Be ready five minutes ago."

"Fine." We hung up. "O'Brien wants me at the hospital badly enough to come get me," I announced. "He'll be here five minutes ago."

"That sounds like him." Mallory chuckled. "Can we do anything for you?"

"Let me have some phone numbers in case I have to reach someone." I ran to the office and grabbed my shoulder bag. Carmella wrote her mother's number in my notebook. I hurriedly closed it and stashed it in my bag.

When O'Brien arrived, Mallory walked me out to the car.

"I don't know what you're up to, but be careful," he told me. He opened the door for me and leaned in for a last word. "Danny, call me if she needs anything. Understood?"

Hearing the tone Mallory used, I half expected O'Brien to salute him. A curt nod comprised his reply. However, as we left the curved driveway, O'Brien muttered something under his breath.

"Sorry, I didn't catch that," I told him.

"You weren't meant to."

I let it drop. "Is the nurse in place?" I asked instead.

"Yes, and she's been briefed. She also has a syringe loaded with sterile water for you."

"How's Ash?"

"Getting restless. I'm about ready to suggest he be put back into the coma." O'Brien briefly glanced at me. "Thank you for not spilling this to Robert."

"How did you know?"

"Simple deduction. The roof is still on the mansion. Let's go over the program."

"I give the shot of water into the IV line. You arrest me. Ash gets worse. Becca should be called to his bedside. Dr. Rossiter can give another shot of water into the line."

"So, we don't give Ash anything real?"

"Absolutely not! Ash doesn't respond. We arrange for Ash to be alone and wait to see what happens."

"What if nothing does?"

"We go to Plan B."

"Which is?"

"He dies after we leave his grieving wife alone with him."

"She won't buy that. She's not stupid and he'll be breathing."

"Of course, he'll be breathing." I snickered. "Trust me, though. I doubt if she will get that close, and if she does, she won't see it. I stood at the bier onstage, leaning over him, and *I* couldn't see it. He's made it an art."

"If you say so."

"Even unconscious, it was hard to tell, believe me."

"You think Rebecca Chernak is the butler."

"She had the best access to Ash's medication."

"Kaye, she wasn't even supposed to be here. She was only called in when the other gal fell ill."

"That's one thing I keep tripping over. Also, I saw Ash wobble several times before Becca arrived on the scene. However, he brought at least three vials of insulin with him that we know of, probably more. Maybe the three we have were doctored before he left the city." A comment of Carmella's replayed in my mind. "One thing Carmella told me is guest professionals usually aren't a part of the whole rehearsal process. Ash and company were with us the entire time, and they stayed at the hotel out here rather than going back to the city every day.

Who knows how many vials he initially brought with him?"

"When did you start to notice his decline?"

"It started so gradually it's hard to say. Bear in mind, I didn't know him at all when this began. I can't peg it to a specific day. He was energetic when we met, but he started acting noticeably tired about a month ago. It's been steadily getting worse since then."

O'Brien nodded. "Let's change tacks. Who else has a motive?"

"That's another stumbling block." I sighed. "Any chance of cracking the giant clam you took into custody?"

"I've got one of my best men working on him. So far, he's breathing through his nose and making faces at us."

"I'd give a box of Red Rose teabags to know who hired him."

"A whole box? For you that's a major bribe. I'm waiting to see if anyone inquires as to his whereabouts, but he's a night orderly so he may not have been missed yet. Anything else?"

"Mr. Mallory has friends nosing around opera circles to see if there are any closets with a skeleton or two of motive."

"I hope he turns up something." A deep sigh underscored his grimace. "I'm out of my depth with these people. They move in a different world, much more rarified."

"I know what you mean. I'm trying to convince myself I was on that stage. I told David Peterman I got signatures on my program so I could prove to myself it really happened."

"You did well. I know Robert's proud of you."

"I'd like to think so." I put my head back on the seat. "By the way, Norm Brier is going to speak to my advisor and the dean on Monday and report I fulfilled my requirement. He's the supervising professor, and he's giving me an A."

"Not an A-plus?"

"I don't think it works that way." I sighed and turned my head to face him. "Do me a favor?"

"I'll consider it."

"When you arrest me, don't cuff me."

"I wasn't planning to. I also think we should stay at the hospital rather than going to the station. We need to be available."

"I can agree with that. You might even decide to let Becca see me after my arrest."

"I don't want any fist fights."

"With Becca it's more likely to be scratching and biting, but I doubt it. She's one cool customer."

"If she's involved, I hope we can crack that shell, or this isn't going to work." O'Brien reached into his pocket and handed me a familiar paper bag. "You should have this on you."

I dropped it into my satchel.

Staged for Death

17

All players, fully briefed with assigned places and roles, stood ready fifteen minutes later. The nurse, Anne Gerard, looked impeccable. In her cap, crisp white uniform, and white stockings and shoes, she appeared professional and unflappable. Her brown hair was correctly tucked in a bun under her cap.

"Let me make sure I have this correct. I'm to answer the phone and door, screen visitors, and guard my patient until I'm told otherwise," Anne recounted.

"Yes." O'Brien loved communicating in monosyllables.

The nurse regarded her patient, who reclined on his pillows with a wide grin. "I admit I'm an opera buff. Having Ashton Harper as my charge is a real treat."

"Wait until you have to control him," O'Brien cautioned with a smirk.

I audibly snickered while she settled into her chair on the far side of the bed with a book.

"Not that I'm going to be able to concentrate on a book. I've got a front row seat in a police investigation, I'm sitting with someone I've seen onstage, and I'm getting paid to be here." The nurse chuckled, her blue eyes twinkling. "I love it! Let me know when I need to leave."

Evans, not nearly as thrilled at spending his time in a bathroom, confided his gratitude about one aspect of his assignment to me while we checked his view.

"I may ask Miss Gerard out when this is over," he told me.

"That would be nice. She's a wonderfully capable nurse,

according to Dr. Rossiter."

The syringe filled with sterile water rested in my jacket pocket. That vial resided in Miss Gerard's keeping since it would not do to leave it lying around.

O'Brien agreed to let me know when Becca arrived at the hospital. His job consisted of escorting her to the room. Once she caught me in the act of injecting the fluid, he would place me under arrest. Harper, under orders to lie back and be semi-conscious to all visitors except me, meekly acquiesced to his part. I reflected that the plan as sketched out was thorough yet left room for any improvisation we needed to make on the fly.

Harper and I chatted quietly until a knock sounded on the door. I sat in a chair near the head of the bed while he assumed his pose. Anne opened the door at my nod and blocked the entrance. From that position, her line of sight included me, without turning her head.

"May I come in?" a male voice asked. "I'm Jeff Sebring, a friend of Mr. Harper's from the opera company."

I nodded. She stood back and allowed Sebring to enter.

"Lauren? I thought Becca would be here." He gave my shoulder a squeeze. "I thought I'd drop by before I grabbed some breakfast. How's he doing?"

"He's in and out of consciousness," I somberly reported. "Honestly, I keep hoping he'll sit up and call me Auntie and ask me to join him at Wilfrid's."

The baritone chuckled. "That's our boy." He glanced at Anne Gerard. "A private nurse?"

"Dr. Rossiter felt one was necessary since Ash's condition has been fluctuating so badly," I improvised. "The floor staff can't be here all the time, and so far, he's been through two crises."

"I'm glad someone is thinking," he commented, "and Ash can afford it."

"I didn't realize you guys were so well-paid."

"We're not. Ash was born into money."

"Oh? I didn't know." *This could make a motive easier to find.*

"Don't misunderstand," he said. "Ash worked his way up the ladder like the rest of us, starting in the chorus and working his tail off to win featured parts. He moved up to leads in the past couple of years. Tenors, really good ones, are rare." He gazed sadly down at his friend. "He's still working up to his peak. You probably don't know he had his choice of roles in this production."

"No, I didn't. You mean he chose to play Tybalt?"

Sebring nodded. "You know we all have established roles for these productions."

"Carmella told me that," I acknowledged.

"Ash performs both Tybalt and Romeo. He could have had either role in this show. He wanted to give Wendell a break to play a romantic lead, so he took Tybalt. He joked it's more fun to get skewered than die by poisoning, but the gesture was typical of him."

"How long have you been with the company?"

"A little over four years. Ash saw me in a community theater musical in Boston and brought me down to New York. I was pretty green, all voice with little acting skill. He encouraged me to drop popular music and go into opera training. He helped me adjust to life in the big city, gave me tips on how to emote, found me an acting coach, that sort of thing. Ash has been much more than a friend. He's my mentor and teacher."

"Alan told me he has a good eye for talent," I admitted. "Of course, I haven't known him long. I do know he pushed to get Carmella her role when the other girl dropped it and made sure she was heard by your director. He also helped the Gianellos start their restaurant."

"I've been hearing about Susan's Place for years but last night was the first time I've been there." Sebring smiled. "I guarantee it won't be the last. I can't understand why Becca didn't want him to do it."

"She seems to be hard to get to know. How long have they

been married?"

"Almost four years, although they dated for about two years before that. I've always thought that was odd, too. Becca was seeing both Ash and Des, and we all thought she'd marry Des."

Harper moaned softly and his feet moved. Anne jumped up, gently held his wrist, and took a pulse, playing her part exactly the way O'Brien instructed.

"You might try talking to him," she told me.

"Ash?" I leaned in and pitched my voice low.

"Becca?" His faint voice quavered.

"Ash, it's Lauren. Jeff is here, too."

"L-Lauren? Wh-what's—" His eyes fluttered open.

"You're in the hospital, buddy," Sebring told him, reaching down to pat his shoulder. "How do you feel?"

"Weak. Tired." He struggled to speak. "Jeff. Laszlo—did he see—Carmella?"

"Oh, yes! He and Joseph were both in the audience. Laszlo is quite impressed with your latest find." Sebring leaned over the bed, one hand on the back of my chair. "Ash, she's got the scholarship. Laszlo called the party and offered it as soon as he and Joseph had talked it over."

Harper faintly smiled. "She's—a—good—kid."

"We're all going to take care of her," Sebring replied. "She's going to be something very special."

"She already—is—" Harper's voice dropped off.

"He's fading out again," I told Sebring, turning to look up at him. "We'd better not tire him too much."

I rose and we moved away from the bed. Anne straightened out her patient's covers before she sat down on the far side of the bed and picked up her book.

"Lauren, what time is Carmella's party?"

"Her mother wants us there around two."

"Alan and Lisa are going to take Emilie, Wendell, and me. Do you need a ride?"

"No, I'll either drive or Mr. Mallory will take me over there with his daughter." I smiled. "Carmella and Julie are fast becoming good friends. I think they giggled half the night."

"Mallory's a great guy, and his daughter is a real doll. Carmella needed to unwind, and it sounds like they had a good time." Sebring glanced back at the bed when Harper softly moaned again. "Have you eaten?"

"I had breakfast with Julie and Carmella," I replied. *A lie within a truth.*

"Oh." The baritone sounded genuinely disappointed. "I was going to ask you to join me. You could have coffee or something. I'd really appreciate the company."

"Thank you for the invitation, Jeff. Maybe some other time? I think I'll stay here for a while. When he does come around, it seems to help if someone he knows is with him. Your timing was terrific." I smiled. "Let me have a rain check."

"No problem." Sebring glanced back at the bed again. "It hurts to see him like this. He's been a wonderful friend. I'm glad I got to talk to him. I hope it helped." He gave me a quick hug. "See you at the party!"

"I'll be there," I assured him. He left and I closed the door.

The nurse stood at the bedside, staring open-mouthed at her patient.

Harper sat up and folded his legs Indian-style. He impishly grinned at her.

"Please, Miss Gerard, whatever you do, don't tell him he's good at this," I cautioned with a smile of my own. "We'll never hear the end of it."

"Well? Was I okay?" he demanded of me.

"I was afraid you'd overdo it, but your performance was acceptable."

"Like your performance last night was acceptable, I suppose," he grumbled.

I rolled my eyes. "Ash, I told O'Brien you are an actor above everything else."

"Guilty. Like most of my fellows, I'm always insecure about

my performances," he lightly retorted. "You asked Bill about how you were doing, after all."

"Truce! You should have known by the expression on Miss Gerard's face that you did well above her expectations, and she's a nurse."

"I figured Becca would be here by now," he groused. "Jeff was a good test, though. Speaking of Jeff, I think he feels like a bit of a fifth wheel. Emilie and Wendell seem to be hitting it off. Maybe you should have gone with him."

"I thought he was being polite. Perhaps I should have, but you realize I'm going to be busy." I frowned. "Jeff has always been nice to me. However, I'm not opera, and I'm not interested in any relationships. Between work and school, I haven't got the time."

"Oh, Auntie, if you would give me one day to get past your defenses, we could be great together." Harper stretched out again with his eyes closed and a sly smile formed on his handsome face.

I shook my head in resignation. The nurse laughed.

"Miss Gerard, you'll find Ash comes on like a locomotive at full steam," I told her. "You will shortly meet his wife."

"Make it Anne," she suggested. "This is way more fun that my usual assignments. I'm enjoying it!"

"I need to get up," Harper informed us. "Bathroom time."

"You can't get out of bed." Anne handed him the urinal. "Use this."

He opened his mouth to protest.

"Ash," I snapped out in low tones, "we can't risk someone coming in here while you're up and in the bathroom."

"You're worse than a staging director," he complained. After wiggling around under the covers, he handed the container back to Anne and watched while she checked his sugar levels.

"So far so good," she reported. "No wonder you're feeling restless."

Evans vacated the bathroom to give her room to work. "This is so fascinating," he commented with a heavy dose of irony. He stretched. "I'm glad I can snatch a break. Just so you'll know, I can see and hear anything around the bed. Bye for now," he drawled. He disappeared back to his post once the nurse finished.

"I think I ought to tell you that O'Brien is considering having Dr. Rossiter sedate you," I informed Harper. "Don't push your luck."

The room phone rang. Following O'Brien's instructions, Anne answered it.

"Room 405. May I help you?" She listened for a moment before hanging up. "That was Captain O'Brien. Rebecca Chernak and Desmond Raphael have arrived. He and Dr. Rossiter will be coming up with them. He suggests you postpone your action for the moment."

"Did he give a reason?" I glanced at the clock; it showed twelve twenty-five.

"He told me to tell you to trust him."

"Swell," I muttered. "Ash, your acid test is about to walk in the door." He drooped appropriately on his bed. I moved around and joined Anne on the far side of it. She stood level with his chest while I stayed close to the foot.

A knock sounded and the door opened with no other warning. Dr. Rossiter ushered in Becca and Raphael. Becca spotted me while she advanced toward the bed. Rossiter took up a position near me at the foot of it. O'Brien sidled into the room and stood where he could keep an eye on Becca. A flicker of emotion crossed her impeccably groomed face. From where I stood, it seemed to be contempt. I did not know quite what I expected from her.

"You must be Miss Gerard, the nurse Dr. Rossiter recommended we hire," Becca coolly greeted her. She totally ignored me; her attitude indicated I no longer existed. *Maybe I should be grateful.*

"Yes, Miss Chernak," Anne replied. She went around the bed and drew the chair up near Harper's head for the singer and resumed her place with me.

Becca, beautifully dressed and every inch the opera diva,

wore a navy-blue silk suit, pale blue blouse, dark navy gloves, and small hat with a veil that came down to her forehead. She perched on the edge of the seat and held her navy blue clutch purse in her lap. Raphael stayed on his feet behind her. "Ash? It's Becca."

Harper moaned, barely moving his head.

Becca gasped. "Ash? Des is here with me." She turned toward Raphael with an imploring expression.

"Ash? How are you doing?" the bass asked and put his hand on Becca's shoulder. She reached up and clasped it, clinging to it.

Harper took in a deep, slow breath, almost shuddering at one point. O'Brien tensed and shot a quick, questioning glance at me. I slowly lowered and raised one eyelid; he gave me the tiniest nod.

"B-B-ecca?" Harper's eyes fluttered open briefly and he tried to try to focus on her face. His left hand lifted a bit then fell back to the bed.

"Yes, Ash, it's me." She bent closer to him. She took her hand from Raphael and almost touched her husband's face; her hand fell back in her lap before she made the contact.

"Sorry—so much trouble—" Harper's faint voice was barely audible to me.

"Ash, you were wonderful as Tybalt!" Becca told him, her expression sincere. "I think it was the best performance I've ever heard you give."

"You–w—w—were there?" Harper struggled to open his eyes.

"Of course, I was." She turned to the physician. "You mean he doesn't remember I was there? Or here last night?" She reached up and clutched Raphael's hand again. "Oh, God!" she moaned. "This is unbearable. Oh, God!"

"It's hard to tell, Miss Chernak. He's not fully conscious, as you can see."

"Doctor, will he pull through?" Raphael asked. He freed his

hand from Becca's grasp and put his arm around her shoulders. She leaned back against him.

"It's going to depend upon the next few hours." Rossiter's voice and attitude held concern.

"Des?" Harper weakly asked. His eyes opened, and he tried to smile.

"Right here. How are you feeling?"

"I'm not sure—weak. What happened?" Harper tried to sit up. Anne immediately moved forward and gently eased him back onto his pillows.

"Please, lie quietly and save your strength," she told her patient in a low, professional voice. "Don't try to sit up."

"You collapsed on stage after the duel with Wendell," Raphael told the tenor. "Don't you remember?"

"I–I—tried to tell Lauren to—to keep going—" His weak voice trailed off.

"We finished the performance, Ash, just as you asked."

"Lauren? She—she—"

"Lauren was a real trooper, Ash." Raphael glanced at me and smiled. "She told us to carry on, and we all did."

"Didn't want to spoil—" His voice faded again.

"Ash!" Becca put some force behind his name, her voice tinged with alarm. She raised her hand to touch him, but once more, it fell back.

"Glad—you're here." His eyes closed. "I hope—" His body sagged and relaxed.

"Doctor?" Becca's voice held a note of panic. *"Doctor! Please?"*

Rossiter moved past them and checked his patient. "He may be losing consciousness again," the doctor told them. "He's been doing this most of the day."

"I can't bear to see him like this," Becca whined. "Des, please, take me out of here," she pleaded, her voice cracking. Her face contorted. "I can't stand this," she added in quavering tones bordering on hysterics. "Please?"

"Mr. Raphael, why don't you take Miss Chernak to the visitor's lounge? It's down the hall on the right. I want to examine Mr. Harper, and I'll join you in a few moments."

"Come on, Becca, we'll wait for Dr. Rossiter in the lounge." Raphael helped her stand and put his arm around her waist and supported her. She clung to him as he escorted her to the door. Neither one looked back.

O'Brien opened it for the couple and watched as they went down the hall. Once satisfied they were out of earshot, he closed the door.

"Ash, that was masterful," the police captain told him.

"I'm glad I knew it was an act," agreed the physician.

Evans poked his head out of the bathroom. "I'd like to I add my congratulations."

Harper grinned at me. "At least *some* people appreciate acting talent when they see it."

"Becca has trouble dealing with sick people, doesn't she," I pondered aloud, ignoring the singer's jibe.

"She can't stand being in the same room with someone who is ill," Harper admitted. "She's always had trouble with illness of any kind. I love her, but she shies away from me if I'm having a bad day. I do all my shots in the bathroom. It bothers her to see me give myself an injection."

I suppressed a shudder and sternly reminded myself to keep my mouth shut. The more I learned about Becca, the harder that became.

"Anne, let me see his latest reading," Rossiter requested. He studied the chart she handed him. "Ash, you're doing very well."

"Can I get out of here?"

"No," O'Brien and I strongly stated in unison.

Harper raised both hands in a gesture of surrender. "It was just a thought."

"Doctor, I'd like you to report that his condition is stable for the moment while you emphasize the notion that the least little thing could send him back into a crisis," O'Brien suggested as guidelines. "Stress the thought that you consider these moments of consciousness to be a hopeful sign."

"Hiding the lie within truths." The physician's face clouded. "I'd prefer to be honest."

"Doctor, is Ash's condition stable?" I blandly inquired. "Aren't his moments of consciousness a good sign?"

"Yes, to both," Rossiter replied, frowning, "of course." The point I made clicked, and he smiled. "Oh! I see. Of course. I'm not really lying."

"You're simply allowing them to infer from your words what they think they discerned here in the room," I asserted.

"She likes to prove she's a writer," O'Brien acerbically commented. "Anyone else would have said you tell them a few facts and let them form their own conclusions."

Anne snickered and winked at me. I grinned back.

"Dr. Rossiter, when can I have another snack?" demanded Harper. "Your leftovers were okay, but I'm hungry. This," he rattled the IV bottles, "doesn't cut it."

"I'll see you get something as soon as we can." Rossiter smiled at him. "Your wife was right about one thing. Your performance last night was superb."

"Thank you." Harper dipped his head.

"Is there anything else you want me to tell the lady?" Rossiter asked O'Brien.

"Not at this point." O'Brien's gaze rested on me for a moment and returned to Rossiter. "I'd like to talk with your nurse for a moment. You start your conference with Becca. I'll follow you shortly, since I also want a chat with her."

Rossiter nodded and left.

"Miss Gerard, I have some instructions for you," O'Brien announced. He quickly outlined what he wanted her to do. "When the time comes, yell for me by name."

"I want you both to notice he didn't tell the doctor what we are doing," I pointed out.

"I'm merely insuring the doctor's reactions will be genuine,"

O'Brien responded, with a low-end glare.

"Yet he tells me with a straight face that *my* mind is devious," I protested to Harper. "Anne, I would suggest you inform me you'll be gone about five minutes."

"Be sure to come back in two," added O'Brien.

"Understood." Anne gazed at each of us in turn. "Are these two like this all the time?" she asked the tenor.

"I met them recently, but I'd be willing to guess yes. The good news is they're on my side." Harper grinned at me again. "Lauren tore into me once, using words I had to look up in a dictionary. Once was enough. I don't think I'd want either of them as an enemy."

"That sounds like an interesting anecdote, but I agree about keeping them friendly," Anne replied.

"If you people are finished chit-chatting, I'll wander down to the conference." O'Brien stated, unperturbed and at ease. "I'm going to enjoy arresting you," he said as he passed by me.

"Don't count on ever being able to do it again," I countered as he reached the door.

He growled and shut the door, this time with him outside.

"Let's give him a couple of minutes to get down there and sit," I suggested. "Walt? Are you up to this?"

His head emerged from his hidey-hole. "Count on it. I'm not sure why you asked for me, but I'm glad you did."

"You'll be needed later. Anne cannot be expected to go without coffee forever. There's bound to be a scuffle. Whatever happens, don't react with Becca and Des in the room."

"Right. Before I vanish, Mr. Harper, I want you to know my parents were in the audience last night, and they told me the production was wonderful." He pulled the door to its slightly open position.

"It sounds like I missed a great show last night," Anne commented. "I had tickets, but I was called to work and gave them away."

"The auditorium was sold out," Harper proudly informed her.

"It was a terrific audience."

"It's been a unique experience for me," I confessed.

"One of the students in the production is going to be a major opera star within six years," Harper added. He tapped my hand. "Speaking of Carmella. What's this about a party this afternoon?"

"Her mother is having a celebration for her," I explained. "Carmella invited all of us last night. She wanted the cast there because she's afraid her mother won't believe her about the scholarship. The party should start in a little over an hour."

"Wish I could be there." He sighed, his expression wistful. "After all, the scholarship was my idea."

"Carmella knows you initiated it, don't worry." I grew serious. "Ash, listen to me," I ordered. I waited until his eyes found mine. "Once you are comatose, things are going to start jumping. O'Brien is going to arrest me, and you can't react. Got that?"

"I don't like it."

"Neither of us is thrilled, but that's the plan." I insisted. "You could blow the whole operation if you react. Ash, will you do this?"

"Lauren, I promise, I'll be good. Comatose?"

"For now. You may have to die later, but you'll be informed of when and in front of whom." I regarded him with a smile. "This is the most important role you've ever played."

"Got it." He grinned at me and collapsed into his pillows. One eye opened as he addressed his nurse. "Oh, Miss Anne? While I'm out of it, be careful."

"Careful?" she questioned. Her eyebrows drew tight, wrinkling her forehead. "Forgive me, but I'm puzzled. I'm always careful with my patients."

"I mean if you have to move me or something like that. I'm extremely ticklish. I don't know if I can ignore being tickled and stay comatose or dead." He winked at her before lying inert.

"Oh, bother! I'm glad he remembered that. He's right. It only takes a tiny touch to set him off," I confirmed with a sigh of relief. "That could have bollixed up everything. Anne, I think it's about time for you to tell me you've got to run an errand at the nurses' station." The clock showed fifteen minutes shy of one o'clock.

Anne moved to the doorway. "Thank you," she called back into the room. "I should be about five minutes."

"She's good," Harper muttered, eyes closed. "By the way, Auntie, what's in that syringe?"

"Sterile water. Now be quiet and don't make me wish it was a sedative."

I kept an eye on the large timepiece on the wall, the syringe in my hand. At the minute mark, I pulled the cap off, inserted it into the piggyback port in the tubing, and slowly pushed the plunger.

Right on cue, Anne walked in on me.

"That didn't take as long as I thought—" She broke off to take a deep breath. "*What are you doing? Get away from him!*" she shrieked before she yelled at the top of her lungs, "*CAPTAIN O'BRIEN!*"

She and I struggled for the few moments it took O'Brien to come charging down the hall. Rossiter and Raphael were close behind him.

"*KAYE!*" O'Brien roared. He grabbed both my arms from behind. The move pinned my back to his chest. "Miss Gerard! Get the syringe!"

"It's empty," Anne reported. She bit her lip as she pulled it out of the tubing and showed it to him.

"This could have been anything," Rossiter declared, taking it from her. He began to check Harper. He pinched Ash's arm and got no response. "He's going deeper," he announced. He and Anne proceeded to monitor vital signs and do a neurological check.

"Lauren! What's going on?" Raphael demanded. "What did she do?" he asked the nurse.

"Miss Gerard? What happened?" O'Brien maintained a

forceful grasp on me while I squirmed.

"I asked Miss Kaye if she would stay with Mr. Harper while I ran down to the nurses' station to get some paperwork. I told her I'd be gone for about five minutes, but it didn't take that long. I got back here and saw her injecting fluid into the intravenous line."

"It's a good thing you came in when you did," Rossiter chimed in while he worked. "At least we know something went into the line." He turned to O'Brien. "I need to know what was in here. Can you get it analyzed?" He handed over the syringe. "The faster the better."

"Certainly," O'Brien agreed. With one hand clamped on my arm, he used his other one to snap open a handkerchief. Rossiter carefully wrapped the syringe, and O'Brien pocketed it.

"Well, well, well," Becca stated quietly from the doorway. "I knew it. Captain, I told you she had done it." A satisfied, smug smile formed on her face. If her expression got any more smug, I would have broken free from O'Brien and slapped her.

"It seems you may have been correct, Miss Chernak," he replied, formal and all business. "Lauren Kaye, I am taking you into custody."

"You don't know what was in the syringe," I spat at him. I tried hard to appear guilty. "As the doctor said, it could have been anything. For all you know it could have been water!" *Bother! If I'm not careful, he'll suggest acting lessons!*

"Don't give me that crap," he snapped back. He patted me down, and finding nothing, pulled my bag open. "And what, pray tell, is this?" He lifted out the bottle of insulin. "Since when do you use insulin?"

"I have no idea how that came into my possession," I countered. "Anyone could have planted it on me at any time."

"You're lucky. I could charge you with attempted murder. Right now, I'll settle for taking you into custody as a material witness, pending results of analysis on the syringe and testing for prints on the bottle. You are under arrest."

Staged for Death

18

We made a quick trip to the station. He did not book me, although we agreed to let our cast of characters assume it had been done. We slipped into the rear entrance of the facility and occupied a small conference room. Once a patient room about four doors down from where Harper lay comatose, the hospital rebuilt it after a broken pipe flooded it. It served as a more secluded meeting place for staff conferences than the inadequate cubbyhole behind the nurses' station. The nursing supervisor on duty offered it to O'Brien when he requested someplace he could use as on-site headquarters.

A long conference-style table with a telephone, several padded conference chairs, and a water cooler made up the simple furnishings. A second table provided a spot for a coffee pot and paper cup service. At the moment, there was only a stack of cups.

I helped myself to a cup of water and sat down. O'Brien did the same and stared at me from across the table. I thought about twiddling my thumbs but decided not to aggravate him.

"I can't get over how good Harper is," O'Brien volunteered. "I swear he literally sank deeper into the bedclothes as we were leaving the room."

"He probably did," I agreed. "I told you if he has to die, you could stand a foot away from him and not realize he was breathing."

"So, are we any further along than we were before you played Florence Nightingale from Hades?"

"I think I am," I confessed. "I admit I'm not sure what to do about it."

"You are? Would you care to let me in on it? Just do me a favor and don't tell me I saw what you saw," he tartly added. "We've had that conversation. More than once."

"Becca isn't the butler."

"Explain." Succinct as always, O'Brien rarely wasted breath on unnecessary words.

"Becca wouldn't even touch Ash, either in the dressing room last night or here today. Can you see her dealing with syringes and vials?"

"Frankly, no."

"She may not be completely in the clear," I frowned. "I mean, we have no idea who hired the goon. I can't see her tampering with the insulin or the IV. The picture does not focus."

"Who put the insulin in your costume pocket?"

"There was a lot of traffic in and out of Ash's dressing room last night. I noticed a bottle was missing after Ash was taken out on the stretcher because I had seen two bottles when I drew the shot for the doctor. I also noticed the refrigerator door slightly ajar. Twice." I sighed. "Anyone could have removed the bottle, put it in the paper bag, and tucked it into my skirt. Becca was standing next to me in front of the refrigerator while Dr. Rossiter was attending Ash. Des walked me up the stairs to the stage. Let's face it. Even you could have done it."

"Me?"

"Sure. It's not even a stretch of opportunity. You and Mr. Mallory were in the dressing room after I left to go back onstage. You could have taken the vial out then. You both walked me up the stairs before curtain calls. Remember, I was still in costume."

"I see what you mean. I could have, or Robert could have. Okay, we scrap opportunity for the moment and get back to motive. Anything new?"

"I have a little more, but I warn you, the overall picture remains murky. I did get a few facts from Jeff Sebring which might help." I related what the baritone told me.

"Interesting," he observed. "Money. Always a good motive. If Harper dies, Becca inherits. I think we can assume Des Raphael is set to step in and claim her."

"I'm struggling not to infer more than surface traits based on what I've seen. She hates illness but married a man who has a chronic disease. I think that's the one thing pricking at me the most. If she knew about it from the first, and it bothers her, why in heaven's name did she do it?"

"You told me Robert is doing some digging. I wonder if he has come up with anything?"

"I have a feeling we are going to find out in the next half hour or so." I pointed at the clock. "Carmella's party starts in forty-five minutes. I'm not there, and he's going to want to know why. Probably soon. You know him. What do you think he'll do?"

"When he hears I've taken you in as a material witness, he'll come out swinging, at least figuratively, at me."

"If he makes it literal, whom do I back with my hard-earned money?"

He ignored my crack. "With luck, he'll call over here first."

"I'm going to catch it for not calling him from the station." I sighed. "I wonder how Dr. Rossiter is doing."

"Let's ask." He pulled the telephone toward him and got connected to the sickroom. After he asked the initial question, I listened to a series of grunts which ended with, "When you have a moment, Doctor, I'd appreciate a consultation. I'm in the conference room down the hall." O'Brien hung up. "Becca is doing her wifely duty, sitting at his bedside. Obviously, Rossiter couldn't say much with her in the room, but he'll come down here when he can."

"We could place bets on how long Becca stays at Ash's bedside."

"You do seem determined to risk your lucre today. Another thought. I could pull her out and have her confront you." He surprised me with an impish grin. "Either one could be fun."

"I suppose." I yawned. "The nagging question remains. Why

is our butler determined to kill Ash Harper?"

"We have the old standbys. Money and jealousy."

"Jealous of what? His flirting? His singing? I don't think this is a re-run of the chicanery we dealt with at the resort," I said, referring to the incidents which first drew us together. I shook my head. "We're dancing in the dark."

"Could it be a matter of wanting him out of the way?"

"Out of the way, for instance, like if he's gone, it leaves room for someone or something else?"

"When you put it that way it makes more sense, yet it's not precisely jealousy." O'Brien sighed. "Yes. If Ash Harper dies, who benefits and how? Wife becomes widow, inherits money, possibly the beneficiary of a life insurance policy, and so forth. We need more to go on."

I pondered the choices. A knock sounded on the door.

"Is it legally acceptable for me to be here?"

O'Brien nodded "Come in."

Dr. Rossiter joined us. "I'm here to report—"

The phone rang, interrupting him.

"O'Brien." The police captain listened and thanked the person on the other end as if he meant it. "You were saying, Doctor?"

"I walked Miss Chernak to the front entrance and put her in a cab to go back to her hotel. Raphael is waiting for her there. Ash is in his room with my nurse and your man."

"Medically, how is he?"

"He's fine. If he wasn't comatose, I'd send him home," the physician stated.

I snickered. The expression on his face darkened and I immediately apologized. "Sorry, Doctor. I'm not laughing at you, I promise. Your statement, taken at face value, sounded absurd."

"You're entirely correct," he conceded, with a wry grin. "However, I meant every word of it. Anne has her hands full keeping him in bed."

O'Brien, who also cracked a smile, sobered. "We need to ask

him a few questions."

"Agreed. Who was on the phone?" Cooperation between us tended to be rare. I took advantage of it while I could, curious to see how long he allowed it.

"One of my men. I'm keeping an eye on some of our players. If this goes sour, I want to know where everyone is."

"No chances again. That's comforting. When you talk to Ash, do I get to come with you?"

"You're my prisoner. You go where I tell you to go." O'Brien leered, then rose and indicated the door. "Shall we?"

The phone rang again. He reached across the table and grabbed the receiver.

"O'Brien." He immediately sat down in the nearest chair with a hard thump. "I—" His face slowly turned beet red. He repeatedly tried breaking into the conversation with no success. "Will you—Just a—just a min—will you—wait a—min—*Wait!*" he roared into the handset.

"Lauren, what's going on?" Rossiter asked in a whisper while O'Brien's sputtering continued.

"You haven't met him officially, but I'd wager a year of my salary Robert Mallory is on the other end of the line," I quietly replied. "From the sounds we're hearing I would also guess he found out I've been taken in as a material witness."

"*HOLD!*" O'Brien finally bawled into the phone. "She's perfectly all right. She's a material witness. The case is *not* closed! I'm—" He listened some more while he ran his fingers through his hair. "I said I'd let you know when she needs a lawyer. She hasn't officially been charged with anything. I want—" O'Brien glowered at the phone in his hand before he banged it down on its cradle.

"Apparently he doesn't care what you want," I observed. "Mr. Mallory, of course?"

"He called the hotel to ask if anyone needed a ride to Carmella's party. He spoke to Des Raphael, who was in Becca's room. Raphael told him you're under arrest." O'Brien shook his head. "He's upset."

"That has got to be one of the most massive understatements of the decade," I cynically observed. "On another aspect of this, it has occurred to me that the party will be a big help. Most of the people involved are going. Hopefully, at least, it will make it easier to keep track of them."

"I have someone watching the house," he stated, once more keeping the answer vague. He glanced up and cleared his throat. "I'm sorry we've monopolized all your time, Doctor," O'Brien sincerely told the physician. "You've been invaluable."

"I called my partner and he's taking any emergencies. All I had to tell him was my patient's name." Rossiter paused. "Have either of you seen the Sunday edition of the *Daily Gleaner?*"

"Nope. That is, at least I haven't," I told him. "Did Ash's collapse make the newspaper?"

"Oh, yes. They didn't print anything about it being attempted murder, just the collapse itself. It's on the front page. The arts editor wrote a glowing review of the production, and it's the lead of the front page of the Sunday section."

"I'll arrange copies for everyone through my boss. *Blast and bother!*" I yelped as I suddenly slapped the table, which startled both men. "O'Brien, you realize I'm a news reporter, correct?"

"I've heard rumors," he acknowledged with a smirk.

"Will you give me a job in the police department if I get sacked for not reporting these events as a news story to my editor?"

"I'm sure we can work something out," he reassured me, his tone bland. "Doctor, are you game to continue working with us?"

"Are you kidding? I told you that my primary concern is my patient's well-being. If I can help find the answers, I'll be happy to help." Rossiter beamed, reveling in his new role. "I didn't pull him through last night only to watch him get killed. What do you want me to do?"

O'Brien took a deep breath and told him. Steven Rossiter proved to not simply be willing but added a few touches of his own.

"Sounds hopeful, but if this doesn't work, we do have one more card to play," I said. "Congratulations, Doctor. You have a genuinely warped way of thinking."

"Blame Agatha Christie and Rex Stout," he preened, obviously pleased.

"We're going to have to brief Robert Mallory," I announced, "otherwise he's going to come after O'Brien with a meat cleaver. Let me take the blame for not including him."

"I can't do that," O'Brien mildly protested. "For one thing, he'd never believe I let you overrule my judgment."

"Where is he now?"

"Best guess? On his way up here to finish chewing me out."

"Where's Julie?"

"She's with Carmella at the party."

"Good. She'd have kittens if she knew—"

The door of the room flew open. It banged against the wall hard enough to make us all jump. Mallory stood on the threshold. From his stance with feet slightly apart and shoulders tense with hands at his side in fists, he was ready to tear something apart. His gaze focused on the police captain. Nothing else existed.

"O'Brien!" His voice low, his tone was as icy as the expression in his blue eyes. A glacier would have seemed tropical by comparison.

O'Brien rose slowly to his feet, hands also clenched. The image of two Old West gunslingers ready for a showdown at high noon crossed my mind.

I stood and moved into Mallory's direct line of vision.

"Please join us," I suggested.

I suddenly realized I never appreciated the phrase, *stopped cold*, before that moment. Mallory, intent on confronting O'Brien, abruptly and forcibly regrouped. The masterful effort played out across his face. He took two strides into the room and gathered me into a hug so tight I could barely breathe.

"What in blue blazes is going on?" he demanded of O'Brien.

His voice remained cold enough to freeze a pond into an ice-skating rink.

I tapped his shoulder, and without dropping his gaze from O'Brien's face, he released me, although he kept a hand on my shoulder.

O'Brien calmly shut the door before he addressed his long-time friend.

"As you can see, she's fine." He sat down at the table and indicated we should too. "So is Harper. You remember Dr. Steven Rossiter?"

"Of course." Mallory fought to regain his equilibrium.

He seated me in a chair and took the one next to me, sitting ramrod straight. His emotions, barely under control, played on his face. His shoulders remained taut, and the muscles in his jaw tightened. "Forgive my behavior, Doctor. I have known Lauren for a long time, and I have come to regard her as a member of my family."

"She's a remarkable young lady," Rossiter agreed.

"Danny, you can start explaining any time," Mallory bluntly stated. "You're running a bluff?"

"Not exactly," O'Brien returned. "More like a sting."

"Raphael told me you had arrested Lauren." He tossed it out as a fact, not a question. Mallory's posture, as tense as a coiled spring, underlined his cool voice.

"Becca was in the room when I took her into custody as a material witness."

"You took her down to the station." More fact.

"Briefly. I did not, however, put her through the booking process."

Mallory's shoulders relaxed a bit. "Why keep me out of it?"

"You had to react naturally. That still goes," O'Brien warned.

Mallory nodded. "Understood."

"Are Des and Becca planning on attending Carmella's party?" I asked.

"Wouldn't that be a little cold-blooded?" O'Brien countered.

"Maybe not. They might figure that they could go and give an update on Ash's condition."

"You have the principals under surveillance?" Mallory inquired.

O'Brien nodded. "Kaye and I were going to head to Harper's room. Would you care to join us?"

"Thank you, I believe I shall," Mallory replied and gestured for Rossiter to precede him. "Doctor?"

The four of us rose and left the conference room.

"Doctor, did you remember to get Ash a snack?" I queried on the walk down the hall. He stopped, and sheepishly shrugged. "I'll take that as a no. Why don't you get something on a tray and say it's yours?"

"Good idea." He headed down the hallway toward the elevators.

"Danny, was it entirely necessary?" Mallory quietly asked. He stopped before we entered Ash's patient room to give the police veteran time to respond.

"Yes." O'Brien regarded his friend. "Accept it and bear in mind I made sure she doesn't have a record."

Mallory nodded. O'Brien knocked; I noticed the absence of the police guard. Anne opened the door, smiled, and moved aside for us to enter. Since she did not speak, I figured Harper would be comatose. I approved. Mallory needed to see him in action.

Ash Harper lay on the bed, limp and lifeless. I could see breathing because he made one out of every three or four breaths deep and shuddering. Mallory, appropriately stunned, stopped inside the door before he slowly advanced two steps.

"Ash," I softly called from behind Mallory once Anne shut the door.

Harper moaned and moved his legs a tiny bit. I exchanged grins with Anne, who stood with her back to the door. She rolled her eyes.

"Ash, O'Brien has questions for you," I informed him while I walked to his bedside. "If you don't respond, I'll tickle you."

"Oh, Auntie, anything but that," he replied with a snicker and sat up. "Where's Dr. Rossiter?"

"Rustling up a snack for you." I turned and saw a bewildered expression on Mallory's face. "Got you, didn't he."

"Good lord, that's incredible," Mallory murmured. His relief at seeing it had been staged clearly showed. "Well done! I'm glad it's acting, too. The last time I saw you, it was too real." He offered his hand to Harper, who shook it.

"Aren't you under arrest?" Harper asked me.

"She's in custody as a material witness," O'Brien replied with another leer at me. "I took her down to the station."

"You didn't take her fingerprints," Harper observed.

"Hold! How did you know he didn't print her?" Mallory asked the tenor.

"Her fingers are clean. I've had my prints taken." He saw O'Brien's quizzical expression, and added, "Nothing criminal, Danny, I promise. Sometimes a foreign tour has odd requirements. I sang in Berlin a year ago as part of an exchange program. It took me a full day to get rid of that ink."

"You don't miss much either," Mallory commented with a side glance at me. The singer flashed a satisfied smile.

"Ash, as Kaye mentioned, we have questions and some are personal," O'Brien began. "We're trying to work out motives."

"Danny, if I can help straighten this out, ask anything you need. It's driving me nuts. I hate this feeling of not knowing."

"Kaye, you know what we need. Go ahead," the police captain ordered.

Startled for a moment at this major sign of acceptance, I took a deep breath. "Ash, do you have a will?"

"Yes. Becca gets two-thirds of my estate. The rest goes to New York City Opera for scholarships. Since my father's death four years ago, I'm worth something in the neighborhood of a million dollars."

"Heaven help us! Does everyone involved know this?"

"Becca knows. Laszlo is aware the company gets a share, but

he doesn't know the amount." Harper shrugged. "I'm not going to have any children, and my sister has money of her own. Becca wasn't too upset when I told her she wasn't getting the whole estate once she realized I wanted to set up scholarships for the company. I've already set up one fund. It's the one which will provide Carmella's tuition."

"Do you have a life insurance policy?" I continued without comment on an undoubtedly pertinent point.

"NYCO insists on it for all their principal performers. Mine is for one hundred thousand dollars, and it's also split. Becca gets half, the company gets a fourth, and my sister's kids get the remaining fourth."

"Have you made any enemies in your time with the opera company?" O'Brien questioned.

"Me? Definitely not. I'm the least offensive person in the organization," Harper asserted. "I spend a lot of time and effort in finding and nurturing new talent. Jeff and Carmella are good examples. I'm famous for flirting, and while it's possible it has sparked some jealousy here and there, I doubt it has enraged someone enough to kill me."

"That tallies with what Jeff told me earlier," I reminded O'Brien. "You discovered Jeff," I added to Harper.

"He was buried in the chorus of a community theater musical. It was barely college-level quality, but he didn't blend well." He smiled. "I met him and auditioned him. You've heard his voice. It's powerful, but when we met it was raw and cried out for training. I facilitated the necessary meetings. He always gives me too much credit. Jeff joined the company about the same time my father passed away."

"That was also when you married Becca," I added.

He nodded. "It was a year of ups and downs for me."

A knock sounded on the door. Harper immediately went limp, startling Mallory. Anne opened it for Dr. Rossiter, who carried a tray. He entered and the moment she closed the door, Harper bounced up again.

"Oh, goodie! Food!" He eagerly reached for the tray. His IV tubing rattled the bottles against the stand when he extended his arm.

"Down boy," Anne laughed. She took the tray from Rossiter and placed it on the over-the-bed table. "Be careful or you'll end up wearing it."

"Sorry, but I'm starving," he complained. "It's hard work playing comatose. I need this." He uncovered the plate and inhaled. "Tuna!" We all chuckled while he dug into a scoop of tuna salad on a bed of lettuce, attacking it the way Roland Beesley would cut into a steak if no one watched him.

"Ash, I have a question, if you don't mind," I said after a couple of minutes, "but I don't want to interrupt you."

"Auntie, ask away. I'm savoring again." He smiled with his eyes closed as he chewed.

"You mentioned you aren't going to have any children. Was this a joint decision with Becca?"

"It was my decision. There's a risk of inheriting diabetes, and I don't want to pass it along." He suddenly became serious. "I wouldn't want to watch a child go through this."

"What about Becca?" Mallory asked. "Did she know of your decision?"

"Robert, Becca and I discussed this at length before we married. I would never have married otherwise. To me, it would not have been fair. At dinner the other evening I told Lauren, at heart, I'm a gentleman." He finished his salad, leaned back on his pillows, and tossed his napkin on the tray. "I suspect the enjoyment of the snack was enhanced by the fact I was starving. When may I have a real meal?"

"With luck, later today," O'Brien assured him.

"I'll hold you to that. Meanwhile, what's the plan now?"

"Evans!" O'Brien sang out.

The familiar head popped out of the bathroom. "Yes, sir?"

"Do you want to be relieved? You've been in there for hours."

"Captain, if it's all the same to you, I'd like to stay for the finish." The detective smiled. "I've had worse stakeouts."

"We're going back to the conference room, leaving you with Harper and Miss Gerard," his boss informed him. "I've pulled the guard off the door."

"Understood, sir. I'm to stay hidden unless a threat presents itself, correct?"

"Yes." O'Brien turned to Anne. "You should take a quick break to get some coffee, but don't go far. If Harper has a visitor, come get me. We're down the hall in the small conference room."

"I understand."

O'Brien herded us out and back to our on-site headquarters.

We sat and stared at each other while we waited for further events to unfold. I realized we anticipated something which might not occur. The wait itself got boring and frustrating.

O'Brien again brought up the idea of motives.

"*Why* is this happening? We have more information now."

"The idea of money is always valid," Mallory offered. "The inheritance and insurance amounts are certainly large enough."

"Mr. Mallory, you said you have sources checking on a few items. Any luck?"

"Not so far."

"Cheese and rice!" O'Brien's favorite epithet underlined his scowl. He ran his fingers through his hair. "We are getting nowhere fast. Motive is usually the most obvious part of an investigation like this."

"We'll get there," Mallory affirmed. "The question is whether it will be in time."

"Speaking of time," I spoke up, "it's almost two o'clock. Mr. Mallory, you ought to call Carmella's mother and explain you're going to be late. If you don't, I'm afraid Julie will talk someone into driving her over here."

He responded by reaching for the telephone which rang the

moment he touched it. O'Brien grabbed it.

"O'Brien." His face contorted into a grimace and slowly turned red. His grey eyes got darker. "How?" he bellowed into the handset. His free hand opened and closed rhythmically in a fist. "I want facts, not excuses! I also want to know how word got out when my explicit instructions were that no one from the outside was to talk to him." He lowered his voice and demanded, "Tell me you put a tail on him!" He listened for a moment and struggled to control his anger. "Okay, okay, it happened. Have Walsh get over here in plain clothes but armed." He slammed the phone down. *"Cheese and rice!"*

"The phony doctor was sprung?" I surmised based on his reactions.

"Yeah, and I can't figure out how anyone knew he was there in the first place," the veteran policeman fumed. "He may not be on his way back up here, but you heard me ask for an armed guard."

I nodded. I opened my mouth but hesitated while I tried to gauge his mood. He saw the expression on my face.

"Go ahead." He growled it.

"The guard is great, however maybe someone should slip into Ash's room and warn them he's loose."

The phone went off again, like a broken alarm clock.

"O'Bri—" He cut it off; this time his red face turned white. He swallowed hard, twice. "Is Walsh on his way up here? Good. Get everything you can from the scene. I want to know what happened and I want it ten minutes ago." He banged the phone onto its cradle. "We don't need to warn them about Stone. They found him in a car in the station's parking lot. He's dead." He pushed the phone toward Mallory. "Before it rings with more bad news, call Mrs. Viscotti."

"Give me the number," Mallory requested, addressing me.

I realized I didn't know it. "I'm sorry, Mr. Mallory. It wasn't spoken aloud, and I barely glanced at it. I have it written down, though." I reached down for my bag and my hand groped air. "My bag is in Ash's room. I'll be right back."

I trotted down the hall. No guard yet. I knocked softly, opened the door, and took two steps into the room.

19

The left side of my face pressed against something hard and cold. I slowly figured out I was lying face down on the floor with absolutely no memory of how I got there. The back of my neck throbbed. My head pounded in time with it. One shoulder decided to join them. I gradually became aware of a voice. *No. Plural. Voices.* Something dug into the ribs on the right side of my chest. The vocal noises began to sort into words. The words gradually started to make sense.

"Please, may I examine Miss Kaye?" Anne pleaded. "You could have killed her!"

"Leave her where she is," a man coldly stated.

The butler? I tried to focus my thoughts.

His voice sounded familiar. *No help there—we had not eliminated anyone.* My memory for voices would not function properly yet. I knew the voice, but I could not place it.

"Please!" Anne begged again. Apparently, the butler gave another negative response; she moaned with a stifled sob.

Bewildered, I wondered if Evans planned on intervening. I also wondered how I ended up on the floor. The *why* would wait.

"Pssst." The low hissing sound came from the vicinity of my right elbow.

What? Having been cracked over the head with resulting foggy thoughts, it took me a moment to work out my current position. *Okay, I'm lying on the floor across the opening of the bathroom.* Feeling ridiculously proud of myself for working that much out, I decided the corner of the door of the bathroom and object digging into my threatened ribs were the same.

"Pssst." The tiny, low sound repeated.

Evans! Heaven help us! I'm in his way! I slowly moved my right arm. The throbbing in my shoulder increased. I prayed my assailant stood with his back to me with his attention on Anne and Harper. Evans tapped my hand, and I lifted my index finger. *Evans must be on the floor on his side of the bathroom door.*

"If you can slide over about a foot I can get out," he whispered. "Take it slow."

Slow defined the only way it would happen. I felt incapable of sudden moves. I made sure all parts worked and started to carefully wiggle away from the partially opened door. I hoped if Anne saw me move she would keep the butler occupied. The door followed me gently but with no pressure as Evans patiently waited for the opening to enlarge enough to let him out.

The sergeant burst out of the bathroom. At the same moment, someone entered the room.

"What in blazes is—" a gruff voice started to say.

O'Brien!

Sounds of a major scuffle were punctuated by a series of grunts. Three voices loudly protested and lots of footsteps echoed. Something hit the deck next to me with a crash. I decided to stay put rather than join the chaos. Somehow, the floor felt safer than trying to stand up in the middle of a fight.

"*Hold!*" O'Brien barked the command. Instantly, silence fell in the room so completely the clock could be heard ticking. "Where's Kaye?" he demanded.

"Floor behind you," Evans informed him. I speculated he had taken a course in brevity from his captain.

"Here," I called out. I gingerly raised my head off the floor. "Walt, I'm sorry I blocked you."

"Gerard, check her," ordered O'Brien.

Anne crouched down beside me. "Does everything work?" Her eyes reflected her professional concern.

"I think so. Let me turn over and sit up." I did, with her help.

A strange tableau greeted my eyes. Evans held a gun on Jeff Sebring. Sebring regarded me with palpable disgust. Harper, bless him, lay comatose on the bed. The overturned chair missed me by four inches. O'Brien assumed a position from which he could keep an eye on everything.

I took a breath. "Jeff, why?"

"You were going to kill Ash. I couldn't let you do that."

"WHAT?" Gerard, Evans, and O'Brien chorused before breaking into babble as all three started speaking at once.

I held up my hand. "Hold!" They fell silent. "Thank you." I turned my head—slowly and carefully because it felt like it might fall off—toward the nurse. "Anne, what happened?"

"Mr. Sebring arrived for a visit. We chatted for a moment, and I asked if he would stay while I got a cup of coffee at the nurses' station. I opened the door, saw you coming down the hallway, and mentioned it. Mr. Sebring told me to be quiet. He stood behind the door and hit you across the back of the neck when you came in."

"Jeff, you assumed I was going to kill Ash. Why?" I made a note to congratulate Anne on her concise reporting skills.

"You were caught trying to do it earlier."

I started to laugh. I stopped short because it hurt. "O'Brien, he bought the package. He's protecting Ash, not trying to finish the job."

The door opened again. Dr. Rossiter and Mallory were standing in the hallway with a third man, an officer. The latter stayed outside.

Mallory crouched, righted the chair, and lifted me onto it. Positioning himself beside me, he stared at O'Brien and raised one eyebrow. His implicit question did not need words.

"It was a giant misunderstanding," O'Brien reported, visibly chagrined for once. "Sebring thought Kaye was going to try again and clobbered her."

"You mean she's not the killer?" Sebring burst out.

"No more than you are," I answered. "I promise, Jeff."

"Oh, Lauren, I'm so sorry!" Consternation flooded his voice, shaded by relief. "When I heard you had been arrested, I didn't want to believe it, but when you came in here by yourself, I figured you had gotten away somehow. Forgive me, I'm sorry," he sheepishly repeated. "I guess I should have known better."

"Don't be sorry," I said soothingly, "you acted in good faith."

"Why didn't Evans respond?" Mallory reasonably cut to the facts.

"Sir, I did as soon as I could. Mr. Sebring hit Lauren, rendering her unconscious. She fell prone and landed directly in front of the bathroom. I couldn't shove the door because it was in her side." Evans smiled at me. "I didn't want to break her ribs. Once she came to, she was able to move enough for me to get out."

O'Brien glowered at me, which I thought unfair, since none of my actions deserved it. "Are you all right?"

"I'll live." I addressed the baritone. "Jeff, are you on your way to the party?" He nodded. "I thought Alan and Lisa were going to take you."

"I got a cab. They have Becca and Des, so I thought I'd stop by here and check on Ash before going over, so I could let everyone know how he was doing." He gazed at me. "I should have known you weren't a killer, but is someone really trying to kill Ash?" At my nod, he swore softly to himself.

"I took the liberty of stationing Walsh at the end of the hallway," Mallory reported to O'Brien. "He appears to be a forlorn, worried visitor."

"Good." O'Brien glanced at me. "Doctor, would you check Kaye?"

"Gladly." He gently probed the back of my neck, made sure both eyes reacted to light evenly, and insisted I find my nose with my eyes shut. "Bruise on the back of her neck, no signs of concussion. How's your head?"

"It hurts." I shrugged and immediately decided to not do it again. "I'll be fine."

"How is Ash?" O'Brien asked.

"The same. No better, but no worse," Rossiter solemnly replied.

"Let's give Miss Gerard a break and move back to the conference room. Kaye, where's your bag?"

Anne dug it out from under the bed. "Here. I saw it get kicked in the scuffle."

Mallory took it. "You don't need this on your shoulder," he murmured, giving me his hand.

"No argument," I gratefully agreed.

"Evans?" O'Brien growled.

"Yes, sir?"

"Business as usual." The police captain actually smiled at Anne. "You make quite a competent and credible witness."

"Thank you, Captain. I've done a fair amount of reporting to doctors."

Once back at the conference table, I pulled out my notebook, opened it to the appropriate page, and handed it to Mallory.

"Call before it rings again. Reassure your daughter."

He quickly got Julie. After her first barrage of words erupted in his ear, she deigned to let him speak. He kept it brief.

"Julie, I understand your concerns. Honey, I'm still up at the hospital. Ash is no better and no worse than he was two hours ago. Right now, I'm going to see what I can do for Lauren. I'll get to the party as soon as I can, I promise." He paused. "Of course, I'll let you know." He hung up.

"She calmed down?" I asked.

"She's not thrilled, but that should do until I get there." He turned to O'Brien. "All of the principals, except Jeff, are at the Viscotti home. Wendell arrived with Emilie. Everyone is delighted with the news Ash is still alive and stunned at the thought that Lauren tried to kill him."

"So, nerves are on edge," I observed.

"I think that's safe to say. Jeff, if we let you go to the party will you be able to keep Lauren's innocence quiet?" Mallory questioned.

The baritone nodded.

"I have an idea," I interrupted as O'Brien started to speak. "Jeff, how good an actor are you?"

"I rate myself fairly high," he replied with a smile.

"Now what are you driving at?" grumbled O'Brien.

"Send Jeff with Mr. Mallory to the party to give the latest report on Ash. That he isn't gaining ground, and Dr. Rossiter is getting concerned."

"Tell?" O'Brien asked.

"Unsure."

"Why?"

"Dissembling."

"Pressure?"

"Yes." I liked speaking in short-hand. *Short-speak?*

Mallory, who had followed our exchange like the match point of a Wimbledon championship game, forced us to pause. "Will you two please make sense?"

"You mean we weren't?" O'Brien's eyes glinted with mischief.

"Mr. Mallory, you're the one who first speculated we'd work well together." I winked at O'Brien.

O'Brien allowed himself a brief flash of a smile. "She's got you there. However, I'm not sure her idea will work. I think he'll have to be told."

"Which is why I questioned his acting." I cocked my head to regard the police captain. "Yes or no?"

"Yes."

"You're doing it again," Mallory observed. "What's scaring me is I am beginning to understand it."

"Jeff, come with me." I stood. "Captain, I think you should accompany us. If there's someone else behind the door and I get conked on the head again, I'm trusting you to catch me before I hit the floor."

"No comment."

We walked down the hallway and O'Brien nodded to Walsh, who saluted. I knocked.

"Please, come in," Anne said when she opened the door.

"All is serene, I hope?" I softly queried. "We want to show Mr. Sebring what's going on."

"I'm not used to the abrupt change," she murmured to me and closed the door.

"Jeff, brace yourself for a shock," I cautioned the stocky singer. "Ash, let there be consciousness."

"Hi, Jeff," the tenor sat up and greeted his protégé.

Sebring, shocked at seeing the tenor upright and conscious, stumbled as he approached the bed. "My God! I thought *I* was good! Ash! The whole time?"

"No, the collapse last night was all too real," Harper admitted, "and I did have a major setback after I began to recover. But today, yes." The two shook hands.

"Even when I attacked Lauren?"

"I knew you weren't the butler, but since I couldn't prove that, I had to stay out cold."

"Butler?" Jeff queried. "What butler?"

"My name for whoever is trying to kill Ash," I explained. "I use the term for any unknown, nasty person causing trouble."

Harper studied me. "Are you all right?"

"I'm doing better than you will be," I candidly replied.

"Oh, boy! I get to die?" The grin showed pure boyish enthusiasm.

I nodded.

"Jeff, you told the others you were going to stop by and see Harper before joining the party, is that correct?" O'Brien clarified.

"Yes. I asked Becca if she wanted to come with me and she declined. She admitted she finds it hard to see Ash like this."

Harper nodded. "She's always been that way."

A knock sounded. Sebring gasped when Harper collapsed. I opened the door and Mallory entered.

"Dr. Rossiter has gone down to the cafeteria to get a bite to eat of his own," he reported. "I figured I'd join the conclave."

"Jeff, can you go to the party and sell the idea that Ash is worse?" O'Brien questioned.

"If you have any doubts, Mr. Mallory can either do it or back you up," I added.

"I can do it, but Robert's presence might help."

"Jeff, I know you're good. Play it as a part," Harper advised as he sat up again. "What do you expect to happen?" he asked, addressing O'Brien.

"The whole opera crowd should be given the opportunity to say goodbye. After that we see what happens."

"Leaving him *alone* with these people?" Sebring gasped.

"Never quite alone," Evans piped up from the bathroom doorway. "I would have interrupted you sooner if Lauren hadn't landed in front of the door."

Sebring nodded. "When do we do this?"

"Now." O'Brien regarded me. "You have to stay here."

"I know," I agreed. "Perhaps we can liven things up on this end. You can always cuff me to your wrist."

The policeman snorted.

"Please, let me make sure I have this straight," Sebring implored. "I go to the party and announce Ash is alive but getting worse. I add that he may be going through another crisis. After that, what?"

"Relax, Jeff," Mallory cut in, clapping the singer on the back. "All you have to do is look upset, make the announcement, and the rest should follow. I may follow it by suggesting if people want to see him it would be allowed, yet we don't want to eclipse Carmella's celebration by abandoning her."

"It could actually be helpful if the opera people stayed together," Harper mused. "It would be easier to reach them in case of my death."

"Not a bad thought," Mallory said and turned to me. "When does it end?"

"The party? About four o'clock, unless something has changed."

He checked his watch. "It's a bit after two now. This may work."

"We can stage a confrontation with me in a chair in the waiting area," I suggested to O'Brien.

"This is not a party piece of fluffy entertainment," O'Brien growled.

His growl, one of his standard tones of voice, did not intimidate me.

"You lost one suspect today," I bluntly countered. "Don't you want to keep an eye on me?"

"No comment," he tartly returned. "Gerard, are you willing?"

"Captain, I will be happy to remain with him until I'm no longer needed." Her eyes twinkled.

"Robert, take Sebring to the Viscotti party," O'Brien instructed. "You can also report Kaye remains in custody. Let them know Dr. Rossiter is in constant attendance and he's worried. And so forth." He paused. "Also, a warning if Harper is going to have visitors, now would be the time."

Mallory and Sebring left. Anne asked if she could run down to the cafeteria to grab sandwiches for herself and Evans and left.

O'Brien stared at me for a long moment after her departure. "Kaye, you may have a knack for this."

"Thanks, I think," I replied, surprised at the lack of sarcasm. "I'd like to hope I'm learning."

"May I ask a question?" Harper said. "I don't mean to pry, but I'm curious. How long have you two known each other?"

"We met in June," O'Brien supplied. "She was doing a story out at Northwoods Resort. Robert Mallory was there, and I was his guest. At least that's how it started."

"How does Robert Mallory fit in?"

"Short version? His daughter Julie is my best friend. I've

known them for about eleven years," I explained.

"Do you expect this to work?" Harper glanced between the two of us.

"The visits to your deathbed?" I asked for clarification.

"Uh-huh. How will it help?"

"The problem we're having is evidence," O'Brien said. "We have motives, opportunity, and suspects, but it's all circumstantial. The sole physical evidence leads straight back to Kaye. We've got to unearth something more definite than that."

"You know, you also have a way with words," I mumbled.

"Your turn to use them. I'll bite. I want to hear something from you, since this charade was primarily your brainchild. Specifically, how will it flush out the butler?"

I stared into his grey eyes. "Think about it."

Slowly, almost imperceptibly, he started to smile. It showed primarily in his eyes, but the corners of his mouth twitched.

"Remind me never to make an enemy of you," he told me.

"If you ever do, you'll be the first to know." I gave him a sly grin and snickered.

"I'm lost," Harper complained. "Make that, I'm lost again. Or still."

"This alone may not nail the butler," O'Brien explained, "but it will add into the mix."

Harper sat up straight. "Wait a minute." He crossed his arms over his chest, IV line and all, and frowned. "These people are my wife, my friends, and my colleagues. You're playing with them, and I'm the primary actor."

"Ash, believe me, I don't like the idea of subjecting everyone to this," I gently assured him. "I feel sorry for all but one of them, and right now I don't know whom to leave out. Without proof, I'm half-way to a jail sentence. We're trying to save your life and me from the penitentiary."

"Even now?"

"I have enough circumstantial evidence to officially arrest Kaye and give the district attorney good enough cause to arraign her for attempted murder," O'Brien informed him. His frown deepened to a scowl. "I know she isn't responsible."

"What about the guy who was here this morning?"

"The orderly who tried to attack you?" O'Brien asked. Ash nodded. "He's dead."

"God above!" Harper groaned. "How?"

"We had him under wraps, but word got out and his lawyer got him released. His body was found less than ten minutes later in a car in the station's parking lot. We can't find the lawyer involved, and I'm waiting for the autopsy report." O'Brien sighed and rubbed his face with his hands. "I can't count on finding any threads to follow from that whole string of events."

"I was in custody when Stone was released and killed, but that is the only thing in my favor. Ash, you've said more than once today you hate not knowing," I reminded him, then suddenly yawned. "Pardon me. I plan to sleep for at least two days when this is over."

"I'm still having trouble believing someone is trying to kill me," Harper forlornly mumbled.

Without any knock for a warning, the door started to open. Harper immediately collapsed limply back on the bed. O'Brien yanked the door fully open. A woman wearing a nurse's uniform almost fell into the room with her hand on the handle. Her shoulder bag, not noticeably smaller than mine, banged the door frame.

"Who are you?" he demanded.

"I'm Ruth Franklin. It's shift change. I'm here to relieve Anne Gerard."

I raised my eyebrows. At a nod from O'Brien, I murmured, "I'll be right back." I ran down to the conference room and grabbed the phone. I asked the hospital operator to connect me to the cafeteria. Impatience made it seem like it took ten minutes for the line to ring. In reality, it took a few seconds.

"Please call Dr. Rossiter to the phone. It's urgent." I heard the cashier call out his name. In less than a minute, I had him on the line.

"Dr. Rossiter? Lauren Kaye. Did you request a nurse to relieve Anne Gerard?"

"No." He started to say more but I cut him off.

"Excuse me, but this is critical. Do you know a woman named Ruth Franklin?"

"No."

"Is Anne with you?"

"She was, but she left a few minutes ago to return to Ash's room." He paused. "You mean she's not there?"

"No. Get back up to Ash's room, please? There's a woman claiming to be the relief nurse for Anne."

I hung up. My thoughts raced. On my way back to O'Brien, I conferred with Walsh. "No one in or out without O'Brien's personal okay. Exceptions are Dr. Rossiter and Anne Gerard." He nodded.

I knocked. O'Brien opened the door and raised his eyebrows. I shook my head while I went by him. Ruth Franklin, sitting in a chair away from the bed, dropped her bag on the floor next to her chair. I stationed myself behind her, which allowed the police captain to see my reactions to her replies. I paid attention to his questioning technique. He got results.

"Miss Franklin, who asked you to come up here?" O'Brien civilly began.

"I was assigned by the doctor on duty."

"Which doctor would that be?"

"The doctor on the case."

"His name?" O'Brien's attitude remained casual.

"Dr. Rossiter."

"His first name?" The policeman's voice hardened a bit.

"I'm sorry, sir, I didn't catch it." She crossed her legs.

"Are you a regular employee of the hospital?" He circled in from another direction.

"No, sir. I work for an agency. They send me out whenever I'm needed."

"Your patient's name?"

"Ashburn Harper."

"So, you are saying Dr. Rossiter asked the agency to send out a nurse to relieve Anne Gerard." He ignored her mistake with the name.

"Yes, sir."

"Have you worked for Dr. Rossiter before?"

"Yes, sir." Franklin remained cool. "May I get on with my assignment?" She gestured at the room and the bed with her right hand.

Her long fingernails sported bright red nail polish. No nurse I knew would report for duty that way. Dress code regulations forbade it. I shook my head at O'Brien.

"Not yet," he calmly told her. "I have a few more questions to ask. Oh, and I would like to examine your purse."

"Why?" she asked defiantly. She reached down for it.

I moved a shade faster and got it first. I handed it to O'Brien. He opened it at the moment Rossiter walked into the room—without, I noticed, his identifying lab coat.

"Captain, is there a problem?" the physician asked.

"Hold a moment. Miss Franklin, can you identify this gentleman?"

She swiveled in her chair and glanced at him. "No."

"Sir?" O'Brien's gaze shifted to the doctor.

Rossiter stayed by the door. "I can tell you she's no one I've ever seen."

"What is the name of the nursing agency for which you work?" O'Brien queried. He reached into her bag and pulled out a wallet. Lazily, as if it did not matter, he opened it.

"You can't do that!" she snapped, jumping up. She extended her hands to make a grab for it. "That's mine!"

I gripped her shoulders and pulled her back into the chair from behind, not bothering to be gentle.

"You say you're a nurse. You also claim you have worked with Dr. Rossiter before, yet he doesn't know you and you say you can't identify him," O'Brien commented. He started going through the wallet's contents.

"Well, I'm used to seeing all the physicians in their lab coats. It helps identify them." She gave the lame explanation as convincingly as she could. O'Brien did not bother to respond.

"Captain, there are a few things here I find overly strange," I wondered aloud. "The long nails and the red nail polish are contrary to regulations. She's wearing a uniform, but her stockings are not white, and neither are her shoes. Also, her hair is not styled to be up off her collar."

O'Brien glanced up from the wallet. I spotted a glint in his grey eyes.

"And the answer is?" I prompted, stepping into my role as his assistant.

"Well, well, well," O'Brien intoned. "According to her drivers' license, we have here a woman named Ruth Franklin who is, according to a membership card in here, an actress."

"An actress!" Rossiter exclaimed.

"If she's supposed to be the relief nurse, we should probably worry about what has happened to Anne Gerard," I suggested. The fake nurse wiggled and tried to stand. I used pressure to keep her seated. "Maybe Miss Franklin has some ideas."

"No."

"Not even one?" O'Brien echoed.

She shook her head.

"Captain, have you noticed her nurse's cap is identical to the one Anne Gerard wears?" I asked. I found I enjoyed my new role.

"Now that you mention it, yes."

"I suppose it could be a coincidence. I wonder what nursing school it represents."

Franklin pouted. "I want a lawyer."

"You haven't been charged with anything. Yet." O'Brien leaned over and squarely gazed in her eyes. "What were you supposed to do in here?"

Franklin folded her arms across her chest.

"Is there anything else in her shoulder bag?" I curiously inquired to keep up my half of our team effort.

"Why don't you find out," he encouraged as he handed it to me. "A gentleman knows better than to rummage around in a woman's handbag."

I snickered and took the bag. About the same size as mine, it did not weigh as much. Inside I saw a jumble of items, too many to identify without removing them.

"There's an easy way to do this." I dumped the bag out onto the foot of the bed. Amid various objects, which included a small compact, a lipstick tube, a coin purse, an eyeglass case, and what appeared to be a small rolling pin, I saw a small, hinged case. I pointed to it.

"Any guesses?"

"That looks like a syringe case," offered Rossiter.

"Could be pay dirt!" I grinned at O'Brien. "Since I would rather not give you another set of my fingerprints, you can open it."

The police captain snapped open a handkerchief and picked up the case. Carefully manipulating the hinges, he showed us it held a filled syringe and a vial of medication. O'Brien gingerly lifted the vial so Dr. Rossiter could see it.

"Epinephrine." He whistled. "Captain, this would have killed him."

Heaven help us! What's next? I glanced at O'Brien. His lips tightened into a thin line as he inhaled a bushel of air and let it out slowly in a silent whistle. It was his only visible reaction to this latest jolt.

"Do you always travel with a syringe and epinephrine?" O'Brien inquired. His grey eyes, darker than normal, bored into her defiant ones.

"I'm allergic to bee stings," she sharply retorted. "Prove otherwise."

"I may try," O'Brien told her and turned to me. "Is Walsh outside?"

"He's under instructions no one goes in or out without your personal okay. I gave him two exceptions. Rossiter and Gerard."

O'Brien nodded, picked up the phone, and called the station.

"I need two men up here. Castle and Morse. Morse will be bringing someone back to the station. I'll give him instructions here." He replaced the handset.

"Where is Anne?" Rossiter demanded.

"That's why I sent for Castle. He can start a search. If this woman is really wearing Gerard's cap, it may be necessary." O'Brien turned to the woman in the chair. "I'm afraid we're going to mess up your pretty manicure, Miss Franklin. We use nail polish remover to clean our fingerprint ink."

"You can't arrest me!" she snapped out. "I've done nothing wrong!"

"You're a material witness in a murder case," he informed her. "I'm having you taken into custody. Since the last person who tried to kill this man is dead, you might want to consider this protective custody."

The phone rang. At O'Brien's nod, I picked it up.

"Room 405."

"This is Dr. Brenner down in Emergency. Is Captain O'Brien there?"

"It's a Dr. Brenner," I told O'Brien and handed him the phone.

O'Brien glanced at Rossiter. "Anyone you know?"

"He's one of our emergency room physicians," Rossiter confirmed.

"O'Brien." He listened for a moment. "Miss Gerard? How is she?" He nodded to us. "If she's able, I'd like to see her up here. Thank you." He hung up.

"Anne?" Rossiter anxiously asked.

"She reported to the emergency room about ten minutes ago. Someone hit her over the head when she exited the elevator. When she came to, she decided to stop by emergency to make sure she's okay. Brenner says she's fine, no signs of concussion."

"Thank goodness," the physician said, relieved. "I had no idea her assignment would place her in any jeopardy. You're sure she's not hurt?"

"From what Brenner told me, she's more mad than injured."

"I'd be willing to wager Anne doesn't have her nurse's cap," I murmured. "Captain, can you get prints off the small rolling pin from Miss Franklin's shoulder bag?" I pointed to it. "It looks like it could deliver a disabling blow to a head."

"There you go again," he told me, not quite growling. "Noticing things."

"Well, can you?" I repeated with a shrug to his comment.

He nodded.

A knock on the door sounded. Walsh identified himself and opened it to let Anne Gerard into the room. "Castle and Morse are here, too, sir."

Anne stopped in front of Ruth Franklin and glared at the seated woman. "Captain O'Brien," she blurted, "that's *my* cap!"

I walked around the actress and lifted the cap off her head, bobby pins and all. "Here you are, Anne." She took it to the mirror and pinned it back on.

"Did you see your assailant?" O'Brien questioned the genuine nurse.

"I'm sorry, Captain," Anne said. "I can't identify her, other than to state she had my cap. I was hit from behind."

"That's perfectly all right, Miss Gerard," his response almost cordial. I glanced up in surprise at his geniality. He generally barked at me. "We found more than enough in her purse to hold her. I need two bags for evidence."

She opened the top drawer of the chest and pulled out two small waxed-paper bags. "Will these do?"

"Admirably." O'Brien dropped the wooden roller in one; the case with the vial and syringe went into the other. He leaned out the door. "Morse? I have a prisoner to be transported to the station. Keep her in an interrogation room. No calls, no visitors, and *don't leave her alone*." He stuffed all her remaining belongings back into the shoulder bag and grabbed the bogus nurse by the arm. "Enjoy being protected," he told her while he propelled her out the door to Morse, who took the bag.

20

O'Brien, Rossiter, Anne, and I exchanged looks and sighed as one person. Evans poked his head out. "Anne?"

"I'm okay, Walt," she reassured him. "Oh, here. I did get your sandwiches." She handed him a rumpled white paper bag. "They may be a bit squashed."

"That won't bother me," he said with a wink. "I'm so hungry I might eat them right through the bag."

"Ash, you can open your eyes," I said, slightly above a whisper.

"God above!" he uttered, "Anne, I am so sorry!"

"You didn't crack me over the head," she reminded him. "The doctor in emergency told me my hairstyle may have saved me from a concussion. I never dreamed putting it up in a bun would stave off anything more than a reprimand from a supervisor." She grinned at her patient.

The phone rang in the silence which followed, and we all jumped.

"Room 405," Anne answered. "That will be fine." She hung up the phone and faced us with a slightly dazed expression.

"Now what?" O'Brien asked.

"That was Mr. Mallory. Mr. Harper will shortly have some visitors. His wife is coming over with Alan and Lisa Brockton. They just left the party."

"It's crisis time," I announced.

"We act as if the actress succeeded?" O'Brien anticipated me.

I nodded. "We need some window dressing."

"Doctor? This is your department," O'Brien gave the physician the floor.

"Anne, get a basin of water and start sponging off his face and upper torso, as if he were sweaty," ordered Rossiter.

Anne raised her eyebrows. "I beg your pardon, Doctor? Sweaty?"

"Oh, I'm sorry. I forgot you weren't here. The phony nurse had a syringe and a vial of epinephrine. You can report his pulse is racing."

"Yes, Doctor."

"Ash, I want you to quiver every now and then in addition to your occasional and extremely effective shuddering breaths," Rossiter instructed.

Harper flopped. He sank into his breathing and twitched a bit.

"Excellent. Epinephrine, or adrenaline, injected into the line would be making you hot and flushed. I don't think you need to pant, but when you're not shuddering, keep the breathing rapid and light."

"Got it." Ash sat up. "May I have some water? Plus, I need to use the—" Anne handed him precisely what he required. "How am I doing?"

Anne took a moment to run the test. "Marginal, on the low side." She questioned Rossiter with raised eyebrows.

"I think we'll be okay with the drip, Ash. We'll get you something to eat afterwards."

"I won't ask for it in writing." He turned his attention to me. "Auntie, when should I die?"

"Good question." I passed it on. "O'Brien?"

"Gerard, let the Brocktons come in first, but keep it short. Ash, do your tricks and add a moan or two if you wish."

"I'll see how they react." Harper turned to me as I opened my mouth to speak. "I won't overdo it." I nodded and he grinned.

"After they leave," O'Brien continued to Anne, "I want you to let Becca in."

The nurse dipped her head to acknowledge the order, and the

policeman continued his instructions.

"Ash, I'd suggest you die while your wife is in the room."

"I may have to make it fast. She could take one look, turn, and run. She has an aversion to illness. No telling how she'll handle this."

"Use your judgment but do it while she is in here. Doctor, you can play your part however you wish. If you want to, pull Gerard out with you, and leave them alone. Evans will be alert." O'Brien turned toward the bathroom. "Won't you, Evans?"

"Yes, sir," Evans softly called back. His voice carried a slight reverberation from his vantage point.

"Kaye and I will be in the conference room. I'll have Walsh come get us after the Brocktons leave. I'll bring her down here in time for a confrontation between her and Becca."

Back in the conference room once all our players were ready, I stared at the clock.

"Three-o-five?"

"What's wrong with three-o-five?" O'Brien sensibly queried. "I could put it as five minutes past three, if it would make you feel better."

"Shouldn't it be later?"

"Why? Because we've been racing to keep ahead of our butler for the past eighteen hours?"

I sank into a chair. I put my arms on the table, folded them, and cradled my head on my arms. "You know, that's exactly what we've been doing."

"Someone wants our tenor out of the way badly enough to hire or coerce two outside people into killing. It has been sheer luck we've been able to confound them." He got us each a cup of water, downed his, and paced.

"It's times like these I wish I smoked," I muttered.

"It's times like these I wish I hadn't quit," he returned with a sly smile.

"Okay, no cigarettes," I acknowledged. I raised my head and took a drink. "I keep asking myself how I get tangled up in these things. Honestly, I don't seek them out."

"You did the first time," he reminded me. "I even warned you about it."

"Okay, you have me there. But not this time. I was simply fulfilling a graduation requirement."

"I hate to admit it, but Ash Harper does owe you his life," O'Brien conceded. "I suppose I should thank you, too."

"Nah, it's out of character." I gave him a sly smile. "Do you want to cuff me?"

"I'm tempted, but we should probably skip it. If Becca flies at you in a rage, you would be a bit hampered. Also, I'd hate to get caught in the middle."

"True, although I can't see Becca in a rage. She strikes me as the cold, icy type but it would be my luck if this fired her up." I sighed. It led to a yawn I thought would crack my jaw. "Oh well. No cat fight."

"Sorry if that disappoints you," he said.

"You're being nice to me," I observed with a slight frown.

"So?"

"It's making me nervous."

O'Brien chuckled. "If it helps keep you awake, terrific. I could compound things by calling you Elizabeth." He finally sat down. "I like it better than Lauren."

"It is my middle name," I acknowledged. "This has *got* to work. If we can't get the butler out in the open, Ash is as good as dead. Unless he gives up after these failures."

"I don't think we'd be that lucky. I wonder if Robert's sources uncovered anything."

"We've been so busy blocking attempts on Ash's life, I forgot to ask him to double-check with them," I admitted. "It would be nice to have a second leg to stand on. Can Ruth Franklin be tied to anyone in our merry little group?"

"She was hired."

"Probably, but maybe not." I yawned again. "I have a question."

"You usually do." For once, his voice did not drip with acid.

"Could the butler be uncovered without the setup?"

"Good question."

"Thank you. I try to maintain a high level of quality." I cocked my head to one side and regarded him. "Got a good answer?"

"We'd get him eventually," he admitted. "Our one problem would be doing it in time to save Harper. These moves did buy us time." He gave me a crooked smile. "If you quote that, I'll deny saying it."

"Relax—I wouldn't dream of quoting you. However, that's the conclusion I reached."

A knock sounded on the door; Walsh leaned into the room. "The Brocktons are in the waiting room and Miss Chernak is with her husband."

"This is when it gets interesting," O'Brien murmured. He took my arm and marched me down the hall.

"Any instructions?" I whispered.

"Play it by ear," he whispered back.

"Gee, thanks. That's *so* helpful," I muttered. I took a deep breath while O'Brien knocked.

Anne opened it.

"I'd like a word with Dr. Rossiter, if it's possible," O'Brien told her.

In a moment, Rossiter stepped out, closing the door behind him.

"Captain, what may I do for you?" he asked. After a moment, he opened the door and called softly, "Anne, would you join us out here please?" He turned to us and lowered his voice further when the nurse joined us. "Miss Chernak is sitting by his bed, staring out the window."

A long moment of silence hung in the air. Once again, we waited for something to break. One minute grew into two, then three—

"*DOCTOR!*" Becca shrieked with all the volume and projection of an accomplished singer.

Rossiter went back in with his nurse, leaving the door ajar. O'Brien went in ahead of me. I edged inside to the foot of the bed to stand next to O'Brien.

I decided this performance ranked as Harper's greatest role. After working with Ashton Harper for all the weeks of our rehearsals, I recognized he was an actor of considerable skill in addition to being a wonderfully talented singer. Now, as he laid on his hospital bed, he gave an utterly and totally convincing performance of a dying man, with every aspect perfect.

Rebecca Chernak made no move to touch or console her husband. She stood back three feet from the bed close to his head. Her eyes were wide and riveted on his face. She held her right hand in a clenched fist over her heart. Her left hand clutched her purse with a grip that turned her knuckles white.

"Miss Chernak, it would comfort him if you would kiss his forehead," Rossiter gently encouraged.

Without moving, the diva seemed to shrink back from the bed.

"Please, at least take his hand?" the physician hopefully urged.

"No." She breathed the word softly, shaking her head. "I can't. No, I'm sorry."

The physician reached out and placed his hand on her shoulder. She shuddered and pulled away.

"No, please," she whispered. "I—I—I can't," she begged. "I simply can't. I would if I could, but no. No, please, no," she whimpered as she cringed.

Anne, stationed on the far side of the bed with her fingers on her patient's wrist, fixed her eyes on his chest. Rossiter moved past Becca to stand closer to the bedside. His gaze focused down; I could not tell for certain where.

Harper took one slow deep breath, shuddered, and let it out.

Anne, her fingers on his wrist, looked up at Rossiter and somberly shook her head. Rossiter picked up his patient's other wrist. Getting no pulse, he placed a finger on the tenor's neck to palpate a carotid pulse. Finally, he listened to the dying man's chest with his stethoscope. He glanced up at the clock.

"Death occurred at three-fourteen," he solemnly pronounced. He pulled the sheet up. "Miss Chernak, I'm so sorry for your loss."

The widow gasped. A spasm of pain crossed her face. She turned pale and hugged herself as if she might be ill. She backed farther away from the bed, swiveled, and spotted me.

"This is all your fault," she acidly hissed. Her grey-green eyes glinted like flint and her voice filled with venom. "You did this," she snarled.

"Miss Chernak," Dr. Rossiter came up behind her, "under the circumstances, we will have to do an autopsy."

She tore her eyes away from me and looked at the physician.

"No." She responded in a flat and strangely emotionless tone. "I refuse to give my permission."

"Becca, any death under suspicious circumstances must be investigated," O'Brien calmly informed her. "I'd like to extend my condolences, and if there is anything my office can do to make this difficult time easier for you, please let me know."

"You can lock her up and throw away the key," she vehemently suggested, once again glaring at me. She approached me and sneered. "People believe you're friendly and fun, but you're really a selfish and nasty little hussy." She moved closer, studying my face. Without warning she raised her right hand and slapped me across the face. *Hard.* She turned and calmly left the room.

"Anne, the Brocktons are in the waiting area. See that she joins them," Rossiter ordered, "and then come back here."

"I'll be there in a moment," O'Brien added.

The nurse nodded and left. The door closed.

"Ollie-ollie-oxen-free," I intoned. I gingerly touched the left side of my face. It stung.

Harper sat up and Evans stepped out of the bathroom. Even Rossiter appeared startled to see Harper sitting up.

"Good heavens, Ash! If I hadn't felt your pulse and heard your heart beating, I would have sworn you had died," the physician commented.

"I don't think I've ever had a bigger compliment," the tenor replied with a grin. His expression changed when he regarded me. "Lauren, I'm sorry. Becca had no right to do that." Harper closely eyed my face.

"I'm taking it as proof she's on edge." I sighed and moved to sit on a corner of the bed.

Anne slipped back into the room. "Miss Chernak is with the Brocktons. She's sobbing, and they are consoling her."

"Did Becca do anything while she was alone in here?" O'Brien demanded from Evans.

"No, sir."

"Blast it!"

"Can't have everything," I wryly stated. "Frankly, I didn't expect much from her. Okay, what's next?"

"Doctor, now might be a good time for Harper to get dressed and have something to eat," the policeman offered.

"Danny, now might be an even better time to remember that I don't have any clothes. I have what I'm wearing," Harper gestured to the standard issue hospital gown, "and the costume I wore onstage last night. Somehow I don't think either one would be appropriate."

"We're going to have to take you out on a stretcher anyway," Rossiter replied with a glint of mischief in his eyes. "You can spring back to life in the elevator. Once we're off this floor, I can get you some clothes from the orderly room."

"Which is where?" O'Brien asked. "We still have one more act of this."

"The finale?" Harper piped up.

"Wherein, hopefully, the mask will fall off the butler," I intoned.

"Lauren, do you know who it is?" Harper asked.

"Yes, I think I do."

Staged for Death

21

"Who is it?" Harper demanded. He sat dangling his legs over the side of the bed, impatiently fidgeting. Dr. Rossiter shook his head while he attempted to remove the intravenous line. Harper's antics hampered the effort.

"Ash, if you don't keep still, I will end up tearing the vein," the physician warned. "Please bear in mind I can't take you into the operating room to repair anything. You're dead."

"Sorry, Doc. This is aggravating. I want to know who is trying to kill me." Harper gave me a hard glare. "Give me the name. I don't even want an explanation. One name."

I shook my head. "Nope. Not yet."

"I understand your frustration, Ash," Rossiter said. "Believe me, I'm just as curious, but you *must* hold still for one more minute." He grimaced with the effort and gave up. "Anne, hold his arm."

The nurse steadied the appropriate limb, and the physician got the needle out. Anne took the IV pole and assorted tubing into the bathroom.

Harper stared expectantly at me. "Well?"

"I'm sorry, Ash, I can't tell you. There's a chance I may be wrong." I faced O'Brien. "Even if I'm right, we don't have any proof yet. Do we?"

"I'm with you, and unless I'm reading this wrong. I think you've got it." He turned to Harper. "However, Ash, she's correct in saying we have no proof."

I frowned. "We also have a few details to work out."

"I'm aware of that. We have got to get everyone with the opera company over to Carmella's party for a start."

"I thought everyone was already there," Harper muttered.

"Not quite. We also need to discover if any of Mallory's sources discovered anything to support a motive." O'Brien took in another bushel of air for his silent whistle.

Anne came out of the bathroom with a wet washcloth. "Try holding this against your cheek for a couple of minutes."

I nodded my thanks. The cool wet cloth felt soothing against the stinging area.

"Are you two sure you're not related?" Dr. Rossiter inquired. His eyes went from O'Brien to me and back again.

"Not as far as I know." I shuddered. "What a thought."

O'Brien frowned at me for a moment before he fired out his orders. "Doctor, find our deceased friend some clothes."

"And something to eat!" demanded our lively corpse.

"And something to eat. Enough to hold him for a while. Evans, you're our prisoner escort. Follow me. We should all meet back in the conference room in twenty minutes."

"If you're really lucky, Walt, I may even come quietly," I assured him. He grinned. I handed Anne the washcloth and put my hand to my face, which tingled. "Do I want to check it in a mirror?"

"No!" the four men chorused.

I glanced at Anne. She smiled and shook her head. "Better skip it."

Rossiter called for a gurney and told the orderly he'd take it from there.

"Anne, you've been wonderful," Harper said as he jumped onto the gurney. "With your permission, I'd like to give you tickets to my next performance."

"That's the best tip I've ever received," she said with a big smile. "Dr. Rossiter has my address."

"I'd like to add my thanks," I said while the doctor pulled the sheet over Harper's face.

Rossiter maneuvered the gurney out the door.

Evans grasped my upper arm and we trotted after O'Brien, who moved like he accepted the lead in a reenactment of the Charge of the Light Brigade.

My time in the waiting room lasted less than a minute.

"Remove her or I leave," Becca royally issued her command when we entered the area, her voice ice-cold. "I will *not* have her around me!"

"That's understandable," O'Brien soothed. "Evans, take Kaye to the conference room."

"That was easy," I commented with a sigh as I sank into a chair. "I may as well call Mr. Mallory." I pulled the phone toward me. At my touch, it rang. I jumped and glanced at Evans. "I'm really getting tired of this. You answer it."

He grinned again. "Sergeant Evans," he told the receiver. "Just a moment, she's right here." He extended it. "For you. Mr. Mallory. He saved you the trouble."

"Kaye." *Oh well, it's habit-forming.*

"Lizzie, Alan Brockton called a minute ago to say Ash Harper died a short time ago."

"Yes, he didn't." I let him assimilate my quip. "I was going to call to ask if word had spread. It was amazing. Dr. Rossiter was impressed, and I admit I was startled myself."

"I see." Mallory did not continue.

"Ah, let me guess. You can't talk, but I can," I offered.

"Exactly."

"Have any of your friends in opera high places turned up useful tidbits? At this point, we'll take gossip. We're flying blind on motives. We've got lots of speculation, but no facts."

"Oh yes, they've been most helpful. Do you need a lawyer?"

"No, but I can think of someone who does. You missed the final attempt on Ash's life." I gave him a thumbnail sketch. "We took advantage of it for the death scene. I'd be interested in knowing if anyone in our cast is connected with our phony nurse. Dr. Rossiter said it would definitely have been the final curtain for Ash."

"Good lord!"

"She's on ice, and if anyone slips up this time, O'Brien will start swinging a machete at a few necks to make heads roll."

"And now?" he asked.

O'Brien walked into the room.

"Mallory?"

I nodded and held out the handset.

"I'm sending the Brocktons and Becca over to you," he said. "We'll follow in a few minutes. Ash needed clothes and a snack." He paused for what I assumed constituted some form of acknowledgement. "Keep everyone there. I'll apologize to Carmella later." He passed the phone back to me.

"Yes?"

"You're coming?" Mallory's low, even voice came over the wire.

"I'm part of the finale. I think O'Brien plans to walk in first and I'll be brought in by Evans with Ash as my second guard. Nerves there are frayed to the breaking point?"

"Assuredly. I couldn't have put it better myself."

I hung up and reported to O'Brien. "It's hunch time," I offered after I finished.

"I guess it was inevitable." He sighed in resignation. "What is it this time?"

I started to voice my thought when the door opened again, and Harper stepped into the room.

"Doctor Kildare, I presume?" I greeted him. I nodded approvingly at his appearance. Clad in slacks, shirt, tie, a white lab coat, and carrying a sports coat over his arm, he gave off a professional presence. "Too bad you don't look more like Lew Ayres."

"And here I thought I could pass for him. This is the best we could do." He bowed and smiled.

"We spoke to Mallory at Carmella's celebration. You might like to know that you are officially dead there, too. I sent Becca and the Brocktons back to the party." O'Brien directed his grey eyes to me. "You said something about a hunch?"

"Find out if our fake nurse was also our fake lawyer."

O'Brien called the station, asked a few questions, hung up, and turned on me. "*Cheese and rice!* How in blue blazes did you know?" he demanded, almost angry. He ran his fingers through his hair and glowered at me.

"I told you. I had a hunch." I frowned. It took less energy than a scowl. "Think about it and you'll see it makes sense. She's an actress, and she pulled it off. Once he was released, she used her handy little hypo with the epinephrine. Stone's autopsy won't show anything but heart failure."

"The same way mine would have?" Harper shuddered. "God above, I keep feeling like I'm trapped in a B-movie mystery. All that's missing is a big, creaky house and a ghost."

I nodded. "Ash, it's natural for you to be reluctant to accept someone close to you wants you permanently out of the way. Keep in mind, however, the butler has one death in his column. Stone was undoubtedly killed on his orders, or instructions if you prefer, even if the butler didn't actually do the deed himself." I smiled. "Our ace now is he thinks he succeeded."

"Our butler can't be Becca," he murmured. "She'd never stoop to this."

"Don't try to worm it out of me." I resisted a strong urge to comment on what Becca might or might not do. "I've stood up to more experienced interrogators than you, and I'm impervious to the tactics." I smiled serenely at O'Brien.

He snorted. "I'm going to ignore that. Are we ready?"

The Viscotti home, a lovely two-story house on an older, tree-lined street in Merrick, was easy to spot. We pulled up in two cars, one marked and one not. Carmella's family outdid themselves. The raised porch was festively decorated, covered with balloons and streamers. To erase any lingering doubts, a banner stretched across the entrance which read, *Opera Debut Celebration!* Parked cars lined both sides of the wide pavement. The party, which Carmella said would run from two o'clock to four o'clock, finished breaking up while we sat there. Several people came down the front steps and paused to stare at the police car before getting into their vehicles.

We watched O'Brien approach the main door. It opened as he raised his hand to knock. The doorway widened and he disappeared inside.

"Now we wait," Evans announced, checking his watch. "We are to give him ten minutes."

Fidgeting punctuated our wait. Evans drummed his fingers on the steering wheel, his eyes locked on the home's front door. Harper gave visible evidence of plain, simple nervousness. He shifted in his seat, fussed with his tie, and bounced his heels on the floor. I struggled to stay awake. After my third glance at it, I swore my watch stopped.

"I've never been declared dead before," Harper murmured when the silence in the car grew too much to bear. "This feels weird."

"Ash, remember you said something about a ghost? You're it," I told him.

"God above, thanks," he groaned.

"Door opening," Evans stated.

Mallory descended the steps and casually strolled to our unmarked vehicle. Evans cranked his window down.

"Greetings," Mallory said. "I've been sent to get the prisoner and her two escorts, but Danny wanted to add one touch to Ash's attire." He walked past our vehicle to his car and returned with a brown fedora.

"A hat?" Harper asked dubiously as he took it. "This doesn't seem like much of a disguise."

"It doesn't need to be," I assured him. "People see what they expect to see. No one will be expecting you."

"She's right. It should hide enough of your face to help.

Remember, as far as they know, you are on a slab in the morgue."
Mallory opened the door and helped me out. "The way this has
been staged, no one will even notice you."

"Walt, why don't you lead in with me, and Ash can hang back
as if guarding any possible exit I might make. Nobody pays
attention to the man in the rear." I turned to Mallory. "What are
we going to see?"

"Most of Carmella's friends left shortly after we got word of
Ash's death. The last ones departed moments ago. The opera
people stayed, drawn together out of respect for Ash. Once
O'Brien arrived, he asked Mrs. Viscotti's permission for us to
remain. She agreed, and he made it official. No one leaves the
premises. You are being brought in to see if the investigation can
be concluded."

"Is anyone else still here?" I inquired as we crossed the street.
He knew exactly why I asked.

"A handful of her family members," Mallory replied.
"Besides Carmella's parents, her brother, and the Gianellos, there
is one gentleman from her mother's side."

I stopped suddenly in the middle of the street, and he
chuckled. "You can relax. You haven't met him. Your
acquaintance sent a representative." He took my arm and guided
me to the curb.

I did not realize I held my breath until I let it out. Her uncle,
after sending the bouquet of flowers opening night to Carmella,
conceivably might have decided to attend her party. Mallory's
statement about a representative served to shortcut my curiosity,
making it unnecessary for me to voice my actual question.

"Huh?" Harper probably did not realize he said it.

"Never mind, Ash," Mallory told him. "Carmella, by the way,
flatly refuses to believe Lauren had anything to do with your
death."

"That's like her," I observed. "How's Julie doing?"

"She accosted me, demanded to know why I wasn't doing
anything to help you, and hasn't spoken to me since. She and

Carmella are sitting together. Be prepared to be literally bowled over."

"Here we go," Evans commented when we entered the house.

I took a deep breath and crossed the threshold. *Heaven help us, I feel like Jonathan Harker entering Dracula's castle.*

O'Brien met us in the foyer alcove. He gave us the tiniest flicker of a smile before forcibly taking my arm. With Evans on my other side and Harper behind us, he guided me down to a large, paneled basement recreation room decorated with more balloons and streamers. A glance around told me the family congregated on one side of the room. I spotted a man off in a corner on his own, sitting in shadows. *Must be the family member.* The opera crowd congregated on the other side. A buffet table against one wall had serving dishes on it. The tables and chairs showed evidence of a party.

One glance was all I had time for. A petite form rushed across the room. She almost knocked me flat in the process of giving me a hug.

"Lauren," Carmella cried, "tell me you didn't do this!"

"I didn't," I confirmed quietly, "I promise."

Julie followed right behind her. "I knew that," she loyally declared. "Daddy, make them stop treating her like a criminal!"

"Julie, Captain O'Brien is just doing his job." I held up my hands. "See? No handcuffs. It's okay."

Babble broke out for a few moments. It sounded more like a cumulative effect of many different voices speaking in low tones.

"Captain! Why is this woman here? Why isn't she in jail?" Becca's voice, projected professionally, cut across the background conversations. "I *demand* she be taken to jail!"

"Becca, I didn't have any part in it," I told her. "I wish you could believe me."

She rose and majestically glided across the room. She shouldered her way roughly between the two girls, knocking them aside without apologies, and faced me. "I don't. Your fingerprints were on those bottles of Ash's insulin."

"I admitted I drew two shots from it. I drew the first one because Ash asked me to when he collapsed after the opening night performance. I drew the other one following Dr. Rossiter's instructions last night."

"A likely story." Her cold voice echoed the hard, bitter expression in her eyes. "Ash never told you to do any such thing. He hated for anyone to know he had an illness he thought was a weakness. I walked in on you in his dressing room, and I saw what was going on. You wanted him, and he wouldn't leave me, so you killed him."

"You saw what you wanted to see." I kept my voice as calm as I could under the circumstances. I wanted to do to her cheek what she had done to mine and then turn her head so I could equally address her other one. I felt I owed myself that much. "I repeat. The night Ash passed out in the green room, he asked me to draw a shot when orange juice made him worse."

"You lie!" Becca cracked her voice like a whip.

Raphael, his forehead creased with confusion, walked slowly up behind her. "Even assuming you're telling the truth, Lauren, there's still the question of who killed Ash. If you didn't, who did?"

"Des, all I can do at the moment is swear I had nothing to do with it."

"You were onstage with him when he collapsed. I know he didn't sing his last line to Alan."

"He couldn't, Des. He knew he was sinking, and he was struggling to speak." I shuddered at the memory. *No acting required. That memory will always make me shiver.*

"Another story as likely as the one about the shot," Becca contemptuously spat at me. "You say he spoke to you? What did he say?" She underlined her demand by crossing her arms over her chest.

"Can you remember his exact words?" O'Brien harshly prompted me; his grey eyes boring into me.

"His first words were *Keep the show going—Must go on.*

After a moment, he continued, *Becca—did—* He gasped and added, *Becca–did my–my—sorry so weak—* before he passed out."

"Don't you *dare* try to tell me Ash accused me," Becca hissed, her gaze icily penetrating like a cold blast of arctic air. "We only have your word for any of this. Did anyone else hear it? You could have tampered with the insulin as easily as anyone."

"Becca, he's gone," Raphael gently told her. He put his hands on her shoulders. "You can't bring him back."

"I want justice for him," she cried. She shook free from Raphael's hands and turned to face him. "Don't you understand? Ash loved me." A sob broke from her and emphasized her emotionally-charged words.

I reminded myself that both of the singers who confronted me were also consummate actors.

Becca pivoted again and took two steps forward to stand nose to nose with me. "Ash understood me. You robbed me of that. My husband is dead. You murdered him. You are a liar and a killer, and you deserve to die. You can't convince me of anything otherwise." Her grey-green eyes were full of bone-chilling hatred. "The evidence points straight to you. I'll see that you pay for what you did!"

"Becca, Dr. Rossiter has corroborated that he asked Lauren to draw a shot from that vial," O'Brien informed her. "That's why her fingerprints are on it."

"What about today?" she fired at the policeman. "She was caught with a syringe in his IV tube, wasn't she?"

I clenched my hands into fists at my sides and forced myself to take long slow breaths. To face Becca at close quarters was arduous. An argument would be useless—she would not budge from her histrionics. I wondered why O'Brien delayed springing the trap and how much longer it would be.

"Becca, everything I've done has been to help Ash."

"No, you murdered him, and you are lying about it," she

repeated with a sneer, enunciating each word in staccato-fashion.

"I've been trying to help find whoever is responsible."

We stared at each other for a long moment, our eyes locked.

"Actually, Becca, it's all perfectly true." Harper stepped out from behind me, removed his hat, and slipped his arm around my shoulders. "Far from trying to kill me, she actually saved my life."

The room stayed perfectly quiet for a slow count of ten; that silence broke when a few people gasped. I kept staring into Becca's eyes, which widened as she shifted her gaze from my eyes to the man at my side.

"No! Nooo! *NOOOO!*" It started as a low moan and built into a shrill shriek. She staggered back, her lovely face contorting with ugly agony. Tears, frustration, and anger etched her expression in a parade of emotions. She sagged against Raphael. "I thought you said he was dead," she whimpered to him. A sound broke from her, a combination of a sob and a moan. "You told me he was dead."

"Ruth killed you!" The tall bass gasped as he stared at Ash, his hands on the soprano's shoulders. "The plan was perfect!"

Becca whirled. "You *bungler*!" she snapped at Raphael. "You promised you'd take care of it. You *failed!*" She slapped him across the face exactly the way she had hit me.

The sound of her hand hitting his face became the signal for pandemonium to break out.

Staged for Death

22

After O'Brien placed both singers under arrest, his men escorted Desmond Raphael and Rebecca Chernak into the waiting police cars. Those of us left at the gathering re-grouped to try to understand the events which had transpired.

Mrs. Viscotti's cousin stopped to have a quiet word with Mallory before he left. On his way out, he nodded to me, although he never introduced himself. I nodded my reply. My carnation aside, I remained more than content to leave my relations with Carmella's uncle at cordially distant.

Norman Brier and David Peterman reluctantly claimed other commitments and approached me. I suddenly found myself flanked by Harper and Mallory.

"Lauren, I couldn't see you as a killer," Peterman told me, giving me a hug. "Robert, I keep forgetting that life with you around is never dull." They shook hands.

"Ash, I am so glad you are alive and well!" Brier smiled. "We didn't want to be known as the production that killed off a good tenor." He shook hands with Harper and Mallory, then turned to me. "If you decide to abandon writing for acting, please let me know."

I gave him an over-exaggerated grimace, and he burst out laughing.

Carmella's parents moved a long table into the center of the room. The Gianellos helped arrange food and plates on it so we could all sit down and talk. Jim Pomeroy, obviously at home here, glanced around the room and placed the chairs we needed around the table. Mallory moved off to speak to Julie. She gave him a hug, so evidently, she forgave him.

Susan took a moment to speak to Harper. "Mr. Ashton, I'm *verklempt*—full of emotion, sad and happy at the same time." She had tears in her eyes. "Time you'll need, but you'll come to realize you can still be happy. Be glad you're alive."

Harper gave her a hug. "I'm still in shock, but yes, I'm very glad to be alive."

Susan shook her finger at me. "The only thing not surprising me is finding you in the middle of this. *Oy vey!* Did you remember to eat today?"

"I had breakfast. I even have witnesses to it."

"*Feh!* Hours ago." She dismissed it with a wave. "It doesn't count."

Harper laughed and offered me his arm. "Auntie, may I see you to the table?"

I caught Mallory's eye. He gestured to three seats, and I took the middle one. Mallory sat in the one to my left. Harper helped me off with my coat and took the seat to my right, which put him in the center of the table. Julie settled in the seat on the other side of her father, while Carmella sat between Harper and Pomeroy with her mother on his right. Carmella's father took the head of the table, with Susan to his right and Gianni to her right. Lisa and Alan Brockton faced us, with Jeff Sebring, Emilie St. Clair, and Wendell Thorne filling the rest of their side.

O'Brien stood behind the chair at the foot of the table. We all looked up at him expectantly and waited.

"I know some of you may have a question or two—" O'Brien declared.

At least eight of the people present spoke at once, cutting him off.

"Danny," Mallory chuckled, "you are a master of understatement. Even I have a few."

"Okay, so everyone has them. First, I want to apologize for putting you through the agony of thinking Ash had died. All I can do now is assure you it was necessary, and we appreciate your forbearance. Next," O'Brien's eyes sought out Carmella's, and he smiled, "I especially want to apologize to Carmella and her parents for intruding on her special celebration." He sat.

"Hear, hear!" Harper seconded the sentiment. "Carmella, can you forgive me for spoiling your party?"

"Anything, as long as you didn't die." She beamed at him. "I was really upset, mostly because I couldn't thank you for getting me the scholarship. Ash, I'll work very hard, and I won't let you down." She blushed and shyly kissed him on the cheek. "But Captain, why did you arrest Lauren? She had nothing to do with it."

"The meager physical evidence we had pointed straight to her." O'Brien gave a slight shrug. "We had to lull the butler into a sense of security."

"Who is this butler?" Emilie asked. Other heads nodded.

"Lauren came up with it as a general name for any criminal who hasn't been identified yet," Mallory explained.

"As in, *The Butler Did It,*" Harper added with a smile at me. "It comes from all the old films where the butler is the prime suspect."

"It'll grow on you," O'Brien sarcastically commented. "After a while, it even starts to make sense."

"When did you know it was Des?" Harper asked me.

"After I worked out that Becca wouldn't be comfortable handling needles and vials of medicine, I started wondering who might be. Our butler had to be someone close to you, and by implication, to her. Des Raphael was closest to her. I surmised she told him about your condition, and I reasoned he is familiar with injections."

"He is?" Mallory questioned.

"I can only speculate about this bit, but I'm guessing that there's a close tie between Des and Ruth Franklin we haven't uncovered yet. Ruth's an actress, and she was a busy girl today between playing lawyer and nurse. When a bottle of epinephrine and a syringe turned up in her purse, she told O'Brien she always had them with her." I shrugged. "Like I said, it's a theory, but it fits the facts."

"Ruth Franklin told us she's allergic to bee stings," O'Brien supplied.

"She probably is. I think Des knew exactly whom to call. Ruth arrived fully equipped to perform."

"Excuse me, please." Brockton cleared his throat. "You realize the rest of us," he gestured around the table, "have no idea what you're talking about. Who is Ruth Franklin?"

"Yes, and what happened?" Emilie asked.

"Danny, I think we should back up a bit," Mallory suggested with a smile. "After what we have put these people through, it's a matter of courtesy."

"How far back do we go?"

"Let's fill in some of the blanks," I offered. I stifled a yawn.

"Ruth Franklin is, as Lauren mentioned, an actress who became involved in all this. I'm not sure how she ties in with Des Raphael, but I agree with Lauren that she does," Mallory offered.

"We do know Franklin pretended to be both a lawyer and a nurse today," the veteran police officer stated. "We got that far."

"Can you give us a short version of the events? From the beginning?" Brockton asked. "You are now saying Des wanted to kill Ash. That's hard for us to take. I mean, most of us have known and worked with him for years."

"Okay, let's backtrack," O'Brien said. "There were four attempts on Ash's life over the past two days. One of them began weeks ago." He waited until the gasps and exclamations subsided. "Taking them backwards, we can call them Plan D, C, B, and A. The fourth attempt, Plan D, was supposed to be a syringe full of epinephrine injected into Ash's IV line. It would have been untraceable."

I nodded. "Des would have to know how to draw a shot in an emergency because of his close relationship with Ruth, whatever it is. I'm wondering if they are brother and sister. I think we'll also find that Ruth had some sort of tie with Stone, probably theater. She used him as her dupe, whether paid or unpaid, for the third try when the first two attempts failed. Plan C was to be a large injection of air into the IV line, which would also have been untraceable."

"Why do all this during a production?" Sebring wanted to know.

"People around Ash would be focused on the show," I replied, "and distracted."

"Why this one?" Brockton asked.

"That's the easy part. Des was trying to protect and shield Becca from the knowledge of what he was actually doing. He chose this one because Becca wasn't supposed to be here at all. Des could strike at Ash with no suspicion falling on her." O'Brien smiled at Emilie. "When Emilie fell sick and Becca was called in, she was happy to see Des, but he must have been torn. However, his plan was in motion and there wasn't much he could do except let it play out."

"Captain, what was that plan—the first one?" Julie questioned.

A phone rang, and O'Brien was summoned to take the call.

"Answers," he said. "At least, I hope this will give us a few. Kaye can answer your question, Julie." He handed it off to me while he left.

"The original plan, which we are calling Plan A, was quite simple and extremely effective. Although most of the rest of the company were unaware of it, Ash has diabetes and uses insulin injections to control it. Des diluted Ash's insulin supply. He drew off some of the drug and replaced that drawn-off volume with sterile water. Ash brought a supply of vials of insulin with him for the production and at least the last five or six had been altered. Each one grew progressively weaker. Between the diluted medication and the stress of a performance, he would almost certainly collapse. Given enough time, it would be fatal."

"I did," Harper spoke up. "I felt lousy, tired all the time."

"I have to admit that plan, the gradually weakened insulin, was close to foolproof. The onset of symptoms would be insidiously slow, and the tampering could be detected or confirmed by analysis of the contents of the vials, not something which would have been routinely done. Dr. Rossiter admitted earlier today that if Ash had succumbed in the emergency room, his death would have been taken as natural metabolic failure."

"God above!" Harper gasped. "Lauren, I guess I didn't realize that before."

"I caught on that something was not right, but since the effects happened over time, I didn't put it together at first." I smiled at Harper. "Saturday night, when Ash collapsed on stage at the end of the duel with Wendell, he told me to keep the show going. By the end of the scene, he was genuinely unconscious. Des must have been immensely pleased. From his viewpoint, the timing was close to perfect." I shuddered. "All I wanted to do was scream for everything to stop so we could get him to a doctor."

"But you didn't," Brockton told me. "You handled it like a seasoned performer." He addressed Harper. "She told me you weren't acting, and I sang my lines without you."

"I did it because I realized that in the panic I would have caused if I had screamed, it would have taken twice as long to get help in addition to closing the show."

"That is one of the marks of a professional." Harper smiled at me. "So was continuing and finishing the performance." He grinned at Brockton. "I'm not going to bring up acting lessons again, though."

"Me neither. She could probably find a bar of soap here," quipped Lord Capulet's alter ego. "No one else knew anything had gone wrong until the scene ended, and you didn't jump off the bier."

"We got Ash to his dressing room, and the doctor gave him two shots of insulin," I continued, ignoring the jibes, "but they didn't work. I drew the second shot he gave to Ash."

"Then that shot came from the bottle of insulin we've heard

about?" Carmella asked. "The one that had your fingerprints on it? Why were you framed?"

"I was handy, and Des mistook my friendship with Ash for something else." I grimaced. "I think at some point he also realized he needed a patsy in case anyone got suspicious. He wanted to keep Becca out of it, but he realized he needed her help to complete the frame-up. She was in Ash's dressing room, standing next to me near the refrigerator. It's my guess she probably took the bottle then. She probably didn't know my prints were on it—that was a welcome bonus."

"Her prints weren't on the bottle," Mallory objected, "and they should have been."

"Gloves." I yawned, cutting off the rest of my thought.

"She always wears gloves with her evening dresses," Harper elaborated on my solitary word. "What I want to know is who put the bottle in your pocket?"

"Again, I can only give you a theory. My best guess is Becca passed the bottle to Des, who was outside the door. She had a golden opportunity when she left the dressing room while they were putting Ash on the stretcher. She even asked me to stay with Ash while she ran into the hallway to speak to him. She left with Ash in the ambulance. Des could easily have dropped it in a bag and into my pocket while we went up the stairs for Juliette's death scene." I yawned again. "Pardon me. According to Dr. Rossiter, by the time Ash got to the hospital, he was close to slipping into an irreversible coma, exactly the outcome Des planned."

"I know he started to improve at the hospital," Sebring stated, "but why did he get worse again that night?"

"I'm not going to pretend we have all the answers, Jeff," I admitted. "My guess is when Des called Becca from the restaurant, she told him Ash was showing signs of regaining consciousness. Since she was now in on the entire plan, she knew he was supposed to die, not recover. Becca probably wasn't gentle about it, either, and undoubtedly demanded he do something. Remember, he made that call from the payphone outside. No one else heard either side of it."

"I wondered at the time why he didn't use Susan's hostess phone, but I figured he wanted more privacy," Mallory observed.

"Des needed that added privacy," I agreed. "When he joined her at the hospital and the doctor had Ash moved to a private room, I suppose Des realized he had to try something else. He improvised a second attempt with what he had at hand."

"But he didn't take anything with him when he left the party," Brockton said.

"Alan, there was something in Ash's room that Des figured would work. Again, my theory, and Dr. Rossiter agreed it would have worked, is he probably put a dextrose solution into the IV line before they left the hospital to come back to the party. You saw the two bottles hanging on the IV pole in the room. The second one was not hooked into the infusion tubing and was there in case a counter to insulin was needed. It's commonly known as D5W, a five percent solution of dextrose in water. It would have been child's play to draw a couple of syringes full from that bottle and inject them directly into the active IV line." I turned to Mallory. "I haven't asked, but I'm also guessing that when O'Brien took Des up to the hospital to pick up Becca, he stayed in the hallway rather than going into the room."

"That's what he told me," Mallory confirmed. "So, Des would have had a clear shot at manipulating the IVs."

"It wouldn't have taken much to send Ash back to oblivion. The effect was delayed until they had arrived at Susan's, which was safer for them."

"So, Plan A was the diluted insulin and Plan B was the dextrose into my IV line." Harper frowned as he attempted to put it all together.

I nodded.

"So, what was Plan C?" Sebring wanted to know.

"Stone, an orderly pretending to be a doctor, entered Ash's hospital room prepared to shoot a large amount of air into the IV line. I'll give them credit—it would also have been tagged as a natural death in view of the ups and downs Ash had been having." I took a sip from the mug of tea which had miraculously appeared in front of me. I glanced around the table. Susan smiled and shook her finger at me. I nodded my thanks.

"And finally Plan D would have been the epinephrine injection by the phony nurse," Harper recounted. He shuddered when I nodded. "God above!"

"May I ask a question?" Emilie ventured.

"Of course." I got a nod from O'Brien when he sat down again.

"How did you know Becca wasn't behind this?"

"Emilie, I never said she wasn't behind it. Somehow, though, she got Des to do the dirty work for her." I glanced at Harper. "She was too squeamish to make the attempts herself. I saw that when Ash collapsed. She came into the dressing room, she reached out, but she couldn't quite touch him. Today, when she thought he was dying, she couldn't bring herself to kiss his forehead or hold his hand. She may not have handled the drugs directly, but that doesn't mean she wasn't involved." I leaned back and closed my eyes.

"I have a question for you." O'Brien spoke up.

"I thought you were getting answers," I sourly stated. I sat up and forced my eyes open.

"I have a few. But I do have a question."

"O'Brien, *I* have one. For Ash," I retorted.

"What's *your* question?" Harper asked me.

"We know Des was the butler. He masterminded all four attempts. His motive was simple and obvious. He adores Becca, and he did all this for her. The big question concerns *her* motive." I swiveled to face him. "Ash, why did Becca want you out of the way?"

"I had time to think about it while I was playing possum. Becca is a complicated person. It goes back to her upbringing. She grew up in a slum area of Chicago with an alcoholic father. Becca never had anything as a kid except a remarkable singing voice, and she used it to claw her way out of that hellhole. Like many people who grew up with nothing, she wanted everything. If she wanted me gone, my guess would be my money."

"What about divorce?" Sebring asked.

"It's not in her nature. Becca doesn't share. She's an 'all or nothing' type of person. I would have happily given her a divorce with a good settlement. I guess I knew how she felt about Des, and I genuinely would have wished them well. But a divorce would also leave me free to find someone else, and she wouldn't allow that even if she didn't want me. I loved her passionately at first." Harper shrugged in resignation. "It gradually faded over the course of the first year of our marriage. Even then, though, she knew I at least understood her. Beyond that, I don't know."

"I have acquaintances in the opera world," Mallory offered in the silence which followed while we all pondered Harper's words. "When Lauren came under suspicion, I made a few calls to friends for information. Money was the theory I heard the most, but the last person who called me back was a woman who knows Becca fairly well. She suggested Becca wanted something besides her freedom. She married Ash knowing he would not have children. My source said Becca once confided she wanted something all her own. A child."

"God above, help us! She's much too selfish!" Harper groaned.

"It's a strong motive," I pointed out, "regardless of whether or not she would have been a good mother. That desire would be a powerful force, especially as she got older."

"I thought I knew Des," Brockton sadly commented. "This doesn't make any sense. I know he was infatuated with her, the entire NYCO organization knew it. I've known them both for years, even before Ash joined the company. I guess I'm having trouble with the idea Des would murder for her. It's way too much to comprehend!"

"Becca dazzled him," Harper conceded. "He put her on a pedestal when they first met, and that's where she stayed. He adored her to the point of worship. She loved that attention and adulation, and she played on it. I guess he was willing to do anything for her, including murder."

"We heard that she had dated both of you," Carmella said. "Forgive me for asking, Ash, but if she liked the way he treated her, why did she marry you instead?"

"Honestly, I never asked. We got married shortly after my father died and I inherited a fortune. I knew the money was a factor. I guess I didn't realize how big a factor. She knew I didn't want children. I told Lauren and Danny I made that plain before we dated seriously. We talked about it again before we married. My death would have given her money, and then she could marry Des and have a child."

"That's one of the answers I did get," O'Brien said. "Although Des Raphael would have done anything in the world for her, there were two things he *couldn't* do. For one, he couldn't marry her."

"What?" During the discussion, I leaned back in my chair and started to relax. O'Brien's statement brought me upright, and I opened both eyes at the same time. "Ruth Franklin is his *wife*?"

"I think I missed something," Harper glanced between me and O'Brien. "All he said was Des couldn't marry Becca."

"It's logical reasoning." I yawned again. "Knowing how Des feels about her, the one thing that could block a marriage between them if you were gone would be an existing one of his."

O'Brien nodded. "Des and Ruth have been married for almost ten years. He played around, something Ruth accepted. She was aware of how he felt about Becca, and she put up with it. But Des never had any intention of permanently leaving his wife."

"You said there were two things he couldn't do," I frowned in concentration. "The other must be—" I paused to think, and a yawn escaped me. "Des can't have children?"

"He tried with his wife and was told he can't. Apparently, he contracted mumps when he was thirteen, and there were complications. Ash, your death was all he could give her."

"No wonder Ruth was willing to play both lawyer and nurse for him." I sighed. "They must have figured Becca would be generous with them for helping her. Did Becca know about Ruth or his inability to father a baby?"

"According to what I was told on the phone, she did not. She does now, however, and she's furious. Once she found out, she screamed she'd been betrayed."

"It won't be pretty," Harper offered. "She's awfully vindictive. Poor Becca. I wouldn't give her a child and Des couldn't." Harper's voice filled with sadness. "She's always been ambitious. I saw that, and tried to help her, take care of her. I guess it wasn't enough."

"Ash, she tried to have you killed," Emilie gently reminded him.

"I'm guessing she never asked for that outright," I said. "She probably told Des she had a problem and let him decide how he wanted to take care of it."

"Evans has been with her since she was taken to the station," O'Brien said. "According to him, once she found out that Des was married, she sang like an opera diva, if you'll pardon the phrase. Evans told me that one of the things she keeps repeating was she never told Des to kill you, merely get you out of her way."

"I wonder what she thought Des was supposed to do to accomplish that if not murder." I yawned again. "Maybe she simply decided she didn't want to know what he was going to do and blocked it from her mind. Possibly, though, she is starting to work on a defense plan to get out of her current quagmire with the least damage."

"Poor Des," Sebring murmured. "Caught between his wife and Becca."

"I still have to wonder why Des went along with this," Lisa Brockton said. "An affair, although improper, could be excused, but we're talking about murder. He couldn't marry her, and even assuming he was totally infatuated with her, why in the world would he agree to kill Ash?"

"I can offer one possible motive for speculation," I mused. I paused to sip my tea.

"Don't stop there, Auntie!" Harper emphasized his statement by slipping his arm around my shoulders and shaking me a bit. "Give!"

"I think with a little digging you'll find Des badly needed money," I offered, aiming my eyes at O'Brien.

"Why?" Mallory queried, using one of O'Brien's favorite words.

"Why did he do it, or why would he need money?"

"What makes you think he needed money?"

"Yesterday before the performance, I went around getting autographs in my program book." I stopped for a moment. "Heaven help us! Was that really last night!" I shook my head.

"Hard to believe, isn't it," Mallory commented while the rest laughed.

"I've had a four-hour nap since I got off-stage," I grumbled. "I could easily believe it's still yesterday."

"Get back to why you think Raphael needs money," O'Brien prompted with a growl that carried a marked degree of force.

"Fine," I said with a yawn. "Pardon me. I knocked on Des' dressing room door and he called to me to come in. Becca was with him, which was not unusual, but she was sitting on his lap. To give them a minute to sort themselves out, I turned and studied the room. I saw several newsprint sheets with odd names and a picture of a horse under a box of Kleenex on his makeup table. I finally realized they were horse-racing tip sheets."

"*Cheese and rice, Kaye!*" O'Brien burst out. "Someday you're going to hang on to a tidbit of information too long, and it's going to cost you! Why didn't you tell me this earlier?"

"Daniel O'Brien, you were in and out of that room at least twice," I bounced his wrath back to him like a slammed ping-pong ball. "You saw it. As for mentioning it, well, frankly, I forgot."

"You *forgot!*" O'Brien folded his arms across his chest and treated me to one of his darkest glowers. I was too tired to be intimidated.

"Danny, give up and get used to it," Mallory told his friend. "Not much gets by her."

"God above, thank all the heavens for that!" Harper fervently agreed. "Lauren saved my life at least three times in the past three days."

"I guess she has her moments," O'Brien reluctantly conceded.

"Thank you, I think," I mumbled while Mallory chuckled at the interplay between us.

"Captain, what will happen to Des, his wife, and Becca?" Wendell Thorne spoke for the first time since sitting down at the table, although he followed the tawdry details with interest.

"It's not my call, but I made some recommendations to the district attorney. In my opinion, Des should be charged with attempted murder and conspiracy to murder. Becca should be charged with complicity and as an accessory to conspiracy to murder. However, the exact charges will be up to the district attorney. Finally, I know Ruth Franklin will be tried for the murder of Ken Stone."

"Who is Ken Stone?" Lisa Brockton asked.

"Yes, who is he?" Julie chimed in as others nodded. "You mentioned him before."

"He worked as a night orderly at the hospital," I explained. "My theory is Ruth Franklin coerced him into making the third attempt on Ash's life." I caught the blank expression on Julie's face. "Plan C, the third attempt, was the syringe full of air." She nodded, and I continued. "Later, Ruth acted as his lawyer, got him released, and killed him using a syringe full of adrenaline."

"That's how she planned to kill me," Harper added. "Stone said he was a doctor, and Ruth Franklin said she was a nurse. Lauren caught on to them both."

"How?" Thorne asked. "Lauren, don't misunderstand me.

I'm glad you did, but I'm curious."

"I guess I have a knack for small details. Dirty fingernails on a doctor whose lab coat didn't fit, bright red fingernail polish and regular stockings on a nurse. These things tend to jump out at me. It's hard to explain. I look, that's all."

Mallory chuckled again.

"O'Brien, you need to uncover the tie between Ruth and Stone. Try nosing around her theater activities." I yawned again; too widely to be polite. "Pardon me. There must have been a tie of some sort unless she chose him at random."

"We're working on it. Right now, I need to get back to the station." He rose and bowed to Carmella's mother. "Again, Mrs. Viscotti, my apologies for turning the celebration party into an investigation. You have my thanks for your patience."

"We were glad to help," she replied. "It was a sorry situation, but it had to be done."

"I can find my own way out." O'Brien shot a stern glance at me. "May I make a suggestion?"

"You will anyway, whether I agree or not."

"Get some sleep." He left.

Conversations began to focus on other things, and I ignored them all while I picked at the food on my plate. My heart wasn't in it. Eating took energy and mine had run out.

"Danny was right, you know." Mallory leaned toward me after watching me for a few minutes. "You're out on your feet."

I yawned, apologized, and promptly did it again.

"I'm going to take you back to the house and have Mrs. Fiddler put you to bed." Mallory picked up my satchel.

"It's not even six o'clock in the evening," I protested although Mallory used a tone of voice which left no room for argument.

"Lauren, give up," Julie advised with a laugh. "You know that voice."

"I haven't had anything to eat since breakfast," I added in desperation right before I yawned.

"Auntie, can you eat in your sleep?" Harper grinned.

"I may find out."

"Lizzie, you may as well give up gracefully," Mallory suggested.

He pulled my chair back. Harper stood and held my coat for me while I put it on. Mallory took my arm.

"Mr. Mallory, we have food packed to go," Mrs. Viscotti piped up. She rose and went to a side table. Susan joined her. "Make sure she has something to eat first so she can sleep well."

"You are so right," Susan agreed. "All the time I tell her that she'll never catch a husband if she's skin and bones." Mrs. Viscotti nodded. They stood side by side and gazed at me.

"Heaven help us all, now there are two of them," I groused as we exited the house. "The only difference is the accent!"

23

The phone on my office desk rang.

I picked it up. "Lauren Kaye."

"I need your story on the opera murders. I'm putting this edition to bed in five minutes."

"I'm finishing it up now." I balanced the handset on my shoulder while I furiously typed. All the words appeared with typos and misspellings. The typewriter keys jammed. I pulled the sheet of paper out and inserted a clean page.

"If you can't do this properly and on time, I will have Rollie dictate it to a copy editor. He has your notes."

"*What?* How in blazes did he get my notes?"

"He took them from your desk on my instructions."

"He'll wreck the story!"

"Get it to me now, or it goes to him."

"That won't be necessary, Mr. Slater. I am almost done."

"Too late," he replied.

"That's not fair! It's *my* story! Let me bring what I have, and I can dictate the rest—"

"It should already be in the hands of the typesetters."

The phone fell off my shoulder. It landed on the floor with a clunk. I grabbed it.

"Boss? Boss! Are you still there?" Desperate, I yelled into the receiver, "*MR. SLATER!*"

The effort of shouting woke me from my nightmare. I shook my head to clear it. The bad dream eerily echoed the way my morning had gone the day I met with my advisor. My story, however, was complete in my head and ready to write. I simply needed to type it.

I looked around. My gaze took in the familiar décor of my room at the Mallory mansion. Dressed in a nightgown, I saw my robe draped across the foot of the bed. I felt no surprise at being there, but for the life of me I could not recall how it happened. I remembered leaving Carmella's party and Mallory putting me in his car, but nothing after that.

The bedside clock on the nightstand said eight. The dark sky outside the window indicated evening. I hoped I had not slept through until Monday evening. I grabbed my robe, stuck my feet in my slippers, and headed downstairs to Mallory's office with the intention of borrowing his typewriter to dash the story out in time for the morning edition. I got to the foyer without seeing anyone. The double doors to his office were open, and I stopped to peer in. Mallory and O'Brien relaxed with drinks in the two comfortable chairs in front of the desk. My boss sat behind it with the typewriter.

"Am I interrupting something?" I queried from the doorway. I tried to appear nonchalant as I took in the tranquil scene.

"I told you she wouldn't forget," Mallory observed to Slater. He waved his hand toward the desk. "Bernie even put the paper in for you."

"I think I wrote the story in my sleep," I informed them. "I'll call it *Murder in Act Three*. Or, if you'd prefer, *A Tale of Four Tries*."

"How about *The Butler Sang at the Opera*?" O'Brien suggested, his grey eyes dancing with laughter.

"Hold it! I was going to suggest that," Mallory protested with a chuckle. "Think of your own title!"

"If you gentlemen are finished, I promise *I'll* think of something if you will give me some privacy."

"Make it fast, and I'll take it with me," Slater informed me. "We have a deadline, you know."

He vacated the chair and gestured for me to take it.

"Boss, all this started with me trading a day class in music appreciation for being a supernumerary in the opera. I did it was to keep my job," I reminded him as I started to hit the keys. "I guess now I've got to get this on paper and handed in to you for the same reason."

They refrained from laughing until the door closed behind them, but I heard it over the clatter of the keys as I typed my heading:

Staged for Death by Lauren Kaye.

More exciting titles from

JUMPMASTER PRESS™

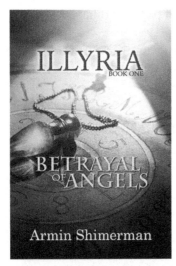

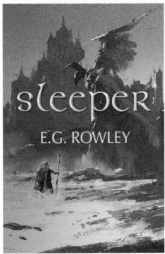

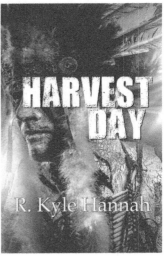

About the Author

Dale Kesterson

A native of New York City, Dale is a writer, actress, singer, and character voice artist currently living in the middle of nowhere in a Kansas town so small it doesn't have a red-yellow-green traffic light. Although a science major in college, she enjoys the creative side of life.

Staged for Death is the second novel in the Lauren Kaye Mystery series; it follows the debut novel, *Resort to Murder*, published in 2021. Other published works include her first science fiction short story in the award-winning *Tales of the Interstellar Bartenders Guild* and she co-authored a two-part time travel series with Aubrey Stephens: *The Devil to Pay: Time Guards Volume One* and *Four Score and Seven: Time Guards Book Two.*

Besides writing, Dale is active in her local community theaters. Her most recent stage role was as Cornelia Sawyer, the store psychologist in *The Miracle on 34th Street;* she has been stage manager and assistant director for two productions.

A professional photographer and seasoned traveler, Dale lives with her husband of over thirty years and their hairless cats, and if she's not otherwise busy she does handcrafts—she hates being bored!

More in the Lauren Kaye Mystery Series

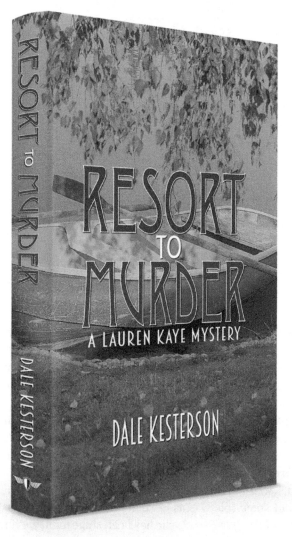

Made in United States
Orlando, FL
28 May 2022